W9-CBP-398

THE BLOCK PARTY

THE
BLOCK PARTY

A Novel

JAMIE DAY

ST. MARTIN'S PRESS
New York

First published in the United States by St. Martin's Press, an imprint of St. Martin's Publishing Group

THE BLOCK PARTY. Copyright © 2023 by J.D. Publications LLC. All rights reserved. Printed in the United States of America. For information, address St. Martin's Publishing Group, 120 Broadway, New York, NY 10271.

www.stmartins.com

Designed by Donna Sinisgalli Noetzel

Library of Congress Cataloging-in-Publication Data

Names: Day, Jamie, author.
Title: The block party : a novel / Jamie Day.
Description: First edition. | New York : St. Martin's Press, 2023. |
Identifiers: LCCN 2023009265 | ISBN 9781250283191
    (hardcover) | ISBN 9781250283269 (ebook)
Subjects: LCGFT: Detective and mystery fiction. | Novels.
Classification: LCC PS3604.A986565 2023 | DDC 813/.6—
    dc23/eng/20230308
LC record available at https://lccn.loc.gov/2023009265

Our books may be purchased in bulk for promotional, educational, or business use. Please contact your local bookseller or the Macmillan Corporate and Premium Sales Department at 1-800-221-7945, extension 5442, or by email at MacmillanSpecialMarkets@macmillan.com.

First Edition: 2023

10 9 8 7 6 5 4 3 2 1

For Kathleen

and all she did to make this party happen

MEMORIAL DAY, PRESENT DAY

Chapter 1

Alexandra Fox meant to have only a couple of drinks at the block party. Three, tops.

Oh well. Woman plans, God laughs.

But God didn't have to put this party together. She did. The neighborhood slogan might as well have been: *Go ask Alex, I think she'll know.* Basically a lyric from a sixties drug song. Hence the drink in her hand. If Alice from Wonderland needed pills to function properly—well, Alex from Meadowbrook, Massachusetts, could imbibe some wine.

"What happened to the blue tablecloths?" one neighbor asked.

Alex startled at the sound of her voice.

"Those were so pretty."

Alex eyed the red tablecloths as if she couldn't believe their horrible aesthetic. "Hundred percent agree," she said with just the right touch of disgust. If she'd been able to find the blue ones in her basement, she'd have used those instead. But there was a good chance she'd thrown them out by mistake months ago.

"Such a good call," Alex continued. "I'll remember them next year." She almost made an air kiss to seal the deal, but she wasn't that drunk yet.

Instead of pointing out what's not working for you, she thought, *perhaps you could have helped me send out the eighteen invites . . . or put out the food or set up the badminton court. But no—shame on the red tablecloths.*

"Oh, you must try Emily's potato salad," Alex said in hopes of sending this person away. "Utterly to die for."

She directed the neighbor's attention to the folding tables piled high with dessert trays and bowls of chips, which offered crumbs that daring birds would occasionally swoop down to snatch. Platters of meat sizzled in the sun.

Off went the neighbor, and *finally* Alex had a free moment to herself, nobody asking for anything, which meant she could drink from her red Solo cup in peace.

Tomorrow she'd restart her sobriety. Worse things had happened. It wouldn't be a big problem as long as she could avoid her husband, Nick—at least until she sobered up.

Sounds of children at play filled the air, while their respective parents chatted in clusters or lounged on beach chairs dotting the island of the cul-de-sac. Alex resisted the urge to scoff.

If you all knew what I know, she thought, almost grinning at the idea, *you'd be running from this party as fast as you could, not playing cornhole, that's for sure.*

She felt a gentle tug on the back of her shirt. Turning, she set her blurry vision on a young girl who lived four doors down on Alton Road. She knew the face, but for the life of her couldn't remember this child's name.

"Are the hot dogs ready yet?" asked the little girl—or was it girls? Was she seeing double?

Damn.

Alex pointed at the distant row of grills manned by a line of sweaty dads. "How am I supposed to know if the hot dogs are done, sweetheart?" she said. "I'm not working the grill, am I?"

The little girl's eyes went wide. Alex feared the child might burst into tears. She hadn't meant to be unkind, just factual. The approach worked well with her divorce mediation clients, but was obviously less effective with a kid at a neighborhood barbecue.

"Come with me," she said, her voice cheerier.

Molly. This girl's name is Molly Sanders. There. Not drunk.

She took the girl's hand. The child's flimsy grip made it easier to stay upright. "We'll go check on the hot dogs together."

A blaze of sunshine coaxed beads of sweat onto Alex's skin. *Water. I need water.*

The hot dogs on the grill were in fact done. Alex was not. She reached into the kiddie pool and fished about the icy depths, eventually retrieving a pony-size plastic bottle of white wine. She filled her red cup almost to the brim. She also got herself a bottle of water, as if that might even things out.

Alex kept an eye out for Nick. They hadn't spoken much since their big fight two days ago. As luck would have it, she'd picked the grill farthest from the rattan tiki bar. Behind that bar, Nick Fox mixed the more elaborate cocktails, none of which he'd have permitted Alex to drink. Good thing she'd stocked the bar for him that morning. He had promised to do it but didn't, leaving her to do the job. She felt more than deserving of the drink she'd helped herself to in the process. Didn't matter that it was before noon. The freestanding structure, one Nick had bought at a flea market some years back, leaned to one side as if it were about to topple over.

Alex could relate.

This would be her last glass until the evening, she promised herself. *Water and coffee from now until then.* She was still fully functional. She could carry on a conversation. Nobody was looking at her funny, were they?

The street was quite active now and would stay that way late into the evening. If Alex paced herself—steering clear of Nick, of course—she could party with her neighbors to her heart's content.

The party was controlled pandemonium, with fifteen families (three no-shows) and thirty-something kids. Classic rock blasted from a pair of speakers purchased exclusively for this annual happening. Yard games abounded, with the lawn of Alex's sprawling home functioning as the badminton court.

She surveyed the houses along the cul-de-sac's perimeter. Nick, an architect by trade, had designed their beautiful home. But now she saw these dwellings for what they really were: empty husks, an illusion of normalcy and security. If those walls could talk—oh boy, the secrets and lies they'd share.

How did it all change so much in a single year?

Drink in hand, Alex retreated to the shade of a nearby canopy tent, safely out of the view of prying eyes.

A moment later, a man entered the tent, someone Alex did not wish to see.

She didn't know his given name, but everyone in town called him Bug Man. Bug Man was a pest control salesman and a neighborhood pest himself. He was tall and lanky, with stooped shoulders and protruding eyes like those of the flies he was hired to exterminate. His uniform, an all-green jumpsuit with a matching green cap adorned with some colorful bug motif logo, said he was here to work. Certainly he hadn't been invited.

Alex gave him a scowl. "What are you doing here?" she asked. "This is a private party."

Bug Man offered an awkward grin. "I'm advertising my new business." He presented Alex with a flyer, which she did not accept. Not that she could have read it, anyway, with her vision going in and out of focus. "I'm working for myself these days," he said.

"Is that so?" Alex's tone was cool.

"Yeah, I lost my job after someone on this very street made some unfavorable calls about me," Bug Man said. "Guess my sales tactics didn't go over well with your neighbors."

"I purchased your services once," Alex said. "But only after you scared me into doing so. Perhaps there's some truth to those complaints."

Bug Man shrugged. "I was simply explaining that once I treated your neighbor's home, the pests most likely would seek shelter in your residence. Pests don't care who's paying the mortgage. They go where there's no poison. I was merely trying to be helpful."

"In some places, they'd call that kind of help scare tactics," Alex said. "Look, you weren't invited, and I don't want you hounding my neighbors—ringing doorbells like there's a fire outside, scaring people half to death, papering cars with your flyers, or breaking windows when you don't get your way."

Bug Man looked indignant. "What are you talking about?" he asked. "I kill bugs. I don't break windows."

Alex's expression only hardened. "We both know you're the one who tossed that rock with the note attached through my brother-in-law's window. If he sees you around here, you won't be safe. You do remember that he owns a gun? I wouldn't go knocking on his door if I were you."

Alex didn't wait for a reply. She marched out of the canopy tent—right into Nick. They collided with force, enough to spill the wine in Alex's Solo cup all over her husband.

"Jesus, Alex," Nick said. He looked down at the massive wet spot on his polo shirt with disgust. "Have you been drinking?" he asked.

"No," said Alex, using some newly discovered muscles to keep from swaying.

Nick sniffed the air. "I can smell it on your breath," he snapped. "God, Alex, we *talked* about this."

"It's one party, Nick," Alex said. "Lighten up, will you? You're not my *mother.*"

"Thank God for that," Nick muttered under his breath.

Alex tried not to let the sting show. "What's that supposed to mean?" she asked.

"It means you say what you want, do what you want, and damn the consequences. You promised, Alex—you *promised,* no more drinking."

"I have some fun for one day . . ." Alex slurred. In case Nick hadn't understood, she held up a single finger.

Nick's eyes, normally a sweet shade of brown, darkened to charcoal. He stepped back to appraise her.

Alex stepped back as well, barely catching herself from rolling an ankle in her wedge heels. She didn't want to be near him. Nick latched his hands on his hips, with the same look on his face he used to lecture Lettie.

"I'm just having a good time, honey," Alex said. "Leave it alone, will you? Setting up the party was a lot of work. And Lettie—she's leaving soon for college, and I'm still pretty upset about our argument. Can't I blow off some steam without you watching me like a hawk?"

"Not this way you can't," Nick answered, his tone clipped.

Alex waved him off. She didn't need to be lectured. Didn't want a talking-to. She was a grown-ass woman who could make her own life decisions. "I really don't appreciate being treated like a child," she said. "I think I deserve a little gratitude from my damn husband, not a lecture—or do you think the red tablecloths are shit as well?"

Nick looked utterly perplexed. "What on earth do tablecloths have to do with you being blotto at the block party?"

"Whatever," said Alex angrily. She twisted the David Yurman bracelet Nick had bought for their twelfth anniversary, resisting the urge to rip it off and throw it at him. Too much nuance was in play for Nick to grasp. She'd rather be with her girlfriends, anyway. They'd understand her far better than her husband ever could.

She took one step backward, but it proved to be one step too many. Alex's foot connected with the side of the kiddie pool full of water, ice, and beverages. One second, she was backing away, and the next she was on her ass, covered in water and ice, with drinks floating all around her.

Heads turned. People stopped talking. All eyes fell on Alex.

She leapt out of the pool as if it were electrified, raising her hands overhead triumphantly to signal that she'd meant to do that. "It was getting hot out here," Alex shouted at the gawkers. "I'm good. All cool now. Literally and figuratively."

That was a clever recovery, she thought.

A smattering of applause followed, but it couldn't overpower the whispered talk and sniggers of laughter.

Nick gripped Alex's arm. "What the hell, Alex? You are such a disgrace," he said between his teeth. "Get control over yourself, will you? Go home. Sleep it off before you embarrass yourself further. Lettie shouldn't have to see you like this. And, Alex, whatever you do—*don't* come back."

Well, that hurt.

Alex managed to keep her smile plastered on as she made her way home. It was hard to walk in sodden jeans. Her wet shirt offered a veiled preview of her midriff, but thankfully nothing more.

"I'm fine. I'm fine," she told anyone who asked. "Can't a girl fall into a pool these days?"

Once inside, Alex undressed in the bathroom. She placed her soaking clothes in the hamper. She was angry about Nick's remarks, but more upset that she hadn't thought to grab another bottle of wine from the pool. The house had been dry since March. *Probably for the best.* She'd sleep for a bit and go back to the party later. Nick didn't control her.

Alex settled on the couch. The air conditioner was on, chilling her skin. She pulled a fuzzy blanket up to her chin. Her mind replayed the incident, unleashing torrents of shame.

You're better than this, Alex told herself. *Nick was right to be horrified. What an ass I made of myself. What's wrong with me? Thank God Lettie wasn't around to see that.*

Alex's eyes eventually closed. Soon she sank into a dreamless slumber.

Sometime later she awoke with a start. Daylight still seeped from beneath the curtain, informing Alex that she hadn't slept through the party.

She bolted upright—too quickly—and the room began to spin. It took a moment for her ears to attune to the sound blasting outside the window. Something was wrong. Over the years she'd heard it all—fireworks, laughter, music—but police sirens at the Alton Road block party?

That was a first for sure.

Meadowbrook Online Community Page

Post from Regina Arthur

Does anyone know what's going on? Just heard what sounded like a hundred sirens go by.

> **Ed Callahan**
>
> Might help if we knew where you lived! Think much?
>
>> **Reply from Tom Beck**
>>
>> Ah, Ed's back. Who the heck unblocked you, Ed?
>
> **Laura Ballwell**
>
> I hear them, too. I think something is happening on Alton Road.
>
>> **Reply from Susanne Horton**
>>
>> Something happening to The Flauntin' Altons? Surprised they haven't deployed the National Guard. LOL!
>>
>> **Reply from Joseani Wilkins**
>>
>> That's not funny. Something serious is going on.
>
> **Regina Arthur**
>
> I've never heard so many sirens.
>
> **Janet Pinkham**
>
> Is anyone else having problems with the town garbage bags splitting at the seams? It's happened four times now, so I have to double-bag them, not to mention the mess it's made.
>
>> **Reply from Katherine Leavitt**
>>
>> Janet, please start a new post for that. There's a serious situation on Alton Road. Isn't today their annual Memorial Day block party?
>>
>> **Reply from Laura Ballwell**
>>
>> Yes!!! My husband is trying to get the police scanner to work. Stay tuned!
>
> **Christine Doddy**
>
> Sending thoughts and prayers.

Reply from Susanne Horton

While you're at it, send the local assessor, too. They should be paying higher taxes. Ha-ha.

Henry St. John

I think there may be a fire or something. I just saw three fire trucks go by my house.

Tom Beck

Anyone living near Alton Road see smoke?

Reply from Ross Weinbrenner

Only smoke I've seen is from their flotilla of BBQ grills. Who here's ever been invited to the Altonites' big Memorial Day block party??

Reply from Ross Weinbrenner

They don't even invite people on Tucker Street. That's TWO streets over. Isn't two streets close enough to be part of the block?

Reply from Ed Callahan

Um, no.

Reply from Susanne Horton

Altonites!! Ha-ha

Laura Ballwell

Everyone please!! This is serious. Maybe there was a bad accident or something?

Regina Arthur

My husband just heard code 187 on the scanner.

Reply from Susanne Horton

Is that the code for being stuck up?

Reply from Tom Beck

No, you idiot. It's the code for a homicide.

MEMORIAL DAY, ONE YEAR AGO

Chapter 2

From her shady vantage point, Alex watched Nick arrange a pile of burlap sacks into a perfectly straight line on their neighbor's meticulously manicured lawn. She admired her husband's dad bod from afar, fully aware it wasn't the party atmosphere making her heart patter. Those cargo shorts aside, Nick was the love of her life.

But Alex couldn't sit idle, admiring her husband. She had work to do. She was the organizer of the block party, which came with a host of responsibilities.

She checked her phone. It wouldn't be long before those sacks were filled with children racing about like giant jumping beans. She smiled at a memory of Lettie doing just that. The days were long, but the years were short—a cliché, but that didn't make it untrue.

Even though the party was in full swing, with people everywhere drinking, eating, and playing games, Alex had no trouble spotting her daughter. True to form, Lettie was the only one at the block party clad in all black, her Doc Martens a stark contrast to the sneakers and sandals everyone else wore. She ambled past her father without so much as a glance, nonchalantly sipping from her red Solo cup.

Alex hoped it contained only soda.

"Lettie," Alex called, "why don't you share your playlist with Uncle Ken? We could use some newer music."

As if on cue, the Doobie Brothers came blasting through the speakers that Alex's brother-in-law, Ken Adair, had hauled up from his basement. Ken, who had once played guitar in a high school band, had promised to form some kind of musical group to perform at the block party. Luckily for all, he hadn't found the time or the neighborhood talent to make good on his threat.

Lettie dismissed her mother with a wave. "I was into helping with the music at this party, like, four years ago, back when I cared," she said. "And now I don't."

She raised her Solo cup in a salute before marching away. Lettie was under orders to attend the block party, but that didn't mean she had to socialize.

"She'll come back around. Give it time," said a voice behind Alex's back.

Alex turned to see Willow Thompson, a tall, thin woman in her thirties with dark blond hair full of annoyingly perfect ringlet curls. It was Willow's lawn that would host the sack races. Technically, it was Willow and Evan's lawn, at least until their divorce was finalized.

"Come around when?" Alex said. "After she has a baby and needs me again?"

Willow offered only a shrug.

For someone who'd never had a career, who made money working part-time jobs here and there—the last one being at a day care—Willow always dressed to impress. Decked out in form-fitting capri pants, strappy sandals, and a loose-fitting silk blouse perfect for the warm weather, she looked ready to command a crowd, even at a barbecue.

"It'll get easier when this thing at school blows over," said Willow. "If it helps any, Riley feels bad about what happened. She doesn't support the vandalism, but she supports the *idea* behind it."

"Good to know," said Alex. She didn't sound all that appreciative.

Riley Thompson, Willow's only child, was president of the student body council and the equivalent of an A-list celebrity among Meadowbrook's youth. She was also Lettie's childhood best friend turned tormentor, but Alex didn't carry a grudge. Girl friendships held more drama than a Shakespeare festival. It was the more recent events that Alex found a little harder to overlook.

"I should go check on the burgers," said Alex, bounding off before Willow had a chance to change topics to her pending divorce, a favorite subject. "Let's catch up later, okay?" Alex offered a friendly wave. Off she went to the tent where Willow's soon-to-be ex-husband, a well-known but hotheaded fashion photographer named Evan Thompson, was grilling the meat.

Evan looked like Willow's counterpart in his snazzy button-down shirt, perfect shorts, and footwear that was likely straight out of the box. As a couple, they looked beautiful together, but their personalities clashed like plaids and stripes. Willow was something of a homebody, while Evan always wanted to be on the road. It didn't help that his frequent sojourns to New York and various exotic locales to photograph hot models made it difficult for Willow to trust him. Add to that his excessive partying and general irresponsibility while Willow took care of everything, and the couple ended up with a combustible marriage.

Even though the decision to divorce was firm, the paperwork had yet to be filed. For Riley's sake, Willow and Evan had agreed to continue cohabitating until after graduation, when the house would be sold. But that couple made the "till death do us part" vow sound like a threat.

"So what did the biggest mistake of my life have to say?" Evan indicated Willow with a nod while his hands were busy plating burgers.

Alex plastered on a smile. "You mean the mother of your precious daughter?"

"She might look like her mom, but thank goodness Riley has more of my personality."

"We're all still friends, Evan." Alex suppressed a sigh. "We're trying to support you both. Let's keep it cordial." She stuck a meat thermometer into the thickest part of a burger Evan had plated. The digital readout displayed 110 degrees.

"This burger barely has the wind knocked out of it," Alex said. "Let's not serve *E. coli* to the children, okay? Thanks so much." She gave Evan a gentle pat on the cheek.

"You want anything to eat?" asked Evan. "I'll charbroil something just for you."

"No, I'm good," said Alex. "Maybe in a bit." She didn't want Lettie to see her devouring a former sentient being. She wasn't in the mood for a lecture.

"What's Lettie having for lunch?" Evan asked. "I'll make her something special."

"My heart," Alex called over her shoulder, walking away.

The party would mostly run itself from this point, but not without small fires for Alex to put out along the way. By four o'clock that afternoon, she had addressed a buns crisis (she found more packages in her basement freezer) and a shouting match between ten-year-olds (she located their respective mothers), and she'd made a run to the store for more chocolate bars after Nick left a package too close to the fire.

She was finally able to take a breather. Alex put her feet up on a chaise longue, ready to savor her wine. Moments later, she spied her younger sister, Emily, pulling into the driveway of 13 Alton Road with her Audi. A gleaming silver Lexus drove in behind her.

Number thirteen was now unoccupied, as the Weaver family had downsized after their youngest had graduated from college. The stately brick manor had gone on the market only days ago, and already had an eager buyer.

Emily looked poised and confident in casual business attire. Her bright smile all but said, "This house is sold." As one of Meadowbrook's most sought-after real estate agents, Emily Adair—like her husband, star software salesman, Ken Adair—loved the thrill of the deal.

From the Lexus emerged Emily's clients, a handsome Indian man and his striking blond companion, probably his wife. Accompanying the couple was a young man in his late teens, maybe early twenties, who had dark hair and dark eyes and was most likely their son.

Emily caught Alex's eyes across the street and waved eagerly for her to join them. "Alex," said Emily, still beaming, "this is the Kumar family—Samir, Mandy, and their son, Jay. Everyone, this is my sister and, lucky for me, my next-door neighbor, Alexandra Fox, Alex for short."

One might not guess the relationship between Alex and Emily with even a lengthy appraisal. While the sisters shared the same shiny dark hair and light hazel eyes, Emily was petite, whereas Alex was taller by several inches, with a stronger build. Emily got their father's small round nose, and Alex had inherited their mother's more striking bone structure. Genetic differences aside, both women had their own classic beauty.

"So, good news," said Emily. "The Kumars are very interested in making an offer, and I suggested we do the second viewing today so I could show them the neighborhood."

That rising pitch Alex knew so well was a not-so-subtle cue that the deal was all but done.

"You picked a perfect day to come," said Alex.

Samir made no motion to shake her hand. In contrast, Mandy offered a warm handshake—firm, too. Jay stood disengaged and off to the side.

"We're all here for our annual block party," Alex continued.

"Sweetheart," Nick called to Alex from across the street, "we're out of mustard!"

"Okay," she called back, forcing cheer into her voice, "I'll call the police. Not to worry." She sent Mandy a tight smile. "That's my husband, Nick," she said. "He's a great guy, very handy with a toolbox—less so with condiments."

Mandy, who had glowing skin and a radiant smile, returned a polite laugh as she took in the scene with her piercing blue eyes. Her husband, Samir, directed his attention to the mammoth house that Alex thought was far more home than three people needed.

"The party seems like so much fun. What a great tradition," said Mandy, who matched Willow when it came to style.

Samir was no shabby dresser himself. Alex could tell he was fastidious about his appearance, taking note of his wrinkle-free dress shirt and slacks, his well-manicured hands, the shine on his loafers, the gleam to his watchband, and his clean-shaven face.

"Remind me, what are the taxes here?" Samir asked Emily, his tone suggesting that whatever number she quoted, it was going to be too much.

"I have that on the listing sheet," said Emily, without missing a beat.

"So many children," observed Mandy, still taking in the sights.

Alex heard something melancholic in Mandy's voice, which she attributed to having a son who, like Lettie, was long past the days of backyard games.

"Ken," Emily called to her husband, who was standing within earshot, "come here, honey. Let me introduce you."

"So much house," grumbled Samir. "Who needs this much house at our age?"

"It's gorgeous," said Mandy, who did a good job ignoring her husband's complaint, if she even heard it.

Alex watched Ken cross the street like a conquering emperor—his chest stuck out, sporting his best damn-glad-to-meet-you smile. He had charm, and Alex loved him as family, but her bullshit radar always pinged loudly in Ken's presence. He still looked fit in his blue polo, she had to give him that. Hitting the gym religiously five days a week had held age somewhat at bay, while offering a glimpse of the athlete he'd been. Handsome almost to a fault, Ken radiated a magnetism that drew people to his side, including Emily.

Ken came over carrying his treasured bottle of Johnnie Walker Blue Label. Now Alex knew this was staged. At over two hundred dollars a bottle, this was a prize Ken typically kept to himself. Shock of shocks, he carried three glasses in his hands.

"Mandy, Samir, this is my husband, Ken Adair," said Emily.

In Ken's usual fashion, he addressed the man first. In his mind it was still a man's world, and Samir would be the one with the checkbook, who'd be making the final decision.

"I'm pretty selfish with my expensive whisky," Ken said, looking only at Samir. "It's become a block party tradition of mine to indulge in it only *once* a year. And ever since I started the tradition, I have a little superstition about sharing it."

"Little?" Emily interrupted. "He never shares a drop—never."

"That's right," Ken confirmed. "But my very persuasive wife talked me into offering some to our new neighbors as a welcoming toast. So—may I pour you a drink?"

Samir gave a little chuckle. "Well, it's a little early for me to partake, but thank you for the offer."

"No problem," Ken said. "And just so you know, I have pull on the town planning board if you're interested in doing any renovations. I'm converting our garage into an in-law apartment for my mother-in-law, in fact. Going to crush me on the taxes, but she's worth it. Family's everything, right, honey?"

"Sure," said Emily without her sales charm.

"Yeah, I'll do anything for my family. Put a few hundred thousand miles on the F-150 driving my kid from one lacrosse tourney to another over the years, but now he's a starting midfielder at Syracuse. That's a D1 program, if you didn't know. Got a full ride, too."

Emily cleared her throat. "We have another son, Dylan, who plays sports for Meadowbrook High as well," she said.

Ken looked slightly abashed. "Yeah, yeah, that's right. D's a great player, too. Really tries hard!"

Tries hard? Tries hard to shine as brightly as Logan, thought Alex, who had a flash of pouring Ken's fancy whisky all over his head.

She let the urge pass. Ken's obsession with Logan's accomplishments was nothing more than reflected glory, but that didn't make it any easier to swallow.

Ken finally turned to Samir's wife, as if noticing her for the first time. "How about you? Mandy, was it? Would you like a drink?"

When their eyes met, Ken went perfectly still. Alex wasn't sure what to make of the expression on his face. He was known for his appreciation of women, especially the attractive ones, but he appeared struck by Mandy's beauty. *Enraptured* was the word that came to mind. And Mandy's expression showed a spark as well—one that certainly hadn't been there before. It was as if a little explosion had gone off between them. Alex could feel a charge in the atmosphere. From the look on her sister's face, Alex could see that Emily had noticed it, too.

Chapter 3

Lettie

I know what most of the moms at the block party are thinking, at least the ones with younger kids. I can see judgment in their eyes. Because I'm wearing black and not decked out in spring colors, they think *troubled, depressed, moody, angry, defiant, and drug-using teen.* Hey, five out of six isn't bad. I don't use drugs. Never tried them. Never had a drink of alcohol, either. In other news, I don't go to many parties.

To be honest, I don't care about my popularity. I'm not a prude about mind-altering substances, either. My friends on the school's climate crisis committee always spark up after our weekly meeting, and I don't mind. I get it. Who wouldn't need a little stress relief after two hours talking about melting ice caps, perilous heat waves, food shortages, and endless droughts?

I'm pretty sure the Meadowbrook Moms don't think much about our warming planet from the comfort of their air-conditioned homes or while driving around in massive SUVs, but they sure are big on appearances. They see my dark cutoff shorts, legs white as toothpaste, all attitude in my Doc Martens, with no makeup, long hair in a ponytail, and believe the same won't happen to their precious kids.

Whatever helps you sleep better, I guess.

My dad calls me over. I can predict what he's going to say before he says it.

"Lettie," he'll call out in that deep dad voice, "have you had anything to eat?"

I march right over.

"Lettie," he says. "Have you had anything to eat?"

Bingo.

"I'm not hungry."

Three words. Half my daily quota.

"Well, how about a veggie burger?" asks Dad. He knows I won't touch meat. Doesn't like it, though. Thinks I'm protein deprived. I'm not. Plant protein is just as good, I've told him countless times, but he doesn't listen to facts when he's got his mind made up.

"I'm good, thanks," I say.

Six words already and the day is still young. Drat. I'll make up for it tomorrow.

"Egg toss?" asks Dad.

He points to himself, then over to me, as if I didn't know he wants us to be teammates.

It takes everything I have, all the willpower I can summon, not to grimace. I can't break my dad's heart, but the egg toss? Oh god no. From the age of eight to the age of thirteen, I teamed up with Dad and we went unbeaten. We're like the Tom Brady/Rob Gronkowski of the egg toss. Somewhere in the basement is a box of ridiculous plastic trophies that my uncle Ken buys every year to hand out as awards for various games, the egg toss included. However, much to my father's dismay, I've retired from competition after I experienced what I've come to think of as my awakening—i.e., when I awoke to how dumb these contests are. Year after year, Dad tries valiantly to get me to unretire. He thinks another trophy will bring us closer.

Bless his sweet heart.

It's not like I haven't tried to engage with my father. Really, I have. I'm not the teen who thinks her parents are stupid and have nothing to offer. My dad is crazy smart. He's a great guy, too, and yes, I love him. But he doesn't want to talk about things that matter to me: our warming planet, the immigration problem, gun control, gender issues—the list goes on.

Now we're on a collision course of a different sort. College is looming and the cost of my education has become his favorite topic of conversation. He thinks it's a waste of money to spend an obscene amount on a BA. I think I don't want to go to UMass. California is calling my name! Most progressive state in the nation, where I'd get to work on the climate crisis from the front lines. If my father won't pay for USC, I'll take out loans. He'll tell me I don't understand how interest works. Fearmonger about me drowning in debt. Good luck getting a car or a house, he'll say.

Whatever. If I do get a car, it'll be an eco-friendly van I can live out of. No Meadowbrook-type carbon-spewing McMansions for me.

"Maybe next year for the egg toss," I say to Dad, throwing him a bone. I see the hurt in his eyes. Since *sorry* isn't in my vocabulary, I apologize to him on the inside.

I do give him a quick hug that more than makes up for my denial. I'm hoping my hug also conveys that I don't hold a grudge, even though he's grounded me for half the summer. If I had been my kid, I'd have done the same.

I venture off to find some privacy, doing my best to avoid eye contact. This shindig was never that fun to begin with, but since I'm now the talk of the town, thanks to that school security camera, I'm in need of a hideout.

Unfortunately I can't seek sanctuary in my bedroom, which is where I wish to be. I'm kind of lacking bargaining power on account of my being unquestionably guilty of a rather major transgression.

Burger grease perfumes the air as I wander to the back of the Thompsons' house, which stands next to ours at the far end of the cul-de-sac. I'm thinking of sticking my feet in the Thompsons' pool, but instead I have the bad luck of running into my first cousin, Dylan Adair. Startled, Dylan springs off the lounge chair like a frightened cat when he sees me, revealing the full form of Riley Thompson, who was hidden beneath him.

Dylan stands up straighter. Regretfully my eyes go down. I see what I see, what he knows is there, too. He gets red in the face, as do I, before he leaps into the pool, acting as if he'd meant to do that all along.

"Yo, what's up, Lettie?" Dylan says nonchalantly, trying to sound cool and casual. He rests his elbows on the edge of the pool, lifting his torso up so water cascades down his muscular chest. He's been hitting the gym extra hard ever since his brother, Logan, made all-conference for lacrosse in his junior year of college. Dylan might not be the star player Logan is, but his dark and brooding good looks, along with his athletic prowess, are good enough to earn him the affections of the undeniably most beautiful girl in our school, Riley Thompson—who happens to be the person I most want to punch in the face.

Riley rises from the lounge chair like Venus exiting her clamshell. She's got on a white bikini that would look half the size on my wider, thicker frame. Don't get me wrong; I'm not obsessed with body image. I like how I look well enough, but I'm also aware that Riley is utterly gorgeous, and I'll never have a body like hers no matter how many hours I spend in the gym (too few), or how many honey-glazed doughnuts I forgo (maybe not enough).

"Hi, Lettie," Riley says, cocking her head to the right as if a tendon in her neck suddenly snapped. "What's up?"

I could say *food shortages* or *income inequality*, but instead I answer, "Nothing."

And then we look at each other curiously, trying to decide what comes next. The answer appears to be silence.

I could confront Riley, let her know that I know she's the one who ratted me out, but what good will that do? Dylan, of all people, told me it was Riley who identified me in the security camera photos the Meadowbrook police posted to social media. The police wanted to nab the school vandal, and Riley wanted to play the hero. It's good to know that family loyalty trumps blow jobs.

"I'll catch you later," I say to them both.

"Bye, Lettie," Riley says with a wave.

Dylan and I lock eyes briefly. I can tell he's worried I'm going to confront Riley, screw things up for them. While I want to get back at her, I won't do it at the expense of my cousin.

I walk past Brooke Bailey's house. Brooke would be the hot mom on the street if only she had kids. Doesn't have a husband because he's dead—took a fall off a cruise ship. Police called it an accident. Rumors implicated Brooke. Like an independent voter, I remain undecided.

I cross over onto the lawn of the vacant house next to Brooke's place. I'm trying to forget most of what just happened when I see an attractive Indian dude, about my age, using the swing set that once belonged to the Weaver family. Smoke billows from his mouth after he pulls a Juul from his lips. His handsome head becomes enshrouded in fog. Since I've never seen this guy before, I assume he's looking to buy the Weavers' place, but he seems too young to be house hunting, and I get the sense he's too smart to be vaping, which makes him troubled.

Call me intrigued. I'm not shy. "Hey," I say.

He raises his head. Lord, those brown eyes! He's better looking than any boy at school, but not by Meadowbrook standards, which give preferential treatment to the more traditional jock types.

"Hey, yourself," he says. He takes a second hit, expunging a cloud of white vapor that evaporates quickly in the warm air. He offers me the Juul.

"No thanks," I say. "I don't know you."

"I'm Jay," he says, offering the Juul again as if that took us from strangers to vape buddies.

I smile when I decline. "Lettie," I say.

We skip the handshake.

"I don't think I've heard that name before," says Jay.

"It's short for Elizabeth—well, sort of," I say. "When I was little, I pronounced my name Lettiebeth, and Lettie kind of stuck. Nobody calls me Elizabeth. I'm just Lettie now."

Jay takes a hit, and out comes the vapor.

"Do you know a single Juul pod contains as much nicotine as a pack of twenty regular cigarettes?" I say.

Jay smirks. "Why do you think I use one?"

He pats his hand on the swing beside him, an invitation I take him up on. Do I like swinging? A lot more than tossing eggs, that's for sure. I squeeze my body into the plastic swing, which compresses like a straitjacket under my weight. I can still hear the block party commotion from the back of the Weavers' place—Uncle Ken's bad music blaring, kids shouting as they run about, general party mayhem drowning out the birdsong that's our usual background noise.

I plant my feet on the ground, using leverage to build up a little momentum, happy to have an outlet for my nervous energy. I can tell Jay is older than I am, but only by a few years. I like his shaggy hair and casual style—jeans, white tee under an open, untucked button-down shirt. He wears white Nikes, no socks.

"So, Lettie," says Jay, "what's your story?"

"That's a big ask for a first question."

"I don't have much time," says Jay. "My parents are looking to buy this house and it won't take long."

"Pretty sure home buying isn't a quick purchase," I counter.

Now it's Jay who laughs.

"You don't know my mom," he says before giving me an endearing smile. "When my mother has her mind set on something—and she's got her mind set on buying this place—it happens, and it happens quickly."

I sharpen my focus on his mustache with trimmed scruff. Normally I wouldn't be attracted to that look, but it works for Jay.

"Are you going to live here with them?" I ask, hoping the answer is yes.

"Yeah," he says a bit gloomily, like he'd rather not.

"Do you have brothers or sisters?" I glance at the brick monstrosity in front of us. It's a lot of house for three, especially when the one "kid" seems old enough to have his own apartment.

A distant look invades Jay's eyes, a heaviness not present moments ago. There's a story there, but I'm not about to pry. My face grows hot. I feel slightly queasy, fearing I've said the wrong thing. Jay's expression softens, saving me from further embarrassment.

"Nope, just me," he says.

"Are you going to go to Meadowbrook High?" I ask.

Jay chuckles. "I got the boot from Northeastern six months ago."

The boot? He's been kicked out of college? Naturally a thousand thoughts enter my mind, enough so I stop swinging. What did he do? Was it grades? Drugs? I'm excited at the prospect that Jay might make this neighborhood a whole lot more interesting, but I'm hoping it's nothing really bad. Even so, I'm not about to ask.

"What about you?" Jay says. "Do you go to Meadowbrook?"

"I did," I tell him.

"So, you're graduating. Congrats."

"No, I'm going to be a senior next year," I explain. "I just got suspended for the last two weeks of school, that's all."

Jay looks impressed, like we might be kindred spirits. "Tell me about it," he says, a twinkle in his chocolate eyes.

I think: *Why the heck not?*

I show him my phone, specifically the default display picture.

"Is this you?" he asks.

I nod. You can't make out my face in the photograph. My eyes glow so brightly from the security camera's sensitive optics it's blurred my features. The can of spray paint in my hand is still quite apparent.

"Graffiti?" asks Jay.

I nod again before telling him the story about how I went to school wearing a T-shirt that read: *Bite Me!* The shirt had a picture of an apple with a big bite taken out of it. Evidently the graphic violated school decency standards, something about threatening speech. I was given a mandate: my mom could bring me a new shirt, or I'd have to go home and miss an important test.

"I'm like, whatever! Do you people need examples of real hate speech?" My indignation game is strong.

"I'm guessing they didn't buy that argument," says Jay.

"Not in the least," I say. "And I'm thinking about the injustice of it all—not for myself, but for the *real* problems the school should care about: greenhouse gas emissions, class sizes, mental health counseling, bullying, poverty, child abuse, gender issues, race issues, but no, my dumb T-shirt is the *big* problem that must be addressed."

"Did your mom bring you a shirt?"

"She did," I confess, "but the next day I created an online petition stating my shirt wasn't indecent and the whole standard needed to be rewritten. Naturally, I supplied the new language. I got three hundred signatures in a couple weeks, even from some middle school kids."

"So, what happened?" asks Jay, sounding intrigued.

"My petition was voted down at the school board meeting."

"I'm guessing this is where the graffiti comes into play," Jay says.

"That picture I showed you is me spray-painting 'Bite Me!' and an apple with a bite out of it on the door of the school gymnasium."

"Oh," says Jay, his eyes widening.

"I probably would have gotten away with it, too, but my cousin's girlfriend identified me to the authorities."

"How so?" says Jay. "That picture could be any female."

I open the photo on my phone, using my fingers to zoom in on the image, specifically the hand holding the can of spray paint. What's clear now is a discoloration on my wrist—a birthmark. I show Jay the same mark on my skin.

"Riley Thompson lives over there." I point to Riley's house. "She was my best friend when we were little girls, and my birthmark was a big topic of conversation. It fascinated her. She doesn't have a blemish on her body."

"What did she get out of reporting you? Cash reward?"

Not sure why, but I get the sense money is very important to Jay.

"No cash. But she's president of the student body. Maybe she felt obligated. Or she wanted to improve her credibility with the powers that be. She's always been attracted to prestige."

"Do you have to be in summer school?" Jay wants to know.

"No, I can still turn in my homework and take tests, so I won't fail the quarter. It's not the worst thing."

"How'd your parents take it?"

"Not well," I say. "I'm grounded for half the summer. I can get a job, go to work, come home, and that's it. Oh, and I can go to this dumb block party, probably because my parents know I don't want to be here." I motion to the big happening taking place on the other side of the house.

"Talk about layering on the punishment," says Jay with a laugh. "Well, you can talk to me this summer, assuming I move in."

I'd like that, but I don't share that with him.

"You're not the only misfit in Meadowbrook," Jay adds, pointing to himself.

We're swinging now, going higher. The chains creak under our collective weight.

"Who says I'm a misfit?" I retort.

Jay sends me a look that calls my bluff.

"Okay, I'm a misfit," I admit.

"And I'm twenty years old, still living with my parents," he says before taking another hit of his Juul. "We can be friends."

We don't shake on it, but that's just a formality.

"How will you pass the time in home confinement when I'm not around to distract you from your plight?" asks Jay.

I shrug. "I might get a jump start on my summer paper for my AP Psychology class," I tell him. "I'm writing about revenge. Riley inspired me."

I offer up a devious grin. Jay doesn't have much reaction at all.

"Writing about revenge is cool, I guess," he says indifferently. In the next breath, though, his expression shifts to a chilling smile. "But taking revenge . . . now, that's something to truly savor."

Chapter 4

Morning sun streamed through the kitchen windows like a beacon announcing the arrival of a new day. For Alex, that meant back to the routine—not quite the grind, as she worked for herself. She was one of several Alton Road residents who had argued (unsuccessfully) to hold the block party on a Sunday, not the Monday of Memorial Day. She just wanted an extra day for recovery.

She took her first desperate gulp of coffee, too aware of the pounding in her head, regretting her choice to cap off the party with that final late-night glass of wine. She'd enjoyed yesterday's festivities well enough, but was glad it would be another year before they'd unpack the supplies to do it again.

She'd barely gotten her first rejuvenating jolt of caffeine when into the kitchen trotted Zoe, the family dog, a brownish, whitish, yellowish mutt that everyone loved and only one person fed. Zoe had come from the local animal shelter after months of Lettie begging for a pet. Nick was resistant, given their busy schedules, but Alex felt continually guilty that Lettie was an only. Eventually Nick warmed to the idea, but he never thought of Zoe as his responsibility. In his mind, this was Lettie's dog.

In a way he was right. Without Lettie, there'd be no Zoe. Whenever Lettie cried about not having a sister or brother, Alex broke inside. It wasn't by choice, but that was too much to explain to a child. By the time Lettie was old enough to understand, she'd grown accustomed to her status. Once she stopped asking for a sibling and started asking for a dog, Alex jumped on it. Lettie got a playmate, and Alex didn't have to answer any uncomfortable questions.

Alex filled Zoe's food bowl, noticing that the water bowl needed filling, too.

Nick appeared in the kitchen, doing up his tie.

"Zoe's water bowl was empty again," Alex said.

"And good morning to you," said Nick. "Any post-party regrets?"

"None," Alex lied. She felt like John Henry was trying to hammer his way out of her skull.

"Lucky," said Nick, rubbing his temples. "I think I'm getting too old for the block party."

Feeling no sympathy, Alex again pointed to the empty water dish. "Are you too old to pay more attention to Zoe? That's kind of what I'm asking here. I've got a lot on my plate."

"Right. And I don't?"

"Okay, that's not what I'm saying, Nick. I'm asking for your help, is all."

"You do have a daughter who wanted a dog. How about asking her?"

Alex's hands moved to her hips. She could feel her blood pressure starting to spike. Too early for that.

Calm. Stay calm, Alex told herself. *No reason to take this stupid conversation to unnecessary heights . . . or lows.*

"I'm sorry, are you refusing to help?"

Nick took the bowl over to the sink and filled it with water. "No, I'm merely pointing out that you have a daughter who begged for a dog and you *never* ask her to help with Zoe. Never. It's like you're afraid to confront her with anything these days. She's not a fragile egg, Alex. You don't need to handle her with kid gloves. You can push her and she'll still love you."

Alex's mouth dropped open. She wanted the perfect retort, something that would really sting, but her vast vocabulary yielded only a single "Harrumph."

Eventually she found some words. "How did this conversation turn into how I parent Lettie? And I think I've confronted her plenty," said Alex, harboring visions of tossing Zoe's water bowl at Nick's head like a Frisbee.

"Really? You didn't even want to punish her for getting suspended."

"That's not true."

But it was true. Alex had felt that the suspension was punishment enough, but suggested grounding her for two weeks when Nick pushed back. Eventually she'd had to apply the same mediation tactics she used on her clients to herself. They came up with a compromise—no winners, no losers—grounding Lettie for six weeks instead of Nick's proposal of the entire summer.

With coffee in hand, Nick departed the kitchen as Lettie came strolling in, her face fixated on her phone. She was grounded, but not without a lifeline to the world.

Alex did a fast reset. She didn't want Lettie to know that she and her dad had been exchanging tense words. She could almost hear Nick's reprimand—*you can't keep protecting her from real life.*

"How'd you sleep, hon?" Alex asked.

"Fine," said Lettie, not bothering with eye contact.

"Are you able to get your homework? Principal Corey said—"

"Mom—I'm fine," Lettie said.

"Right," said Alex. *Why is it that talking to teens feels like handling a live grenade?*

"Did Aunt Emily sell the Weaver house to that family?"

Lettie's question took Alex by surprise. "Did you see the Kumars looking at the house yesterday?"

Before Lettie could answer, Emily, who'd let herself in as always, barged into the kitchen through the side door.

"I have a real problem," she announced. She snatched a muffin from a plate that Alex had set out for breakfast. Emily took a bite and only then looked to Alex for permission, which she gave with a genial nod.

"Morning, Lettie," said Emily, her mouth full of muffin.

"Morning, Aunt Emily," Lettie responded. "Say, did you sell the Weavers' house to that family?"

"Not yet," answered Emily a bit tersely.

Alex knew the tone well and could guess the source of her sister's distress.

"Cool," said Lettie with an indifference that didn't quite jell with her initial interest. Out went Lettie, while Emily, strangely enough, hefted the white trash bag out of the freestanding kitchen trash can.

"Um, what are you doing, Sis?" Alex asked.

"Ken went to the dump," Emily said, as if that explained everything.

"And are you taking my trash there as well?"

"Not exactly," said Emily, and fled out the door.

Alex didn't hesitate to follow. "Em, where are you going with that?"

Emily didn't answer. She was too busy crossing the street, headed for the Weavers' house.

Alex had a mediation session scheduled for first thing that morning. She didn't have time for her sister to have a full-on meltdown, but that was what appeared to be coming. She raced to catch up with Emily, who was moving at a pace close to a trot, the garbage bag swaying in her grasp.

"What on earth are you doing?" Alex asked as Emily entered the code on the lockbox to retrieve the key.

"I need to figure out a way to keep the Kumars from buying this house," Emily said. She unlocked the door, entering the vacant home with urgency.

Alex followed her into the echoing foyer. The sparsely furnished rooms were staged for showing.

"Did the Kumars make an offer?"

"Twenty thousand over asking, and it's a cash deal." Emily made it sound like the sale had fallen through.

Alex trailed Emily down a flight of stairs into the basement, still baffled about why her sister would bring a trash bag from her home down here.

"What's your concern?" asked Alex, moving quickly to keep pace. "Is there something wrong with the house you haven't disclosed?"

Alex hoped that would be the case, because Emily in an emotional crisis meant a crisis for Alex as well.

"Not yet there isn't," Emily said.

The basement was unfinished but quite clean, with a gray concrete floor, smooth and flat as a skating rink. Emily hurried over to a corner, where she untied the trash bag. For reasons Alex couldn't fathom, Emily proceeded to dump the trash onto the floor. Out spilled wrappers and crinkled packages, soaked coffee grounds that spread like a coating of measles, wadded paper towels and plastics that should have been recycled.

"Emily, my god!" Alex said. "What the hell are you doing?"

Emily didn't answer. She was too busy fishing through the trash, searching with serious intent as though she might find something of value. Eventually she stood, holding—of all things—a browning banana peel.

"This will do," she said. She left the mess on the floor and bounded back up the stairs, forcing Alex to follow.

"Emily, stop it!" cried Alex, directing her plea to her sister's back. "What is going on with you?"

Alex followed Emily into the brightly lit living room. She recalled the sales copy advertising great sunlight, and it hadn't lied.

Rising on tiptoes, Emily stretched to unhook a burnished metal curtain rod from its wall-mounted holder. She began to unscrew the end cap while still holding on to the banana peel.

"Emily, hon," Alex said in a far gentler tone, "do I need to call an ambulance? Have you lost your mind?"

Emily was too busy fussing with the end cap of the curtain rod to respond. As soon as it came off, she tried to stuff the banana peel into the hollow rod, but it wouldn't fit.

"Damn it, it's too thick," she lamented. "It needs to be shrimp, and I don't have any shrimp. I'll have to go to the store."

"Why on earth would you put shrimp inside a curtain rod?" Alex demanded. "Whatever it is you're doing, you need to stop it right now and talk to me."

Emily slumped onto the hardwood floor, her body trembling. The curtain rod rolled away with a clatter. She dropped the banana peel onto her lap and buried her face in her hands.

"It's going to happen again," Emily moaned. "I can feel it."

Alex had a good idea what *it* meant. She also could guess what Emily was up to with the trash. "Are you trying to sabotage this sale? *Your* sale?"

Emily nodded glumly. "I read a story on the internet about a woman who put some shrimp inside the curtain rods of her former marital home before she moved out. Nobody could find the source of the stench. Drove them all mad."

"Oh, Em," said Alex with a heavy sigh.

"I was thinking I'd plaster some wet cardboard on the walls too, try to grow black mold, but I don't think I'll have time before the inspection. I've only got three days!"

Alex sank to the floor and placed an arm around her sister's shoulder. "You are completely unhinged, you know that?"

"I know," Emily admitted, but didn't really seem to care.

"This is about Mandy Kumar, isn't it?" Alex's face showed the perfect blend of empathy and love.

"I've seen lingering looks in my day," Emily said. "But Ken's eyes basically popped out of his head. I mean, Mandy is pretty—and she's got a great figure, I'll give her that—but I didn't expect to need a cup to catch my husband's drool."

"Are you sure it happened like that?" Alex asked the question even though she'd seen it happen, just like that.

"Even worse, Mandy was all gaga for Ken," Emily said.

"Ken is really handsome. A lot of women have that reaction to meeting him, but it doesn't mean anything."

Emily's expression only soured. "I know the difference between someone casually checking out my husband and something more—and *that* was something more."

"I really think you're creating a tempest in a teapot," said Alex. "Maybe they worked together or something? He could have recognized her, and it was just innocuous."

"I already asked him that, and he said no, definitely not. And it would have come up in conversation if that was the case, right? Instead, Ken took my question as an opportunity to lecture me about my jealous streak. I don't care what he says. It's going to happen again, and it's going to happen with her. I feel it in my bones."

"Ken and Mandy?"

"Yes, Ken and Mandy," Emily snarled. "I have the same feeling I had before."

Before. Alex didn't need any clarification.

"You can't know that for certain," said Alex.

"I knew he was sleeping with his secretary. I knew when he told me that he wouldn't do something so clichéd that he was in fact doing something *that* clichéd."

"That was fifteen years ago. You two have been good since then. You worked through all that."

"Once a cheater, always a cheater," said Emily.

Alex rose to standing, pulling Emily up with her. She set her hands on her sister's shoulders so that Emily couldn't hide from her stare. "Honey," Alex said in her most compassionate voice. "You and Ken are doing well now. You did the hard work and pulled through."

It was true. It had taken a year and a half of hard work, but Emily and Ken managed to recover from his infidelity. It had been a painful process for both, one that took humility, compromise, and uncomfortable honesty. Ken had no choice but to quit his job, sell the house, and move, which was how Emily came to live on the same street as her sister.

When Ken's affair came to light, nobody encouraged Emily to stay with him, including Alex. Emily arrived at that decision after extensive therapy. Remorsefully, Ken agreed to hand over his phone as well as his account passwords to his wife, while begging for a second chance. It had taken years to rebuild trust and put the marriage back on stable footing.

Or so Alex believed.

"One look shouldn't get you this upset." Alex held up the banana peel, a scent of rotting fruit tickling her nose.

Emily rolled her eyes the way Lettie might. "Really? You're honestly telling me you didn't see it."

Alex frowned, wishing honesty wasn't the best policy. "Okay, I did see something," she admitted. "But I can't say it was anything more than some initial chemistry."

"I'd say that's enough for me to sabotage this deal."

"Didn't you take some kind of professional oath or something?"

"We take a pledge. I don't think that's the same thing."

"It's sort of the same. And regardless, what you're doing here could put you in a lot of legal hot water. So I'm going home to get a broom, and we're going to clean this mess up together. You can put the curtain rod back."

"Fine," Emily agreed. She seemed settled, back to her senses, as if a fast-moving storm had come and gone.

"Just promise me, Alex, promise you won't lie to me. If you see something, say something, okay? I need my own Homeland Security system. I can't handle another round."

It was hard for Alex to view her sister as a mature equal. Instead, she saw Emily through an old lens, remembering her sister as a troubled teen—one who still could snap and do something crazy, like spreading trash in a home she was about to sell.

"Of course I'll say something," Alex said, knowing that the evidence of Ken's betrayal would have to be unquestionable and irrefutable to make this a promise she could keep.

Chapter 5

Lettie

From my bedroom window I watch the moving truck arrive. It's a large truck, but then again, it is a big house. A silver Lexus pulls into the driveway and Samir Kumar gets out. He's dressed like he might go golfing—khaki pants and a nice button-down short-sleeved shirt. He advances up his new walkway, hands on his hips, looking around, before shaking his head in dismay. I get the sense he can't believe he bought the place.

Mandy Kumar couldn't have had a more different reaction. She springs out of the car like school just got out for summer, looking summery herself in a sky-blue dress with her sunny beam of blond hair pulled into a tight ponytail.

I'm wondering about Jay, if he cares enough about his new home to show up on move-in day. Or perhaps I'm hoping he cares enough about me to make an appearance. We didn't exchange phone numbers, but I found him online. While I didn't summon the courage to make a friend request, that doesn't end my interest in him.

Just as that thought arises, a gleaming blue Subaru barrels down Alton Road, too fast for the moms on the block. The car comes to a hard stop next to the Lexus. A moment later, Jay emerges. My heart flips at the sight of him.

My earliest crushes were Disney princes, and there's definitely some semblance of a princely character in Jay as he swaggers over to his parents, tall and lean. He stands next to his father. They share a quick laugh about something, which surprises me. Jay had given me the impression that he was a profound disappointment to his parents, something we had in common. Interesting.

Moments after his arrival, Jay is helping his father unload the car. That says something about his character. It could mean he's not lazy, but then again, he did get kicked out of college. Perhaps it wasn't his grades? I think about what he said to me at the block party—about revenge being something to savor. I wonder if he arrived at that conclusion based on personal experience.

Revenge, of course, brings thoughts of Riley Thompson. If anyone deserves payback, it's Riley, and that's not just because she ratted me out as the school vandal. No, I've been on the receiving end of her cruel heart many times before.

I can see Riley's bedroom window from mine. There was a time we'd communicate using our bedroom lights to send Morse code. Back then, I naively assumed our friendship would go on forever. Then came middle school, and with it, the start of Riley's bullying.

In hindsight, I shouldn't have been surprised by the turn of events. We'd become friends only as a matter of proximity, not personality. Given that we were the same age and gender, and were both only children, Riley and I were thrust into each other's lives.

For a number of years, we were inseparable. Riley was my best friend, my steadfast trick-or-treat companion. We always wore complementary costumes on Halloween. For our last costume combo, I went as a baseball and she was a bat. Talk about foreshadowing! One year we were locked arm in arm, going house to house, getting all the candy we could carry, and the next, I'm at Riley's front door without her because she'd abandoned me for a new group of meanies. Willow tossed a few extra packages of Reese's Pieces into my pillowcase that year. Pity Pieces, I called them. They ended up in the trash.

Of course I was hurt, but what was I going to do? Riley had found a new group of friends, all of them the popular girls who would never have accepted me as one of their own. I didn't dress right, didn't obsess over the same things or care which boy was doing what. Even back then I was starting to think more about deforestation than lip gloss and fashionable leggings.

The beginning of the end came when Riley stopped saying hello to me at school. In girl-speak, the silent treatment is essentially a formal declaration of war. Being ignored was one thing. I could handle that. Once Riley started operating under a "pack mentality," when she and her cohorts isolated me, I was transformed from a person into prey. That's the first time I experienced real shame in my life.

Oh, sure, we got plenty of lectures in school about the terrible consequences of bullying. Phrases like *lift each other up, be compassionate, empower each other, choose kindness,* and blah-blah-blah got drilled into us from September on, but Riley and her crew were impervious to the old saying that "If you don't have something nice to say, don't say anything at all."

Guys who bully tend to punch or shove, but girls are far more insidious. They're emotional ninjas, delivering stealth wounds you don't see or feel until you're already bleeding out and near social death.

Unbeknownst to me, Riley and her gang had put me under surveillance—waiting, watching, hoping I'd make the wrong move. It didn't take long for me to give them the goods. My big blunder was being nice to a kid in math class who was close to the bottom rung on the school's social hierarchy. The boy's name was Matthew Bird—nice enough kid, but he didn't have the brand-name clothes, the athletic skills, or the right friends to make him popular. What he did have was an unruly tangle of dark hair that earned him the nickname Bird's Nest.

After Matt helped me with a math assignment when I missed school one day, I innocently returned the favor. I guess Riley saw us together in the library. That was all it took. The very next day we were called "lovebirds," and I got my new nickname—Loony Lettie. The loon being an actual bird made the taunt both cruel and clever, a perfect combo.

I remember what I was eating for lunch the day I first heard my new name—pizza, green beans, and a little cup of applesauce. Trauma does that to you. It makes sure you recall every painful detail of the triggering event so it can roost in your psyche and live there forever.

Loony Lettie and Bird's Nest became an overnight sensation at

Meadowbrook Middle School. The jokes started flying. Get it—flying? Are you nesting with Matt at lunch? Migrating south for vacation? Someone even put a pile of twigs inside my desk at school. Okay, I admit that one was kind of funny. Girls would say they liked my feathers when they meant my clothes. I found myself laughing along with them, thinking if I could be in on the jokes that they wouldn't hurt so much.

Didn't work.

Not everyone shunned me, and that's probably what saved me. The theater kids were always welcoming, and a bunch of them were into various causes, which furthered my activism. I never stopped being friends with Matt Bird, either, but he moved away at the start of eighth grade. I haven't heard from him since. I suppose Meadowbrook holds painful memories for him, so I don't begrudge him for cutting ties.

With Matt gone, the bird jokes came to an end—thank God for that—but by that point, the ice between Riley and me had grown miles thick.

Then one day a miracle happened. Riley invited me to go shopping with her and her friends. I couldn't have been happier. I didn't like being an outcast, and the invitation felt sincere. I thought my worst days might be behind me.

As we were leaving a store, one that sold glittery things teen girls can't resist, I heard a loud beep, beep, beep. Something had set off the store's alarm system. Next thing I knew, the cashier was coming out from behind the counter to confront us. A manager showed up and demanded we empty our backpacks. We did as we were told, and I was stunned—horrified, really—to find three items in my backpack that I certainly hadn't placed there.

Next thing I knew, the manager had called mall security, and they called my parents. I cried like I was going to be carted off to prison on the ride home. I swore up and down that I didn't steal anything. I insisted that one of the other girls had put the items in my backpack as a prank, but my parents didn't believe me at first. They assumed I'd tried to impress a group of new friends.

Mom, not Dad, gave me the benefit of the doubt. She confronted Willow with the allegation. Later that night, Riley was on my doorstep crying. I'd heard the expression *crocodile tears* before, but suddenly it had real meaning.

A little pressure from her mom was all it took for Riley to crack like Humpty Dumpty. My punishment was immediately revoked. Riley got grounded. She had to write me a letter of apology, too.

Things shifted at school after that. Riley and her friends stayed cliquey, but they mostly left me alone. The jokes stopped and the bullying stopped, too. I had my friends, Riley had hers. A chilly truce ensued, one that's lasted years. I eventually started speaking to Riley again, but only after she and my cousin Dylan began dating. He didn't listen to my pleas.

Now, in thinking about recent events, I'm willing to bet that Riley didn't let bygones be bygones. When she saw my birthmark on that security camera photo, she saw an opportunity for a little retribution. That whole school council president thing just gave her a good cover to turn me in. And I'm sure she knew Dylan would never keep her confidence. We're family, after all. No, Riley *wanted* me to know the name of the rat.

A pulse of anger surges through me, thinking of her smug smile when she told the school administration what she knew. Because of her I've had to endure an embarrassing school suspension—which could impact my college prospects! Granted, I was wrong to deface school property, but that dress code is utterly ridiculous. Something had to be done. If I thought for one second Riley had honorable motives, I might let it all go. But she didn't, so I can't. This was payback for middle school bullshit. Well, payback is a two-way street, bitches!

Outside I go, crossing Alton Road to where Jay is moving boxes from the car into the house. His parents aren't around, so we can talk privately.

Jay struts over with a broad smile that showcases his dimples. "What's up, Lettie?" he asks. "Good to see you again."

It's harder than I thought to meet his gaze. "Nothing much," I say back. "How's the move going?"

"Good," says Jay.

Well now, I didn't expect that to be a conversation stopper. I wonder where my confidence has gone? Irrationally, I blame a dodgeball game in fourth grade. I'm worried my expression says that I'm as dark and brooding as my clothes, or worse, that I have on the same outfit I did the day of the block party.

I take in a breath. Upon exhale, I finally find my voice. "Remember what you said about revenge being something to savor?"

"Sure," says Jay, as a devious little twinkle dances in his eyes.

"I guess I'd like your help with something."

Jay's smile broadens, becoming slightly sinister. I feel a chill, despite the warmth of the day.

"Glad you asked, Lettie," he says. "I'd be happy to help."

"So how do we start?" I ask.

Jay doesn't give it a moment's thought.

"First we have to learn everything we can about your neighbor—where she goes, what she does, who she hangs out with, that sort of thing."

"Why's that?" I want to know.

"If there's one thing I've learned, doing what I do . . . it's that everyone has secrets."

Meadowbrook Online Community Page

Ross Weinbrenner

I say we work backwards and figure out who got arrested.

> **Laura Ballwell**
>
> I say you let the police do their job.
>
> **Susanne Horton**
>
> How about don't tell others what to do because, ya know, "America."
>
> **Christine Doddy**
>
> This whole thing is so bizarre. I mean Meadowbrook doesn't have murders.
>
> > **Reply from Ross Weinbrenner**
> >
> > Well, it does now, **Christine Doddy**. Who on that street has marital problems? That's where I'd start looking. It's always the person closest to you who does you in.
> >
> > **Reply from Ed Callahan**
> >
> > Is this Real Housewives of Meadowbrook? Ha-ha
> >
> > **Reply from Janet Pinkham**
> >
> > Oh, I love that series! Is it still on? Are they filming in town?
> >
> > **Reply from Ed Callahan**
> >
> > **Janet Pinkham** Please check your meds.

Ross Weinbrenner

I'm serious. A strained marriage is like a gas-soaked pile of wood. All it needs is one little spark to set the whole thing ablaze. So which couples on Alton Road had marital problems?

> > **Reply from Christine Doddy**
> >
> > A better question is which ones didn't.

SUMMER

Chapter 6

On a bright Tuesday morning, Alex came strolling up Alton Road after a two-mile walk. Zoe padded alongside with a proud look on her face, tail wagging, tongue hanging out the corner of her mouth.

Alex knew fresh air and exercise were good for her, but she also felt the pressure of her busy schedule. Lettie should be the one to take Zoe for her walk, but Alex wasn't in the mood to badger. Nick's criticism about how she handled Lettie with kid gloves came to mind. Alex didn't need his armchair parenting. Nick himself could push a little harder as well, but no need to create friction with your daughter when the onus could be placed elsewhere.

Oh well. Since she was the one walking Zoe, Alex committed herself to making the most of this outing, which offered one of the few times in her week to literally stop and smell the roses. Several of her neighbors were expert gardeners, so she took her time admiring the dazzling array of colors that sprouted from impossibly tiny seeds.

This morning marked the start of what would be yet another chaotic day for Alex, one that included a rather contentious divorce mediation—this one featuring a father who had let his thirteen-year-old daughter drive his car around the block, of all things. Pausing in front of a lush flowerbed, relishing the simple act of inhaling the rich aroma of lilies made her forget, if only for a moment, that the world was full of poor decisions.

For Alex, choosing a new career path wasn't among them. Three years ago, she'd been approaching meltdown territory as a family lawyer. The hours were brutal, and prepping for court made a best friend out of Pepto-Bismol. Switching to full-time divorce mediation had changed Alex into a kinder, more patient, less frazzled version of herself.

She had loved learning about the law, but practicing law was nothing like being in the classroom. Now instead of trying to win, beat her opponents into submission, get the best deal for her clients, she was focused on making sure both parties felt like winners *and* losers. So why then, Alex asked herself, did she need wine at night to decompress? Was Nick right about Lettie's leaving in a year triggering some suppressed emotions? Or was she afraid of what life as an empty-nesting parent might be like?

She and Nick had talked for years about what they'd do once they were liberated from the day-to-day parental obligations, but now that they were at odds, sniping at each other, lacking affection, etc., the idea of more time alone with her husband held less appeal. Could they be headed for the same place her clients found themselves? Alex hadn't thought so until recently. He was so uptight these days, but maybe he, like Alex, was lamenting that soon his only child would fly the nest.

Eventually Alex found herself in front of the Kumars' house. Zoe raised her leg, marking her territory on a glorious rose bush in full bloom. The momentary peace Alex enjoyed soon gave way to thoughts of Emily, bringing fresh worries about how her sister was adjusting to the presence of Mandy Kumar in the neighborhood. No shrimp smell, so that was a good sign.

Since the day the Kumars moved in, all had been quiet, as far as Alex knew. That didn't mean Emily was at ease. The trouble with cheaters was that they knew how to slither unseen through the grass—and Ken, at least at one time in his life, had been as snakelike as they come.

"Alex, do you have a minute?" Willow Thompson's anxious voice tore through Alex's thoughts. Willow crossed the street and immediately launched right into her worries. "I need your advice," she said. "I've noticed large cash withdrawals from the checking account, and I'm starting to panic."

Alex switched into professional mode, the way a superhero dons a cloak. "Have you officially filed for divorce like I suggested?" she asked.

Embarrassment showed on Willow's face. "I was going to do it, but Evan keeps insisting we wait until the end of next school year. Less upheaval for Riley, he says."

Alex managed to keep the groan to herself, while thinking: *How can smart people be so dumb?*

"I guess I can understand his point," said Alex in a measured tone. "But to hold off even filing?" She looked baffled. "It muddies the waters financially—and that's just the start. You both need to start working on clear boundaries and a plan. Did you contact any of the lawyers I recommended?"

"Not yet," Willow admitted. "I was going to, but things got in the way."

What could be more important than this? Alex wanted to shout.

"Look, honey, I'm not trying to worry you." Alex placed a hand on Willow's shoulder. "But you need someone in your corner fighting for you when issues come up."

"So can he just take money from the account?" asked Willow, as if she hadn't heard a single word Alex had just said.

"Until you've filed, and there are court orders in place, there's nothing stopping either of you from using the money in your joint accounts. I don't understand why you won't just hire a lawyer and file. You can do that—file—even without a lawyer. All you need are the forms and a notary, which I happen to be, and I'll happily do the paperwork with you. It's really not a problem."

Willow seemed uncertain.

Alex didn't have the time to convince her otherwise.

"I don't think I should do that," Willow said, after giving it some thought. Her shifting gaze and tightening expression suggested more to the story than she'd shared. "Evan's threatening me with the prenup. He was being reasonable about the money at first, said he understood my situation, appreciates what I've sacrificed for our family, but when I confronted him about the withdrawals, he went crazy. You wouldn't believe how upset he was."

Alex had seen Willow's prenup enough times to have it partially memorized. A second-year law student could tell the damn thing was ironclad. Evan's well-to-do family had made sure of that. She shouldn't have signed it, but young love and naïveté go together like cookies and milk.

"Oh, Willow, I'm so sorry." Alex gave her neighbor's hand a squeeze. She didn't harbor any grudges toward Willow—or Riley, for that matter. All that bullying nonsense was in the past, leaving plenty of room in Alex's heart for compassion.

Alex often forgot how young Willow was compared with the rest of the moms on Alton Road. Riley was seventeen, the same age as Lettie, which meant Willow was only twenty when her daughter was born, still in college. As far as Alex knew, Willow never did get her diploma. Getting a job that would pay a Meadowbrook mortgage would be difficult.

But Evan could swing it. He boasted about his family money as if he'd actually earned it. He was—what? Five years older than Willow? Six? Alex knew only that Willow had been in college and Evan already a professional photographer when they met at an art show. Regardless, he should be thanking Willow. She doted on Riley while he gallivanted about the globe for his glamorous job.

"So, final word, can he do that? Take the money without recourse?" Willow asked, her brow furrowing.

Alex thought she looked more worried than angry. "How much are we talking?" she asked.

"I'd say an extra thousand."

"A month?"

"A week," Willow clarified.

"Jesus," Alex muttered. If she had an extra grand lying around it would find its way into Lettie's 529, not up the nose of some hot model, which was probably where Evan was putting his withdrawals.

"File. And file now," Alex urged. "You won't be left destitute."

Willow shook her head. "Riley is turning eighteen this winter, and the prenup limits alimony to fifteen hundred a month. I can't stay in Meadowbrook on that, and have you seen rents these days? I'll probably need a roommate. Imagine *that* Craigslist ad: thirty-seven-year-old divorcée seeks non-smoking, cat-tolerant roommate because her bitter, childish, thieving, model-whoring ex-husband won't treat her with any decency after she spent eighteen years of being his devoted wife. I'm sure my inbox will be *flooded* with responses."

"Willow, you don't have a cat," said Alex, trying to bring a little lightness to the moment.

"Not yet I don't. I'm projecting. I've no doubt I'll need the emotional support."

"What about moving in with Brooke for a time? She's single. I'm sure she'd welcome the company."

"Brooke Bailey?" Willow made it sound like she'd never met her neighbor. "She's too perfect, too gorgeous, and I'd feel constantly insecure. And besides, she's not single, she's widowed. There's a difference, and—well, you know."

A dark edge invaded Willow's voice along with a raised eyebrow, both subtle nods to a long-standing neighborhood rumor that Jerry Bailey's accidental death hadn't been so accidental, and Brooke's grieving widow bit might have been something of an act.

"You *may* need to get a job," Alex tossed in. "Riley will be heading off to college. It's a good time to explore Willow 2.0."

Willow threw her head back to let out a sardonic laugh. "I'll make sure to put extra caramel in your macchiato," she said.

"It won't come to that," said Alex, thinking it might come to that.

"You've been awesome, as always." Willow leaned in to give Alex a quick peck on the cheek. "Thanks for the advice. I'll let you know how it turns out."

Spinning on her heels, Willow hurried back to her abode, where Alex suspected she would not confront Evan with her concerns—or call a lawyer.

Alex was headed for home as well, passing the Kumars' house, when she heard an odd rustling sound behind her. Zoe heard it, too, and barked out a warning. Turning, Alex focused her gaze on a copse of trees at the far end of the Kumars' back lawn. She expected to see some animal passing—a deer, most likely—but to her surprise she glimpsed what was most certainly the outline of a man, sneaking out of the Kumars' yard to enter the woodlands behind their house, moving like a commando on a night mission.

Alex's heart skipped several beats at the thought of a prowler close by, but confusion soon replaced her fear. Even from a distance, Alex could tell who was entering the hiking path that ran behind the Kumars' house, one that led to a quasi-private lake a quarter mile away.

It was her brother-in-law, Ken Adair.

Chapter 7

Lettie

I haven't heard from Jay, not since he made his offer to help me plot my revenge against Riley. I'm wondering what he's cooking up. If I'm being honest, I'm nervous about it. I don't want to do anything too drastic—just want to dish out a little payback that would make me feel better about my current situation.

Being grounded for six whole weeks, just at the start of summer no less, feels like a life sentence. I'd never given the practice of putting people into isolation much thought until it was relevant to my life, which is so ironic because we talk about that kind of narrow thinking in my climate crisis committee. Until the fire is raging around your house or the floodwaters are rising or there's nothing in the well to drink, climate change doesn't seem like such a big deal. Then all of a sudden—BAM!—it sucks to be you.

And right now it sucks to be me—lonely, isolated, feeling sorry for myself, bored out of my mind, thinking about the plight of prisoners for the first time in my life. In a way, it feels like I've run into a metaphorical brick wall. One minute I'm full speed ahead, ending junior year on a high note. I make one utterly, absolutely benign wardrobe choice and suddenly I'm hidden away like Quasimodo.

Sure, I get to sleep on a plush mattress, not in a bell tower, but the feelings of isolation and loneliness can't be all that different. At least that's how it feels to me. I spend my days surrounded by the same voices, the same sounds and smells, not to mention the obvious tension between my parents. I've caught snippets from arguments. Not sure what that's all about, but Mom buying wine by the case can't be a good sign.

At least my friends are being supportive—or they were. They tagged me in all the FREE LETTIE memes that made the rounds on social, sent me funny DMs and short videos from the Target parking lot, where many of us congregate on a Friday night. (Meadowbrook lacks excitement as well as things to do.)

"WE LOVE YOU LETTIE!" they'd shouted in unison at the camera. "We miss you! Come back to us!"

A short while later, they grew bored and the DMs stopped. Lately I hardly hear from them at all. One minute you're the hero of the school, a beloved vigilante, the poster child for free speech, and the next you're yesterday's trending hashtag.

All of which brings me back to my bedroom, where I'm looking out the window expecting to see Jay Kumar drive down the street any moment now. Am I obsessed with him? Maybe slightly. But I'm not psycho obsessed. I mean, I wouldn't be spying if I weren't grounded.

Sadly, I've been doing so much watching, I've noticed a little pattern with Jay. Every morning around ten-thirty, he drives off and comes back twenty minutes later with a coffee and some baked goods from Starbucks.

Which is why I'm looking out my window at 10:45 in the morning, waiting for Jay. Sure enough, I hear a car coming down Alton Road, and no surprise, it's his Subaru. Jays pulls to a stop, gets out of his car holding a coffee in one hand and a brown bag in the other. Is he a danish guy or a muffin man? These are the monumental questions I ponder as I basically stalk my new neighbor.

I've been resisting the urge to shoot him a text ever since we exchanged numbers. I don't want to seem desperate, even though I am—just a little. Jay's probably forgotten all about me and my revenge plot.

No sooner do I think that than he looks up at my window and sends me a little wave. I can't resist the urge to duck down like I'm hiding from the cops. I lie flat on my bed, breathing hard, terrified to peek out the window again.

Next, my phone buzzes. I check it without changing my position. It's an incoming call from Jay. Shit. I answer.

"Hey, Lettie," he says. "Fall off your perch?"

My throat goes completely dry. It's as if I've lost the ability to speak.

"Why don't you come on out?" he says. "We should talk."

"Okay," I tell him. "I'll be down in a minute."

"I have an extra croissant if you want one."

I think: *A croissant man?* Never would have guessed.

I race downstairs. Outside, I blink away the morning sun as I march down our redbrick pathway, regretting that I hadn't worn sunglasses or put on a cuter outfit. There's no time to change now.

"Are you still grounded?" Jay asks.

"Yeah," I tell him, appreciating the perfect ratio of scattered scruff to his clean swarthy skin.

From the pocket of his jeans, Jay extracts his vape pen. He offers it to me, which I decline with a shake of my head.

"Oh, I forgot," he said. "You don't."

I feel a pulse of excitement watching him inhale.

"Do your parents mind?" I point to the cloud of vapor he blows out. "I mean, there are healthier breakfast choices."

His face brightens, but he doesn't quite laugh. Suddenly I feel rather small.

"Them?" He thumbs behind himself to his house. "They mind everything I do."

"Yeah," I say, like we have so much in common, but getting grounded isn't quite like getting kicked out of college.

"How do you like the neighborhood?" I ask, hating the tremor in my voice.

"Same shit, different street," he tells me after taking another hit. "My dad is a bit worse here, I think."

"Worse? Like, what do you mean, worse?"

"Let's just say there's a Kumar way and I don't follow it. My mom's a psychologist, so she has diagnosed my 'issues,' and Dad's a psychiatrist, so he's got the medicine to fix me. A nightmare parental combination, if ever there was one. But my dad is the one pushing hardest for me to get my life together."

I have so many questions, but I don't feel comfortable prying.

"What do you do all day?" I ask, stuffing my hands in my pockets. "Do you just get your coffee and hang out?"

Jay peers over my shoulder. His gaze travels up to my bedroom window. I wince, not having known embarrassment could actually hurt.

"Have you been spying on me?" he asks. A sly grin comes to his face.

A terrible sinking feeling washes over me. Any words I might have seem to have slipped from my mouth down into my stomach.

"Don't worry," he tells me. "If I was grounded, I'd be looking for any source of entertainment. Sorry I'm not more interesting."

I want to say that he's the most interesting person in Meadowbrook, maybe the most interesting person I've ever met, but I manage to find some restraint. "All I know is that you go to Starbucks and you don't seem to do much else." I keep it vague, hoping that's enough to get him talking.

Jay offers me a casual smile. "I code. All day. Every day. That's what I do."

"Yeah, what are you coding?"

"Something that's going to make me a billionaire."

My eyes grow wide.

"That's a lot of Juul pods," I tell him, and he laughs. "Are you making an app? Everyone makes apps these days."

"If I told you—"

"You'd have to kill me," I say, finishing the thought for him.

Grounded or not, I'm sure my mom wouldn't want me making friends with the handsome older vaping college dropout.

As if reading my thoughts, Jay turns his head when he takes a hit, blowing the vapor toward his house, not mine. He does so with attitude, like he's making a statement, a blatant show of disrespect for his parents perhaps.

He puts his Juul away and takes out his phone, which he then holds up for me to see. "I want to show you something," he tells me.

He launches a video recording. I recognize the person in the frame as Jay's father, a close-up image of his broad face that fills the display.

"I'm not going to let him just hang out in the basement all day doing nothing with his life and time," Jay's father says to someone, but I can't see who.

He stops the playback with his thumb. "He's talking to my mom," Jay tells me. "They do this a lot—complain about me."

"And you . . . recorded it?" I gasp, then lower my voice. "Is this in their bedroom? Are you recording them doing it? Because if so, that is seriously messed up."

Jay makes a face like he's going to be sick. "Hell no," he says. "My parents don't have sex. My father hasn't filled his Viagra prescription in three years."

"You know your dad takes Viagra?"

"I told you, Lettie, everyone has secrets . . . and secrets are hard to keep in this day and age." Jay tilts his head to the side. "So, are you ready to find out Riley's? We're all set on my end."

I stammer before I can speak. "All set? What's all set? What do you mean by that?" My heart feels fluttery as I grow a bit light-headed.

"Riley. Your big revenge plot," he says. "You asked for this, Lettie." Jay's voice takes on an edge I hadn't heard before. "Are you backing out on me? I've put in all the legwork to get you what you want. Don't tell me you've got cold feet now?"

I hear the subtext loud and clear: *back out and we're done.* He won't ever talk to me again. I'll be just a dumb little girl in his eyes. I think of all I've suffered because of Riley. A little payback can't hurt, right?

"I'm not backing out," I tell him, though my voice lacks conviction. "What's the plan?"

"The plan is that I've got good intel that Riley is going out tonight, and you and I are going to see where she goes and what she does."

"How can you know that?" I ask. Then I think of the secret recording he made of his parents. Who knows what Jay is capable of?

"You're not the only one who's been doing reconnaissance work on the neighbors," he says with a grin.

The panicky feeling in my chest deepens. "I can't go tonight," I blurt out. "I'm grounded. Remember?"

I feel so juvenile that I can't meet his gaze, so I stare at my feet instead.

"Lettie," Jay says, gently lifting my chin with one long, elegant finger until I'm looking him in the eyes, "when it comes to taking revenge, you won't get anywhere by playing it safe."

Chapter 8

God knew they could have used a date night, but getting ready felt like more hassle than it was worth. Alex hated every outfit she tried on for a concert Nick was more excited about attending than she was—some nineties band trying to revisit their glory days.

A glass of wine on the couch was the only date she needed. She'd spent the day in a grueling mediation session between a divorcing couple who used their money and time to bash each other rather than agree on a vacation schedule. She'd always been inured to her clients' marital strife, but now she seemed to be taking her work home in the worst possible way. The conflicts that played out in her office were somehow skewing her perspective, making it hard to tell the difference between reality and a projection of fears and anxieties for her own marriage.

At least the house was quiet. Alex busied herself getting ready for the evening. Nick wasn't home from work yet. She assumed Lettie was in her room, where she'd been spending most of her time while grounded.

To this day, Alex regretted compromising with Nick on Lettie's punishment. It was too much, and she wanted to rethink the whole damn thing. She'd address it with Nick later, try to get her daughter's sentence reduced for good behavior. *Let him accuse me of being too soft a parent,* she thought. *It's not like he has all the answers.*

It was a bit early for a drink, but Alex found herself opening a bottle of wine and filling a glass to the very top. Although Nick enjoyed a cocktail here and there, she was glad he wasn't home to watch her imbibe. She didn't want to throw out the "it's five o'clock somewhere" line again unless absolutely necessary. The world was divided into twenty-four different time zones, and there was a good chance she'd used that excuse often enough to cover every one of them.

At the expected hour, Alex heard Nick's car pulling into the driveway as she was pouring herself a refill. She took a long drink, then another, and rather than try to finish it all, poured the rest of her glass down the sink. She rinsed the glass clean, aware she was getting rid of evidence, not sure why she was taking such measures to hide a drink—or two.

Moments later, Nick strode into the kitchen through the side entrance, followed close behind by Emily.

Alex always welcomed her sister's pop-in visits, but this was one she could do without. It had been a few days since she'd seen Ken traipsing through the woods behind the Kumars' house. She'd had ample opportunities to share what she saw, but Alex feared it would do more harm than good.

She was hoping Emily would preempt any conversation by offering some grand explanation, a crazy story about Ken having to race over to the Kumars' place to help put out a grease fire or something—anything—but no such luck.

As far as Alex was concerned, revealing what she'd witnessed might start an avalanche of accusations that could be the undoing of Emily and Ken. The weight of that responsibility felt too much to bear, so Alex was counting on time to take care of the issue for her.

"Hey, sweetheart," Alex said, giving Nick a kiss on the cheek to lessen the chance he'd smell wine on her breath. "Are you excited for the show?"

"Very!" Nick said with kid-like glee.

"Who are you seeing?" asked Emily.

"I don't know," said Alex, "the Wiggles or something."

Nick shot Alex an incredulous look. "Weezer," he corrected. "We're seeing *Weezer* tonight. Not the Wiggles. Good god, did I waste this ticket on you?"

"Whatever. I don't care about the band." She said this lightly, even though she meant it. "But I certainly hope you don't think taking your wife out on a date is a waste of anything."

"No, of course not," said Nick. He placed an arm around her shoulder to give her a half hug. "I should get ready. It's getting late, and we'll hit traffic."

Nick worried about these sorts of things—traffic, parking, gas (he never let a car get below a quarter of a tank)—while Alex was more fly by the seat of her pants. His stress frequently became Alex's, which always added a little anxiety to their date nights.

After Nick left the room, Alex turned her attention to Emily. "So what brings you here, Sis?"

Instead of answering, Emily leaned forward, prying apart the lapels of her silk blouse to reveal a stunning emerald pendant dangling from a platinum chain. "Thought you'd like to see this," said Emily, whose radiant smile was worthy of any red carpet.

Alex's breath caught. "It's gorgeous."

"It's from Ken," said Emily, who did a little shake/shimmy dance to express her delight. "I know you've been worried about me, so I wanted to make sure you know everything is okay at home now."

"More than okay, I'd say," Alex said. "So what's the occasion?" Emily's birthday was close to Christmas.

"No special reason, just that he loves me," said Emily with a sparkling smile. "Guess I should feel a little guilty for thinking the worst," she added.

"Or trashing the Kumars' basement," said Alex.

"Not my finest hour, I admit," Emily said. "But I'm letting all that go now. It's in the past. By the way, I saw Lettie heading off with the new boy on the street."

Alex gave her sister a confused look. "What are you talking about? Lettie is up in her room, or at least I thought she was."

Nick returned to the kitchen, bending at the knees to pet Zoe.

"Honey, Emily just told me that she saw Lettie driving off with the new neighbor. Is she sneaking out on us?"

Nick cleared his throat. "Oh, I didn't get a chance to tell you," he said, "but Lettie begged me to let her go out to a movie with Jay Kumar. I felt like she doesn't have friends in the neighborhood like she once did, and this would be a good opportunity to fix that."

A flash of anger turned Alex's vision momentarily white. "Isn't that something that maybe you and I should have discussed beforehand?"

Nick's eyes said yes, even though he'd done the opposite. "She's been really cooped up lately," he said.

"It's called grounded," Alex snapped. "A punishment you and I agreed on. In fact, didn't you just the other day criticize me for not being firm enough? And as for an added 'What were you thinking?' isn't Jay Kumar, like, thirty?"

"Twenty," Emily chimed in.

Alex's eyes grew fierce. "You sent our grounded daughter out on a date with a twenty-year-old who we hardly know? I'm sorry, Nick— and *please* feel free to take this the wrong way—but what the hell is wrong with you?"

Nick struck a defensive posture, his back literally up against the kitchen wall. Anger sparked in his eyes but dimmed before Alex's furious stare. "I'm sorry," he said, looking and sounding genuinely contrite. "You're right. I should have consulted you, but you were in a mediation session and couldn't be reached, and I was just so busy. I made a quick decision."

"By *quick*, do you mean without any thought whatsoever?" Alex's anger was still rising.

This time Nick didn't back down. "Give me *some* credit, will you?" he said. "Yeah, maybe I didn't think it all the way through, but it's not like I didn't give it any thought. Lettie is getting older, and sometimes we need to trust her judgment. She's going to be in college in a year, hanging out with kids of all ages. She's a smart girl . . . I guess she and Jay have been talking, and she's gotten to know him better. She trusts him, and despite some mistakes she's made, it's important Lettie knows that we still have faith in her. And besides, you were the one in favor of a lighter punishment. I didn't think it would be such a big deal. But I am sorry. I should have made more of an effort to reach you. That was wrong of me."

Alex took a deep breath. This wasn't the hill she wanted to die on. Given her profession, she was well aware that how couples fought could be the deciding factor in the health of their marriage. She and Nick were hardly a paragon of matrimony, especially these days, but in the end, each always tried to see the other's point of view.

"Okay, I get it . . . and thank you for apologizing. Let's just move on and have a good night out," Alex offered as an olive branch. "I have an idea," she said. "How about a drink before we go? Nick, can you pour the wine while I get changed? I don't like what I have on. I'll hurry. We won't be late."

It was about forty minutes into the concert before Nick embarrassed Alex to the point where she wanted to crawl under her seat. Prior to that, she'd been having a good time—to a degree. The band was loud enough to make her head hurt (or was it cocktail number whatever?) and many of the concertgoers could have been Lettie's friends, but a number of people from her generation were in attendance as well— including one especially exuberant gentleman in the row behind them decked out in flannel and a Weezer T-shirt, as if grunge were still in fashion.

The guy whooped it up with unabashed enthusiasm at the start of each song. Unfortunately, he didn't stop whooping until the end of each song. Then he'd swill his beer. Start all over again. "Hell, yeah! Weezer rules! Yeah, Weezer! Rivers! 'Beverly Hills'! 'Beverly Hills'!"

Evidently, "Beverly Hills" was a reference to one of the band's hit songs, and Rivers was the band's lead singer, who most certainly didn't care what this guy had to say.

Nick, however, did care. He cared a great deal, in fact. After the fourth song with nonstop screaming, Nick whirled around to glare at the much larger, far more physically intimating man behind him.

Alex's whole body tensed. She'd been in the car with Nick enough times to know when his anger would turn into road rage. Was concert rage a thing?

"Hey, dude," Nick shouted, pointing his finger at the man, "will you shut the fuck up so we can enjoy the show?" He said it loudly enough that Rivers might have actually heard him.

Applause broke out from most everyone nearby.

The man's eyes came aglow. The dark hairs of his thick beard twitched as if they'd caught an electric current. A stare-down ensued, Old West style, and Nick showed no signs of backing down.

Alex harbored visions of riding in the ambulance with him, calling his mother to get his blood type.

The bearded man raised his plastic cup, perhaps to toss the contents at Nick. "Whatever, dude," he grumbled. He put the cup to his lips, and that was the end of it.

Alex should have been proud of her husband for taking a stand. Instead, layers of embarrassment settled inside her. She couldn't bring herself to turn around again, so she spent the rest of the concert in her seat, with her eyes forward, fearing that at any moment the man Nick had confronted would retaliate. A trip to the concession stand for a glass of wine eased her nerves somewhat. Maybe if she was lucky, she'd forget the evening entirely come morning.

Alex was still revved up on the rainy ride home, while Nick was all smiles and joy. He'd always been this way—calm one second, a tempest the next. She'd grown accustomed to his mercurial tendencies, but that didn't make them a pleasure to live with.

True to form, Nick streamed a Weezer playlist of the concert they'd just seen. As far as he was concerned, the altercation was a thing of the past. The concert, however, would continue for the duration of the drive home.

"Haven't you had enough Weezer?" asked Alex.

"Never," said Nick, turning up the volume when "Beverly Hills" came on.

Alex wanted to shut off the music but didn't want to spark an argument. Instead, she found a subject that might interest him. She told him about seeing Ken sneaking around the Kumars' place.

"That's strange, for sure," said Nick, "and it's not the only odd occurrence involving our new neighbors."

"Oh? What else?"

"I went over to the Kumars' on Thursday to invite Samir to poker night."

"When is that again?"

"Next week," Nick said.

"Is he coming?" asked Alex.

"That's the thing. At first I thought so. At least he seemed interested. He asked me what games we played, and I told him mostly it's Texas Hold'em, but we mix it up some."

"Is Samir okay with gambling?" Alex asked. "I know in some parts of India it's not acceptable."

Nick gave a shrug. "I don't know how long he's been living in America or what his cultural practices are. But he does know how to play Texas Hold'em, because he asked me about the blinds."

"You talked about window treatments?" Alex looked confused.

"No, not those blinds," Nick said with a chuckle. "It's a poker term for a rule when there's no ante in a game."

Alex didn't quite understand, but she let it go. Poker wasn't her thing, but she was glad Nick got together with the neighbors to have some fun. As for Nick, it was no surprise to her that he would be welcoming to Samir Kumar and try to include him in their game night.

"So what happened?" she asked.

"Like I said, he seemed interested, but then he asked where we were getting together. Soon as I told him it was at Ken's place, he got really tense, and then he told me he had plans and had to take a rain check. But he seemed upset. I don't think he even said thanks for the invite. He basically closed the door in my face, kind of abruptly, and that was that."

"Which day was this again?"

"Thursday," said Nick.

"So this was after I saw Ken sneaking away from their home," Alex said thoughtfully. "Wonder if it's connected."

"Could be," Nick said.

Alex drifted into thought as Weezer sang on. Perhaps the only way to get some answers was to pay a visit to Mandy Kumar. It was a good thing that the neighborhood women had their get-togethers, too.

Chapter 9

Lettie

Do I find it strange to be in Jay Kumar's Subaru, driving some-where—don't know where—on some half-baked revenge plot against my cousin's girlfriend? Um, you betcha.

It's a minor miracle that my father agreed to let me go in the first place. If he'd said no, I would have gone to my mom. If she said no, I was fully prepared to sneak out. As Jay said, revenge isn't a play-it-safe kind of thing.

Speaking of safe, it's a foggy, drizzly kind of evening. Jay is a good driver, though he consistently goes ten miles over the speed limit, even in the rain. That's got to be intentional, like he knows just the right amount so that he never gets pulled over. He doesn't curse under his breath at other drivers the way my father does. No, Jay is calm. He projects an air of total control.

A new-car smell wafts up from the polished black leather seats. The dashboard glows red and features all kinds of high-tech gizmos. Jay has cradled his phone in a holder that latches onto one of the air vents. He's running a GPS app that seems to be leading us to the location of another vehicle, specifically Riley's BMW.

Yeah, that's right, Riley has a BMW, same as her dad. Whatever.

"Tell me again how you know where she is?" I ask as the rain comes down.

Electronic dance music blasts from Jay's seat-shaking car stereo system. I'm glad he plays his music really loud so we don't have to endure the awkwardness of small talk. We can just drive and follow the path to where Riley is parked. But again, I'm curious. How does he know her location?

"It's called a GPS tracker," Jay tells me. "I put a small device inside Riley's car, and it broadcasts a signal back to me so I can know her whereabouts."

I gulp as a knot of worry blossoms in my chest, but I let the feeling pass, because what am I going to do now? Beg Jay to let me out on the side of the road, in the rain no less, just because he's breaking eight or nine different laws? Yeah, I probably should, but I don't. I'm seventeen and technically my brain is still forming, so instead of doing the smart thing, I say, "You do know I can't really write this into my paper on revenge. Pretty sure my teacher would call the cops on you if I did."

Jay laughs it off. "I wouldn't write anything incriminating about yourself. Besides, Riley's not going to know it's there," he assures me. "And I'll get it out of her car tonight after she goes to bed."

Now it's finally clicking for me. "Wait, did you *break into* Riley's car?"

Jay shoots me an incredulous look. "How else was I going to put the tracker in there?"

He says it like I should have known, but I'm still putting the pieces together. Here's what I conclude: Jay is a criminal. He's a digital bad boy, which is probably the only kind of bad boy I can handle. I'm really not into the tatted-up in-your-face rough and tough types. Guess I like my outlaws to be quicker with the mouse than the draw.

I strongly suspect if my mother knew what Jay is all about—how he hacked into his parents' computer, broke into a neighbor's car, seldom left his basement hideout, got kicked out of college, vaped like Puff the Magic Dragon—she'd put a hard stop to our burgeoning friendship. If my dad found out, I suspect we'd be moving.

I glance at the tracker app on Jay's phone, which directs us to Riley's parked car some ten miles away in what is known as the Metro Region. Here the big houses and sprawling lawns give way to crowded streets lined with bars, restaurants, and a good deal of nightlife. What the heck is Riley doing out here? Meadowbrook kids never troll the Metro Region. This is the stomping ground for college frats and recent postgrad types, which may explain why Jay looks supremely confident navigating these streets. He drives, tokes on his vape, letting in a little rain as he blows smoke out the window, checks the GPS, and does it all with ease.

I'm a bit surprised and perhaps a tad unnerved that I find myself even *more* attracted to Jay. I'm worried it's because he flaunts the rules in ways I never would.

Without warning, Jay swerves his car to the right, hard enough to make my stomach lurch as he changes lanes. A moment later, he's expertly navigating his Subaru into a tight space using the kind of parallel parking skills I suspect I'll never possess.

"Her car is parked up there," Jay tells me. He points to the other side of the street, about five cars ahead of us.

There it is: the back end of a black car that could be Riley's Beamer, but I can't be certain in the rain and fog.

"I had no idea Riley hung out here," I say.

"There's a lot about Riley you don't know. But that's why we're here, right? Find out her secrets . . . and exploit them."

"Where do you think she is?" I ask, looking at the sea of neon surrounding us.

"She could be anywhere," Jay tells me. "We'll just wait it out."

A stab of panic hits me. No music. No driving. No distractions. We have to *talk* to each other. Jay leaves his car idling while we wait, and out of habit I lean over and push the button that kills the engine. It's something I do with my mother whenever she does the same.

Jay shoots me a look, one tinged with grievance.

I'm utterly mortified. "Sorry," I stammer. "I should have asked. I'm kind of conditioned to do that." I want to make myself small enough to crawl into the glove compartment.

Jay takes a toke. "No worries," he says, blowing vapor into the air that hangs cloudlike around his head. "I was being thoughtless."

"It's just that there's more carbon dioxide in our atmosphere now than at any time in human history," I blurt out, unprompted. Some habits are hard to break.

"Is that so?" Jay's smile implies he's not afraid of the looming climate apocalypse.

"Preindustrial levels were 278 parts per million. Now it's past 400 parts per million, which is most definitely human-caused. I'm sorry if you're a natural cycle believer, but that's just utter bullshit. We did it."

"I'm not disagreeing," he says.

"Last time there was this much carbon dioxide in the atmosphere, trees grew on the South Pole."

"Are you always this cheery a conversationalist?" asks Jay.

I feel myself die inside.

Jay's laugh pulls me from my mental abyss. "It's fine," he tells me. "I need to think about these things more than I do."

"I guess when you're trying to become the next tech billionaire, things like breathable air don't really matter that much," I say, wondering if I'll ever learn to shut my mouth.

"What else inspires you, Lettie? Beside our warming planet?" Jay leans toward me.

I smell his cologne (did he put that on for me?) and can feel the body heat radiating off him as my own internal temperature ticks up a degree or two.

I want to give him a good answer, something that will make him think I'm worldly and all that, but I come up blank instead. What *does* inspire me?

"Why are we here?" Jay presses. "Why do you want this so bad?"

I'm thinking: *Loony Lettie, security alarms, all that girlhood bullying,* but I keep my response general. "She deserves it," I say.

"Not really an inspired answer."

I'm saved from explaining myself further by the sight of a young woman who comes stumbling out of a bar called McCormick's. It takes me a moment to realize that the off-kilter patron who's wearing no jacket, only a blue dress that appears to have been painted on, is actually the person we'd come here to find.

Riley grabs onto a nearby parking meter like it's her dance partner. Her feet leave the curb as she swings out into the street before returning to the sidewalk after completing one full revolution. She might be upright, but that doesn't make her steady. She sways back and forth, oblivious to the rain dampening her clothes and hair. One moment I think she'll topple left, and the next I think she'll go right.

Before she can fall, a tall guy in a sports coat and jeans bursts out of McCormick's. He hunches forward to shield himself from the rain as he runs to catch up with Riley, who's begun walking away from her car.

Jay hits the wipers, but I can't get a good look at Riley's companion. The rain is making him blurry, and to make matters worse, he opens an umbrella that he uses to keep them both dry.

How chivalrous of him.

Riley shows her appreciation of Umbrella Man by wrapping her arms around him.

The umbrella comes down like a shield, blocking my view of what's happening on the other side, but I can see the guy's hand is low enough to be cupping a part of Riley's rear anatomy where Dylan would not think it belonged. The umbrella comes down even more so I can watch a drunken kiss. Honestly, I've seen mating rituals in wildlife documentaries that were classier.

Jay has his phone out. It takes me a moment to realize he's recording the whole encounter. I'm not sure how much he can capture on video given that all I can make out is the back of Riley's head.

After the pawing, Umbrella Guy escorts Riley to the passenger side of her car. I'm thinking it's a good thing she's not driving; I feel safer with *this* guy behind the wheel. At least he can walk a straight line. One second, they're parked, and the next they're driving out of sight. It happened that fast.

Jay pulls out and we're back to following them, but there's no need for the GPS if we can keep them in sight.

I feel a little less guilty about tailing Riley covertly because now we'll know that she gets home safely. I check the time on the dash. The movie I'm not at just got out. We follow the Beamer for a few minutes.

"They're not heading back to Meadowbrook," Jay tells me.

"We have to keep following her and make sure she's okay," I answer. "That guy she's with is definitely *not* in high school."

"It's okay, we got enough," Jay says.

"Enough for what?" I ask, not liking the nervous edge in my voice.

"Revenge," he says. "We put the video and pictures online, tag Riley, and that should turn her life upside down."

I gulp, thinking that'll turn Dylan's life upside down as well. "You can't do that," I snap. "Dylan will be crushed."

Jay bangs a U-turn at the light and starts driving *away* from Riley.

"Where are you going?" I shout. "We're headed the wrong way!"

Jay doesn't change course. "I'm not wasting any more of my time on this, Lettie. We have a plan. Doesn't seem like you can go through with it, though. No worries. I'm not going to force you."

I feel all kinds of panicky. "I need you to turn this car around, Jay, right now." My tone is older and bolder than I am.

"So you're okay if I post the pictures?" Jay wants to know.

"No," I say sharply. Then suddenly I get it. I know exactly what Jay is thinking. "If I tell you to post the pictures you'll turn around?"

"That's right," Jay says.

"And if I say no posting, we drive home?"

"Right again," says Jay. "This is how revenge works, Lettie. You have to make some difficult choices."

I can't let him post. "What if something happens to her?" I cry out. "Who's that guy she's with? She could be in trouble. We can't just leave her."

Jay shoots me a sideways glance. "Did she look in distress to you?"

He makes a good point.

"She's fine, Lettie," he says with utter confidence. "And I don't think you've got this revenge thing figured out just yet. You're supposed to *want* bad things to happen to your target."

"But not rape!" I shout. "I don't want her to get hurt. And I don't want Dylan getting hurt, either."

"Again, that's just not how revenge works."

"We're going to have to come up with something else then," I insist. My heart is beating so hard I worry it might burst.

"It's fine," Jay says. "Let's forget all about it and just go home. She can handle herself, and clearly that wasn't the first time she's been with that guy."

"We should still follow her," I say.

"Why? To see what Motel 6 they're crashing at? I'd rather save the gas."

"How do you know where he's taking her? What if he takes advantage of her?" I ask. "She's clearly under the influence."

"Okay, then give me the green light to post the pictures, and we'll spend as long as you want following Riley around. Those are your two choices. So what do you want to do, Lettie?"

I want to punch Jay in the face, that's what, but he's driving. I dig my fingers into my legs instead. How did I let myself get into this mess? I asked for it, that's how. I study my knuckles. What the hell should I do? Post the pictures and maybe save Riley, or don't and spare Dylan.

So far, getting revenge really blows.

"Relax, Lettie. This isn't Riley's first night on the town. I can assure you."

"You've followed her before?"

"Let's just say I've done a little initial reconnaissance work. She's fully aware of what she's doing."

I admit that puts me somewhat at ease. At least it'll buy me time to decide what to do with the recording.

"If it makes you feel any better," Jay says, "I'll keep an eye on the GPS tracker. Make sure she gets home safely."

What more could I do? I can't control what happens on her date without crashing the party. I figure it's out of my hands, and at least Jay will know her whereabouts so I can sleep tonight.

"Shoot me a text when she's home, okay?"

"No problem," Jays assures me. "But chances are she's not coming back until morning. I'm sure her mom thinks she's sleeping at a friend's house—that's what I would have told my parents back in the day."

"Good point," I say.

"And Lettie, you should know this isn't the *only* secret Riley's keeping."

"What else?" I ask. "What are you talking about?"

He opens up the center console to his Subaru and takes out an amber-colored pill bottle. There's no label, but Jay shakes it and the bottle rattles like a maraca. "I found this in Riley's car," he says. "Maybe I'll put it back—or maybe I'll make her think she lost it. These beauties are no joke."

"What are they?"

"Quality opioids," he says with delight. "Unless she's recently had back surgery, it seems our little Riley isn't just into booze and boys. She's into the hard stuff as well."

Jay presses down on the gas. His car zooms forward as my stomach flattens from the force of acceleration. I glance at the speedometer, watching the needle climb until it stops at about twenty miles an hour over the speed limit.

In the GPS tracker I can still see Riley's car continuing in the opposite direction, headed to who knows where with some stranger.

The rain is coming down harder now.

Chapter 10

Work had kept Alex so busy that it took her three weeks even to think about organizing a neighborhood get-together—just the ladies this time. When she finally got around to it, she called Willow to get a night that worked for her schedule.

"What's the occasion?" Willow asked.

"None, really. Just a chance for us to welcome Mandy to the neighborhood and have a few drinks and some laughs."

"You're not going to make it a theme night, are you?" The potential of that clearly horrified Willow.

"Why not?" asked Alex, who had already sourced some theme ideas on Pinterest.

"Because we're not twelve," said Willow crisply. "I went to a friend's house a few weeks ago, and it was a pajama party. I've now officially had my fill of forty-something-year-old women in their jammies."

"Too bad—that actually sounds like fun," said Alex. "We get into our cozy pajamas and drink mai tais. What's not to like about that?"

"Too much merriment for my current situation," Willow said. "Divorce has soured me on fun of all kinds. I'm taking my drinking *very* seriously these days."

Alex had a glass of wine in her hand and cookies in the oven. She understood Willow's position all too well. Any time she made it to six o'clock still in one piece, she felt proud of the accomplishment and deserving of her reward, which she always uncorked with serious intent.

"We'll skip the pj's and focus on the drinks and banter. Deal?" said Alex.

"Of course I'll be there," Willow said. "You pick the day. You're all I have left."

She ended the call before Alex could dig into *that* layer cake. Alex wondered if Willow was implying that she had trouble at home with Riley as well as Evan. In the past, Alex had unfairly compared Willow and Riley's closeness to her relationship with Lettie. She and Lettie had a different kind of bond, Alex told herself. She didn't have the time to devote her every waking minute to Lettie's whims and needs. That child would have rebelled against such attention anyway. Lettie possessed an independent streak far too wide for Alex to get her arms around, which was why it shouldn't have been a surprise to feel her daughter pulling away. And yet it felt like a surprise, or maybe surprise wasn't quite the right word. Maybe it was just plain old hurt. She had one child, and that child would be leaving home—soon.

Alex felt a pulse of grief. She lamented more than ever having agreed to Nick's punishment. And yet instead of standing up to Nick, she'd once again put on a united front for the sake of the family. When was she going to find her voice? She had it everywhere else—why not at home?

Because Nick had a temper? Because she always wanted to keep the peace? Such a weak excuse. She was no pushover. And by letting Lettie go out with Jay like that, Nick got to play the hero in his daughter's eyes. The way Alex saw it, boys with experience came with one thing—expectations. But what was she to do about that? Put her foot down again and say no more seeing Jay Kumar? Good luck with that. All she'd get would be more distance between them. It simply wasn't fair. She and Nick needed to have some words.

But first she needed a drink.

The doorbell drew Alex away from the kitchen, the oven, and the cookies—but not her wine, which she carried with her out into the hallway. She figured it was UPS. None of her friends ever bothered announcing themselves before coming in.

To Alex's surprise, Brooke Bailey was standing on her front stoop. True to form, Brooke had arrived gorgeous as ever. Alex wondered if she used a stylist and makeup artist before leaving the house.

But the truth was that Brooke could make anything look good on her. Her skin tone was the most sensuous olive shade imaginable. With her figure, she could wear a potato sack as a dress and make it look like a fashion statement. However she did it, Brooke Bailey was always effortlessly chic—and to make matters worse, she was incredibly nice and extremely bright as well.

She entered Alex's home with a friendly smile, walking in sleek black heels as if they were loafers. Her patterned skirt featured mood-boosting polka dots that she paired with a simple white tee. Alex knew from Nick that the guys in the neighborhood wondered if Brooke's breasts were real, to which she would retort, "What does it matter? They're *really* impressive."

Brooke arrived carrying a brown bakery box that was sealed with decorative green and pink ribbon.

"These are for you," she said, offering Alex quick kisses on the cheek. While she and Brooke weren't particularly close, they were neighbors and friendly enough that the gesture felt as warm as it was welcome.

"Well now," Alex said, balancing the wine and the bakery box in her hands, "what's in here?"

"Just back from New York," Brooke said as she trailed Alex into the kitchen. Even her voice was sultry, an enveloping deep timbre that offered hints of romance and mystery. "I stopped at Supermoon Bakehouse. They make these to-die-for raspberry eclairs with maple butter pastry cream, and I thought to bring you a box. You do so much for everyone else around here, I figured someone should do something nice for you."

Alex set the eclairs on the counter. "That's so sweet of you to think of me," she said. "And you were on my mind, actually. I was just going to call you. I'm having a girls' night, and—"

Alex cut herself off when she noticed Brooke's troubled expression. Brooke sniffed the air, looking around for the source of some offending odor.

At that moment, Alex caught a whiff of it, too.

"Is something burning?" asked Brooke, eyeing the oven suspiciously.

Alex nearly shrieked. Fast as she could, she fished a potholder from a drawer. When she opened the oven door, a wall of smoke hit her in the face, and a second later the smoke detector started blaring. From somewhere in the house, Zoe was barking madly, pleading for the noise to stop.

Brooke covered her ears, but to her credit didn't let the piercing alarm bother her for long. She jumped into action, shutting off the oven, then opening windows to let the smoke escape. More smoke came out when Alex extracted a tray of charred cookies from the oven.

Positioning a chair beneath the smoke detector, Brooke effortlessly climbed up—in her heels, no less—to hit a button that silenced the alarm. Just what Alex needed, another hero to make her feel worse about herself, but she *was* grateful for Brooke's timely arrival.

"Hey, glad you're here to try my new recipe for homemade hockey pucks," Alex said, making a big show of her tray of blackened ovals.

Brooke laughed as she got down off the chair.

Alex set aside her brief twinge of jealousy at gorgeous Brooke, her perfect dessert, and the way she so calmly managed the stressful situation, to focus on discarding the burnt remnants of her cookies into the trash.

"I was going to bring these over to Mandy Kumar as a little welcome-to-the-neighborhood gift, and at the same time invite her to the party I was just telling you about." Alex waved her hand in front of her face to fan away some lingering smoke.

Brooke retrieved the box of eclairs from the counter. "I'm sure they're not as good as your homemade cookies would have been, but why don't we share these with Mandy," said Brooke. "I'll go with you. I haven't met her or her husband."

After downing another healthy gulp of wine, Alex headed outside with Brooke. It was a quick jaunt across the street to the stately brick colonial the Kumars now occupied. Perhaps Mandy would offer some explanation of why Ken appeared to be her back-door man. Thank goodness Brooke was there to offer a buffer.

The doorbell's regal chime echoed quite loudly. Through a side-light, Alex got her first good look inside the Kumars' new house. She noticed it was lacking in furniture and personal touches. It gave off a cold, unwelcoming feeling, but she assumed the family needed more time to settle in.

Brooke produced a friendly smile when Mandy Kumar opened the door. She wore a fashionable, tailored suit, which cast her in a professional light.

What did this woman do for a living? Alex wondered.

"Hi there," Mandy said. Her bright eyes shimmered as they caught light from the late-afternoon sun. "What a nice surprise."

"Hi," said Brooke, extending the box of eclairs. "I'm Brooke Bailey, your next-door neighbor. Sorry it's taken so long to meet you. It's just been busy. Alex and I brought these for you as a belated welcome-to-the-neighborhood treat."

Mandy set the bakery box on an end table in her cavernous foyer. "Thank you both so much. How thoughtful," she said. "Would you like to come in?"

"Thanks, but next time," said Brooke. "I just got back from a business trip to New York and I've a lot to catch up on."

"Oh? What do you do that sent you to New York?" asked Mandy.

Normal question, thought Alex, though she caught a strange look that came over Brooke's face, one that implied the subject wasn't a favorite topic.

"Sales and marketing mostly," Brooke offered a bit vaguely.

Alex realized she didn't know the name of Brooke's employer. It had never come up in conversation.

"How do you like Meadowbrook so far?" Brooke asked.

"It's perfect," Mandy said. "It's . . ." Her voice trailed off as her gaze softened. She glanced about the cul-de-sac at the resplendent homes belonging to her new neighbors—Brooke, Willow, Emily, and Alex. "It's just what I was looking for," she offered with a wistful smile.

"Is it closer to your work?" Brooke asked. "I love the suit, by the way."

Alex suddenly felt quite frumpy in her jeans and loose-fitting sweater.

"Actually, it's a bit farther, but I don't mind," said Mandy. "I commute with Samir and it's more time for us to be together."

"That's nice," said Brooke. "Where do you work?"

"I'm a staff psychologist in the obsessive-compulsive disorder unit at McLean Hospital," said Mandy.

Alex looked impressed. "That must be fascinating," she said.

"Rewarding for sure, but it has its challenges," Mandy replied. "I can talk your ears off about exposure response prevention, but I'll save that for another time."

"And I thought my work was intense," said Alex. "Divorcing couples obsessively and compulsively dislike each other, but I don't have to try to fix it. I just need them to come to an agreement."

"Oh, so you're a mediator?"

"Former divorce attorney turned mediator," Alex clarified. "I needed a break from the courtroom."

"I get that," said Mandy. "Legal battles are nothing but stress and pressure, even if you're fighting them for other people."

"Very true," Alex agreed. "So, did you and Samir meet at work?" she probed.

"No," replied Mandy. "We got together in college, and our career paths just happened to overlap about ten years ago. Funny how that works. I was at McLean's first, and then Samir applied for a job a year or so later. Now he's the medical director."

"Well, it must be nice to be together so often," said Alex. She couldn't imagine working with Nick in the same office, then coming home to the same house as well. Having a little space from each other was sacred, in her opinion.

"I remember you were very eager to get this house," Alex continued, thinking back to the block party. "What drew you here?"

Mandy returned a tight smile. Color seemed to drain from her vibrant blue eyes. "We needed a change in scenery," she eventually offered. "Call it . . . a new start."

"Well, we're glad you picked our neighborhood," said Alex. "In fact, we came over to invite you to a ladies' night at my place. Wanted to check your schedule."

Mandy perked up at the offer, breaking into a smile that showcased pearly white teeth. "Oh, thank you. I'd love that."

Before Alex could offer a date that might work, Samir Kumar appeared in the foyer, standing behind Mandy. "Hello," he said, eyeing Alex and Brooke with the same piercing intensity he'd displayed on the day they'd first met. "Is there a problem?" he asked.

It was an icy blast of arctic air. Samir, again dressed impeccably—a shine to his loafers, not a crease in his khakis or dress shirt, gold wedding band gleaming like it was freshly polished—stood with his arms folded tightly across his chest, glaring at his wife as if she'd done something wrong. His look made Alex pull back slightly, an unconscious reaction to create more distance between herself and the Kumars.

"Samir, this is Brooke Bailey, our next-door neighbor. Brooke and Alex invited me to a get-together at Alex's home. Isn't that nice, darling?"

Alex noted the prompt, which struck her as odd. Samir was certainly bright enough to recognize a neighborly gesture.

"Well, we are quite busy," Samir snapped.

Alex and Brooke exchanged a questioning glance.

"We haven't picked a date yet," Brooke said tentatively.

A dark and flustered look came to Samir's face. The air around him picked up a charge. He moved closer to Mandy, so that their shoulders were touching. His well-manicured hand soon found the back of Mandy's arm. It didn't look like a gentle hold—more like a hard grip.

"As I said, we're quite busy. We haven't had much time to get ourselves organized. I'm afraid we're going to have to take a rain check."

We? thought Alex. She wanted to say that Samir wasn't invited, but held her tongue.

Alex peered over Samir's shoulder into the home. She saw no boxes, no clutter to unpack, nothing to organize, which made his excuse that much stranger.

Then, Alex caught a suggestion of something in Mandy's eyes that was hard to identify. Was it apologetic? No, not quite. Her posture had stiffened, as though a fight-or-flight reaction had kicked in.

At last she got it. It was a look of fear.

"Oh, yes, I'm so sorry. My excitement got the better of me," said Mandy rather flatly. "I'm not with it these days—the move, work, you know the drill. I promised Samir we'd focus on the house until every-thing was more settled. He wasn't as keen on this move as I was, so I hope you understand. Rain check?"

Alex shifted her gaze over to Samir, whose dark eyes held a look of triumph. His mouth twitched ever so slightly, as if he were fighting back a sneer.

"Yes, of course," said Alex, uncertain how else to respond. "And feel free to drop by anytime you need . . . a break," she added.

"Thank you," Mandy said, clasping her hands in front of her waist, the knuckles of her entwined fingers bloodlessly white. "I'll get back to you when it's a better time."

"Great," said Brooke, who expelled her unease with a shaky breath. "Let us know. Enjoy the desserts, and again, welcome to the neigh-borhood."

Samir didn't look at the box even though Brooke had tried to di-rect his attention to the end table that held the welcome gift.

"Thank you," he said, not sounding the least bit grateful. His hand never left Mandy's arm. He pulled her back ever so gently. His eyes fixated on Alex, his hard, unyielding stare probing her in a most un-pleasant way.

He closed the door with a soft click, neither of them bothering with a goodbye.

Chapter 11

Lettie

I have a job at Kimball Farm. It's been a family-owned business since before my parents were born. The owners are nice people who don't lather on the pesticides, and try to support sustainable farming practices by mostly selling what they grow. I'm helping the environment by biking to work, which I do even in the rain. I'm still riding the bike my parents bought for my thirteenth birthday—a source of pride, as I'm trying to limit my consumption. I know my efforts to end global warming won't keep the polar bears on ice, but it's better than nothing, I suppose.

It's my third summer working here. The owners baked me a cake to celebrate the official end of my home confinement. Cute. There wasn't any formal celebration to mark my release from parental custody back home; it just ended when I went out with Jay.

Speaking of, it's been weeks since he and I went trolling for Riley's secrets. I did receive his promised text letting me know Riley had returned home safely, but it didn't come until ten o'clock the next morning. Where she'd gone and with whom wasn't included in his message.

I'm not sure how I feel about the revenge thing anymore. I'm not sure about a lot of things, actually. I mean, who is Riley Thompson? I thought I knew her—didn't think much of her, to be honest. Now? She's cheating on my cousin and deserves some payback. Too bad I don't have the stomach to dish it out.

That's a problem, though. Revenge is my one connection to Jay, and I'm not willing to let it go—let him go. I'm just not sure how to move forward.

I decide to switch my focus from getting revenge to writing about it.

So far everything I've read suggests the Old Testament's "eye for an eye" won't bring me any closure or catharsis. It's increasingly unclear to me why people even bother. According to my research, I'd get a fleeting feeling of superiority, soon followed by a hollow pit in my stomach as I ended up feeling worse about myself. Some evolutionary benefit to the act of revenge is hardwired into our brains, but I'm not far enough into my paper to know more.

But I don't need a PhD in psychology to know pill-popping, run-around Riley isn't good for my cousin—that's obvious. Making gaga Dylan aware of that fact without breaking his heart or revealing that Jay and I were spying on his girlfriend is going to take some tact.

Dylan's been away at a lacrosse camp, but he's home now. My goal is to convince him to take a hiatus from Riley, but first I need to help the last customer of my shift.

It takes longer to explain how to use the credit-card reader than it does to bag her purchase of asparagus, broccoli, blueberries, and basil. I don't let my aggravation show. It's actually a confusing contraption. As she's leaving, the customer slips two dollars into the "For College" tip jar. I return a heartfelt thank-you.

"Where do you go to school?" she asks.

I explain I'm going to be a senior at Meadowbrook High. Her next question is easily anticipated. "Do you know where you want to go?"

"I'm hoping for USC," I say. "I want to study environmental science."

She's mildly surprised, I can tell. Nobody thinks smart kids sell produce. "Well, good luck, dear," she says, and off she goes.

Luck is nice, but help convincing my overly principled father to pay the hefty price tag for my dream school would be far more useful. We're destined for a showdown because I'm getting into USC, but that's for later. It's too bad Mom always takes Dad's side, because I could really use her support for once.

After my shift is over, I hop on my bike and head back home. I get there in a little under fifteen minutes. My legs are burning by the end of the trip, because Meadowbrook is quite hilly and my bike is in desperate need of . . . well, a new bike. But I'm not going to cave in to consumerism.

I do the home thing: talk to my dad using a grand total of twenty-seven words that honestly convey everything that needs to be said. The last time we had a real "talk," I was young enough to cry over a scraped knee. I'm a perfectly normal rising senior, which means that long meaningful chats with my father, in which I absorb his wisdom and immediately apply it to my own life, would happen only in the movies.

"Where are you going, Lettie?" Dad asks as I'm heading out the kitchen door. He's got that "let's do something together" look in his eyes. Poor thing.

"I'm going to find Dylan," I tell him, and out I go.

I can feel my father's self-doubt follow me outside. He's wondering if he missed some key opportunity to forge a stronger father-daughter bond. I should tell him we're fine—at least until the college debate hits. He should really focus on Mom, not me. Has he ever checked the recycling bin? Her drinking seems to be getting worse. My mother of old didn't have grape breath before the sun went down.

I find Dylan in his backyard using a lacrosse rebounder to play catch with himself. Here he is, fresh back from lacrosse camp, still trying to get better, up his game. It's a mating ritual of sorts. The better he is on the field, the more impressed Riley will be. Poor guy has no clue his love life is really a sham.

I breathe out a sigh as I approach. "What's up, D?" I call out to him.

Dylan turns. His expression brightens. "Yo, 'sup, Lettie."

He sends a ball at an impossibly fast speed into the rebounder, which sends it back to him just as fast. Somehow it ends up in the pocket of his stick. I don't get this sport. If the players were on broomsticks, chasing the Golden Snitch, then I'd be a fan.

"Got a second?" I ask.

"Sure," he says. He comes over, pushing his sweaty long hair out of his face. He smells like a gym sock. "What's up?" he repeats.

Dylan's never been a great conversationalist.

"How's it going?" I say. I've no idea how to ease my way into this topic.

"Um, good," he answers.

An uncomfortable silence ensues. I suspect he's said all he has to say on the matter of his well-being. Dylan and I may have some DNA in common, but it hasn't brought about a strong emotional connection. I've come to view my cousin the way I might a zoo animal—something to eye with a bit of curiosity and sadness. What makes him tick? If he has any real feelings, they're buried so deep in his subconscious I'm not sure a backhoe could dig them out.

If I could unspool his thoughts, see them laid out before me, I suspect they wouldn't be all that different from Zoe's: ball, food, sleep, and in his case, sex. Zoe doesn't give that last one much consideration, as she's been spayed, which by the way is the responsible thing to do.

"How's lacrosse going?" I ask, still fumbling.

"Camp was awesome. Summer league just started up," he tells me.

"Has Riley come to watch you play?" It's an awkward segue, but it will have to do.

"No," he says, and I catch something in his eyes, a glimpse of that hidden depth I've wondered about. Maybe he already knows about his girlfriend, and this will sort itself out without my involvement.

"All good with you two?" I blurt out.

He looks at me like I've said something in Mandarin. "Um, yeah, we're cool," he tells me.

Crap. I'm on a train to nowhere. "You know . . ." I say, giving it a moment's pause, "a lot of girls at school think you're cute."

He stares at me blankly. I don't blame him. Talk about non sequiturs.

"Yeah? That's cool, I guess."

Ball meets rebounder, meets net, meets rebounder again—and so on.

"I mean, I get that you and Riley are tight and all, but it's senior year, D. Why not spread your wings and take flight, try something new?"

I can't believe it when I actually find myself flapping my arms like they're the wings of a bird.

Dylan looks at me like I've taken some psychedelic.

I stop flapping. "I'm just saying, if you want to meet someone new, just say the word and I'll make it happen." I issue my offer with an air of supreme confidence that I've no business projecting.

In my head I'm having an entirely different conversation: *Dylan, I have to tell you something. Riley is cheating on you with another guy, and she's got a drug problem, too. How do I know all this? Um . . . well, you see, I followed her using a GPS tracker and . . .*

This is where my Good Samaritan desires and the harsh reality of the truth clash to induce my silence.

"All right, then," Dylan says awkwardly—and understandably. "I'll let you know if I need any help with my love life, Lettie."

He goes back to the rebounder and I slink away, feeling utterly foolish.

As I'm walking home, I see a Mercedes pull into the driveway of the house next door. Brooke Bailey emerges from the car looking more put together than a completed jigsaw puzzle. She's got a dazzling array of bangles sparkling on her toned olive arms. Her breasts appear to be five steps in front of her, and if her hips in those tight jeans swayed any more, they might generate a breeze.

Brooke catches my eye and waves politely, giving me a good look at her manicured nails painted bloodred.

We exchange pleasant greetings, but I'm not feeling very pleasant. Instead, I'm thinking that Riley is a young version of Brooke Bailey, a fledgling femme fatale.

Everyone knows about that cruise and her missing husband Jerry. Everyone thinks the same thing, too. My big fear now is that one day Riley will grow up and do to Dylan what I'm pretty sure Brooke did to her husband: toss him overboard from a cruise ship and get away with murder.

Chapter 12

L adies' night began promptly at seven o'clock. First pour was wine, even though Alex knew the rhyme about that before liquor. She'd arranged for at least a little privacy. Nick was out for the night, and Lettie was upstairs in her bedroom, headphones on, not coming out unless dragged. Neither of them wanted to be there for the festivities, anyway.

It was rare for Alex to have a moment's peace, let alone a whole night of it. Good thing tomorrow was a Sunday so she could recover.

Zoe greeted each guest with her trademark bark and eager tail wag, eventually settling down with a plush toy on the living room rug. For a time, the women chatted pleasantly while picking at the cheese plate Alex had prepared. Everyone contributed, bringing something to share. Willow made hors d'oeuvres with bacon and blue cheese that were swoon-worthy. Emily, true to form, went overboard (as she always did at parties) preparing the bruschetta, and a caprese salad that went quickly as well. It wasn't Brooke's style to make a fuss in the kitchen, but she didn't mind splurging for top-notch catering—in this case, shrimp cocktails served in fancy-looking crystal glasses. And naturally, they decided to forgo the desserts to leave more calories for alcohol.

"I need to keep eating to absorb all the booze. I'm so out of practice," Emily said as she prepared a pitcher of margaritas without referencing a recipe.

Alex had made certain to have Lettie show her how to play Spotify through the Bluetooth speakers. The night started off with chill jazz, which Alex paired with her favorite Cabernet. But as the drinks flowed, the conversation veered away from summer vacation plans to stupid things men do (a subject that got the most laughs).

It was Brooke who suggested the music should be amped up a bit. In response, Alex played some Eagles, leading to a rousing sing-along of "Take It to the Limit," perhaps sung in four different keys, but the drinks made it sound perfectly in tune to Alex's untrained ears.

Eventually Willow brought up the subject of Mandy. "I thought this night was for her," she said, looking around as if Mandy might emerge from another room any moment now. "Is she coming?"

Alex and Brooke exchanged wary glances.

"We had a weird encounter with Mandy and Samir," Alex eventually said.

"Weird how?" Emily asked as she poured margaritas into salt-rimmed glasses.

"She was fine, but the husband was something else," Brooke replied, a note of disdain in her voice.

Alex picked up on the irony of Brooke initiating the rumors about their new neighbors, considering how the neighborhood typically gossiped about her. Everyone on Alton Road, it seemed, had some opinion of Brooke Bailey—the women either harbored a fear that their husbands were enamored with her or suspected that Jerry Bailey hadn't suffered a drunken fatal fall without a shove.

"Samir Kumar's behavior was very odd," Alex said. "Kind of controlling, I'd say."

"Kind of?" Brooke exclaimed. "I'd say *very* controlling. Mandy wanted to come tonight and he wouldn't allow it. Simple as that."

Willow recoiled slightly. "Are you sure?"

Alex said, "We saw what we saw. She actually looked . . . frightened."

"He was gripping Mandy's arm," Brooke added, "like he was sending her a message. And Mandy told us they work for the same hospital—and he started there *after* she did." Brooke's pregnant pause implied that only controlling people would do that. "Seems like they're together all of the time—and he still won't give her a night to herself to get to know her new neighbors." Her eyebrows rose.

"What do you make of that?" Emily asked.

Brooke and Alex shared another silent exchange.

Eventually Brooke spoke up. "I'm worried that Mandy could be in an unhealthy situation—controlling behavior is often a sign of abuse. I'm familiar with the warning signals. The way he spoke over her, gripped her arm, made excuses to keep her from making new friends . . . there's something not right there. I'm certain of it."

"I suppose all relationships have a dark side," Willow said, as if she was ruminating on her own marriage.

"That may be," said Emily, "but we still shouldn't rush to judgment, not without having all the facts. It's easy to misinterpret events that way."

"Emily's right," said Willow. "Before we go judging Samir and Mandy, maybe we should judge ourselves against our own dark secrets. I mean, we all have them, right?" Willow's gaze traveled the room. "I know I do."

"Do tell," said Emily. A devilish glint caught in her eyes.

"Hold on a second," said Brooke, standing to draw attention to herself. "This is ladies' night, right? We're here to have fun, not just dump our dirty laundry all over the place."

"What do you suggest we talk about, then?" Emily sounded more than a little disappointed.

"Oh, I think we spill the beans," said Brooke cheerily. "But let's have fun doing it."

No one seemed to disagree.

"And what would make it more fun?" asked Alex, feeling emboldened thanks to the tequila in her veins.

"We've got the truth serum," said Brooke, tipping her glass to her mouth. "I say we play a game and use it to get us to share things we might not otherwise."

"I'm in," said Willow without hesitation. "What's the game?"

"It's called Two Truths and a Lie," said Brooke. "We each make three claims, and everyone has to guess which is the lie. I'll start."

Brooke bowed her head as if in deep thought. A moment later she raised her chin, revealing an inscrutable expression.

"I worked as an exotic dancer," she began in a monotone voice. "I have a stalker. And I killed my husband."

Chapter 13

A heavy silence filled the room, broken only by Emily, who cleared her throat as if to dislodge her discomfort. "Well, that kicks things off with a bang," she said, giving herself a generous pour from the margarita pitcher.

"And *one* of those is a lie?" asked Alex disbelievingly. "Only one?" Under the circumstances, she certainly hoped Brooke had been an exotic dancer. And as creepy as the idea of a stalker was, it was better than an admission of murder.

"I've given you only one lie," Brooke announced, her poker face replaced with a devious grin. "Those are the rules."

"I mean, look at your body," said Willow, leaning forward in her chair to make a closer inspection. "Obviously you danced. Give you a pole, and I'd slip a dollar under your G-string."

Emily spit out a laugh.

"Only a dollar?" said Brooke, who seemed offended. As if to put an exclamation mark on the slight, Brooke stood, holding her hands out in front of her as though gripping an imaginary pole. She began to sway her hips in slow motion, making suggestive, sexy moves in time to the upbeat music now playing. She kept her pole-gripping pantomime going as she splayed her legs wide, slowly lowering herself down to the floor. Alex could easily imagine her being onstage. Rising with the same sultry grace, Brooke capped off her demonstration with an alluring, over-the-shoulder look sent Willow's way.

"Okay, make it ten dollars," said Willow, and all burst out laughing.

"I'm going to go out on a limb and say former exotic dancer is definitely true," said Alex, who was glad Nick hadn't been there to watch Brooke's display.

"And thank God you didn't dance like that on any of our trips," said Emily.

Brooke laughed a little uneasily while Alex nodded. Ken and Jerry had been close friends growing up, went to high school together. It was no coincidence when Jerry bought the house on the same street as Ken. Given the long history between the two, it was only natural for the couples to vacation together.

"When and where was this period of your life?" Willow asked.

"In my twenties," said Brooke. "While I was living in New York. I danced at a gentleman's club in Chelsea."

"Not sure that's dancing, and *gentleman's club*? That's trying hard to make it sound classy," Emily said.

"And that's a bit judgmental," Brooke countered without sounding offended. "I provided a service to an upscale clientele."

"By *service*, you mean lap dances," Willow clarified.

"And I got well compensated for my skills," answered Brooke proudly.

"How much of your earnings came from married guys?" Emily asked, as if this touched a nerve. Alex didn't know whether Ken ever visited gentleman's clubs, but she now had her suspicions.

"I don't think that's cheating," Willow said.

"Agreed," Brooke said. "So what? I gave married guys a little thrill. I let them ogle my boobs and enjoy some dirty thoughts about me. It's just a fantasy—I never crossed the line with a client. I mean, a lot of guys watch porn. Are they all jerks?"

Nobody jumped to the men's defense. Alex was ambivalent at best on the subject of pornography. She had never gone snooping into Nick's private behavior, but he claimed to abstain. Even if he indulged from time to time, she wasn't sure it was a big deal, as long as it didn't become an obsession that interfered with their intimacy. It seemed to provide a safe sexual outlet for most men, or maybe even gave them new ideas for the bedroom.

Alex's mediation practice had offered too many examples of couples that had fallen apart fighting about sex for her to be closed-minded about her own husband. As long as there wasn't any touching, she'd be understanding about an occasional strip club visit, too. But she certainly wouldn't want Brooke to be the star performer.

A small worry danced in and out of Alex's thoughts. They'd had a lull in the bedroom these past few months, what with Lettie's troubles, stress at work, and tension at home. Could he be harboring resentment? It was possible, though he hadn't voiced any complaints. She'd never questioned Nick's fidelity, but suddenly she could hear doubts knocking.

"We all know most guys are jerks, especially my soon-to-be ex," Willow said. "I'm actually a little impressed, Brooke. I wouldn't have been that bold, and it must have been an exhilarating and somewhat freeing experience." Willow said this with a touch of reverence. "And better to have been a classier joint than some seedy biker bar."

"I don't discriminate. If the bikers can pay, they can play." Brooke ran her hands up and down her body like a magician's reveal.

All toasted the sentiment.

"So, I kind of feel terrible for saying this," Alex blurted out, "but I honestly hope someone *is* stalking you."

"And for god's sake, I pray it's not my husband," Emily said, burying her face in her hands.

"Cheers to that," said Willow, who took a lengthy swig of her drink.

"I never said that the stalker lives on Alton Road," said Brooke.

Alex felt a chill. The way Brooke said it made her think that was *exactly* where the stalker resided.

What if it was Ken? Alex didn't think her brother-in-law's extra-curricular activities involved stalking, but she had caught him in the shadows behind Mandy's house.

"It doesn't matter who it is," Brooke said in a way that downplayed the seriousness of her allegation. "I'm handling it."

"So that's not a lie?" asked Emily a bit dimly.

Brooke sent Emily a come-on-now look. "Do you really think I murdered my husband and decided to come out as a killer at girls' night?"

Alex swallowed a gulp. Brooke's snarky retort hadn't dispelled all doubt.

"What kind of stalking are we talking about?" asked Willow.

"Honestly, I'd rather not go into details," Brooke said. "Like I said, I'm handling it."

Everyone sat with the unease provoked by the thought of a stalker in the neighborhood. It was quiet enough that Alex could hear ice cubes knocking together as she tipped the margarita glass to her lips.

Eventually it was Emily who again broke the heavy silence.

"I'll go next," she said boldly, but a bit apprehensively, too. "Let me see, thinking . . . thinking."

After a few moments of nothing happening, Willow started to hum the theme music to *Jeopardy!* and everyone soon joined in.

"Don't pressure me," Emily pleaded, but the humming continued, getting increasingly louder.

Alex couldn't imagine what her sister might drum up. Emily was pretty straitlaced—a bit uptight, certainly not one to reveal her dark secrets even if she had them. Alex expected something quite benign.

After another minute, Emily was ready. "Okay, here we go," she said, clapping her hands together. "I once dated a girl. I've been arrested for drunk driving. And I hired a private investigator to spy on my husband."

So much for benign, thought Alex.

Brooke's eyes widened with delighted surprise, while Willow's held a new degree of respect. Alex refrained from blurting out the lie, which she knew without equivocation. Of course Emily had spied on Ken—he deserved nothing less—and the girl's name was Leanne.

"You're too smart to drink and drive," Willow said as she probed Emily with the keen eye of a seasoned detective. "So even though I can't picture it, I'm guessing you had a girlfriend . . . and that you also spied on your husband."

"I agree," Brooke said.

"Alex, what's your guess?" Willow asked.

"She can't guess, she already knows," said Emily. "And you got it right on the first try. I'm obviously pretty transparent."

Willow's whole face lit up. "I'd say you making out with a girl is pretty unexpected . . . and also kind of hot," she said. "What was her name? More to the point, is she still into girls? After Evan, I'm not sure I can stand the sight of another penis."

This gave everyone a good laugh.

"Well, I'm glad to know you weren't arrested," Brooke said. "But I hope whoever you hired to spy on Ken didn't find anything worth reporting."

"I've made my peace with it," said Emily, her words slurring slightly. "Ken owned up to what he did. He was extremely remorseful, and we dove into counseling."

"So you just forgave him?" Willow sounded incredulous.

"We all have the potential to grow and change," Emily said. "We weren't being intimate for some time before it happened."

Like Nick and I aren't being intimate, thought Alex.

"Sounds like you're blaming *yourself* for what *he* did?" Willow made a show of her disapproval.

"No, not at all," Emily answered. "But it's not all black-and-white. He could have been an unfaithful husband, and I could have con-tributed to problems in the marriage. Both things can be true. We'd grown apart, and honestly, Ken's affair brought us closer together. It can happen, you know—forgiveness and all."

"Well, I for one am in awe," said Brooke. "And my respect for you has increased tenfold. Forgiveness does not come easy."

"Amen to that," said Willow.

"I think we've all bought into the narrative that relationships have to be a certain way." Brooke set her drink on a coaster. "Love should be funneled into the perfect and very narrow path of matrimony. And then we expect our spouse to be everything *to* us and *for* us—care for us when we're sick, lift us up when we're down, be our best friend, be charming and witty, a great cook and great in bed. It's too much pressure, and it's not realistic. We're human, and we make mistakes. Good for you for understanding that it's much more complicated than all that." Brooke rose and came to Emily's side, bending down to give her a big hug. "That said, men can be real shits." She gave the room a wry smile.

"This is getting a bit intense," said Willow, who wobbled when she stood to offer Emily a hug of her own. "Alex, it's your turn."

Alex felt unmoored and not the least bit interested in sharing anything as personal as what Emily and Brooke had divulged. Lost in thought, she realized everyone was looking at her expectantly.

"Okay," she announced, "here goes. I'm left-handed. I've never been to Disneyland. And my parents wouldn't let me date until I was seventeen."

Willow playacted a loud yawn. "Girl, we are going deep here," she said. "I don't care which one of those is a lie. They're all dull. I demand a do-over."

"Second that," said Brooke.

"Third," said Emily. "You can do better, Sis. And there's a picture of your family at Disney on the mantel."

"That's Disney *World*," Alex said, with a scathing stare that was really for show.

"And Mom and Dad didn't care when you dated, because you were too shy to date *anybody* until college," Emily said.

"I still say that's your warm-up round," Willow said. "We want more. This is our true-confession night now. We've got a stalker and a cheater. What's your big secret?"

Alex didn't know what to share, wasn't sure she had anything fitting a big reveal, but then it came to her. Before better judgment could get in the way, she gave three other possibilities, only one of which was a lie.

"Nick and I once had sex in a McDonald's bathroom," Alex began. "We took magic mushrooms together. And I had three miscarriages after Lettie was born."

Emily scoffed. "That's too easy. Obviously, you're lying about the miscarriages—a bit bizarre, but whatever. We're all drunk, or at least on the way there."

"Why are you so certain?" Brooke inquired.

"Because I'm her sister. I'd have known if she'd miscarried— multiple times at that."

"You're quite sure of yourself," said Willow before directing her attention over to Alex, who maintained a placid expression.

Emily leaned forward in her seat. "Alex? Really?"

Brooke cocked her head slightly to one side before announcing that she thought the bathroom sex was the lie.

"I agree," said Willow. "There are so many better places for a kinky outing. And if you have any more of those magic mushrooms lying about, you better share."

"Is it true?" Emily said to Alex as if she hadn't heard the others. "Did you have three miscarriages?"

Alex returned a solemn nod. She could feel her arms grow heavy as if the weight of that grief had come rushing back all at once. Water flooded her eyes. *Oh shit.* She hadn't been prepared to share such a scarring experience, not with everyone. *What the hell was I thinking?*

"I can't believe you didn't tell me," Emily said.

"It felt very personal at the time," said Alex. "It still does."

Emily was looking like she was the one who'd suffered a loss.

"Nick and I both wanted more children, but I couldn't keep try-ing. After three losses it just seemed like we were meant to be a family of three, and by the time I again thought, okay, another child would be nice, I felt too old to explore IVF or adoption. We settled into our routine, and that was that."

"But why wouldn't you have told me?" Emily pressed. "I'm your sister. I love you. That's something I should have known, don't you think?"

"Well, at the time, no," Alex answered. "I didn't think anybody needed to know. I didn't want anybody's pity, especially yours. You were going through a rough patch with Ken as it was. Besides, I didn't want you to treat me differently, so I kept it private. I'm sorry I didn't tell you. Maybe I should have. Honestly, I've compartmentalized that part of my life. I had to, in order to move on."

The first miscarriage had been the worst experience of her life—and then it happened again, and again after that. Three in a row, all of them spontaneous, a heavy period that ushered in profound bouts of sadness. She'd cried her tears to Nick and no one else.

"You sure picked a fine time for a big share," Emily said a bit tersely. She finished the last of her drink, her aspect softening. "I just wish I could have been a support for you."

"Oh, you two need to hug it out," Brooke said. "I wish my sister wanted to live next door to me. She doesn't even live in the same country, and we talk maybe three, four times a year. Don't let this come between you."

"Agreed," Willow said.

Emily stayed rooted in her chair, but Brooke wasn't backing down. "Hug," she demanded.

With some trepidation, Alex rose and approached her sister with open arms. It took a bit for Emily to relent, but eventually she caved in to the embrace.

Even after they broke apart, Emily looked a bit shaken. "Does Mom know?" she asked.

"No," said Alex. "Dad had just died when we had the first loss. When the next loss came, it felt wrong to bring up the first. Besides, you know Mom. She'd have said something unhelpful like, 'Just keep trying,' as if that's all there was to it."

"No more keeping secrets from me," Emily said in a scolding tone. "I'm your sister, and I love you tremendously."

"I love you, too," said Alex. "My next crisis, I promise I'll let you suffer right along with me."

"Hear, hear." Brooke raised her glass in a toast. "Here's to owning our truths."

"To our truths," Willow said before taking a drink. "And now for mine."

Everyone settled back in their respective seats, all eyes on Willow.

"I've had time to think about what to say," she said. "So here goes.

I never signed a prenup. Evan isn't Riley's father. And I'd kill Evan if I could get away with murder, because it's the only way I won't be left broke after my divorce."

Alex was floored. "Willow, I've read your prenup," she said. "You *asked* me to read it."

"Well then," said Willow, "I guess that's the lie."

Memorial Day (Present Day)

Meadowbrook Online Community Page

Susanne Horton

I bet I know who's dead.

> **Laura Ballwell**
> I think it is inappropriate to be making guesses. There's
> obviously a tragedy on Alton Road. Somebody has been
> murdered, for goodness sakes!
>
> > **Reply from Susanne Horton**
> > Last I checked it's not against the law to have a theory.
> >
> > **Reply from Ed Callahan**
> > Right on that! Everything is policed these days. Ever hear
> > of free speech?
>
> **Ross Weinbrenner**
> So who's dead, **Susanne Horton**??
>
> > **Reply from Susanne Horton**
> > The Bug Man.
>
> **Janet Pinkham**
> Oh, the bugs are such a problem, I agree!! I've had more ants
> this spring than last year. Does anyone know why that might be?
>
> > **Reply from Ed Callahan**
> > Ant Viagra? ha-ha
> >
> > **Reply from Joseani Wilkins**
> > SMH.
>
> **Christine Doddy**
> Who the hell is the Bug Man?
>
> **Regina Arthur**
> Is that the guy who goes door to door selling his exterminating
> service? If so, he told me he had just sprayed my neighbor's
> place, and if I didn't get the same service too, the bugs would
> end up at my house and possibly eat the foundation, or so he
> said. I don't take to bullies kindly. So I told him where he could

spray his bug stuff! The nerve! Was he pulling that stunt on Alton Road? If so, I'm not surprised somebody did him in.

Reply from Katherine Leavitt
OMG, **Regina**! You sound glad the Bug Man might be dead!

Reply from Henry St. John
Lighten up, **Katherine Leavitt**. That Bug Man banged on my door very violently the other night, scared my wife and me nearly half to death. He should tone down his approach.

Reply from Ed Callahan
Maybe I'm missing something, but I thought good salespeople ARE aggressive? OH, he KNOCKED HARD! He hurt my feelings!! What a bunch of wimps. You don't like salesmen coming to your door, put up a no-solicitation sign or call someone who cares.

Reply from Henry St. John
You weren't there, Ed! So why don't you stop judging and go crawl back under the rock where you came from.

Laura Ballwell
Why do you think it's Bug Man, **Susanne Horton**?

Reply from Susanne Horton
I know for a fact that Ken Adair was very unhappy with his sales tactics. He complained and got the guy fired. And I know Bug Man showed up at the Altonites' block party . . . Just saying I've seen Ken Adair at the shooting range on several occasions. All I can say is, if that guy sets his sights, he isn't going to miss.

Reply from Ross Weinbrenner
That's an interesting theory. But I've heard plenty of stories about the Altonites, and the only thing those people have more of than money are reasons to do each other in.

AUTUMN

Chapter 14

Lettie

School started on the fifth of September this year, though I've been at it for two weeks now. Three months of very little summer fun has made me downright giddy for Mr. Donovan's Honors World Lit class, which many describe as a double Adderall hour. Not that I'd ever grind up the ADD meds and snort them like some kids in my school do. After this summer, I wouldn't be surprised to find out that Riley was among those who partook.

I've seen Riley in the halls a few times now. She's always her usual bubbly self, surrounded by the hippest, coolest kids. Nothing new there, but naturally, I can't help but wonder if there's a chemically induced component to her consistently cheery disposition. I haven't seen any posters advertising Riley Thompson for student council president, but they're coming. Perhaps she'll run on an anti-graffiti platform? Hmmm . . .

Despite being a pill-popping cheat, Riley and Dylan continue to do their Velcro thing, arms draped around each other as if their clothes were sewn together. And why not be all PDA all the time? This is senior year! We are the queens and kings of the castle! Let us rejoice in the greatness of the upper class!

Seniors have certain privileges even with schoolwork. For instance, my psych teacher is all for my continuing the revenge research project throughout the year. He's hippie-dippie enough to make it an independent study worth a quarter of my grade. Who knows? Maybe by the end of the term, I'll have had the guts to take revenge, not just write about it.

My hero status from the previous spring seems all but forgotten. It's as if I never railed against the system, challenged the school board, took matters into my own hands, and got suspended for the effort. I'm still a bit raw at how everyone forgot about me as well, checking in less and less while I was grounded.

But nobody has forgotten about Loony Lettie.

After the incident, as I've come to think of it, my moniker from those glory days got a little revival on social. *Loony Lettie went kinda loony with the spray paint,* one post read.

I guess I've got Riley to thank for my return to the ridicule of my middle school years. Couple that with ratting me out to school officials, and she's more than deserving of a little retribution. To keep Dylan from getting hurt, those pictures of Riley and Umbrella Guy need to stay on Jay's phone where they belong. But I haven't come up with a new plan. And worse, I think Jay's lost interest in the whole thing—and me. Other than the occasional text, which he takes days to reply to, I'm basically being ghosted.

At lunchtime, my friends notice I'm distant. For reasons unknown, I feel on the outside of our inside jokes. It's like I've changed over the summer. I've become a different Lettie. Maybe it's because I've seen a new side of life, taken a bite of the forbidden fruit, so to speak, Jay being my apple.

I don't talk about Jay—not to anybody, because I don't need people judging me. He's a college dropout. He's much older. He might do drugs. He lives in his parents' basement. And he's super hot, and I'm totally obsessed with him. Go figure. Hormones suck.

Meanwhile, Mom and Dad are riding me like the lawn mower these days about college apps. I keep telling them to relax, I have time, even though I probably don't. My friends are taking standardized test after test, feverishly securing recommendations, and working on their essays. Many have discovered a latent altruistic side as they rush to volunteer for whatever worthwhile cause.

As for me, I can't tell where gaining revenge ends and enticing Jay begins. All this is a long way of saying why, after school gets out, and I spy Riley heading for the parking lot instead of the turf field where I know she has field hockey practice, I decide to follow. I'd seen her earlier that day walking with a noticeable limp. I assumed she'd injured herself in pursuit of high school sports glory. The injury would have given her just cause to skip practice, but now, without the eyes of her athletic peers upon her, Riley walks quickly, no sign of any limp.

She gets into her BMW just as I get into my own car—a Hyundai Santa Fe my dad once drove that puts the "jalop" in jalopy. I don't dwell on the differences between my rusty ride and Riley's gleaming one as I follow her out of the school parking lot. If she's up to something, it might spark a new revenge plot, something that might reignite Jay's interest in my school project . . . and more important, in me.

One fact is immediately obvious as we start our drive. Riley is not headed toward home. I don't have Jay's GPS tracker, but my eyes work just as well as the technology. I follow her out of town and onto the highway.

We travel five miles before Riley takes an exit. I do the same. We're driving Route 122, a stretch of road with loads of shopping centers, restaurants, and various businesses. If she stops at a store, perhaps I could sneak something into her purse, trigger the security alarm. I'm sure the Bible would approve. But would that be enough? Maybe for me, but I doubt for Jay.

I'm guessing all of this is for nothing. Riley is probably out on an errand. Maybe she's going to CVS to buy an Ace bandage because she really *did* hurt her ankle.

That theory goes out the window when she drives by a bunch of pharmacies without stopping at any of them. With my curiosity refreshed, I decide to keep following. About fifteen minutes later, I'm back to questioning my sanity.

I'm about to give up and turn around to go home and work on my college apps, do something that whiffs of productivity, when Riley pulls over to the left lane to make a U-turn. I glance over my shoulder in time to catch sight of her heading into the parking lot of a Marriott Residence Inn on the other side of the road.

Well, I can't stop stalking now. Next light, I make a U-turn as well. Before long, I'm in the Marriott parking lot. I catch sight of her walking to the front entrance, but she doesn't see me. If she did, my plan is to tell her I'm getting a job application because I've always dreamed of working for Marriott.

Luckily, it's an excuse I don't have to use. Riley is too focused on a bank of elevators to the right of the check-in desk to notice me. I'm off to the side, using a big fake plant as camouflage. Through the slats of a plastic leafy palm frond, I keep careful watch. Riley doesn't appear nervous. I see no outward signs of stress. Has she done this before? Is this where she goes to buy her drugs?

These aren't questions I ponder for long. The elevator opens and out steps a man. I can't see him clearly with that plant blocking my view. Certainly I don't dare risk exposure by stepping out from behind it. I can tell he's got broad shoulders and dark blond hair. Like the guy at the bar, he's dressed in a sport coat and jeans. Definitely doesn't go to Meadowbrook High. He puts his arm around Riley as he pulls her into the elevator with him. A moment later, they're gone. My thoughts are swirling. Who is this guy? I'm thinking it's Umbrella Man, but I can't be sure because I still haven't gotten a good look at him. Maybe she's got a bunch of guys on the line and that's how she gets her drugs.

Either way, I'm both excited and worried as I head back to my car. I've discovered something truly tantalizing about Riley that Jay will want to know for sure. But I'm concerned for her as well. To my eyes, it looked like she was out of her depth, out of her league, and perhaps even in danger.

Chapter 15

lex was out walking Zoe on a beautiful night, optimally temper-
ate, a black sky speckled with stars, when she heard the commotion. A fight. Yelling. Something wasn't right. It sounded like it had
come from the Kumars' house, so she headed in that direction. Her
breath quickened at the same time Zoe's ears perked up.

The uproar grew louder as she neared. In a heartbeat, she went
from calm to tense. The sound of two people engaged in a heated
argument turned a serene setting into something menacing. She
strained to listen but couldn't make out what was being said. Alex
justified her snooping based on her suspicions of Samir. From the
sounds of it, there could be real trouble.

The squabble soon died down. For a time, Alex heard nothing
more than chirping night critters sending out calls for a mate or a
meal. She glanced across the street to her house, catching a flicker
of blue light through the living room curtains. She imagined Nick
sprawled out on the couch, probably asleep. Baseball never held much
appeal to her; she'd left him with the Red Sox trailing by four runs.

A light was on in Lettie's room as well. Was her daughter working
on her college apps as promised? Doubtful. Alex knew lip service
when she heard it. Was she being overbearing, as Lettie claimed?
Possibly. The conversation got a little heated between them. Alex left
feeling like she had taken out some of her stress on Lettie, unfairly.
She could guess the reason why, too. Girls' night had dredged up a lot
of raw emotions from the past. There should be more kids in the roost,

nesting in other rooms, but only two lights were on in her home, no others. Soon there'd be only one.

Alex felt a tug on her arm as Zoe pulled her toward the Kumars' place. The fighting had picked up again. An angry shout, almost a scream, was loud enough for her to consider calling 911. She took shelter behind the tall, prickly shrubs marking the end of the Kumars' property line. From that point she could hear better but still couldn't see *inside* the home. The voices were muffled, but Samir Kumar's distinctive baritone clearly conveyed his displeasure. She stealthily left the cover of the shrubs to gain a better vantage point.

From her new position, Alex could see figures through the windows but still couldn't hear them clearly, though she easily made out the words *you did* and *not acceptable*.

What's not acceptable? she wondered. Was this about Jay—or Mandy? Either way, Samir's controlling behavior was back on display.

She heard another combative volley, also from Samir. This time she made out *I told you* and *you're not allowed*.

The rest was too muffled and indistinct, but she heard a woman's voice respond—it must have been Mandy's. Was she crying? Could be, given the tone. Samir's bellicose barrage continued until Mandy raised her voice loud enough for Alex to hear it quite clearly.

"Stop it, Samir. I don't have to take orders from you!"

Alex was about to leave. This was a fight, nothing more. It wasn't her business. Then Zoe barked—her loudest, most piercing bark. Panic flooded Alex as she drew Zoe to her side, using her hand to form a makeshift muzzle. An instant later, an outside light came on.

"*Shhh*," she said. "*Shh!*"

Moving stealthily, Alex worked her way back to the cover of the shrubs just as the front door came open. She was stuck. If she moved across the street, Samir would see her, and he'd know she was lurking on his property.

As if to confirm her fears, Samir stepped onto the porch. Alex tried to slow her breathing by counting to five in her head for each inhale.

Zoe squirmed in her grasp, forcing Alex to hold on tighter. The bark likely had drawn him outside. Perhaps he reasoned the dog's owner was close by as well, overhearing conversations he wished to remain private.

Painful needles dug into Alex's back as she pushed deeper into the shrubs for better concealment. As she did, Samir came down one step, then another. She hugged her knees to her chest and closed her eyes, praying he wouldn't traverse his driveway. That would be hard to explain. It was a stroke of good fortune when Samir turned around. He retreated back into his house, closing the door behind him. The outside light went off, plunging Alex into darkness. Out came the breath she didn't realize she'd been holding.

With her heart still racing, Alex whisked Zoe home, but she couldn't debrief with Nick. He was snoring on the couch. She went to her sister's place instead, eager to give her a report. It was only just past nine.

Ken was home, oiling his gun on the kitchen table. Parts were splayed all over newspapers in haphazard fashion. Not a fan of fire-arms, Alex always felt a little uneasy at the sight of Ken's weapon. When Emily poured some wine, Alex took it appreciatively, not bothering to tell her sister that she was already buzzed.

"Did you know guns are the leading cause of death for children?" Alex said to Ken as he was snapping this part into that.

"Is that so?" Ken answered, sounding like he didn't care one bit.

"It's true," Alex said. "They've overtaken car crashes, in fact."

"Good to know," answered Ken, flashing her a cheeky grin baked with insincerity. "But this is going to the range with me tomorrow, not on some shooting spree. So, not to worry." He gave her a wink that was playful but dismissive.

"You know, we keep the gun in a safe in the basement," Emily said. She wasn't a fan of guns, but she'd defend the practice to support her husband. "The statistics always leave out that most gun-related deaths involve recklessness or carelessness."

"Or suicides." Ken examined his handiwork after he'd finished putting the handgun back together.

"That may be so," Alex said. "But I hope for Mandy's sake that Samir Kumar doesn't own one."

That got Ken's attention. "Why's that?" he asked.

Alex revealed what she'd overheard outside the Kumars' home.

Ken got a chicken leg out of the fridge, leaving the gun unattended on the table.

"What were they fighting about?" Emily wanted to know.

"Couldn't hear," said Alex. "But it was definitely intense."

Ken took a big bite off the bone and began to chew slowly. "Why's it any of your business what Samir and Mandy fight about?" he asked with a mouth full of food, his words garbled. "Couples fight. That's not uncommon."

"Certainly not around here," Emily said.

"Touché,'" said Ken. "Hey, thanks for coming over, Alex, and spoiling a perfectly fine evening."

"My pleasure," said Alex.

"Maybe you should be paying more attention to your daughter instead of other people's affairs," Ken said. "That girl is depressed."

Alex returned a fierce stare. "Why? Because she wears black? How would you even know what Lettie thinks or feels?"

"I'm her uncle," said Ken. "I notice things. I care. Besides, I talk to Nick."

Alex folded her arms. She snorted. "So Nick thinks his daughter is depressed? Well, he could tell me."

"Maybe he's tried," said Ken. "Maybe you're too busy nosing around other people's problems to hear him."

"Whoa! Way to go full jerk on me," said Alex without cheer.

"Jerk, huh?" said Ken, tossing the chicken bone into the trash. "Let me show you something."

Alex followed Ken into his first-floor office. Emily came in soon after. The French doors fronting Ken's private workspace were high-priced antiques, as he would let everyone know whether they asked about them or not. His bookcases were stuffed with business tomes— *Think and Grow Rich, The Psychology of Persuasion, The Art of War,* and *How to Win Friends & Influence People.* Clearly, Ken needed to reread that one, but Alex held her tongue.

Shelves sagged with trophies—his and the boys'. Most of the

framed photos adorning the walls were of Logan in his athletic glory. The photos of Dylan that dotted the collection were far fewer. Ken didn't care about the disparity as much as he did Logan's stat line for Syracuse lacrosse, which he could recite verbatim.

A set of blueprints was spread out across his expansive maple desk.

"I'm a big jerk, am I?" Ken tapped a finger against the blueprints. "Who's converting his stand-alone garage into an in-law apartment for your mother? This jerk, that's who." Ken pointed the same finger at his barreled chest. "And the costs keep going up, because your mother evidently wants the Italian marble in the bathroom and Kohler faucets. Fine. Let her live well. Lucky for us, I'm crushing it at work—right, Em?" He said this as if Emily hadn't earned a hefty commission for the Kumars' sale.

"It's not how I really want to spend my money, mind you," continued Ken, "but family first, that's my motto."

"Altruistic is your middle name," said Emily without feeling.

Ken planted a tender kiss on his wife's cheek. "And aren't you lucky you landed me."

"Well, I'm thankful you're going to help out our mom," said Alex, who marveled at Ken's ability to turn a story about someone else into something about himself. "But I'm still worried about Mandy Kumar. They could have been having a normal marital squabble, but there's something off with Samir. He's unsettling. Maybe you could get to know him a bit, Ken. Suss him out for us."

"Happy to try, Alex," said Ken. "But Nick and I both invited him to poker night and he declined. Not sure what more I can do. I say the best thing you can do is leave the Kumars alone."

"I think that's sound advice for you to take as well," said Emily, who kept a death stare on Ken.

"Really? That again?" Ken shot back.

"You told me you think Mandy's pretty," Emily said.

"Only because you grilled me about this supposed 'look' I gave her at the stupid block party—like it was anything, like I care one bit about Mandy Kumar."

Emily ran her fingertips across the blueprints. "Maybe Samir thinks like I do," she said almost to herself before locking eyes with Ken. "Could be that's what they were fighting about."

"Well, I've had enough fun for one evening," Ken said blandly. "I'm going downstairs to watch the Sox."

"They're losing," said Alex.

"I'll watch anyway." He headed for the door.

"Speaking of family first, Dylan has a game tomorrow," Emily reminded Ken.

"Can't make it," said Ken. "Work thing."

"Does he know?" Emily asked.

"I'll text him," Ken said on his way out the door.

"Ken, honey, you're forgetting something," said Emily.

He stopped, turned, clearly confused.

"You left your gun on the kitchen table."

"Right," he said.

"Safety first," said Alex, not taken in at all by Ken's apologetic smile.

Chapter 16

One moment Alex was holding a glass of orange juice, and the next it was streaking toward the floor. The glass landed with a crash. Jagged pieces shot out in all directions.

She noticed that her hands were shaking. *Is that why I lost my grip?*

She fetched a broom from the utility closet, swept and mopped, and discarded the remnants into the blue recycling bin in the garage. The bin was filled near to capacity, mostly with wine bottles.

When did Nick go to the dump last? Two weeks ago? This couldn't be from a single week.

Alex checked her hands again. They were still shaking.

She'd never had a tremor before. Probably wasn't related, but she could pinpoint the source of her headache and dry mouth.

No wine this week, she promised herself. That was that. No big deal.

Alex sent Zoe out the back door unleashed, as usual, to do her morning business. They didn't have a fenced-in yard, but Zoe always came back. She returned some minutes later having decided it was a good idea to roll around in the mud. Alex sequestered her in the laundry room until she had time to clean her up. Zoe barked unrelentingly at her forced confinement, making Alex's headache drum louder.

Make it two weeks dry.

Nick entered the kitchen barefoot. Before Alex had time to warn him, his foot found a glass shard she'd missed. He let out a yelp that frightened Zoe into silence.

"Sorry, honey," Alex called. "There was an accident this morning. Dropped a glass. Thought I swept it all up."

She left out the part about the shakes. As Nick headed for the bathroom to perform first aid on himself, Alex went upstairs for a towel to clean off the dog.

Lettie glided down the hallway like a phantom, an apparition haunting their home, one that couldn't be bothered with a *good morning*.

"Sorry about last night," Alex said, not sure she should be the one apologizing. She hadn't started the fight. It wasn't her college career on the line. "I don't want to put more pressure on you than you already have."

"Okay, then don't," Lettie said.

"Is everything all right? Are you . . . you know, good with everything?" *Way to bring your A game to parenting,* Alex thought.

"Yeah, I'm good," Lettie said morosely.

Fears about her daughter's mental state overtook her. She'd talk to Nick about it later—about what Ken had said, specifically—but now wasn't the time. Everyone was in a rush.

Alex took her coffee to the window overlooking the Kumars' house. She wanted to catch Mandy before she left for work, make sure she was all right. The house looked still and quiet, like all the houses on Alton Road.

She was thinking of some excuse to ring the doorbell when the Kumars' garage door opened. A Lexus rolled out moments later, giving Jay's Subaru in the driveway a wide berth. Alex wasn't surprised to see Mandy's Audi still parked inside. She'd mentioned commuting with Samir. But as sunlight flooded the car, Alex could see only one occupant within, and it wasn't Mandy. Even in the low light she could make out Samir's typical grimace.

Alex finished her coffee. After the goodbye/see you/love you ritual with Nick and Lettie, she grabbed her work bag and left the house. She stopped at her car door.

She'd worry about Mandy all day if she didn't at least try to connect. It would be easiest to text, but Alex never had gotten her number. She vowed to rectify that, but it gave her a reason to stop by. If something was wrong, they had no way to get in touch.

There. That's not being too nosy.

She marched up the steps to the Kumars' front porch. The doorbell echoed louder than most. She took a deep breath. This visit felt intrusive, not neighborly. At least now her hands had a reason to shake.

No one came to the door. She tried the doorbell once more and waited, her anxiety mounting. Her imagination was getting the best of her, just as with Lettie.

Of course Mandy is fine. This is Alton Road, not some Hitchcock film. All couples argue.

Even so, Samir's angry shouts echoed in her mind.

She thought Jay might appear—he could tell her where his mother was—but no such luck. The only Kumar she saw that morning was the one who worried her most.

The day passed in a blur, stuffed with other people's problems. By the time Alex got home, she'd forgotten all about the promise she'd made to herself that morning. She was drinking wine and paying bills when Nick returned from his workday. Lettie was out with friends, so she had a chance to ask him about what he'd said to Ken.

"Maybe I made some comment in passing about her being gloomy, but it wasn't a diagnosis. You know Ken—he's always stirring the pot. Lettie's fine." He kissed her cheek gently, as if that settled matters.

When he left the room, Alex felt profoundly alone. Her daughter was pulling away, and she and Nick were as close as Mars and Pluto these days.

She picked up her phone out of habit. A memory from years ago appeared on Facebook, allowing Alex to relive a day spent apple picking. Lettie's two front teeth were missing. Nick beamed with pride over his family. Alex assessed her appearance back then.

I glowed, she thought. What had dimmed her? She wanted to climb into the photograph, return to that very moment, bite the shiny red apple that Lettie clutched in her impossibly tiny hand. She drank from her glass of wine instead. It didn't taste as sweet.

Alex saw Samir leave for work again the next day. As before, he was alone in his car. When it happened a third day in a row, Alex grew distressed. She called Emily, Willow, and even Brooke, but no one had seen Mandy.

That evening, when Samir drove off alone once again, Alex decided to follow.

She raced to her car, pulled out of the driveway as if making a getaway, and waited until Samir was a safe distance down Alton Road before pursuing. His route was haphazard, as though he were taking her on a leisurely tour of Meadowbrook.

Ken's words from the other day came back to her. Was she butting into other people's affairs, as Ken had charged, or was she just a concerned neighbor, as she herself wanted to believe? In her work mediating divorces and at home with Nick and Lettie, she thought of herself as the problem solver, a peacekeeper, the go-to person for everyone in the neighborhood.

Her conscience was telling her there was an issue at hand, a potentially volatile one at that. She even feared Samir might be leading her to Mandy's body and harbored a vision of being discovered later on in the same roadside ditch as his wife. Then she felt foolish for having those crazy thoughts.

A few moments later, she ended up following Samir into the parking lot of the Big Y supermarket.

Alex felt utterly ridiculous on her drive home. She saw no need to tell Nick of her excursion. He'd only laugh at her, and she was in no mood for ridicule. She was only trying to help, and her intuition kept telling her that something was amiss between the Kumars.

Alex was only half buying her own justification. Maybe she *was* being nosy. Either way, this failed attempt to intervene did not mean that trouble wasn't afoot.

She wanted to confide in someone who'd share her concern. It was a relief to see Emily heading up Alex's walkway as she got home.

Alex lowered her car window.

"Glad you're here! I was coming over to vent," said Emily.

"Good timing, then," Alex said. "I'll make some tea and tell you about my failed reconnaissance mission."

"Were you out looking for Brooke's stalker?" Emily asked.

"No, but maybe I should have been," said Alex with an uneasy laugh. "Between the stalker and Willow's big share, Alton Road has become a lot more interesting, that's for sure."

"Or dangerous," suggested Emily.

The sisters had discussed the party game at length, but weeks later it still felt like fresh ground.

Emily followed Alex into her kitchen and settled herself on one of the cushy stools at the counter. Alex filled a yellow kettle with water for tea.

"This whole stalker situation is really distressing," Emily said. "I'm home alone a lot these days. What if I become a target? With Ken's travel schedule, it's just Dylan and me, and he's off with Riley half the time. In fact, Ken just announced he's taking *another* business trip—which, by the way, is what I came to vent about."

Alex joined Emily at the counter with two mugs of steeping tea.

"Is that a problem? Ken's always traveling somewhere."

"This time it feels different." Emily's voice was laden with worry.

Alex didn't need more details. "You're not thinking that—"

Emily's widening eyes said yes, she was.

"Maybe he and Mandy aren't together, but she could have stirred something in him. I can't explain it exactly. He seemed . . . I dunno, too damn excited about a work trip to New York City. And there was nothing on the calendar, so this was a last-minute thing, or so he said."

"Did he tell you what the meeting is about?"

Emily shook her head. "No, and I didn't ask. It felt too—I don't know . . . accusatory? It's been years since—you know, but suddenly, for no reason, I have this feeling Ken isn't being faithful anymore."

"There *is* a reason," said Alex. "You have that concern about Mandy."

Alex had a different concern regarding Mandy, but now didn't seem a good time to bring up their neighbor's absence.

"There's no proof that anything is going on. It was just a stupid look, right?" Emily sounded like she was reassuring herself.

"Right," said Alex, feeling her stomach knot. She'd withheld information about Ken sneaking off into the woods behind Mandy's house. Should she have said something?

The doorbell sounded. When Alex opened the front door, she saw Samir Kumar standing there.

Alex greeted him with a plastered-on smile. "What a nice surprise," she said, her heart thumping. Remembering Samir's hesitancy to shake hands, Alex kept hers at her side.

"Sorry to intrude," Samir said, offering a barely there smile. "I was hoping to speak with you for just a moment."

"Of course," said Alex. "My sister, Emily, is in the kitchen. Why don't you join us?"

Samir glanced at his fancy watch. "I won't take long," he said.

Wary, Alex led him to the kitchen where Emily, now standing, offered a lukewarm greeting. She noticed the shift in Emily's demeanor as her tepid hello gave way to a more protective stance—arms folded, one leg crossed in front of the other, all indications that she, too, felt unsettled around their new neighbor.

Alex went to the kettle. "Would you like some tea?"

"No, no thank you," Samir said. "I just came to offer my apologies."

Alex's eyebrows rose. "You've nothing to apologize for," she said, resisting the urge to demand, *What have you done with your wife?*

"No, I do," said Samir. "I feel terrible that we haven't been more neighborly. I know Mandy feels sorry that she couldn't come to your party the other night."

"That was actually last month," Emily said.

Samir looked slightly abashed. "My point exactly," he said. "The move has been far more distracting than we were prepared for. We've both been out of sorts, and it's not like us to be neighbors who keep only to ourselves."

"So where is Mandy?" Emily asked.

Alex held a breath.

Samir leaned back on his heels, as though the question had pushed him off balance.

"Mandy's not at home," he said. "But she told me I needed to make this apology myself, as it was more my insistence than hers that she not attend your gathering. I was supposed to do this sooner, but time got away from me. So I'd like to make it up to all and invite you to have dinner at our house. Say two weeks from Friday?"

"Dinner? Yes, of course, I'd like that, but I have to run it by Nick to make sure we're free," said Alex. She was glad to know Mandy was alive—at least allegedly.

"And Emily, you and Ken are of course invited as well," said Samir. "Without your help we wouldn't be living in our lovely new home." He sounded enthusiastic.

Alex probed Samir's eyes, seeing his good intentions as nothing but a front. But what reason could he have to play the nice guy?

"Great," said Emily. "I'll check with Ken as well, and let you know. He's away on business."

"Ah, very good," said Samir, who made a move toward the door. "Since it will be in November, I'll open the invitation up to some of the other neighbors and we'll call it an early Thanksgiving—and there's much to be thankful for, including our new community."

"It'll be a Friendsgiving, then," said Emily.

"Precisely," replied Samir.

Alex didn't miss a beat. Samir had deftly avoided answering Emily's direct question about Mandy's whereabouts. Alex felt compelled not to let it go. "So where *is* Mandy?" she asked, willing cheer into her voice. "Someplace fun, I hope."

What little friendliness Samir had managed to cling to during this visit abandoned him entirely. He gave Alex an icy stare. "She's gone to New York City to see family."

Alex and Emily eyed each other, mouths slightly agape.

Sisters could speak without saying a word. New York was a big city, but was it a coincidence that Ken had gone there as well? Alex had her doubts. Maybe Samir did, too.

"I'll let her know you asked for her," he said. "Have a good evening."

Samir realized he could depart through the kitchen door that Emily always used, making his exit quick and easy. He paused before leaving and turned to give Alex a pointed stare. "Interesting that you take the long way to get to the supermarket as well," he said. "It's nice to know that others appreciate Meadowbrook's more . . . scenic beauty."

He left with a nod and the slightest of smiles. It wasn't friendly.

Chapter 17

Lettie

I'm home in my bedroom, committing to memory the difference between endothermic and exothermic processes, when I notice Jay's car pull into his driveway.

I haven't told Jay about Riley's dalliance at the Marriott Residence Inn. I could have sent him a text, but what if he ignored it? Text him again? Look like I'm desperate for his attention, which I am? For whatever reason, our paths simply haven't crossed on weekend days when I'd have the best chance of running into him.

I race down the stairs, my footsteps pounding. Bursting out the front door, I leave Zoe somewhat perplexed while I dash across our lawn. I call Jay's name, getting his attention before he disappears into his house.

He's dressed like a metrosexual: a long-sleeved patterned shirt that could easily pass for a blouse, dark jeans, and polished loafers with no socks. He's got his Ray-Bans on, and damn, that stubble makes him look like the hot guy on some new Netflix drama. He sends me a smile that makes my heart rattle.

"Hey," I say, embarrassed I'm breathing so heavily. Definitely need to start working out more.

"Hey, yourself," says Jay.

He doesn't take off his glasses, and I wish he would so I could get a better read of him.

"How's it been?" he asks. "How's high school?"

I shrivel up inside. I hate that he says *high school*. It makes me feel like a stupid girl.

"Good, you know. Same old."

"Right," says Jay with a smile that puts a crease in his dimples. He goes for his Juul and takes a puff before languidly exhaling a cloud of vapor. I'm almost tempted to ask for a hit, but that isn't me. My nerves feel on fire, but the feeling isn't bad enough to transform me into someone else.

"Do you have a minute to talk?"

I despise the subtle shake in my voice. Maybe my hair is a mess. Maybe my all-black ensemble makes me look like I'm trying too hard to *not* fit in.

I'm worried Jay is judging everything I say and do. Every little blink and nod I make, any weird twitch, the awkward way I stand, or just how I think my body looks to him—all this makes me feel small and vulnerable. I hate our mismatched balance of power, how I'm so into him and he's probably not into me at all. But none of this is going to keep me from telling him what I saw.

"I've found out more about the 'Secret Life of Riley,'" I say.

Jay doesn't look all that surprised, but I can't tell with his sunglasses on. "So, tell me."

I glance about nervously, as if Riley might be lurking right behind us. "I saw her going into a hotel with an older guy—probably the same guy from the other night, but I still didn't get a good look at him."

"Interesting," he says without sounding interested. "Maybe we should talk. Do you want to come in?" He gestures with a thumb toward his house.

Inside . . .

I panic a little. Are his parents home? Is something going to happen between us? Is this it? The definitive moment of my youth that I'll never forget and probably—maybe after therapy—come to regret?

I nod regardless. A parakeet is flapping inside my chest.

I follow Jay into his home. I've been inside before, but when the Weavers lived here, not since Jay moved in. It's big and echoey, not at all what I expected. It's so quiet in this house that I can almost hear the blood rushing in my veins. The walls are mostly barren, not much carpeting to dampen our footsteps. Nothing close to a personal, homey touch in any of the rooms I can see.

"My parents are a lot more into their work than they are into nesting," he says.

"Oh, I see."

I let it go as I make my way into a spotless kitchen. Stainless-steel appliances gleam as if they'd recently been delivered from the store. The granite counters are surprisingly free of clutter. I don't dare open a cupboard, but I wonder if I'd find food in any of them.

"My parents are actually quite good cooks, but they're so busy they don't spend much time in the kitchen," Jay says.

"What do you eat?" I ask.

"A lot of takeout," he says with an air of indifference. "We don't really eat together."

For reasons I can't explain, his revelation makes me feel profoundly sad for Jay, or maybe for the entire Kumar family.

"I don't get it," I say. "Your mom was so eager to buy this house. Why get such a big place if you're not even going to decorate it—or use it, for that matter?"

Jay shoots me a sideways glance before finally removing his sunglasses, which he slips into the pocket of his fancy shirt. "Do you understand your parents?" he asks.

"Good point," I reply.

The lightness in Jay's eyes transforms into one of longing or wistfulness, something that implies a suppressed sorrow. Seeing his vulnerability opens my heart a bit wider, a gap big enough for me to fall into.

I try to center myself by walking around the spacious kitchen that overlooks the Kumars' meticulously maintained backyard. The grass out back is the lush kind of green that makes me think of Fenway Park, where the Red Sox play.

My father took me to a game once. I don't know why we never went again, but I remember having fun that day. Did I tell him I had a good time? Maybe not. Maybe that's why we never went back.

Somewhere in me is a tiny ache—one that wishes I were closer with my dad, like maybe Jay wishes he could be closer with his family.

Without asking permission, I find myself moving from the kitchen to the dining room. My hands brush over a highly polished table that could double for a mirror. "Have you ever had a single meal in here?" I ask Jay, who's now standing behind me.

I catch his amused reflection in the table's shiny surface. His laugh is rich and warm. I smell pastry and coffee. It takes a moment to realize Jay is the source of this enticing aroma. I'm liking it—a lot, too much probably.

Some crystal glasses and a lovely vase stand on a buffet table that's flush against a wall beneath some windows. Something else catches my eye, the only picture I've seen in the house. It's in an ornate silver frame. When I go to get a closer look, I see the picture is actually of the Kumar family posed for an outdoor portrait, many years ago, when they were all much younger.

Mandy looks utterly gorgeous in her figure-flattering wrap dress, her blond hair getting the best of that day's sunlight. Samir Kumar stands quite rigid. His smile is appropriate, but something in it is not quite genuine. Jay was a super cute kid—no surprise—and I'm guessing he's about four in this photograph. There's another boy in the picture as well, standing next to Jay. I'd say this boy is around two years old.

"That's my brother," Jay tells me, as if he's reading my thoughts.

"Is he in college somewhere?" I ask, thinking he'd be around that age by now.

"No," Jay says. The light in his eyes goes dim. "He's dead." He says this with an utterly blank look on his face, not a trace of sadness or regret.

This is unsettling.

"I'm so sorry," I tell him in a soft voice that I hope conveys my sympathy.

"He died about four months after this picture was taken," Jay tells me, still no emotion in his tone.

I want to ask: *How? What happened?* But I can't seem to find the words.

Jay doesn't need a sixth sense to guess what's on my mind. "He drowned," he tells me. "Fell into a pool at my uncle's party."

"Oh, my god," I say. "That's horrible."

"I was there," Jay says. "I was told not to go to the pool—my mother said I'd be in very big trouble if I did. But I didn't listen to her. I went anyway, and Asher followed me to the water. I had my feet in the shallow end. Asher went to the deep end of the pool. He leaned over and fell in, sank right away because he couldn't swim. I couldn't swim, either, and I didn't really understand drowning, not at that age. I kept thinking I would be in big trouble for coming to the pool without permission, so I tried to rescue my brother instead of going for help right away.

"But what was I going to do? He'd already gone under. I just walked around the edge of the pool, calling for him. I must have done this for a minute, maybe two, before I realized I was doing nothing to help. I could see Asher's body still as could be, flat on the bottom.

"Finally I went to get my parents. My father was the first into the water. He dragged Asher to the surface. He came up gasping for breath. Asher's face was blue. I remember my father screaming at me: 'Jay, what have you done? What have you done?'"

Jay goes quiet. It feels like the heavy pause in a pivotal moment during a climactic scene in a play, only this is no act.

"He performed CPR while my mother called 911," Jay continues. "My uncle had to do the talking. Mother was too hysterical to speak. I can't remember many details, but I've seen therapists who have helped with my recall—or maybe all they did was implant false memories. Who knows? My recollections certainly don't come from my parents. We never talk about this.

"The paramedics arrived in five minutes, but Asher still wasn't breathing on his own. My father gave him to mouth-to-mouth resuscitation, pleading with my brother to come back to him.

"They managed to get a heartbeat in the ambulance, but by then his brain was too badly damaged from lack of oxygen. My parents took him off life support a week later. My mother insisted we donate his organs, though my father was against it. There is nothing in Hinduism, my father's religion, that would have prevented the practice. He just couldn't stand the idea of his son not being whole anymore, of him being . . . given away.

"In the end, my mother won out. We still get Christmas cards from people whose lives Asher saved. This was a long time ago, Lettie." He says this as if that should make what I just heard more bearable, which it doesn't.

I don't know what to say. I'm so beyond sadness, I've no words to offer. This is new emotional territory for me. I want Jay to cry or at least look upset. I'm certain he's bottling up all his feelings.

Then I make a bunch of assumptions that might be totally inaccurate: *Jay still blames himself for Asher's death. He's never gotten over the trauma. He believes his father has never forgiven him, which is why Jay can't forgive himself.*

Now I think I get why brilliant Jay—who can hack anything, who is making an app that I'm certain will make him rich—got booted out of college.

He is suffering, and now I'm suffering with him.

I don't really know what comes over me. One moment I'm standing two feet away from Jay and next thing I know I'm pressed up against his chest. I run my fingers up and down his arms in a caressing way. At first I want to comfort and hold him, but as I touch Jay, empathy starts to turn to desire. My body heats up, and I'm filled with an intense need to kiss him.

I move my mouth toward his, and before I know what's happening, our lips are touching. I feel Jay's resistance at first, but a second later his mouth opens and our tongues meet. He pulls me into his body. My breasts flatten against his chest. I kiss him harder and I'm not thinking at all anymore. I'm lost—completely gone in this moment, utterly absorbed by tenderness and passion.

I'm ready, I say to myself. *I want this. I want him.*

Just when I think we're going to find a couch or a bed, or sneak down to his basement lair and take things further—and damn it, I want to, I really do—Jay's mouth closes tight. His lips press together.

We're not kissing anymore; it's more like I'm pointlessly pressing my face against his.

He pulls away. I feel crushed. I'm crestfallen and utterly confused. I'm sure these feelings are apparent.

"Lettie, no," Jay says, his soft voice conveying much tenderness. "We can't."

I'm beyond mortified. I'm not sure how to describe this profound sense of rejection and embarrassment. I feel so stupid and foolish, about two inches tall. I wish I could blink myself out of this room or into another dimension where I never tried to kiss Jay Kumar. I want to speak, ask him why, but I'm too busy dying inside.

Thankfully, Jay comes to my rescue. "I like you, Lettie. I would very much like to kiss you."

I'm struggling not to cry. I don't think my dignity could take another blow.

"It's the age thing, isn't it?" I ask him, the shake returning to my voice. "I'm not freaked out by it. I'm seventeen. I can consent and you won't be in trouble."

I never thought when I went to kiss Jay that I'd be making a reference to statutory rape, and yet here we are.

I go to kiss him again, but Jay's arms hold me back. Usually I just shut off the caring switch when I experience rejection . . . or else I try to explain it away. Bad grade? It was the teacher's fault. Didn't get some academic honor? Blame the stupid organization. Not invited to a party? Didn't want to go anyway. Rejected by Jay Kumar? Try again. The last time I was this determined to get something, I wanted a hamster.

"No, it's not our age difference," he says. "I like you too much for us to do anything, that's all. I can't allow that."

Jay touches my arm in a way that makes me believe his words, but I still can't make sense of them. "I don't get it," I say. "If you like me, then why not?"

My heart continues to thunder in my chest, but I try to put on a brave face.

Jay takes a step back. His expression is thoughtful.

"Do you know the story of the frog and the scorpion?" he asks.

Definitely *not* where I thought this might be going, but okay, I'm in. "No," I say. "I don't."

"There was a river too wide for the scorpion to cross," Jay begins. "The scorpion comes upon a frog who can easily make it to the other side and asks if he could ride on the frog's back. The frog doesn't hesitate to say no. 'You will sting me,' the frog tells the scorpion. But the scorpion assures the frog that he will not. 'If I do so, we will both drown,' the scorpion says. The frog gives this some thought and eventually agrees to ferry the scorpion to the other side of the river.

"At the halfway mark, the frog feels a powerful sting in its back. Poison makes the frog's legs stop moving. Soon they're sinking. 'What have you done!' cries the frog. 'Now we will both drown. Why would you do this?' The scorpion replies as they both die: 'It's my nature.'"

Jay takes a step back, a signal that his story is finished.

"Is that it?" I say, feeling a spurt of anger. "That's a terrible story. Poor frog! What are you trying to say, that it's in your nature to sting like a scorpion?"

Jay smiles in a way I find a bit unsettling. He rolls up the sleeve of his fancy shirt to show me his forearm, on which I see a black ink tattoo of a scorpion.

Chapter 18

Using the Saffir-Simpson Hurricane Wind Scale to rate the destructiveness of hurricanes, Alex estimated that the former couple whose divorce she was about to mediate would register at a Category 3. That was a good thing, too: the Category 5 cases not only damaged the couple but did a number on their mediator as well. The lawyers always made out better the harder the winds blew, but for Alex big paydays weren't worth her mental health.

The divorcing couple sat stony-faced on opposite sides of the table, each flanked by their respective attorneys. They were young and attractive, somewhere in their thirties, with two children under ten who would soon be subjected to the rules of the parenting plan, assuming they could hammer one out.

Alex started with her usual introduction, delivered in a professional but friendly manner, while offering no pretense that she could cut through the gloom. "Thanks for being here on time. I'm confident we're going to have a good session," she began. "I hope everyone is well rested."

"I dunno," replied the man, a scowl on his handsome face. He leaned forward to glare at his soon-to-be ex-wife. "Did your boyfriend keep you up all night?"

Alex inwardly cringed. "That's a big no-go in here, Jarrod," she said in a stern tone. "Can we agree to refrain from the snipes and snide remarks, please? Everyone?"

Alex wouldn't continue until she got confirmation nods from around the table. "Good. Glad that's settled. Abbie and Jarrod, before I explain what this is going to be, let me explain to you what it's not."

She paused to make sure that she had everyone's attention. In a way, this was like theater, and Alex was a master performer, adept at knowing how to play to her audience without losing the script.

"This isn't a place to air your grievances. It's not a forum for name-calling or mudslinging. We're not here to prove a point or make one person or the other wrong. What I am here to do is look out for both your interests and to facilitate what is best for you given your situation.

"You are not going to leave here feeling like you won. That's not how this works. This is an emotional time for you both, but I'm asking that you take the emotion out of it while we are in this room. You may feel resentful, sad, angry, or all three at once. That's fine, but you need to step outside to vent your frustrations and feelings in private with your respective attorneys, because it's not okay to do so in here. Are we clear?"

Alex managed to elicit subtle nods from both parties. It was her first victory of the day.

"Let's get on with it, shall we?"

If getting married had been as difficult as getting divorced, Alex suspected she'd be out of work in a few years. Over the course of her career, Alex had heard a plethora of complaints that really belonged in a therapist's office. Emotions running hotter than a sauna, strings of grievances on which hung the beads of disillusionment.

He's always working.

She doesn't consider my family at the holidays.

We never have sex.

He doesn't get what the word budget *means.*

These couples were after the same thing all people came into this world needing: connection and acceptance. In some ways, Alex hated that her job put her in the epicenter of so much negative energy, but this was also her calling. She was a firefighter of sorts, extinguishing conflicts here, there, and everywhere.

The next two hours were surprisingly productive. Abbie and Jarrod agreed on a parenting schedule—how they would handle most major holidays, who would be responsible for medical appointments—and some school-related matters.

As they were nearing the scheduled break, Alex noticed she had missed a call from Nick's office. Nick never used that line to call her.

Alex initiated the break early before hurrying into her office to return his call. His cell phone went to voice mail, so she called the office number. Nick's administrator put her through to his line.

"Hi, honey," she said, "I'm just taking my first break. I saw you called. Is something wrong?"

"Yeah," Nick said, "I can't find my phone. Any chance you accidently grabbed it on your way out this morning? I know our phone cases look alike."

Alex checked her purse. Sure enough, there was Nick's phone.

"Aw, babe, I'm so sorry," said Alex. "Guess I was in too big a rush this morning."

That was at least partially true. She'd been frazzled because she'd overslept. Try as she might, Alex didn't recall putting a phone into her purse, let alone two. Her only solid memory from the morning was moving empty wine bottles from the recycling bin into the bottom of the trash so it would be less obvious.

"Okay, no biggie," Nick said. "Glad you have it. But I need a number on it. I have to reschedule a meeting with a new client, and I put his contact information in my phone."

"Isn't it synced to your iCloud?" Alex asked.

Nick groaned. "Honey, I don't understand what any of that means. What's an iCloud?"

"How can you be so smart and yet—"

"Don't say it," said Nick, finally putting a touch of lightness into his voice. "My iCloud is dark and stormy, so just get that number for me, will you?"

He gave her the passcode, and Alex found the number he was looking for.

"Say, while I have your phone, you never sent me that adorable picture you took the other day of Zoe in the yard. Do you mind if I text it to myself?"

"Go ahead," Nick said. "I've gotta call this guy right away. Thanks for all your help. I should marry you."

"Too late," Alex said. "I'm already taken."

She ended the call feeling grateful, or at least highly confident that she and Nick weren't anything like Jarrod and Abbie. Their marriage wasn't perfect—no relationship ever was—but the fundamental components of a healthy union were in place. They were just in a little lull, was all—a passing phase of disconnection, probably triggered by fears of empty nesting.

She opened the photos app on Nick's phone and began scrolling. The images, mostly family photos, blurred before her eyes, a kaleidoscope of her life with Nick. It was all going by too fast. She'd long ago abandoned any regrets that they had stayed a family of three, but with Lettie leaving soon, something was unraveling inside her. Her sadness felt disproportionate for what was a necessary part of life.

You raise them with roots and wings. And yet . . .

Alex eventually located the photo of Zoe, but something else caught her eye as well. She hesitated for a fraction of a second before her trembling finger clicked on an image that seemed glaringly out of place.

She felt unsteady on her feet. Her vision went out of focus, her breathing came to a sputtering stop as she endured a tight squeeze against her heart.

Staring back at her from the screen with an alluring look on her face, dressed scantily in revealing black lace lingerie straight out of an adult magazine, was none other than Brooke Bailey.

Chapter 19

Lettie

I do what any almost-eighteen-year-old girl would do after getting rejected by the sexiest guy on the planet. I turn to Google. My first search leads me to articles about coping with rejection—lots of unhelpful advice about understanding that rejection hurts (no shit), practicing self-care (say little affirmations about how awesome I am—whatever), spending time with people I love, and blah-blah-blah.

I've hardly eaten in the days since Jay revealed that he's some sort of predatory arachnid. In retrospect, that scorpion tattoo feels awfully convenient, like he got the ink just so he could use that dumb frog story to let girls down gently.

All I know for certain is that he's not into me like I'm into him, and he didn't have the heart to break mine. That makes Jay even sweeter and kinder in my eyes, and it makes me want him more. Now, how messed up is that?

I have since come to the nearly unbearable realization that Jay represents all people for all time and that nobody will ever love me. I'm simply unloved and unlovable. My body isn't hot enough. I don't have good enough genes, which technically makes this moment of profound self-pity the fault of my ancestors.

What I need is someone to commiserate with—someone who really gets the humiliation and hurt that follows rejection. But my friends and I have drifted further apart, enough so that our social media banter is limited to quick memes and tweet-sized sound bites.

Zoe is in my bedroom, so I go back to Google and type: "Can dogs feel rejection?"

Turns out that when they do, dogs tuck their tails between their legs and lower their ears to try to make themselves small because they don't want to feel like a burden to their owners. That's exactly what I'd do right now if I had a tail. I want to go small. I want to vanish, stop being a burden, let the world forget about me.

Since that's not really an option, I flop on my bed and cuddle Zoe. I'd read that offering comfort to others was a good way to heal our own wounds. I find myself whispering to my dog: "Do you feel small like me? Do you feel insignificant and utterly alone? Do you feel so embarrassed that you want to die?"

Zoe wags her tail vigorously before licking my face. Her breath smells like she got into the trash.

My plan to take revenge on Riley Thompson feels all kinds of wrong. Yes, she tormented me in middle school, turned me in to the authorities in high school, but I see now that I'm not Jay Kumar. He's willing to go too far, push too hard, because that's his nature. It isn't mine. I simply don't have the stomach for hurting other people.

Crap. I'm definitely getting a B on my psych paper now. The whole point was that I'd get my revenge and write a killer paper using firsthand knowledge of what revenge feels like. But those damn researchers might be right. Even though Riley deserves her payback, I'm certain I won't feel good after giving it to her.

I get up off my bed grumpy as ever. I've been grumpy every morning since enduring what I've come to think of as The Worst Kiss of All Time. I know that I'm being overly dramatic, but so be it.

Mom tries to make small talk with me in the kitchen before school.

"How are your classes going?"

"Fine," I tell her.

"Any big projects coming up?"

"No," I say.

"You need any help with your college applications?"

"No, thanks," I say because I feel like that one deserves a show of gratitude.

"There's a Zoom lecture from a college admissions counselor I thought we could watch together. And I really want to get that list of schools so we can arrange some tours. We're going to run out of time, honey."

I want to tell my mother that my heart is broken. I want to share what happened with Jay, what I've seen Riley doing as well. I want her to know that I'm so full of regret and embarrassment that I might give myself an ulcer or heart disease or something else awful.

Instead, I say, "Yeah, I'll text you my updated list later," and head off to school without a hug goodbye.

School isn't much better than home. I'm carrying around a profound weight that makes my backpack feel light as a bag of feathers. I'm a zombie in most of my classes, replaying my fumbled kiss instead of paying attention to the instruction.

My brain keeps yelling at me. *Why didn't you just try to hold his hand first? He could have pulled away and acted like nothing ever happened. Or here's a better idea, Lettie: Why make a move at all? If he was that into you, he would have done something about it! Stupid, stupid, stupid girl!*

Whatever. Brains can really suck.

I text Jay during lunch. I know I shouldn't, but I can't help myself. *Can we talk?*

He texts back. *Lettie, you gotta let this go.*

I just want to talk.

No. We shouldn't.

Because you're a scorpion?

Something like that.

He's right. I should let this go, but deep down I know that Jay wants to connect. He's still traumatized over Asher's death. I want him to know we can be friends. So I don't hold back, even though my instincts say I should.

I just think it would be good if we talked about things. Maybe you need to open up to someone. I want to be there for you.

There. I'm happy with that. Not pushy, but not letting myself be pushed out of the way, either. I'm hoping when we're together we can talk about this revenge plot of mine (or ours). I'll tell him about my change of heart, and even though we're wired differently, opposites can still attract.

I see three dots. Jay's writing back.

Lettie, I'm not a good guy. I don't want to hurt you. Don't make me show you I can.

Well now, that sure gives me the creeps.

What does that even mean?? I text back. *OK, just forget it.*

Jay doesn't respond, but of course I can't forget it. I'm still trying to decode his meaning when I stumble my way into the upstairs girls' bathroom. Unfortunately, I catch sight of myself in the scratched-up mirror above the equally scratched-up sink. I look terrible. Pasty complexion, puffy cheeks, a pimple even! No wonder Jay was repulsed. I look away quickly as I hear a sound from one of the bathroom stalls.

Someone is in here with me, and she's crying. It's a soft cry, a bit strangled, like she's trying to get control of herself. I want to egg her on to let it all out.

I'm still at the sink, and I guess I'm being too quiet, because the stall door opens and out steps the mystery crier. By the shock on her face, I'm sure she thought she was alone in here. The shock on my face says I didn't think it was Riley Thompson hiding out in that stall. But sure enough, I'm looking at Riley with my mouth wide open.

Riley blushes as she sniffles. Without a word, she turns from me before bolting from the bathroom in a sprint.

I hesitate. I should let her go. Revenge may no longer be my goal, but Riley's cheating on my cousin, and that doesn't fill me with much sympathy.

The moment she's gone, I have a change of heart. She's a person, after all. Obviously, she's hurting about something—probably some guy on her Tinder list dumping her. I'm not callous and uncaring, and I did just turn over a new leaf (thank you, Jay, for opening my eyes!), so I decide to be true to my newish good intentions and go chasing after her.

It's not long before we catch up at the top of the stairwell. "Want some company?" I ask.

Riley turns away from my gaze but doesn't tell me to get lost.

Meanwhile, I'm thinking about Dylan, how crushed he'd be if he knew what I knew.

"What's going on, Rye? Are you okay?"

Obviously not, but we have to start somewhere.

"Yeah, yeah, I'm fine, sorry," Riley says, finally looking at me. She doesn't sound even a little bit fine as she wipes her eyes with her hand. "I'm just dealing with some stuff."

Here's where I could have said, "Okay," and moved on with my day, leaving Riley to her private torment, but back to my new leaf.

"Talk to me, okay?" I implore. "Let me try to help."

This isn't BS. I really *do* care. I even take hold of Riley's hand as I pull her away from the stairwell. We walk down the hall together until we come upon a little alcove where we can converse in private.

We sit on the floor, not saying anything for a minute or two. Then Riley's tears come, and with them heaving sobs that honestly tear at my heart. I put my arm around her shoulder and let her cry. Eventually I get her some of the tissues that my mom keeps stuffing in my backpack. Riley blows her nose and then she blows my mind.

"My dad isn't my real father," she tells me.

Chapter 20

From the basement, Alex retrieved a plastic bin with the hand-written label: HALLOWEEN. She had to weed through a lot of the block party supplies to get to the box she wanted.

It was a mess down there, with storage containers and plastic bags strewn about. She made a promise to herself to get rid of some of the excess. Nobody needs two full bags of tablecloths for one party. How a family of three could accumulate so many possessions, enough to max out the storage space of a sprawling home, was a source of both bemusement and frustration.

The bin she needed was filled with fake cobwebs, some spooky decorative pumpkins, a battery-operated witch with green glowing eyes, and other ghoulish holiday accoutrements. Lettie had lost interest in celebrating Halloween over the past several years, but Alex couldn't let the tradition go. It wasn't the only thing she was holding on to these days.

For the past three nights she had gone to bed thinking of that scantily clad picture of Brooke she'd found on Nick's phone, and each morning, she failed to bring it up to her husband. She didn't believe Nick could be Brooke's stalker, but couldn't completely dispel that notion, either. It was *always* the husband who engaged in some diabolical treachery in those true crime docudramas—the seemingly good guy who does the dastardliest things when he thinks no one is looking.

As Alex carried the bin up the stairs, she heard the front door close shut. Nick must be home.

It was time, she decided. She'd given it enough thought and was going to drive herself crazy if she didn't confront him directly.

She set the box down in the foyer where most of the decorations would go. Then it was off to the kitchen, where she picked up the glass of wine she'd already poured. Down went the alcohol, fueling her resolve.

Alex sent a silent prayer out to the universe that Nick would have a damn fine explanation for that picture. Given the state of her life and this neighborhood—Emily's fears about Ken and Mandy, Samir's menacing vibe, Willow's troubles with Evan, her disappearing daughter—Alex wasn't sure she could manage much more.

Nick entered the kitchen looking a lot less chipper than when he'd left the house hours earlier.

"Tough day?" asked Alex.

"You could say that," said Nick, running his hands through his thick hair. "What's for dinner? I'm wiped out." He opened the fridge.

"Takeout," Alex replied. "I'm doing the decorations tonight."

"Why?" asked Nick. "Aren't we beyond that phase? I was thinking we'd leave out a bowl of candy and go out to a movie."

"You can't do that!" Alex said. "This is Alton Road—the top trick-or-treat neighborhood in Meadowbrook. We can't disappoint the kids like that."

"You just don't want to disappoint their parents and be the talk of the town. 'The Foxes bailed on Halloween—what's up with them?'" Nick said in a mocking tone. "Am I right?"

Alex rolled her eyes, drinking her wine like it was lemonade.

"How does Mommy's candy taste tonight?" he asked as Alex was refilling her glass.

She shot him an angry look. "What's that supposed to mean?"

Nick was rifling through the drawer where they kept all the take-out menus. "Wine might be your main course, but I think I need a little more. Chinese? I haven't had fried rice in ages."

"Chinese is fine. But are you going as a judge for Halloween?"

"I don't think I'm being judgmental. More like factual."

"There's nothing wrong with wine after work," Alex said.

"A little wine is fine, but you seem to be *way* past a little these days."

"I honestly don't appreciate your insinuation, especially when I've done nothing wrong," she snapped. "I'm taking care of everything around here—including Lettie's college applications, which you really could be more involved with."

"I'm not saying you're incompetent," said Nick. "And I know you do more than your fair share. I've just been noticing a lot of wine bottles in the recycling bin, is all."

Shit. Alex regretted not hiding them sooner. She'd known Nick would think the worst. If Alex's business had taught her anything, it was that emotional and physical distance created a lot of space for accusations to fly.

"Actually, you're the one who should be defending yourself," said Alex. "I've been meaning to ask what you've been up to on your 'long work days.' Any chance some of them involved our sexy neighbor Brooke Bailey?" Her look could turn a man into stone.

"What the hell are you talking about?" Nick practically shouted. "Jesus, Alex. You really are drinking too much! What could possibly give you that idea?"

Alex was somewhat prepared for this reaction. Any scenario she'd conjured in preparing for this confrontation ended with his getting defensive. But what defense could he possibly have? At least the image on his phone didn't look like a stalker kind—something snapped through a window or captured via a hidden camera. No, that photo was as posed as it was provocative.

"What could possibly give me that idea?" Alex mused aloud. "Hmm . . . how about sexy photos of Brooke Bailey on your phone? You'd have to be pretty damn close and intimate with her to get a pic like that."

In a blink, Nick's expression, his whole demeanor, softened and relaxed. "Ah, I get it now. Didn't even cross my mind, but if I saw one of those pictures without any explanation I'd think the worst, too."

"And just so you know, I wasn't snooping," Alex said. "You gave me the password when I accidently took your phone." She intentionally omitted the part about being hungover when she'd made that mistake. "So, are you into her? Do you two have something going on?" Her voice shook.

"No . . . no, not at all. We don't even talk."

"Well, are you stalking her?"

Nick laughed. "Good god, you honestly think I'm the creepy dude stalking Brooke?"

Naturally, Alex had shared Brooke's startling revelation the morning after the party. A stalker in the neighborhood was simply too important to keep to herself.

Nick appeared wounded, and perhaps rightly so.

"No," said Alex. "Not really."

"How about no friggin' way," said Nick. "Really, I could use a little more conviction from you. Look, I get it—A plus B equals my loving, devoted husband is a crazed stalker, but honey, I would hope you would think more of me."

"Well, how did that picture get on your phone?" asked Alex.

"Ken sent it to me," Nick said.

"Ken?"

"Yeah. Evidently, he found her on this website called OnlyFans."

Alex knew about the not-safe-for-work social media platform where people sold sexually explicit material, but she'd never visited the site.

"I guess Brooke has a pretty big fan base," Nick continued. "From what I know it's an excellent source of income for top talent, and as I see it, Brooke is free to do as she pleases."

"So how did Ken get the picture?"

"He uses the site—sorry to say—and found her on it."

"Ken uses an adult website?"

Nick's face implied she was being ridiculously naive.

"He's my brother-in-law," Alex protested.

"Technically he's mine, too," said Nick.

"And you? Do you use that site?"

"No, sweetheart. I like my women a bit more accessible."

"I hope not *too* accessible."

"How about I like them married to me."

"Did you ask Ken to see her photos? Were you curious?"

"No, not at all. At our last poker game, Ken announced he had airdropped some pictures to me. All he said was, 'Prepare to be surprised.' I was surprised, all right. Honestly, I thought I'd deleted them all."

"Why didn't you tell me?"

Nick acted as if he'd done nothing wrong. "It's her business, not mine or yours." He raised his eyebrows.

It wasn't an accusation, but that was the way Alex took it: she was being too nosy and over-involved in the affairs of others. It wasn't fair. She didn't *ask* people to come to her with their problems—Willow's divorce, Emily's relationship with Ken—they just did.

Sure, maybe she was inserting herself into Mandy's life without prompting, but from her experience, where there was smoke, there was fire.

"And I didn't want the pictures in the first place. I have no desire to see Brooke in the buff, and like I told you, I thought I deleted them all. I'm sorry, honey, but really, if I had stuff to hide, I wouldn't have asked you to go looking at my phone."

Nick's logic was solid. Alex felt small and silly—probably looked the part, too, standing in the middle of the kitchen, arms dangling limply by her sides.

"You know that things have been distant between us for a while now," she said, "and seeing that picture—well, I guess I couldn't help but think the worst."

Nick took Alex's hand. "Only thing I care about is that you believe me, hon," he said, locking eyes with her. "And I know we've been a little disconnected lately. Lettie's suspension, her going off to college, our usual work stress—all that's taken a toll. And I admit I was a little harsh with the way I called out your drinking, but, Alex, I think it's becoming a problem. You really should try to cut back. It's not good for your health, and it sends Lettie a bad message."

Alex nodded. "Yeah, maybe it's been a bit of a crutch," she said. "I'll go a little lighter."

Nick let go of her hand so he could grip her shoulders gently. In his touch, she felt the sincerity of his love. "And remember it's better to have an awkward conversation than to keep things bottled up for days."

Alex glanced at him sideways. "Have you been reading my self-help books again?"

Nick smiled back before kissing the top of her head. "I get it," he told her. "I really do. It was the perfect storm for a misunderstanding. But we're done with this. Agreed?"

"Will you delete Brooke's photo?" asked Alex, more of a demand than a request.

"It would be my pleasure," said Nick. He found the suspect image and deleted it with exaggerated gusto.

Afterward, Alex fell into his arms. "I get why men want to look at her. Brooke is so beautiful and sexy and I'm so, so . . ." She couldn't find the words.

Nick came to her rescue. "Perfect," he said, pulling her in closer, holding her tighter. "You're perfect for me."

And she believed him. He kissed her tenderly, on the lips this time. Their mouths opened as the kiss deepened, allowing a wave of desire to pass through Alex.

Nick left to get the Chinese food. He'd be a while, so Alex headed out the door, leaving Zoe behind. She wasn't out for a leisurely stroll. She was going to have a little chat with Brooke Bailey.

Chapter 21

Brooke came to her front door in a plush pink bathrobe. Her hair was down, looking tousled, but she was as gorgeous as ever. Alex wondered what she had on underneath that robe. Was she interrupting another photo shoot?

"Hey, there." Brooke offered a bright smile that was definitely camera-ready. "This is a nice surprise. Everything okay?"

Alex didn't do pop-ins at Brooke's, so the question made sense.

"Yes, everything's fine . . . but do you have a minute to talk?"

"Of course." Brooke motioned Alex into her spacious home.

Alex had been inside Brooke's house on several occasions, but it was always a bit painful to see how the childless widow lived, especially when Alex had just come from visiting the overabundance of crap collecting dust in her basement.

The real problem was that Brooke had impeccable taste—a decorator's eye, or at least the budget to afford a high-quality professional. Every room had a functional feel, but the interplay of materials, shapes, patterns, and textures produced a visual wow factor almost as enviable as Brooke's curves.

Pictures of Brooke and Jerry traveling the globe on their seemingly nonstop honeymoon adorned the walls, along with fine art pieces that might have been purchased at Sotheby's. Some of the pictures included Emily and Ken, who often vacationed with Brooke and Jerry.

Ken and Jerry's friendship had dated back to their childhood and was almost as close as the bond Alex shared with her sister. The good vibrations between the husbands never quite extended to the wives.

Alex wondered if the distance between them had something to do with Brooke's aloof nature or Emily's tendency toward jealousy. Probably a mix of the two, she guessed.

It was hard to imagine Brooke having done anything harmful to Jerry, let alone tossing him off a cruise ship, especially after seeing the way he was enshrined in her home. But the rumors were pervasive, and arsonists loved watching their own fires. Alex wondered just how honest Brooke had been at girls' night.

She pushed those thoughts aside. Having already jumped to conclusions about Nick, Alex didn't need to make that mistake again.

"Can I get you something to drink?" Brooke asked when they reached the spacious airy kitchen that had probably never seen a spaghetti sauce spill. "Maybe some wine?"

"Love some, thank you," said Alex. Sure, she'd made a promise to Nick, but it was only to cut back on drinking, not stop entirely. So she didn't see a problem with it.

Brooke poured them two glasses.

"So, what's up?" asked Brooke. "You sure everything's okay? You look worried about something."

Alex didn't mince words. "I know about your side business on some adult website," she began. "It's a long story how I found out, but Nick ended up with a photo of yours that Ken sent him. I'm not judging—honestly, I'm not—but I thought you should know, given your stalker situation and our gossipy neighborhood, that this is circulating around the street, maybe closer to your home than you intended."

If Alex's disclosure distressed her at all, none of it registered on Brooke's face. She sipped her wine, nonchalant, as if Alex were talking about the weather.

"Is that all this is about? Goodness, Alex, you had me worried." A twinkle danced in Brooke's dark brown eyes, conveying that the concern was appreciated but quite unnecessary. "You're sweet to care. I love it. But don't worry about me, not even a little. I wouldn't be putting my pictures out there if I didn't *want* people looking at them. I'm just pissed that Ken shared some. I don't get any money that way."

Alex felt more than a little protective of Emily, who most certainly would not approve of her husband ogling their neighbor and former travel companion.

"I'm not going to tell my sister about Ken using the site, but you heard her at girls' night. She wants to hire a PI. So it may come back around, and I wanted to give you a heads-up in case there's some blowback," Alex said. She could only imagine Emily's reaction if she found out—somewhere between distraught and enraged.

Brooke waved away any concern. "I'm not worried, and honestly that's between Emily and Ken. I'm not responsible for what any of my fans do."

"I get it," said Alex. "But I'm still worried how Emily will react."

"She's a big girl," said Brooke. "Trust me, she'll handle it fine. I'll just remind her it's business, not personal."

Alex didn't disagree, but now she wondered how lucrative Brooke's side gig really was. Down went more wine. Brooke was quick with a refill. Alex reminded herself to start cutting back tomorrow.

"Out of curiosity," said Alex with some trepidation, "how did you get into this line of work? It's a bit—um—unconventional."

Brooke's mouth ticked up ever so slightly. "So is stripping," she said, her smile broadening.

"Fair point," said Alex. "But you told us that was a long time ago."

"And it was," said Brooke. "Honestly, I'm a happily clothed marketer in my day job. But I came across a news report about OnlyFans, and I couldn't believe how much people were making—enough so it's become a full-time job for a lot of the models. I checked out the site and thought, *Well, I should get in on the action.*"

"And . . . are you doing well?" Alex asked.

"Better than you'd ever believe," said Brooke. "Say, if you want in, I can show you how to do it. I set up a photo studio in Jerry's old office and I hire a photographer whenever I need. It's easy to do, and you'll rake in the cash. It's certainly more fun than listening to people's marital problems all day."

"Me? A nude model?" Alex blushed.

"Underwear works, too, or a bathing suit. Heck, you could wear jeans and a turtleneck, but don't expect big checks for that."

Brooke chuckled, but Alex didn't join in. She was still thinking about the work.

"I don't think people would pay money to look at me in any clothing, skimpy or not," she said.

Brooke pooh-poohed Alex's self-deprecation. "Come on now. You're utterly gorgeous, you have a great figure, and Nick knows how lucky he is to have you." Brooke put the wineglass to her lips and drank. "Not so sure we can say the same about Ken and Emily."

"What do you mean by that? Do you know something I should know? More than Ken having your pictures, I mean."

A flurry of questions came to Alex. Was there something more between Ken and Brooke? Had Brooke seen something between Ken and Mandy?

Before she had a chance to inquire further, Brooke's cell phone vibrated on the kitchen counter with an incoming message. A glance at the display put a dark look on Brooke's face. "It seems we are not alone," she announced.

"What does that mean?" asked Alex.

Brooke showed her the message.

Who's in the house with you?

Alex's blood iced over. Spinning to face a bank of tall picture windows, she looked into an impenetrable darkness beyond.

"Is that . . . is it . . . ?" She couldn't manage the rest.

"Yes and yes," said Brooke without fright. "My stalker."

"Oh my god," Alex breathed, leaping off her stool. "He's here. Outside? Brooke, we need to call the police."

Brooke barely reacted. "I'm used to this by now. I told you. He's harmless."

While Brooke sounded confident, Alex wasn't buying it. "How can you be so sure? He's *watching* us. Right now!"

Alex's heart rammed up into her throat. Her legs felt unsteady beneath her. How close was he? Was he right outside the window? Shock and fear rode through Alex like waves of electric current.

"If it makes you feel any safer, I'll walk you home. This isn't the first time he's been in our neighborhood, and it won't be the last. He only cares about me. Nobody else matters to him. He's obsessed with me, for whatever reason."

"Thanks for the offer, but I wouldn't feel comfortable with *you* walking yourself home alone. I'll have Nick come get me."

"Whatever makes you feel most comfortable," Brooke said. "But you've nothing to worry about. I've been dealing with this creep for a while now. He's like all the men in my life these days. He can look, but he cannot touch."

Chapter 22

Lettie

I haven't rung Riley's doorbell since middle school, back when I wanted to wring her neck. Ten minutes ago, she sent me a message. I didn't know she still had my phone number, but suddenly she's texting, asking to talk about something "important." I can guess what topic is on her mind.

I wait for someone to come to the front door, wondering what on earth Riley thinks I can do to help. I try to put myself in her shoes—imagining how it would feel to find out this late in life that my father wasn't my father. Well, I suppose that's a bit unfair. He'd have raised me and all that, so I don't think DNA should negate years of noteworthy effort. But still, I get it—there's a certain identity that comes from knowing *exactly* where you come from.

I never did get the full story of how she found out. The bell rang the day she confided in me, and we were rudely interrupted by hordes of students who streamed into the hall. I've been curious to know more since then, but not enough to reach out to her.

Now that I'm at her house, I have this thought that we'll drag out the Barbies like the old days, use them to role-play the looming confrontation with her parents.

Evan, the non-bio-dad, opens the door. His blue denim shirt, stylishly paired with black jeans, is unbuttoned, and I see way too much Evan Thompson for my liking. His eyes are red-rimmed and bloodshot. A scattering of scruff can't hide his pale complexion. All in all, he looks handsome as always, but he's a bit strung out, like a guy who should have left the nightclub hours ago.

He's holding a glass tumbler that's a quarter full of a brown liquid that smells like lighter fluid. I have a passing thought that Evan has a stash of drugs in the house that's helping to feed Riley's habit. It's something I would have discussed with Jay if only we were talking or texting. We haven't communicated since our last odd exchange.

I'm not a good guy. I don't want to hurt you. Don't make me show you I can.

I still don't know what he meant by that. Was it a threat against me, or would he hurt someone I care about to prove a point? Either way, I'm not completely turned off by it or him, and I suppose that's another problem for my future therapist to sort out.

"Lettie," says Evan, clearly surprised I'm there. He doesn't make enough room for me to slip inside without passing close enough to smell alcohol on his breath. Sadly, the odor makes me think of my mother.

"Riley's in her bedroom," he tells me. Even though it's been years, he knows I can find my way. "How've you been?" he asks.

"Good," I say, hoping that will be the full extent of our conversation.

I've always liked Evan, or at least he's always been nice to me, which is partly why I feel extra uncomfortable knowing this secret about him.

I scamper upstairs. Riley's bedroom door is closed. I go inside without knocking.

"Thanks for leaving me alone with your dad," I say sarcastically. "Talk about awkward."

The room looks nothing like I remember. It used to be pink and full of fluffy things. Now it's blue and there are a lot more mirrors.

"Sorry about that," she tells me from her seat at a desk in a corner of the room that was once home to a mountain of stuffed animals. Her ponytail swishes from one shoulder to the other as she gets up from her chair, not to give me a hug but to close the door.

"I was going to meet you downstairs, but I've been avoiding my father, and he got there first."

"Do you think he knows that you know? Does *he* even know?"

I'm sure I could have been more sensitive in how I phrased my questions, but we aren't actually here to play dolls.

"No to both," Riley says. "But I think he's going to find out."

"How so?"

"My mother is going to tell him."

I plop down in a turquoise beanbag chair, which shifts under my weight, while Riley perches herself on the edge of her bed.

"Why do you say that?" I ask.

My gaze darts about the room. I can't help but wonder what's gone on in here—if Riley and Dylan have done the deed on her bed, if she has pills stashed in her desk drawer, or maybe love notes from her secret boy toy, though I suspect those would mostly come by text.

"They're fighting *all* the time now," she tells me.

"They *are* getting a divorce," I say. "Maybe it's, you know, not so great that they're still in the same house?"

"Ya think?" says Riley emphatically.

She looks profoundly sad, and I feel for her in all the ways I haven't. What can I say? Emotions are confusing.

On one hand, I want to revile her choices, but now that I've seen her vulnerable side, I find my judgment softening. Sure, she's my former bully with cheerleader good looks and envy-inducing popularity, but I guess we're all just one secret away from feeling like an outsider.

"I need your help with something—but before that, I have a confession to make." Riley clears her throat like she's about to make an announcement. Then: "It was me . . . I'm the one who identified you as the school vandal. I'm the reason you got suspended last year."

She sounds remorseful, but I saw her in a school play once and she was a pretty good actress. Regardless, I still look surprised, but that's because she actually fessed up to it—the rat.

"I shouldn't have done it," she continues. "I didn't want to get you in trouble."

"Well, what did you *think* would happen?" I ask testily.

"I dunno," she admits. "I guess I wasn't really thinking—or at least I wasn't thinking about you."

Well, that stings, but she's got my attention. "Okay," I say. "So why are you telling me this?"

"I'm trying to apologize, Lettie, okay?!" Red splotches appear on Riley's porcelain smooth cheeks. I think she might cry.

"It helps if you actually use the words *I'm sorry*," I suggest.

"I'm sorry," Riley says as her gaze drops to the floor.

I let Riley stew in her discomfort for a silent minute before I let her off the hook—sort of. "If we're being totally honest, I already knew."

Riley perks up with surprise. "How?" she asks.

I'm not going to sell out Dylan to make my point, so I take a different approach. "The only distinguishing feature in the published image was the splotchy birthmark on my wrist. Nobody's ever commented on it before—nobody except you. You didn't have a blemish on your body when we were kids—still don't—so you were unusually fixated on it. I figured it would have stuck out to you."

Riley looks impressed, like she's in the presence of a great detective.

"But back to the point. Why'd you tell on me?"

A deep sigh exits Riley's mouth, as if to rid herself of all bad feelings, though her guilty expression remains. "I wanted a college reference from Mr. Giuseppe."

My eyebrows go up. "Vice Principal Giuseppe?"

"Yeah, he's pretty stingy with them. I thought if I gave him the vandal, he might give me a recommendation."

Her lame excuse gets a scoff from me. "You sacrificed me in middle school for your popularity, and you did again it in high school for a *reference*, of all things. At least I was standing up for a cause. You only think of yourself—and you always have."

"I'm sorry," Riley says, her voice pleading. "I *really* am."

"Do you know I still get stomach cramps when I hear the word *loony*? And I have an irrational fear of security alarms every time I leave a store. You were horrible to me, Riley—absolutely horrible."

"I know . . . I know," she says, sounding genuinely contrite. "I'm really sorry, Lettie. I was stupid and young."

"You weren't *that* young when you named me as the vandal." I pantomime using spray paint on an imaginary school door.

Riley doesn't know what to say to that. I want to tell her how close I was to giving Jay the green light to share the photos of her and Umbrella Man, but my better judgment prevails.

"I'm asking you for a second chance," Riley begs.

"You betrayed me twice. Why should I give you a chance to do it again?" I counter, squinting at her. "Anyway, what's more important, why did you do it? Not the graffiti—I get that. I'm asking why did you become such a raging bitch to me in middle school? We were friends! Best friends!"

Riley takes a moment to collect her thoughts, as if she's composing herself for some big confession. Once again, her gaze lowers to avoid mine. "I was jealous," she says.

Wide eyes broadcast my astonishment. "Jealous of what? Me?" I point to myself and laugh in disbelief. "I don't have your money, your looks, your friends. What did you have to be jealous of?"

"Your family," Riley says. "You, your mom, your dad—you were all so . . . perfect. My parents, they fought all the time. It was miserable around here—still is. Guess I'm used to it now, but back then I *hated* it—every minute of it."

I flash to our playdates, my mind conjuring echoes of the loud squabbles that evidently tormented Riley.

Tears coat her eyes—kryptonite to my defenses.

"I just wanted what you had—a happy, *normal* family," she says, her voice quavering.

While she's expertly plucked at my heartstrings, I'm still hurt and angry. "That makes no sense," I tell her. "You wanted what I had, so you treated me like crap? How'd that work out? All it did was ruin our friendship and made us *both* miserable."

"It was childish and stupid of me, I know," Riley says.

A hefty sigh releases most of my bad feelings. What's the point in dwelling on them anyway?

"I'm really sorry for what you're going through," I offer, after a brief silence.

Riley dismisses her troubles with a shrug. "It is what it is." That could be either wise and worldly or an avoidance tactic.

"Are you sure about—"

I don't have to finish the thought, as Riley is nodding emphatically. "I took a DNA test," she says. "The kind that looks for ancestors and stuff."

The unfiltered Lettie would say something sarcastic like: "As opposed to the DNA test that reveals your spirit animal?" The sensitive Lettie keeps her mouth shut.

"What made you do that?" I ask.

"Teagan was doing it with her mom for fun, some kind of family tree project. And I thought my mom and I should do it, too."

Teagan is one of my former tormentors—the one who nicknamed me Loony Lettie, in fact. This visit is getting less fun by the second.

"Do you think your mom knows? I mean . . . if she does, why would she want to take the test?"

"She didn't want to take it," Riley says. "Or at least she said she'd get the kits for us, but she never did. I think she was stalling because she knows Evan's not my father. She was probably hoping I'd forget about the whole thing."

So now he's "Evan."

"Whenever I brought it up, my mom would act like it had slipped her mind. The more she put it off, the more curious I became . . . so I ordered the test myself."

Parents just don't get it. The more they want us *not* to do something, the more likely it is we're going to do it. Such thinking is hardwired into our teenage brains.

"When I got the results, they didn't make sense."

Riley hands me her phone. On the screen is a report from a company called MyRoots. I'm looking at a pie chart with one-half colored red. The red part is labeled "Poland."

I think I get Riley's aha moment. Thompson is mostly an English name, and Riley has always said her family is from the UK. This chart says otherwise.

"Evan doesn't have any Polish ancestry, I'm guessing?"

Riley shakes her head.

"My dad is English and Irish. My mom's family is from Scotland. That's what I've been told."

The Scottish ancestry is there, along with a bunch of reports indicating that Riley has a low probability for serious genetic diseases.

Good for her.

"Scroll down," Riley says. "There's more."

And there is more—a table of common relatives. Many of those listed were thought to be fourth and fifth cousins, those who share at least 5cM (centimorgans) of identical DNA. I can't say whether Riley gets the genomics that make up this report, but she doesn't need a STEM background to know what the word *cousin* means. The report is lengthy and a bit overwhelming, but I don't see anything that clearly identifies a close relative, or Riley's biological father.

"There are relatives here I've never heard of. I certainly don't recognize any of the names with Polish ancestry. I'm thinking I should try to contact one of them . . . I want to find my real father."

I cringe again, because I feel bad for Evan. Spitting in a tube has somehow negated his parental status. I think about my own dad. I could never discount his role and influence based on some report.

"I mean, Evan's still your father," I tell her. "No matter what."

"You know what I mean." Riley sounds quite determined. "I want to find the man responsible for creating me."

"What about asking your mom?" I ask.

Riley shakes that off. "My mom is like crazy fragile right now. I don't want to make it worse."

I get it. But I still don't get exactly what I'm doing here. "Rye, what are you asking?" I need her to get to the point. More accurately, I need to get to my math homework.

"You're the smartest person I know," she tells me.

I'm flattered—a little.

"Thanks, but there are a lot of kids at school who are smarter than me," I say. That's not a lie, assuming "a lot" is around six. Maybe seven.

"Yeah, but you're the smartest person I know *well*," she says.

Can't argue with that, I think.

"What do you want from me, Rye?" I ask. "Why am I even here?"

Part of me wants to walk out the door before she has a chance to answer. But I feel for Riley, too. She's made mistakes and so have I. Maybe we all deserve second—or sometimes third—chances.

"Let me guess," I say. "You want me to help you find your bio-dad?"

Riley's face lights up.

I half smile back at her, but on the inside, I'm thinking: *What am I getting myself into?*

Chapter 23

While Alex enjoyed Halloween, Zoe could do without the holiday. Try as she might, Alex couldn't make her dog understand the futility of barking at every trick-or-treater who came to the door. From a canine point of view, the holiday was nothing but one ghoulish threat after another.

The sun was starting to set. Soon the street would be chaos, as Alton Road was *the* place to be in Meadowbrook on Halloween. Alex wasn't about to let her house become the lame one on the block, so she'd bought twelve boxes of full-size Snickers bars and a host of allergy-friendly options as well.

She arranged the candy on silver trays stationed by the front door, a tiny pang tapping at her heart. She couldn't remember Lettie's last costume—it had been that long ago—but she'd never forget her daughter's bouncy energy as the magic hour approached.

Alex tempered the ache of time with another long drink from her glass. In the bathroom, she used the last bit of mouthwash. Nick was due home any minute, so she took the empty bottle of mouthwash to the garage, where she buried it along with the empty bottle of wine at the bottom of the trash. She didn't need him reprimanding her again.

From the doorway, Alex watched a police car drive down Alton Road and make a slow revolution around the cul-de-sac. *Good.* They were doing street patrols, as Alex had requested. She had reported the stalker to them and asked for a thorough investigation plus added security on Halloween.

Redirecting her gaze over to Brooke's house, Alex half expected to catch movement in the woods. She was still shaken from her close encounter with the stalker. Brooke might not have been concerned, but Alex sure was.

It was possible she had upset Brooke by filing the police report, but what choice did she have? *You can't have a strange man lurking in the woods, spying on people, and not do something about it,* Alex had reasoned. *Who knows what might happen?*

Nearby, Emily's house cast a ghoulish glow thanks to Ken's holiday decorations, but Alex knew from speaking with her sister that Halloween fun was in short supply. Emily was still obsessing over Mandy Kumar.

What would have happened, Alex wondered, if she'd come clean about Ken ogling Brooke's photos or seeing him sneaking away from the Kumars' place? A big fight over the former and perhaps divorce over the latter. The relationship was too fragile for her to add fuel to the fire.

If she was honest with herself, Alex felt her relationship with Nick was strained as well. As if to punctuate that worry, Nick called to say he was running late. He had a project to finish for a client and wouldn't be home until sometime after seven. Years ago, that would have been sacrilegious. Now it was par for the course. *Oh, well.*

Lettie was hiding out in her room, where she spent most of her time these days. Alex had been warned that her daughter would vanish during senior year, gracing the family with her presence only occasionally, but the reality was more pronounced than she'd expected.

Alex decided to open a new bottle of wine. She could always use toothpaste as a sub for mouthwash. She selected a demi-sized bottle—375 milliliters, equivalent to two and a half glasses total, which made it easy to store in the cabinet behind the quinoa and pasta collection that hadn't been moved for ages.

She stored a case of wine at her office as well. *Stored.* Yeah, right. *Keep telling yourself that, Alex,* said the voice in her head. The correct word was *hid.*

Thirty minutes before the official start of All Hallows' Eve, Alex let Zoe out the back door to do her business. She was arranging a second row of Snickers bars into a nice display when she realized she hadn't let Zoe back in.

Just an oversight. It happens.

Alex tried to ignore the fuzzy warmth of her wine buzz as she went to the back door where Zoe would normally be waiting, tail wagging, eager to reenter the home. This time, however, her dog was nowhere to be seen.

Fear tickled the nape of Alex's neck. She called Zoe's name but got no response.

Lettie eventually came downstairs. "What's going on?" she asked.

"It's Zoe," Alex said. "She's left the yard."

Lettie's hand flew to her mouth.

Alex noticed a tree branch on the lawn that she didn't think had been there before. A nearby tree showed a sheared limb. A falling branch could have easily startled Zoe, Alex thought.

"She just went out," Alex said, willing calm into her voice. "She couldn't have gone far."

"I'll go across the street, check the woods behind the Kumars'," Lettie said. "Zoe always likes to explore those woods."

Alex was about to agree but remembered Brooke's stalker. She didn't want Lettie searching the woods alone—or at all.

"No, you stay home in case she returns. We'll find her."

Alex sprinted across the cul-de-sac toward the wooded area behind the Kumars'. The most direct route took her through Brooke's yard. One second she was walking on grass; the next, it was leaves and twigs crunching beneath her heavy footsteps. She tried to tread more carefully to better hear any movement, maybe catch the sound of Zoe's barking.

Panic gripped her. If she lost her beloved dog, if something happened to Zoe, she'd never forgive herself.

Alex scanned the woods, but Zoe's brindle coat nearly matched the color of the fallen leaves blanketing the forest floor. Dusk deepened the shadows, making shapes hard to distinguish.

Alex slowed her steps, calling Zoe's name as she went. From nearby she heard a noise, something breaking—a stick, perhaps? Damp earth filled her nose with the smell of decay. Overhead, branches creaked in the blustery wind.

Brooke Bailey's home loomed as an ominous presence in the distance. From where she stood, Alex could see into Brooke's kitchen, with no shades to block her view. She flashed back to the night the stalker texted Brooke, perhaps from this very spot.

Was he out here now? Alex suddenly didn't feel quite so alone. A chill passed through her.

"Zoe?" she called, her voice shaking in the gathering gloom.

Then she heard it again, another soft sound—the ground shifting beneath the weight of a footstep, perhaps? Alex's heart beat a jackhammer rhythm. Blood rushed to her head. She heard it once more, a crunching, brittle leaves turning to dust under the weight and pressure of what she was sure had been a footstep. The sound seemed to come from every direction, impossible to pinpoint.

It was nothing, Alex told herself. Her mind was just playing tricks on her. But damn, she wished she'd brought a flashlight. Sometimes kids used the path through these woods to reach the nearby lake. Maybe a teen party was going on. That had happened before.

The surrounding trees seemed to grow taller, closing in on her. As Alex headed back toward the street, she heard a branch break. This wasn't the creaking sound of windblown boughs, but a distinct snap.

She let go a shuddering breath. She wasn't alone. Turning, she raced for the street. Branches from small saplings lashed at her face as she ran.

The street was in view, and she could see light from the lampposts up ahead. Close to the spot where the woods ended and Brooke's backyard began, Alex's foot caught a root and down she went. Her knees sank into muddy earth still spongy from a recent rain. Sharp pain bolted up her wrists as she used them to brace her fall.

From behind, Alex heard a rustling noise. Something was approaching and seemed to be closing in fast. She crawled forward on her hands and knees, trying to regain her footing as she went. Just when she thought she'd dug her sneaker in hard enough to get upright, her foot skidded out behind her, pushing away wet leaves and loose soil.

Eventually she rose to standing, finishing her sprint with lumbering, off-kilter steps. When she finally broke the tree line, Alex spun around until she faced the forest, mustering the courage to confront the threat head-on. Fear made it hard to breathe. Whoever had been following her was coming—and coming fast.

Rustling sounds grew louder in her ears. A scream bubbled in her throat, about to escape her lips, when Zoe came bursting out of the woods. Her tail wagged like windshield wipers in a driving rain.

Alex's fear gave way to unrestrained joy. She got no more than three or four steps before Zoe was pressing her mud-caked paws against her legs, pleading to be picked up.

Alex scooped Zoe in her arms, cradling her in an embrace. She pressed her face against Zoe's fur and inhaled deeply. Her relief was profound. Alex made another pledge: no more drinking, more focus, more mindfulness, less noise and chaos in her head. She had everything she needed to be happy—a devoted husband, a healthy daughter, a beautiful home, a fulfilling career—but in that moment, nothing mattered to her more than the safety and well-being of her sweet, vulnerable dog.

With her face pressed against Zoe's neck, Alex caught a flash of something white stuck in her collar. Odd. She set Zoe to the ground, surprised to discover a piece of paper folded into a V-shape and tucked securely between the collar and Zoe's fur.

Alex unfolded the paper with a tingle of apprehension. On one side she saw neat handwriting in black pen. A streetlamp cast a yellow glow, bright enough for her to make out the words.

Alex's vision shifted in and out of focus. Even so, she could read the note. She read it several times to make sure she understood the meaning. She got it—loud and clear.

Her reliable dog had not run off. No, someone had taken her in order to deliver a message—a warning, really, presumably from the stalker himself.

The note read: *Back off or you'll regret it.*

Chapter 24

Lettie

Mom came back with Zoe cradled in her arms. I'm beside myself with relief. I was expecting the same from my mom, but instead there's a weightiness to her.

We check Zoe over, tail to nose. She's perfectly fine, no injuries, no need for the vet, but Mom's still not relaxed. Instead, she goes outside to speak with a police officer who's been patrolling our street in preparation for the Halloween mayhem. After words are exchanged, the officer leaves his patrol car, heading for the woods behind Brooke's house where Mom found Zoe.

Strange.

A few minutes later, the police officer emerges from the woods. He and Mom talk some more before he gets back in his patrol car and drives away.

"What's going on?" I ask when Mom returns.

"Nothing," she says. "I just thought I heard somebody in the woods, that's all."

"And? Was anybody there? Did someone try to dognap Zoe?"

"No . . . it's fine," Mom says, not sounding fine at all. "But I want you to stay out of those woods, okay?"

"Sure. Hanging out in the woods isn't really my thing, anyway," I say.

Mom goes up to her room, telling me she has to lie down. These days that usually means "pass out," but she doesn't seem even a little tipsy.

I haven't said anything to my mother about her drinking. Usually it's the other way around—parents lecturing their teens—so I'm not really sure how to broach the subject. I haven't talked to my father about Mom's "Wine Time," either. We barely speak as it is.

All those cute Wine Mom memes littering the internet don't help.

Wine—Because Yoga Can't Fix Everything.

A Day Without Wine Is Like . . . I Have No Idea.

I get that drinking makes things seem better, but maybe it's not so great for a marriage. Even from downstairs, I can hear Mom talking to Dad on the phone. Her tone is tense. Maybe Dad's blaming Mom's drinking for losing Zoe. Maybe they're headed for divorce. I've been preparing for that possibility for the past year now. She and Dad aren't fighting, at least not the screaming kind of fights you see in movies that feature drunken moms, but there's clearly tension between them. Divorce would suck for sure, but then again, I'll be gone and it will be their problem more than mine.

Two minutes after six o'clock, the official start of the trick-or-treating window, the first batch of kids arrive dressed as Spider-Man and Harry Potter. Mom is still upstairs, so I have to dole out the candy. Cars ferrying the costumed rug rats to Alton Road line our street like a funeral procession.

An hour of Halloween passes uneventfully until, through the open door, I hear an angry shout. The cry shatters the night's relative quiet.

Mom comes downstairs, looking startled. "Did you hear that?" she asks.

I step outside into the crisp fall night. Mom follows.

It's too dark to see much beyond our front walk. I search for the patrol car, but go figure—when you need help, it's not around. And the loud shout we hear sounds like trouble.

"Get the hell out of here!" The voice belongs to my uncle Ken.

My mom races ahead. There's a mob of people, maybe ten in total, gathered at the end of Uncle Ken's driveway.

A wall of bodies blocks my view, but I can hear Ken shouting angrily at someone who's shouting back. I don't recognize the other man's high-pitched, nasal voice.

"It's a free country, dude," this mystery person says.

Mom's peering over someone's shoulder to get a better look.

"What's going on?" I ask her.

A glow of blinking lights rises up from the center of the circle.

"I told you to get off my property," Ken demands.

"Technically, I'm not on your property," replies the man with the nasally voice. "I'm on a public road, paid for by tax dollars."

I finally break through the group of onlookers to get my first good look at the individual confronting my uncle. He's tall and thin, dressed in what I initially think is a green costume, but it's really a jumpsuit, a work uniform. He's decorated his uniform with all sorts of LED lights and glow sticks. The lights blink at a variety of speeds, and with different colors, too, mostly reds and blues. He looks like he dressed as a police car for Halloween.

"Oh my god," groans Mom. "It's the Bug Man."

Inwardly, I groan, too.

Everyone in Meadowbrook knows the Bug Man, and pretty much everyone can't stand him. I'm on the community page, so I've seen the complaints. Some of them are pretty damn funny, but apparently they weren't exaggerations. The Bug Man really *is* a pest.

The neon-lit Bug Man says, "Why don't you kick these people off your street, too? I'm dressed for Halloween like they are. I'm handing out candy, too. Here you go, kids. Have some candy!"

Bug Man stuffs flyers from the stack of papers he's holding into the candy bags of the children who are surrounding him. It looks like there's a Tootsie Roll Mini taped to each flyer, and now I get that this whole thing is a super lame promotional stunt.

I don't know why parents and kids are sticking around. Perhaps they think it's a silly Halloween skit, and the candy flyers and angry Ken are part of the routine, and they just want to know how it's going to play out.

Judging by the look on my uncle's face, I'd say it's not going to end well at all.

"You need to take your obnoxious sales tactics somewhere else," Ken insists.

Bug Man pretends to check a watch he's not wearing. "There's at least another hour of trick-or-treating," he says. "This street is fair game, so mind your own business, man."

"Fair game, my ass!" Uncle Ken yells.

The parents finally snap to their senses and pull their children away. Smart move.

"Tonight is for kids to trick-or-treat, not market your damn DDT services."

"DDT is a banned pesticide," Bug Man says calmly. "We use all-natural insecticide oils. I have literature on it if you'd like to know more." He offers Uncle Ken one of his candy flyers.

Ken snatches it from Bug Man, crumpling the paper into a little ball that he then tosses onto the ground.

Looking quite pleased with himself, Bug Man turns his back to Ken and waits for more trick-or-treaters to come by—which they do in short order because this is Alton Road, the greatest street in Meadowbrook for snagging candy. Soon enough, glowing Bug Man places his flyers into bags belonging to a lion, a witch, and maybe a zombie (kind of hard to tell, but definitely a gory outfit).

"Happy Halloween," Bug Man says loudly.

"Thank you," say the kids, and off they go, up Ken's driveway to get even more candy.

Uncle Ken storms into his house, and Mom follows. They're talking, but I stay back, mesmerized by the blinking Bug Man.

"Want a flyer?" he asks me. "Tell your parents about our winter special. Twenty percent off with the purchase of four or more treatments."

"Sure," I say.

He hands me the flyer.

I peel off the Tootsie Roll and pop the candy into my mouth. "Not sure this is the best way to get business," I suggest while chewing.

He smiles at me like he knows I'm right.

"The flyers get tossed out, but the parents remember the company name. Happy Halloween from D&M Pest!"

Bug Man stuffs a flyer into the orange plastic pumpkin of a passing three-year-old dressed as a bumblebee. The bee's mom reminds her daughter to say thank you.

Movement behind Bug Man catches my eye. Uncle Ken is flying down his driveway, with Mom and Aunt Emily trailing close behind. Mom looks anxious and Aunt Emily appears downright panicked.

"Ken, please, stop," Aunt Emily pleads. She grabs hold of Ken's shirt from behind, but he yanks himself free.

When he reaches the end of the driveway, I see the source of everyone's distress.

Uncle Ken has strapped a handgun to his waist. He goes right over to Bug Man with his hands on his hips, like an Old West sheriff.

Bug Man notices the weapon. "Whoa, packing heat for the kids?" he says. "That's quite the treat, man."

"Get out of here," Ken says.

Aunt Emily tries again to pull Ken away. At least he's keeping his gun in its holster.

"Ken, stop it. You shouldn't bring your handgun out here," Emily scolds him, and rightly so.

"Why?" Ken keeps his eyes locked on Bug Man, sending him a hard stare designed to intimidate. "I have a license to open carry. I'm not breaking the law."

"Neither am I," says Bug Man.

"I'm calling the police," I hear my mom say.

"Don't bother."

The voice, a new one, low and menacing, comes out of the dark. A moment later, I see Evan Thompson step into the glow of Bug Man's blinking lights. Willow's there, too, but keeping her distance.

Evan stands tall. His hair is a little disheveled, muscles of his face tight. He approaches with a confident swagger, getting right into Bug Man's personal space.

Aunt Emily stops protesting. Everything becomes quiet and still. The parents know to redirect their kids away from us. Ken may have the gun, but it's Evan who has command.

"You shouldn't be here," Evan tells Bug Man. His words come out in a growl.

"I'll tell you what I told Wyatt Earp," says Bug Man, pointing at Ken. "It's a free country, so I'm staying put." He places his hands on his hips in a defiant pose.

Evan moves closer to Bug Man. His gaze burns a hole into me, and I'm not the one he's staring down. I've never seen this side of Riley's dad before. There's something quite intimidating about him. He's like a human Jenga tower—just barely keeping it together. If one critical block is moved out of place, I can see him coming down with a crash.

"I don't think I've made myself clear," Evan says in his most threatening voice yet. "We're all sick of you. So I'll say it again—get out of here. Now."

Behind us a new crowd has formed. Once again, curiosity has overruled better judgment, and people can't help but watch.

"I don't think I'll go," Bug Man says, looking rather smug.

Evan gets close enough to kiss Bug Man, but obviously that's not what he has in mind.

"Do you know what it's like to snap?" Evan asks. "I mean, when you just lose it? Go nuts? I'm talking a temporary insanity kind of snap?"

Bug Man says nothing.

"Well, I do," continues Evan. "It's happened to me before. Your mind goes kinda blank. Suddenly you don't care about anything. You just let it all go. Everything you've been bottling up, out it comes in one violent action. And when it's happening, you feel nothing but . . . euphoria. You've been desperate for this kind of release for so long. Then . . . the fog lifts, and that's when the regret kicks in. You see the damage you've caused, how you left the other person a bloody mess, like . . . roadkill. Unrecognizable. You feel sick to your stomach, but you can't do anything about it. You can't change the past. So you live with the consequences, and life goes on."

My jaw hangs open during this monologue. I've never heard anyone speak this way.

Bug Man must think the same, because he doesn't have that cocky look in his eyes anymore. It's so quiet we can hear wind rustling the leaves of nearby trees.

"Are you threatening me?" asks Bug Man, finding his voice.

"No," Evan says, dead calm. "At this point I'm begging you to stay right where you are and try, just try, to stick another one of your stupid-ass flyers in some kid's candy bag. Go for it."

Bug Man shifts his weight uneasily from one foot to the other. He gives Evan an appraising look, making his final judgment.

"Okay, okay, man," says Bug Man. "I get you. I'm going. No need to get all wacko on me." He picks up his satchel full of flyers, slings it over his shoulder.

We watch him walk away, blinking as he goes.

Evan says nothing. His expression remains fierce. Looking at him, I feel a chill that makes my heart beat faster. In a night full of spooks, there's no question he's scariest of them all.

Chapter 25

Willow appeared in Alex's kitchen unexpectedly a week after Halloween. While she looked youthful and put together in a cute sweater and jeans tucked into her suede boots, her expression suggested trouble on her mind.

Alex offered her a cup of coffee. The two chatted at the kitchen table about nothing of consequence, but soon enough Willow got to the purpose of her visit.

"I need a way to force Evan out of the house. It's getting worse."

"What's getting worse?" Alex asked, though she could guess the answer based solely on Halloween night.

"Evan's behavior," Willow said, as though it should have been obvious. "Something changed—he's not the same person anymore."

Alex asked the questions she'd pose to anyone in Willow's situation: Is he threatening you? Has he been violent? Do you feel safe at home?

"It's not that bad yet, but I think it could get to that point," Willow said. "He seems unstable to me. And you saw him at Halloween. That was kind of unsettling, right? I mean, Ken brought out a gun, but honestly Evan freaked me out more."

Alex couldn't deny Willow's assessment. "Emily is still livid about the whole gun thing, and I don't blame her," she said. "Apparently, Ken's now trying to get the Bug Man fired."

"Bug Man is lucky he didn't end up dead," said Willow. "Evan was hitting the heavy bag for an hour after he got home. I don't know if it's the drugs making him volatile, but I'm telling you: that man is a time bomb."

Alex had already told Willow about her encounter with the other time bomb in the neighborhood, the stalker in the woods who had attached a threatening note to Zoe's collar. The police had searched the area but found no evidence of anybody lurking behind Brooke's house. Now Nick was considering an upgrade to the alarm system. Willow, Emily, and Mandy had all voiced concern about the stalker. Brooke, who couldn't give the police a name, remained oddly placid about the whole affair.

"He must know that you called the police about him, and he doesn't like it," Brooke had suggested. "Just leave it alone. Eventually he's going to get bored and go away."

Maybe so, thought Alex, but Zoe wouldn't be going outside off leash anytime soon.

"Where are you at with the divorce?" Alex wanted to know. "Can't you just file?"

"And live off what? I'm telling you, Evan will make it a nightmare for me if I do, and we're both still in the house."

"Take a large sum out of one of your bank accounts. Get yourself set up for a new life. At least live a separate life from him."

Willow rolled her eyes. "You think I haven't thought of that already? He doesn't keep that much money in our joint checking, and I don't have access to our investment funds. I'm stuck, Alex. I'm really stuck."

The word that came to Alex's mind was *trapped*.

"You can get a TRO—a temporary restraining order," Alex offered. "Evan won't be able to drain your accounts then. You might even be able to take exclusive occupancy of the marital home. But it's best to file for one when you file your divorce petition. That way you'll be legally protected from the start."

Willow still looked skeptical. "That's just going to inflame the situation," she said. "Evan hasn't overtly threatened me—it's just a bad feeling I have. He's not himself these days, and I don't want to push him over some edge."

Alex peered into her friend's eyes, willing the compassion in her heart to come through. The law wasn't perfect. A restraining order might *not* be enough to force Evan from the home—not without a history of domestic violence. Willow's predicament wasn't an easy one.

"You can always stay with us for as long as you need—Riley, too." Nick would grumble and whine, but he'd also agree.

"Thank you, but no. I'm not going to bring my problems into your house."

It frustrated Alex to be able to offer nothing but sympathy.

"And remember the money?" Willow said. "Those withdrawals I told you about?"

Alex recalled that day vividly. How could she forget? It was the same day she'd seen Ken sneaking away from Mandy Kumar's place.

"Well, it's gotten worse. Evan's been taking out almost fifteen hundred a week."

Alex gasped.

"Weekly," Willow repeated. "When our checking runs low, he moves money to replenish it."

Doing some basic math in her head, Alex came up with eighty grand a year. She knew Evan Thompson had family money, but the figure was still a staggering amount.

"Honey," Alex said, "you can't stop this bleeding without applying some kind of bandage. Lawyer up and fight back. There's no other recourse."

Tears collected in Willow's eyes. Alex rose to grab a tissue.

"It's the damn drugs," Willow said. "He's always had his indulgences, but it's gotten so much worse. He looks bad, too. Skin, eyes—he has this sunken, hollowed-out look."

Alex went quiet. *What a mess,* she thought.

Willow's face crumpled. She was so much younger than the other moms on the block, but it wasn't youthful optimism keeping her stuck. It was the damn system.

"If I didn't think he'd kill us both, I'm inclined to tell Evan the truth about Riley—just to hurt him, just to see him weep," Willow said.

Alex banished the visceral image that came to mind. "You wouldn't, right? Tell me you're just venting. I mean, at this point that would be pouring gas on a fire."

"Of course I'm not going to do that," said Willow, but she sounded disappointed. "That would be suicide. I'd just love to see his face after I tell him, is all."

"Do you think Evan suspects?" Alex asked. "It might explain his behavior—at least his anger. Couples fight about one thing, but often something else is going on. Maybe he's acting out rather than confronting his fears about his daughter."

Willow's expression soured. "I don't think so. He'd have brought it up. No, this is just Evan's partying finally catching up with him."

"I see," said Alex. "In that case, may I ask another question?"

"You want to know about Riley's biological father, is that it?"

"I mean, it's none of my business, but—"

"Oh, don't be shy. I'd be curious, too. Honestly, it's not much of a story. I think Riley's bio-dad would be more surprised to know he was Riley's father than Evan would be to know that he wasn't."

"So it wasn't a real relationship?" Alex asked.

Willow nodded. "Evan and I were on a break after a big fight. He was being super controlling back then—which honestly should have been a red flag, but of course I ignored it. He didn't like that I was going to college parties—and I was like, 'No, I'm still in college and just because we are together doesn't mean I have to give up my social life.' So I told him that we were done, but I felt heartbroken about it. Lord knows why I couldn't just pick a guy who was good-looking *and* treated me well."

Willow paused, as if Alex might have a good answer for that. She didn't.

"Anyway, after Evan and I split up, I did what any brokenhearted young and impressionable college-aged girl would do—I got hammered. And that's when I met Stevie Wachowski, but everyone just called him the Wookiee."

"The Wookiee? Really?"

"Yeah, the Wookiee . . . it was his stage name."

"Oh, let me guess," Alex said, "a musician," making it sound like something less than ideal.

Willow all but swooned at the memory. "Long hair, so hot, and absolutely amazing on the guitar. We had a brief fling, but I quickly realized if I didn't have six strings and a bunch of frets, I wasn't going to get much attention from him."

"And you're sure Riley is the Wookiee's daughter?" That was a sentence Alex hadn't thought she'd say today, if ever.

Willow cocked her head slightly and gave Alex a come-on-now look. "I know when I had sex, and thankfully Evan's not very good at math. Besides, he's so self-absorbed I don't think it even occurred to him there could be someone else." She gave Alex a fractured smile. "It helps that Riley looks so much like me—and Evan and the Wookiee have some similar physical characteristics in common. Guess I have a type."

"So you have no doubt?" Alex pressed.

Willow shook her head. "None. Riley wants to do one of those ancestry DNA tests. Can you say nightmare? I convinced her not to bother, but I worry every day she's going to find out."

"There's just too much volatility in your home for that," said Alex.

"I feel so damn stuck." Willow's voice caught on the words.

Alex felt a weight in her chest. "I'm sorry," she said. "I wish there were more I could do."

"Who knows? Maybe I'll get lucky and Evan will OD, take care of the problem for me."

Alex went cold inside, thinking about the night they played two truths and a lie. She couldn't recall Willow's words verbatim, but it was something to the effect that she would kill Evan if she could get away with murder.

"Anyway, life gives you lemons, right?" said Willow. She got up to go, turning her body in a failed bid to hide the fact that she needed to wipe her eyes. "Thanks for all your support. I've taken up enough of your time today. And I'll see you again soon enough."

Alex's eyebrows arched. Willow seemed to be referring to a plan, not a pop-in visit, but Alex couldn't recall anything on her calendar.

"Why is that?" she asked.

"Samir came over the other day. He invited Evan and me to Friendsgiving, and Evan said yes."

"Just don't go," said Alex.

"Don't be silly," Willow replied. "If Evan gets riled up about some-thing, I might be the only one who can protect you all from him."

Later that night, after dinner was done and the usual routine was over, Alex, weary to the bone, finally joined her husband in bed. She'd planned to have one glass of wine that evening, but that had turned into two or maybe three, and now she had a little headache to go along with her lingering concern for Willow. She sank into Nick's arms, relishing the comfort of his embrace, nestling as close to him as she could get.

Something banged against the window, and Alex jumped. She bolted upright in bed, panicked, her breathing rapid and shallow.

"Whoa, whoa, take it easy," said Nick. "It was probably just an acorn blown by the wind. What are you so skittish about?"

Alex settled. She was up on the second floor, in bed with her hus-band. She was safe. Even so, nothing felt secure anymore.

"I keep thinking Brooke's stalker is out to get me," she said.

Alex was well aware the stalker wasn't her only potential threat. She'd been pushing a lot of people's buttons lately—Samir and Ken specifically. That note could have been from any of them, really. She needed to back off, stop getting involved. Mandy's problems weren't hers to solve. The same went for Brooke, Willow, and Emily. Why was she always trying to fix things, including other people's broken marriages? She should be working harder to fix her own.

"The police searched the woods plenty of times, and they're doing extra patrols," Nick said. "I wouldn't worry so much about it. If anyone, it's Brooke who should be afraid."

"That note was a threat against *me,* Nick—not Brooke," Alex re-minded him. "*Back off or you'll regret it.* What else could it mean?"

"Well, I guess back off, honey. Stay out of those woods and stay out of other people's messy affairs."

"I'd love to," Alex said, "but how can I do that when they keep coming to me with their damn problems?"

She finally had a chance to tell Nick about Willow's visit, then rehashed all of her other worries about their neighbors.

"Emily thinks Mandy is sleeping with Ken, Ken's fascinated by Brooke's erotic pictures on the internet and doing who knows what with them."

"I can guess what he's doing," said Nick.

Alex didn't laugh. "Drug-crazed Evan may or may not know that Riley isn't his biological daughter, Samir might be an abusive husband, and now we've got Brooke's stalker to worry about. Nick, please, please, tell me we're not this screwed up."

"We're *not* this screwed up," Nick said with confidence. To punctuate his declaration, he kissed Alex gently on the lips and gave her a squeeze.

"Thank God for that," said Alex. She pressed her ear against his chest, soothed by the steady rhythm of his beating heart.

"But I will tell you something," Nick said.

"Yeah, what's that?"

"It's going to be one hell of a Friendsgiving."

Chapter 26

Lettie

There's a change in the atmosphere at school, one that always accompanies the approach of Thanksgiving break. Everyone is anxious for a reprieve, me included.

This will be the last Thanksgiving break of my Meadowbrook academic life. Before I know it, the school year will be over, there'll be another Alton Road block party I don't want to attend, and that will be it for high school. A lot will happen in between, of course: midterms to dread, college acceptances to celebrate, and rejections to endure. And I can't forget about the overrated tradition of prom. I'll probably just skip it.

I've thought about asking Jay to prom, but of course I won't. I did, however, break down and text him. I asked if we could hang out, get a coffee, go to a movie, something simple.

Jay wrote back soon after. I was elated for all of two seconds. His reply lacked any emotion or caring. *Busy right now. Coding my ass off. Rain check?*

Talk about leaving a girl hanging. It wasn't a no, but it wasn't a yes. He left me in the horrible middle place where I could go on believing that something more could develop between us.

At least school is keeping me somewhat distracted. I've set aside my long-neglected research paper on revenge to work on my college applications, which I'm doing without any input from Mom or Dad. They like my independence and encourage it, but I think they're both a little hurt I could get it all done—pick my schools, write my essays, fill out my activities, get my teacher recommendations—all that without any hand-holding.

A lot of my classmates, Dylan included, hired college coaches to manage the process because it's too stressful for their parents. Even with a coach, Dylan still sent me his essay to edit, which hit my inbox a few hours before the early decision application to Bucknell was due. Boys!

To my father's dismay, I wrote my essay about my school suspension. Dad thought I was giving the admissions folks a negative first impression, but I disagreed. "I'm explaining how I *learned* from my mistake," I told him.

"Not sure lamenting that you should have created a GoFundMe campaign to pay for a billboard because that would have made a bigger statement than spray-painting on school property is *learning* much of anything," Dad said.

"It's about justice, Dad," I countered, aware my effort to educate him was futile. "A T-shirt that says *Bite Me!* shouldn't be in violation of anything. It's ridiculous, and it's emblematic of a larger social injustice. At best, dress codes violate my freedom of speech. At worst, they teach girls to cover up so we're not a distraction. Someone has to take a stand for what's right. We are only as strong as we are united, as weak as we are divided."

Dad looked impressed. "Are you quoting Churchill?" he asked.

"No. Albus Dumbledore, *Goblet of Fire.*"

With my college apps done, I finally turn my attention to Riley's dilemma. I think I know how to find her bio-dad, but it's not going to be cheap. Good thing she can afford it.

I meet Riley in the staff bathroom. She looks flawless in her white jeans, white top, and pink Vans that go perfectly with her pink earrings. Next to her, I look like Wednesday from the Addams Family. But looks count for nothing. My mom is fond of saying that if everyone threw their problems up in the air, people would race to catch their own. These words resonate with me more now than ever. I sure don't want to catch what Riley is lugging around.

"So how'd it go? What did you find out?" Riley asks, speaking softly even though the staff bathroom locks from the inside.

"Plenty," I tell her. From my backpack, I produce six plastic tubes with stoppers on them. "Hope you brought a good supply of spit."

"I already took a test," she says, as if I forgot.

"Right, I know. But you didn't get enough quality matches. The major DNA companies share databases. But you have to send your DNA to multiple companies to get the most possible family matches, and hopefully some of those are close relatives to your bio-dad. Then you can reach out on the website messaging system. But fair warning, Rye. The people you match with might not *want* to help you find your biological father."

"Why not?" Riley asks. "Won't they be excited to meet me?" The notion seems utterly perplexing to her.

"Secret kids have a way of tearing families apart," I say. "We have no idea about the circumstances. Anything is possible."

I can almost hear the click in Riley's brain.

"So my father—"

"Er—let's call him your birth father. I mean, you don't even know this guy's name."

"So my birth father might not know I exist?" She sounds shaken at the prospect. She might be all put together and insanely pretty, but what I see is a drug-addicted cheater who's more than a little self-centered. She's a hot mess.

Strangely enough, though, I feel better about myself for helping her. While I might not have the heart for revenge, this whole knight in shining armor gig seems to suit me just fine. Who knows—maybe after I find her bio-dad, I'll help Riley get off the pills? I have a passing thought that I might be maturing. Oh well. Worse things could happen, I suppose.

"There's another risk we should consider," I say. "You don't know anything about this new family of yours. What if they want to use you?"

"Use me for what?" Riley asks.

I toss my hands in the air. "I dunno. If they find out who your dad is—that he's loaded—they might try to extort you."

Riley scratches her head. "For money?"

"No, Pokémon cards," I say. "Of course, money. And we all know your dad has a lot of it."

Riley's shoulders sag. "Guess I didn't think of that."

"That's why you pay me the big bucks," I tell her. "You still want to do it?"

She returns my unblinking stare with a barely perceptible nod.

I hand her a tube. "Okay, start spitting."

Dylan is waiting in the hallway outside the bathroom when we exit with six tubes of Riley's spit. He looks profoundly upset. He comes barreling toward Riley as soon as he sees her. Strings of dark hair partially curtain his sunken eyes, which are visibly red. I don't know him to have seasonal allergies, so it's my guess he's been crying. He's breathing hard, too, like he's just finished a race. His jaw is set so tight it might well snap. I can see veins bulging on his neck.

"How could you do this to me?" he asks Riley.

Riley leans back on her heels, as if blown back by the force of his anger. "How'd you know where I was?"

"I saw you in the hallway and I followed you here."

"Dylan, what do you want?" Riley's voice has a nervous shake.

"I want to know who you're screwing behind my back."

"What?" Riley recoils.

Dylan reaches for her arm, gripping it hard as she pulls away.

"Oww!" she cries. "Let go. That hurts!"

Dylan lets go, but only to get out his phone. "Yeah, well, so does this," he snarls, showing her something on the display.

I've never seen someone go catatonic before. Never watched the color drain from a person's face fast as it does from Riley's. For a moment, I think she's going to pass out, but she stays standing. She stares at the phone, mouth hanging open as though she's seen a ghost.

"Who sent this to you?" she asks.

"Do you know anyone named A. Dumas?" Dylan asks. "I sure as hell don't, but that's who sent it."

Riley stammers. She can't find the words.

"Dylan, what are you talking about?" I ask.

Whirling toward me, Dylan thrusts the phone in my face.

"I'm talking about my girlfriend sleeping with some other dude!" he shouts. He looks ready to pounce on us both.

The moment I see the picture, I feel the ground shift beneath my feet. *This can't be,* I'm thinking. *No. No. No.* But even after a number of blinks, the image is still there, no doubt about it. It's one of the photos of Riley taken outside McCormick's on the rainy night Jay and I followed her out of town. Umbrella Man is in the shot, with his back to the camera so you can't see much of him, but you can clearly see his hand on Riley's ass.

The caption reads: *Hey Dylan is this you?*

"So who is he?" Dylan asks, pushing his phone back at Riley. "And who the hell is A. Dumas?"

My stomach shrinks to the size of a walnut. I happened to have read Alexandre Dumas in AP English—author of *The Count of Monte Cristo,* a classic revenge tale if ever there was one. I know damn well who *this* A. Dumas is, and I'm furious, too.

Riley appears stricken. "Dylan, let's talk later, okay? Now isn't a good time." She turns to go, starts down the hallway, but Dylan lunges for her, grabs hold of her arm for a second time, and yanks her back, hard.

I don't like the look in his eyes. A hurricane's swirling in there; his whole expression is a dark and furious storm. I get it, too. His world, or at least his world as I saw it, was composed of a ball, a stick, and Riley. I didn't think his dad's put-downs had affected him any; didn't think he had the depth to feel that wounded. But now I'm seeing it in his sorrowful gaze, the anger in his voice, his deflated stance. I feel for him, but I feel for Riley as well. Clearly she has her issues, so these two probably *need* to take a break. But not this way.

"Who is this guy? Does he even go to this school?"

I'm thinking: *Actually, there's a good chance he's got a mortgage.*

"Dylan, it's over with us," Riley says. "I should have broken up with you before, and I'm sorry. We need to talk about it later, okay?"

"No! Not okay. I want to talk now," Dylan says. His grip on Riley's arm tightens.

She winces in pain.

"Hey, let her go," I plead.

Thank God he listens. Riley pulls her arm to her side like a wounded wing.

"I'm going to find out who he is," Dylan says. His voice rumbles like a roll of thunder. "And when I do—he's going to regret it." He stomps off down the hall.

I'm angry, too. I told Jay in no uncertain terms that I didn't want to hurt Dylan. Now I don't want to hurt Riley, either.

I have some pretty strong words for Jay Kumar, but what really gets me is knowing that I'm not blameless in this mess. I was in the car that night. I asked for Jay's help to expose Riley's secrets. I was the stupid girl trying to impress an older boy.

As Dylan fades from my view, a troubling thought pulses in my head. *If anything happens to my cousin—or to Riley, for that matter—because of the things I've done, I'll never forgive myself.*

Chapter 27

I f a scattering of colorful fall leaves spread out on the console table in
the Kumars' spacious foyer counted, then their home was decorated
for the holiday.

Alex felt a slight shiver as she took off her coat and handed it to
Samir, who greeted them at the door. It wasn't just the cool night air
that chilled her skin. Despite the colorful leaves, Alex was again struck
by the sterility of the rest of the home. The empty vibe was no longer
just from the newness of the move, as the Kumars had had months
to settle in.

"Ah, the last to arrive! So glad you could be here," Samir said. He
looked dapper in his blue sport coat. His smile felt genuine and warm,
but Alex wondered if it was all for show. Was his charm a smoke screen?
She'd come here with an open mind, hoping a close, intimate evening
would provide a new perspective that would let her decide whether he
was controlling at best or abusive at worst.

"Thank you so much for having us over," Alex said.

"It's my pleasure," Samir answered. "We are pleased you both could
come."

"Delighted to be here," said Nick.

Alex remained vigilant. She had followed Samir to the grocery
store like some kind of private investigator, and he knew it, too.
Talk about awkward. As everyone moved away from the foyer, Alex
scanned the walls for family photos, but the white-painted interior
showed nary a nail hole. It felt purposeful, as though they were ac-
tively safeguarding the past.

"Is Jay around?" Alex asked.

"He is out for the evening," Samir said. "We invited him to join us, but he had other plans."

"Oh, that's too bad," said Alex. "We'd love to get to know him better. And I never asked, but do you have other children coming home for the holiday, or is Jay an only? We know so little about you." She forced extra cheer into her voice.

A guarded look entered Samir's eyes, but in a blink, his congenial demeanor returned. It troubled Alex to see someone so adept at regulating his emotions.

"Jay is our only," he said.

Alex got the feeling there was more to the story. Maybe Mandy had suffered miscarriages like she had? But that wasn't dinner conversation. A moment later, she lost that train of thought. From down the hall aromas filled the air, bathing her senses in an abundance of fragrances, only some of which she could place.

Samir noticed Alex sniffing. "We are having a blend of foods tonight," he said. "A roasted chicken Mandy prepared—she didn't want you getting tired of turkey before the holiday—and a few popular dishes from my hometown that have nothing to do with Thanksgiving, but I think you'll find them quite pleasing."

"Where's your hometown?" Nick asked.

"I'm from the north—Ludhiana in Punjab to be exact, the sixteenth largest state in India," Samir said. "I moved to America for graduate studies, met Mandy, and never left. Lucky me."

"Do you go back regularly?" Alex asked. She followed Samir down the hallway, captivated by the scents perfuming the air. As they neared the kitchen, they heard the chatter of the other guests, their friends and neighbors.

"Less and less, I'm afraid. Work has its downside." Samir's voice was flat and expressionless.

From doing mediation, Alex had learned that certain voice inflections could indicate that a client wasn't being entirely forthcoming. She wondered what Samir had to hide.

Before Alex knew it, Mandy, who looked stunning in a fitted black sweater dress adorned with simple gold jewelry, had placed a large glass of wine into her hand.

"Welcome! I hope you like red," Mandy said.

Alex smiled brightly. "I like it all," she answered. "Thank you."

She looked around the room. Everyone was chatting pleasantly, seeming to have a good time. On the surface, everything appeared perfectly normal. Evan was talking with Ken and Emily. Brooke and Willow were paired up near a plate of hors d'oeuvres, sipping wine, laughing occasionally. Just as those decorative leaves gave the occasion a veneer of holiday normalcy, a tense undercurrent permeated the scene. Or maybe Alex just knew too much.

Emily broke away from the men to give her sister a welcoming embrace. Nick soon joined Ken and Evan in lively conversation.

"How are you holding up?" Alex whispered in her sister's ear.

Emily sent a sharp look Mandy's way, then directed a similar look at Brooke, which made Alex nervous. *Does she know about the website?*

She was about to inquire when Samir, who'd been bent over the stove to sample a dish that smelled delightful, stood up to announce that dinner was ready.

A moment later, they were all seated around the long dining room table. The buffet under the windows had been cleared to make room for a self-serve bar complete with a silver ice bucket, wineglasses, and an assortment of spirits, none of which were as high-end as Ken's prized bottle of whisky. A fire crackling in the adjacent living room added a touch of warmth. Mandy and Samir worked as a team to bring in food from the kitchen, and before long a feast lay before everyone.

The bounty elicited effusive praise. Alex took in the sights and smells of a perfectly roasted chicken, the lush green salad, a dish of caramelized cranberry sauce, steaming potatoes drizzled in butter, and a series of small bowls filled with colorful dishes the likes of which she had never seen.

"I won't bother to explain the food to which you are already accustomed," Samir said. "But you may wish to know about my home cooking."

He pointed to an unleavened bread the color of saffron, kept warm inside a copper dish.

"This is makki di roti," he said. "It is a local favorite from the Punjab region. And we eat it with sarson ka saag."

To Alex, the second dish looked like saag paneer, but she wasn't knowledgeable enough about Indian cuisine to know the difference.

"We eat these two dishes together all winter long, and it keeps us very well nourished," Samir said.

There was more—a dish called chole bhature, which Samir described as a spicy chickpea curry. "Normally, you'd eat this with a fried bread, but Mandy insisted we had too much food already."

That they did, mused Alex. The table seemed to groan under the weight of all the plates and bottles.

Food was served in a somewhat chaotic frenzy as more glasses of wine were poured.

Under the table and out of view, Nick set a hand on Alex's leg. His touch felt sweet and intimate, but also surprising. It had once been commonplace for them to be affectionate with each other. She warmed more from his loving gaze than from the wine and the fire. It felt like a rekindling, a momentary reconnection that they could build upon. In stark contrast, Alex observed Willow and Evan, who seemed to be purposefully avoiding eye contact or interaction of any kind.

Ken took a big drink of wine, then used his booming voice to get attention above the din of conversation. "You know, Nick, when you and Alex rang the doorbell, I had this thought it was the Bug Man coming to *bug* us with another visit." He chuckled at his own attempt at humor, but no one else laughed with him.

Ken looked around the table, taking in all the stony expressions. "Too soon?" he asked.

"Way," said Willow, who sent Evan the first real nasty look of the night.

"Who is the Bug Man?" asked Mandy.

"He's a pest control salesman who uses super-aggressive sales tactics," Evan said. "He was outside Ken's house on Halloween, stuffing flyers into the candy bags of trick-or-treaters. That stunt almost got the Bug Man exterminated."

"Well, he should be selling no more," Ken said. "I called the company and lodged a formal complaint. I'm not going to let up, either, until that guy is fired."

Alex saw Mandy's eyes become two slits, as if daggers might shoot from them. If there had been something between her and Ken, that look all but said it was over and done with, and hard feelings lingered.

Mandy didn't leave it at just a look. "Sounds like you're getting overly involved in somebody's life, Ken," she said. "Isn't that kind of like playing judge, jury, and executioner? Has he really disrupted your life to such a degree? What does it matter anyway that he's passing out flyers? It's annoying, for sure, but does it mean you have to get him fired?"

A hush settled over the table. A weight that hadn't been there a moment ago hung in the air like an anvil waiting to drop. It was a conversation stopper, especially coming from the hostess of the party.

Samir placed a hand on Mandy's arm, as if restraining her physically would also rein in her words. Mandy pulled free of his grasp, needing considerable torque to break the hold. Alex caught the challenging look Mandy sent her husband. Samir, however, didn't flinch.

"I say we should not place any judgments on our guests," Samir said. "This is a time for thanks and gratitude. Please, let's all enjoy the meal."

Everyone seemed to regain their composure, enough to fill their plates with food and for Alex to refill her wineglass. This was already quite the evening.

"You're right, Samir," Willow said. "I'm grateful for this meal, and the chance to get to know you and Mandy better. Thank you so much for hosting us all and for this wonderful dinner. I propose a toast."

"Agreed," said Nick. "A toast."

Brooke took that as her cue to reach for the wine bottle. Dressed in a seductive low-cut top that offered an ample glimpse of her striking cleavage, Brooke leaned over the table, past Emily, for the Merlot. In doing so, she flashed Emily the same view that people like Ken, and others online, evidently paid good money to see.

This seemed to be too much for Emily, who muttered, "Quick, Ken, take a picture of *that*."

Alex nearly choked on her drink.

Unflinching, Brooke returned a devilish half-smile and seemed to adjust her body so that Ken and Emily could both enjoy a good look at her endowments. "Go for it," Brooke said. "I see no harm in looking."

"I guess I don't see it the same way you do, Brooke. Especially since my husband's involved," said Emily.

Ken's face turned as red as the wine. He shifted uneasily in his chair. "Emily, this isn't the time or place."

"Oh, whatever," Emily snapped. "You're happy to share your viewing habits with all the guys at the poker table, but I can't make one harmless joke at dinner."

Ken's expression bordered on apoplectic. "I don't see anyone laughing."

Samir appeared baffled. "I don't really understand what's going on here . . . maybe someone would be so kind as to explain it to me?"

"Apparently some people have a problem with my side gig," Brooke said. "I see no issue with putting a few high-quality sexy pictures online and making good money off them."

Now it was Mandy who looked confused. "Do you do porn?" she asked.

"Not porn," Brooke corrected. "It's art. The body is beautiful—all bodies—and I like to celebrate mine. It's a thrill for me that people, men and women, enjoy looking at what I have to share. It's an even bigger thrill when that enjoyment shows up in my bank account."

"It's a website called OnlyFans," Emily said. "And about thirty minutes before we came over here, my husband was looking at Brooke's pictures on the site. I wouldn't have known this fun little fact if I hadn't gone into his office to look for him, but he'd gone to the bathroom—won't say more about that—and left his screen open for me to have a peek.

"I was scrolling through the site when he came back. He got all angry, insisting it was no big deal. He even thought it was funny. But

I know he's just downplaying it because those pictures are super hot, which is why he's more than happy to share them with all his poker buddies. I'm sure Nick and Evan have had a look-see as well."

"Which is fine by me," said Brooke. "Maybe I'll get more paying fans who want my . . . exclusive content."

"What exclusive content?" Evan asked. Alex thought he looked angry—then again, that was his default these days.

Quickly Willow turned to Evan. "So you *have* seen them? Figures." She sounded disgusted.

"Yes, and my interest is strictly professional," Evan said. "If there's some high-end content available, maybe I could give you my honest critique."

"Thanks, but I think I'm all set," Brooke said coolly.

"I've seen them, too," Nick admitted when eyes fell on him. Wisely, he didn't share Alex's knowledge of the photos. She sent him a sly look, a reminder to keep the secret. Brooke stayed quiet as well, understanding the need for discretion without any prompting.

Samir's calm demeanor began to fracture. "So, am I understanding this correctly, that you're posting personal private pictures of yourself . . . on the internet?"

"Well, they're not very private once I put them there." Brooke seemed unperturbed.

Samir went still as he absorbed the information. "Maybe it's not for me to get involved—and I can be more conservative than most in this area—but are you not encouraging the exploitation of women?" he asked. "Haven't you fought long and hard for equal rights, fought to not be sexualized in such a way—the #MeToo movement, all of that? Aren't you at all concerned about the message you're sending to other women?"

Brooke shook off the rebuke. "I think women should decide when they want to be sexualized and when they don't," she said. "In my opinion, the #MeToo movement is all about women having control over their bodies and lives. We shouldn't have men—or anybody, for that matter—decide what we can or cannot do in the privacy of our home, or what we put out there for other people to see and enjoy."

Mandy turned to Samir with a fiery look in her eyes. "I don't think you truly understand what the exploitation of women really means," she said. Her gaze traveled across the table, landing squarely on Ken. "Let me tell you a little more about the exploitation of women."

"Mandy, I need to speak with you in private," Samir snapped. "Now, please." His words reverberated like a gunshot.

Everyone fell silent, unmoving, unblinking even.

Reluctantly Mandy rose from her seat. She followed Samir out of the room.

"I just can't believe you brought this up at the table like that," Ken said to Emily with a scathing stare. "You know . . . I think I've had enough fun for one night." He got up from the table as well. "Please let Samir and Mandy know that I don't feel well."

He left the room with a heavy stomp.

Emily hesitated, but eventually rose to follow her husband.

Alex turned to Nick and said, "I need to go check on Emily. I'll be right back."

She caught up with her sister outside, who was already halfway down the walk. Ken was nowhere in sight.

"I'm fine," Emily said. "It's okay. I feel like we needed this to happen. Maybe now we can start having some honest conversations with each other."

It was dark out. Alex hoped Emily didn't see her gulp hard. Ken wasn't the only one who hadn't been entirely honest with her.

"You can come stay with us if things get bad," Alex said. She flashed on having made the same offer to Willow not too long ago, and imagined her home overrun with people whose relationships were in crisis.

The sisters embraced quickly before Alex retreated back into the Kumars' house and out of the cold. Quietly closing the front door, she made her way toward the dining room, still grateful that Nick knew when to keep his mouth shut. But someone was talking. At the bottom of the stairs, she caught a snippet of conversation from above.

She heard Samir say in a hushed, intense voice: "You need to learn how to control yourself, Mandy. Have you been taking your medication?"

"Actually, *you* need to stop trying to control me," Mandy said bitterly. "I don't want to take those pills. I hate how they make me feel."

"Well, you must take them," Samir commanded.

The floorboards creaked, and Alex realized they were heading downstairs to rejoin the party—minus two guests. Quickly and quietly, she made her way back to the dining room and resumed her seat next to Nick. Despite the tension and awkwardness of the evening, she had gained at least one thing of value—insight into her new and mysterious neighbors.

Samir *was* controlling toward Mandy. And he used medicine—perhaps pills that he himself prescribed—to make sure she did as he wanted.

Chapter 28

Lettie

Jay might be ignoring my texts, but his mother doesn't ignore the doorbell.

"Hi, Lettie," Mandy Kumar says without much inflection. "Looking for Jay?"

Well, I'm not here for tea. I think it, but wisely don't say it.

"Is he home?" I ask. I'm making a big show of being sweet and friendly. Don't want Mom to think her dear son is in any danger.

"He's downstairs," she says, and steps aside to invite me in. There's something icy in Mandy's smile. I've got the sense I'm not the only one putting on a show.

"We had a lovely dinner with your mom and dad," she tells me. "Such a great neighborhood, so many interesting people—and a very *lively* discussion." Her eyes light up strangely.

I nod, not sure what else to say.

"Any plans for college?" she asks.

"Not yet," I say. "Just getting my applications out now."

"Well, good luck," she says. "College is such an amazing time in your life. Treasure it."

"I will," I promise, not sure it's one I can keep. It's kind of a weird thing to say, too.

I certainly don't share which schools I've applied to, or that my top choice is California. All this would open me up for more questions. *California? Why so far from home? What do you plan to study?* We might even get to talking about the high cost of higher education these days, and I could talk about how my dad wants me to go to UMass, but I'll get loans even if I have to go against his wishes. All that's just too much of an info dump for my current state of mind, which is bordering on murderous.

Mandy Kumar seems to sense my growing anxiety. She smiles tightly. Directs me to the basement, which I could have found on my own.

Down I go. There are no lights on, but there's still a glow, like a TV in a dark room. Aside from a rich aroma of coffee, the air feels dank and stale. When I reach the bottom step, I see Jay seated in an office chair with his back turned to me. He's got headphones on, so he doesn't hear me descend. Probably didn't hear me ring the doorbell, either.

Two simple wooden desks are pressed up against a concrete wall on which rest four brightly lit computer monitors. There's a sizable rug beneath the desks, but it doesn't give the space any real ambience. I see no file cabinets. No stacks of papers. Nothing on the walls. Everything Jay wants and needs must be contained within his twin computer towers, which buzz and hum like living beings.

A small table close to Jay holds a coffeemaker, one that can also brew espresso. A half-full pot of coffee is ready to pour, and that's it for the office accoutrements. For some reason, I'd envisioned the lair of a future billionaire to be a bit more . . . luxurious.

"Jay," I say sternly.

He doesn't turn around, probably because he can't hear me.

I tap him hard on the shoulder and say his name again, this time in a growl.

He turns, finally, and off come his headphones. Annoyance flashes in his eyes. I'm not sure if he's angry at the interruption or my presence. I suspect it's a combination of the two.

"Lettie," he says, a bit drawn out. "What brings you here?"

A click of his mouse makes all his screens go dark, not that I could have understood the gibberish he was looking at. I catch a flash of that scorpion tattoo on his wrist. I looked it up online and learned that the scorpion is the symbol of the Egyptian goddess Selket, protector of the dead. I've been wondering if his tattoo has something to do with the tragic death of his younger brother. But now isn't the time for sharing or caring.

I fold my arms across my chest. I'm worried I'll hit him if I keep a hand free. Pissed as I am, I still pick up that special Jay scent I find so damn enticing.

"Why did you do it?" I ask.

"Do what?" says Jay, as if I'm a total idiot.

"A. Dumas? *Count of Monte Cristo.* Really? What the hell, Jay!"

Something of a smirk lifts the corners of his mouth. "What can I say? Your revenge plot inspired me." I hear a note of pride.

That does it. I hit him in the shoulder with a closed fist and I don't pull my punch, either. The contact is hard enough to send a jolt of pain down my arm.

"Ow! That hurts!" Jay rubs the spot where my blow landed. I'm regretting that he doesn't have to rub his chin instead.

"Well, Dylan's hurting, too, you asshole," I snap. "Poor kid has barely come out of his room in a week."

"He'll get over it," Jay answers. "Young love sucks."

"No, you do, Jay," I say. His aloofness doesn't sit well with me. "You sent him that picture."

"Because you asked me to," he says.

That one gives me pause. "Um . . . explain to me how my telling you not to hurt Dylan shifts the blame over to me? Real curious to hear that one."

I can't believe I was ever hooked on this guy. Maybe *I'm* the asshole.

"You want to look up the definition of *hurt,* Lettie?" Jay answers. He's not backing down. "I'll help you out." His hand goes to the mouse. A moment later he's done a Google search for the word *hurt.*

"'To be detrimental to,'" he reads. "'To cause emotional pain or anguish to.'"

"What's your point?" I ask.

"My point is you said not to hurt Dylan. I think his girlfriend running around behind his back with some other dude is a little bit *harmful* to his well-being, don't you think?"

"I, um—" Shit. He's got a point. "I mean yeah, it is, sure, but that's not the issue here," I manage.

Jay's not done. "It's the *only* issue," he says.

"Well, you could have asked me." Not my best comeback, but it's all I've got.

"Why?" Jay asks. "You would have said no. You were all into revenge, and then you got soft for Riley. Those images would have hurt them both, so you'd have done *nothing*. I did you a favor. You should be thanking me, not yelling at me, not hitting me."

"Thanking you? For Dylan locking himself in his room? Riley's all freaked out. Willow and my aunt Emily are acting all weird around each other, sending each other halfhearted waves when I imagine Aunt Emily would rather give Willow the finger. You've made a mess of everyone's lives, Jay! People I care about!"

Jay scoffs. "You were hurting those very people the second you knew facts you didn't share. You were complicit through your silence, Lettie. I waited—waited for you to grow up and do the right thing, but as time went on it was clear to me you were going to bury this thing.

"If I wanted to hurt Dylan and Riley, you honestly think that's what I'd have done? Sent him a photo? Hell, no. I'd have sent those anonymously to your whole damn school. And I could have done it, too—easily, at that. Now, that's some serious humiliation right there. *That's* taking revenge. So obviously I wasn't trying to *hurt* anybody. I was doing what you should have done ages ago.

"Here you are, sitting on the evidence that could set things right, but no, you'd rather have your dear cousin who you claim to care soooo much about go on living like a total idiot. I did what you should have done from the start and saved him from a lot of needless suffering."

I go quiet, turning inward. This isn't what I had expected. I honestly thought I'd have Jay begging for forgiveness. Instead, I'm the one who feels like a jerk. How the hell did that happen?

"There are other ways to have gone about it," I tell him, but I can't think of any at the moment.

Jay calls my bluff with a hard stare.

"He's a mess now," I say. "And I feel totally responsible."

"You're the one who wanted to go digging for secrets, not me," he says. "Sometimes, things are better left unknown. It's never a problem then. Ignorance is bliss, right? It's when you know things you shouldn't that life gets complicated."

I'm thinking I want to be ignorant about Jay Kumar. I wish he never moved here. I'm wishing I didn't know him. Now I'm in deep. I'm responsible. If something happens to Dylan, if he does something stupid like try to track down Umbrella Man and things go haywire, get violent even, it'll be my fault. What if he gets obsessive over Riley? What if he does something *really* crazy? It happens. Sometimes people hurt others because of what they can't have.

All my thinking doesn't change the fact that Jay's made some good points. Dylan shouldn't be in a relationship with someone who's cheating on him. And what the hell am I doing helping Riley find her bio-dad anyway? Why did I suddenly develop a soft spot for my former tormentor? One fumbled kiss has turned me into a sucker, filled me up with empathy for other people, made me forget all the terrible things Riley's done to me—and to Dylan.

I'm suddenly seeing life not in rich color, but in many shades of gray. Riley's not *all* bad. She's free to live and do as she pleases, even if that includes Umbrella Man. And Dylan has no rights to her. Nobody can control what another person does. Clearly, I can't control Jay. But now that this is out in the open, maybe I can still set things right.

"What are you thinking?" asks Jay when I've gone silent long enough.

I'm thinking, *I can fix this,* but I don't tell Jay that. I've just realized helping Riley track down her bio-dad has a hidden advantage for me. I have a chance to get even closer to her. And the closer I get to Riley, the more influence I'll have over her. And maybe, just maybe, I can put everything back exactly the way it was before I got involved.

"Nothing," I eventually say. "I'm not thinking a damn thing."

Jay eyes me coolly.

"Don't lie to me, Lettie. If there's one person you can't keep secrets from . . . it's me."

Meadowbrook Online Community Page

Laura Ballwell

There's always some sort of crisis on Alton Road. Remember over the winter—the ambulance on New Year's Eve?

> **Henry St. John**
>
> I'm a volunteer firefighter. I won't forget that night. You don't forget something like that. Not ever.
>
> **Katherine Leavitt**
>
> Which house was that?
>
> > **Reply from Laura Ballwell**
> >
> > I really shouldn't say. Sorry!
> >
> > **Reply from Ed Callahan**
> >
> > Now you decide to have some decorum? You're a true pillar of the community, **Laura Ballwell**!
> >
> > **Reply from Tom Beck**
> >
> > She's just trying to help. Who kicked your cat, **Ed Callahan**?
> >
> > **Reply from Ed Callahan**
> >
> > Just calling it like I see it!
>
> **Janet Pinkham**
>
> I rode in the back of an ambulance once with my dad who was having chest pains. I thought the whole thing was very scary, but my cousin who's an EMT was working that night. What are the chances? My dad is fine BTW, but he did need a stent put in.
>
> > **Reply from Susanne Horton**
> >
> > OK, glad your dad is fine, but could you get more off topic??
>
> **Ross Weinbrenner**
>
> Those Altonites should have their own damn police and fire department IMHO. They had a town-funded police patrol last Halloween! More taxpayer money down the drain.

Reply from Joseani Wilkins

How about try thoughts and prayers, **Ross Weinbrenner**.
Someone on that street is dead! Good gracious. You
do know that you catch more flies with honey, right?
And BTW, we pay for the police and fire department
regardless how they spend their time. Get a clue and a
grip, will you?!

Reply from Ross Weinbrenner

Joseani Wilkins I'm just saying there's always something
going wrong on Alton Road and we pay for it like it or
not, that's a fact. Even during the holidays, the most
magical time of the year, those Altonites manage to bring
out the worst in each other. Ho. Ho. Ho.

WINTER

Chapter 29

What Alex had been thinking about nearly as much as, if not more than, her Christmas to-do list was Mandy Kumar. Friendsgiving might have been weeks ago, but the memory of what she'd overheard at the bottom of the stairs continued to occupy her thoughts. She was well aware that medications could be used to manage behavior, but was it possible Samir was forcing them on Mandy as a means of control?

She'd brought up the incident to Nick, who did not share her concern. "She probably needs meds and lots of people don't like the side effects," he said.

"But she's a psychologist," Alex reminded him. "I'd think a psychologist would know to take her medications. I'm sure she counsels her patients on medication compliance all the time."

"Do as I say, not as I do," Nick said, smirking slightly, as if that settled the matter. "I don't want to go around thinking the worst about our neighbors. I'm sure it's nothing."

It wasn't exactly the support she was looking for. Then again, he always made light of things when they didn't affect him directly. Alex wasn't ready to let it go. She'd seen too much from Samir, too many odd behaviors—dark expressions, general caginess, arguments, possessiveness—to ignore this episode.

After dinner, Alex used the excuse of delivering a holiday present to engage with Brooke. She hoped her friend would offer a more sympathetic ear than Nick had regarding her concerns over Mandy.

She also felt Brooke deserved some neighborly support after the harsh treatment she'd received at Friendsgiving.

Alex squinted against the low winter light in the late afternoon as she made her way across Alton Road to Brooke's sprawling home, buttoning up her coat to help ward off the chill. Snow swirled across the pavement in hypnotic patterns. As she neared the house, her eyes ventured to the woods beyond, where the stalker lurked. Was he out there now?

As far as she knew, all had been quiet since she'd received that threatening note attached to Zoe's collar. No one had reported any new sightings of the stalker. But police patrols had died down to next to none. As Alex traversed the walkway to Brooke's front door, she had a sense of being watched.

Brooke came to the door with a bright smile. "This is a surprise," she said warmly.

"Merry Christmas," said Alex, presenting her with the small, wrapped gift.

Brooke took the present and started to shake it, but Alex stopped her. "That might break it."

"Ooh, I'm curious," Brooke said. "Do you have time to come in and join me for a drink?"

"Love to," said Alex. She always had time for a drink.

They made their way through the spacious entryway toward the kitchen. Alex noticed a large fake Christmas tree, brightly lit all in blue, shining in the corner of the living room. Even Brooke's Christmas aesthetics were a bit cool and contemporary, veering away from the traditional red and green.

In the kitchen, Alex noticed a bottle of red wine already open on the marble countertop, next to a half-empty glass.

"Let me grab another wineglass," said Brooke. "Make yourself comfortable."

Alex peeked out the window toward the dark woods at the edge of the lawn. A shiver ran through her.

"Any new word from your . . . admirer?" asked Alex as she settled onto an upholstered leather barstool at the counter.

Brooke shook her head. "No. But that doesn't mean he's through.

He's persistent, even if he's been quiet. Hope you haven't received any new threats."

"No, nothing," said Alex, still looking out the window, half expecting a figure to emerge.

She accepted the glass of red Brooke handed her, appreciating the warmth the first sip provided. She hoped it would ease the discomfort she felt as she broached the issues that had been weighing on her.

"I'm sorry about the way everyone judged you at Friendsgiving. I can't imagine how it felt. I have no problem with your decisions, and they're just that—*your decisions*. Fair warning, my gift is a silly attempt to make light of the matter."

Brooke waved it off. "I'm used to those remarks," she said. "But I do appreciate your support. And now I *really* want to see this gift. I can't imagine how you managed to tie the Friendsgiving hubbub into something breakable."

Brooke pulled the bright red ribbon off the gift box. She opened the package, revealing a hand-painted porcelain figurine of a vintage pinup girl in a bikini top and short shorts.

"Oh, I love it!" She held the miniature statue up to her eye level and started to giggle. "She's gorgeous! And I agree—the perfect gift under the circumstances." Her smile glowed.

"So glad you like it. And I meant what I said about not judging."

"Not sure Emily feels the same. I had no idea she was going to drop that bombshell at dinner, and I haven't spoken to her since." Brooke sounded regretful. "Does she hate me?" She grimaced, as if bracing herself for bad news.

"I'm not sure what she's thinking," said Alex. "Right now, Em's focus is on Dylan. He and Riley broke up, and it's hitting him hard."

"Sorry to hear," said Brooke, though her tone wasn't overly concerned. "Dylan's a great kid. I'm sure he'll bounce back."

"I hope so. It's hard for Emily to see her son so despondent. She's already got enough on her plate with Ken."

"My pictures," Brooke lamented. "I really hope they haven't caused any trouble in her marriage. I remember at girls' night, she talked about hiring a PI because she didn't trust him."

Alex's conscience warned her not to overshare Emily's personal travails. But she was still conflicted about what to do with the information she had about Ken. She worried honesty would create more conflict in her sister's marriage, but was she causing more problems by withholding potentially important information? She couldn't tease it out on her own. Perhaps Brooke could help.

She took a deep breath and exhaled with force.

"Their marriage may be in trouble for reasons that have nothing to do with you," Alex said. "I saw Ken sneaking away from the Kumars' house last summer, and I still don't know what to make of it."

"For real?" said Brooke. "Does Emily know?"

"No," Alex said. "It happened not too long after the Kumars moved in, and I just couldn't bring myself to tell her. She'd already convinced herself that Ken and Mandy had something going on. I didn't want to make matters worse without conclusive evidence of an affair. Emily's always been highly emotional—so that alone could have blown up their marriage. You saw her at Friendsgiving, how impulsive she can be. That was hardly the time to get into marital issues, but she lets her feelings get the best of her."

"Why did Emily think something was going on between them in the first place?" Brooke asked.

Alex didn't want to gossip about her sister's personal life, but without any backup from Nick, she felt in need of a confidante. "That first day, at the block party, there was definitely a vibe between them," Alex said. "Emily and I both picked up on it."

"Could it be they already knew each other?" asked Brooke.

Alex shook her head. "Emily asked Ken point-blank, and he said no. If you ask me, Samir sensed something as well. I've heard them fighting, and he hardly lets her out of his sight. And then the afternoon Samir stopped over to invite us to Friendsgiving, he told us that Mandy was away in New York—at the same time Ken had taken a sudden trip to the city."

Brooke's troubled expression deepened. "No wonder that dinner got so weird," she said.

"Samir has been hot and cold with me," Alex said. "I think he's worried I might be onto him as an abuser." She recounted the events that followed Emily and Ken's departure that evening, culminating with what she overheard at the bottom of the stairs.

"Could be innocuous," Brooke said. "A lot of people don't take their meds, even doctors."

"Yeah . . . but it's not just that. It's all his behaviors put together. He's grabbed her arm a few times, dictates who she spends time with—so why wouldn't he be using medication as a means of further control? He's a psychiatrist, so who knows what he's giving her? It makes me wonder if we should be worried for Mandy's safety."

Brooke considered the implications carefully while Alex drained the remnants of her wine, already wanting a refill.

"I suppose there could be something devious going on," she said. "You never know what happens behind closed doors. No one around here ever realized I was the victim of a controlling and abusive husband myself."

"What?" Alex said. "You're right about that. I had no idea. I didn't even know you were married before Jerry."

Brooke laughed scornfully. "Before Jerry? It *was* Jerry."

To this, Alex had no reply. All words seemed to fail her.

Eventually she found her voice. "Wow . . . just . . . wow." Alex's eyes were wide. "I'm honestly stunned, Brooke. I don't get it." She fumbled with her thoughts. "You never said anything to us, there were no hints at all—and you vacationed with Emily and Ken, spent so much time with them . . . I don't think Emily had any idea."

"Abuse is usually a private affair," Brooke said. A heavy pause fell. "Come with me to the living room. I want to show you something."

Alex's footsteps echoed as she followed Brooke into the adjacent room. They stopped in front of a picture of Jerry hanging on the wall. He was sitting on a beach, looking relaxed and self-assured in a linen shirt and cargo shorts. His neatly trimmed salt-and-pepper beard hid his mouth, while sleek Ray-Bans covered his eyes.

"When you look at this picture, what do you think?" asked Brooke.

"I see Jerry on a beach," said Alex.

"Okay, right. Why do you think I hung it up? Why would I have *all* these pictures of Jerry and our various exploits on display?" Brooke gestured at the framed photos adorning her walls.

"I'd say—because you miss your husband?" Alex said.

An expression Alex had never seen before came over Brooke's face, a mixture of contempt, shame, and—was it *relief*?

"Best thing that happened to me was when Jerry Bailey went overboard on that cruise ship," Brooke said.

Alex's breath caught.

"I'm not suggesting I'm responsible for his death, despite what some people think," she clarified. "But I can't say I ever mourned him, not for one second. Trust me when I tell you that my marriage is the perfect example of a relationship not being what it seems."

Her cold, defiant stare pierced Alex. The word *calculating* popped into Alex's mind.

She placed a hand on Brooke's shoulder. "I'm so sorry . . . Do you . . . want to talk about it?"

Brooke seemed unsure, but spoke after a brief silence. "I've kept so much of this to myself, I don't even know where to begin."

They made their way back to the kitchen, settling onto their respective barstools after opening a fresh bottle of wine.

Thank God for that, thought Alex.

"If Jerry was so abusive, why would you keep his pictures on the wall?" she asked.

"At first I was maintaining the lie that I was the grieving widow," Brooke said. "The last thing I needed was to take all the pictures down and have even more suspicion cast on me. Insurance money is grist for the rumor mill. But as I lived with those photos, they came to represent something else—a test of my resilience, I suppose."

"How so?"

"If I could keep looking at them," Brooke said, "and not turn to Jell-O, then it meant *I* was in control. Jerry had no power over me anymore." Her gaze darted to the kitchen door, as if it were Jerry stalking her, not some mysterious stranger in the woods. "Those photos became a symbol of what I'd endured, all my suffering, and a reminder of how *I'd* never let anyone control me and my life again." Brooke shook her head as if to dislodge an unwanted memory. "Having those pictures up, it's like facing my demons on a daily basis—they give me strength, resolve."

Alex tried to maintain a neutral expression. A look of pity crossed her face nonetheless. "I really had no idea," she said softly. "I feel like such a terrible friend and neighbor."

Brooke brushed it away. "Not to worry," she said. "Nobody had a clue. Not even Emily and Ken suspected—well, at least not Emily. Ken and Jerry grew up together, so I suppose Ken knew quite a bit about Jerry's—um, tendencies."

Brooke looked right through Alex as though she were somehow peering into the past itself. "It all started with love-bombing, that fairy-tale romance crap," she continued. "Jerry swept me off my feet. He was unbelievably charming, successful, super confident . . . and it felt so good—no, no, make that incredible—when he focused all of his attention on me."

Alex had never heard Brooke speak so candidly about herself, apart from her OnlyFans work, which she understood was a mask of sorts. This Brooke was honest and open, as unfiltered as the pain etched on her face.

"We fell for each other pretty quickly, got married within six months. Everything seemed perfect . . . for a while, at least. Eventually, though, Jerry's doting turned into something, well—I guess I'd say darker. You might even call it sinister." She looked at Alex. "He insisted on me wearing certain outfits, started dictating not only what I wore and how I spent money, but who I spent time with as well. Sound familiar?" She paused.

"Samir," Alex breathed in a low whisper.

"I had my concerns. I'm no idiot," Brooke continued. "But I ignored my intuition . . . my better judgment, because Jerry and I had such *amazing* chemistry. The sex was so white-hot it was blinding." This put a ghost of a smile on Brooke's face, but it was hardly joyous. "And Jerry was quite adept with his manipulations. I'm sick and angry with myself to this day, all these years later, over how he played me. How I *let* him play me."

Alex had heard clients express similar regrets. Her own sister had said those things, too. She felt horrible for the avalanche of shame that Jerry buried Brooke under, and wished she had the therapist training to help her friend dig herself out. Instead, Alex offered what felt like empty platitudes. "It can happen to anyone. It's Jerry who deserves the blame, not you."

Brooke looked and sounded vulnerable. "He knew just when to give a compliment or how to turn a situation around so my concerns would feel unwarranted—paranoid, even."

"If the stalker doesn't get you rattled, I can't imagine how bad it must have been," Alex mused.

"Oh, it was *bad*," Brooke said. "He made me doubt myself constantly—including making it seem like it was my idea not to have children, or at least that I was on board with his choice."

"You wanted kids?" Alex was genuinely surprised. "I always thought—"

"Thought I was the odd one in Meadowbrook who relished my childless freedom?" Brooke asked with a little laugh.

"You've always been so independent, so calm and collected, while I've been anything but," Alex said. "Even with only one kid, I felt out of control—and I'll admit I've suffered a few bouts of jealousy."

"Over me?" Brooke pointed to herself. "Please. Appearances are so deceiving. I always wanted children. Here you were envying me while I envied you. But I convinced myself that Jerry and I decided together not to have kids. In reality, he didn't want my perfect body getting stretched out and deformed—his words, not mine." Brooke sighed.

"And when I brought up the idea of adoption or even surrogacy, he made it clear he wasn't raising anybody else's kid and he didn't want a stranger to carry his baby. One thing I knew about Jerry: when his mind was made up, there was no changing it. He told me if I got pregnant, he'd make me get an abortion or he'd divorce me. So I never got pregnant."

Alex was speechless.

"But that's not the worst of it," Brooke said. She paused. Collected herself, gathered her resolve, sat more upright on her stool. "Jerry had quite the appetite for sex." She templed her fingers as if in prayer. Prayer for what? A different reality? "He was insatiable when it came to the bedroom, or any room. He wanted sex all the time, and it kept getting more forceful . . . often, violent.

"There were some warning signs. Jerry even told me that he'd been accused of some sexual impropriety. At least that's what he called it—who knows what he did. Told me it was all a bunch of lies designed to embarrass him, some jealous ex-girlfriend wanting revenge for a broken heart. But once I got to know his tendencies myself—well, let's just say I'm certain he was guilty of something.

"Sex was just another outlet for Jerry's anger and exerting his control, his dominance over me. If he didn't get what he wanted, he would just . . . take it." Brooke fell silent.

Emotions came at Alex from all angles. She felt guilt: Why hadn't she been a better friend? How had she not picked up on the signs? Next came waves of worry for Willow, Emily, and Mandy, to whom the expression *under my thumb* applied in varying ways. What had felt somewhat shameful—nosing into the affairs of others, the spying and sneaking about—now seemed to have real purpose. With her friends getting stabbed in the back repeatedly by their trusted partners, somebody needed to be an unbiased observer to call out the warnings.

Brooke put her hand to her chest. Gone was the beauty queen. In her place stood a person—a woman—as raw and vulnerable as Alex had ever seen.

"It's okay," Alex said. "You don't have to go on, but I'm here for you, no matter what."

Brooke closed her eyes. "I was raped, Alex," she whispered, "repeatedly raped by my own husband."

It broke Alex's heart to see her strong, resilient, stoic friend dissolve into tears. There were no words, not really, so Alex simply pulled Brooke into an embrace and gave her a shoulder to cry on.

Chapter 30

Lettie

A few weeks ago I was hanging in Riley's bedroom like my eight-year-old self, and suddenly I'm riding shotgun in her fancy BMW acting as her navigator.

Whatever. Life's weird.

We're on our way to see a woman named Monique LaSalle who lives in Revere. We've been getting DNA match results back at a steady clip. According to one of the ancestry companies, this Monique lady might be a direct relative of Riley's bio-dad, but because of privacy settings we don't have any contact information for her.

Naturally, we looked the name up online and found six possible matches, but only one in Massachusetts. We had a town, but no physical address. From my research into DNA ancestry tracking, I knew we'd get a better response making contact in person, so Rye and I decided on a surprise visit—but first we needed that address.

I turned to Google and found there's this thing called the White Pages. I told my dad about it—not everything, just the White Pages—and he laughed. He said it used to get delivered to his house.

"They printed a book of people's phone numbers and addresses?" I asked, horrified.

"Even better—you used to be able to call a number and they'd tell you the time."

Wow, his life might have been even weirder than mine.

As it turned out, the online White Pages were quite useful. I put the name "Monique LaSalle" into the search field and the town of

Revere. For five bucks we could look up twenty names, which made my dad's printed copy clearly a bargain.

"North of Boston I'm okay with, but I'm not flying to Wisconsin or anywhere else to meet the other Moniques," I told Riley. "If this lead is a dead end, we'll stick to the phone, okay?"

Riley nodded.

"Remember, there might be some reason why she might not want to give up your bio-dad's identity. But once she sees your best pleading look, I'm sure she'll change her mind. Speaking of which, let me see you plead."

Riley makes a face that looks like she just stepped on a Lego.

"Okay, maybe just smile politely," I suggest.

"Thank you again," Riley says, her eyes brimming with gratitude. "I don't know what I'd do without you."

"Well, you wouldn't be going to some sketchy 'hood in Revere, that's for sure," I say, and we share a little laugh.

We have a long drive ahead of us—over an hour—and unfortunately that gives us plenty of time to have nothing to say to each other. We may have a shared mission, but that doesn't give us a bond like Elliott and E.T. I'm not looking forward to a long stretch of doing nothing and saying nothing, so I suggest a Starbucks stop. If the Starbucks Corporation hadn't committed to a resource-positive future, with a stated goal to cut its carbon, water, and waste footprints by half, I would have gone elsewhere.

Fifteen minutes later, we're feeling the first sugar rush from our vanilla lattes (almond milk for me).

The next thing I know, Riley brings up Dylan. "How's he doing?" she asks.

I don't pull any punches. "He's an absolute mess," I say. "Not eating. Not sleeping. He quit the wrestling team, too—my uncle's pissed about that. He's hurting. Basically, it sucks for him."

Sucks for me, too, because I feel responsible.

Riley turns her head so I can see the pain in her eyes. "I feel sick about it," she says, sounding like she means it. "I wish I knew who sent him that picture. I'd kill him."

I'm thinking: *Get in line*. I haven't spoken with Jay since I confronted him. Obviously, I can't let Riley know I was in the car with him that night, but now I can talk openly about Umbrella Man.

"So who is the lucky guy in that picture with you?" I ask. "Someone at our school?"

"No—he doesn't go to school. He's, um, older," she says hesitantly.

"College?" I ask.

Riley gives me a telling look but says nothing more. I'm thinking about the second time I saw Umbrella Man, in the lobby of a hotel. I didn't get a good look at him then, either, but something tells me he had his college diploma already in a frame.

"Riley, you need to be careful," I say.

"I can handle myself." She says it quickly, like a lie she keeps rehearsing.

"Older guys have a different agenda," I say. "They want one thing."

"I already gave that up," Riley says.

I can't help but laugh. "I'm not just talking about sex," I say. "I'm talking about your emotions, about protecting yourself. These guys will use you and dump you like trash."

Riley goes quiet for a time, lost in thought. Eventually she breaks the silence. "Are you one?" she asks me.

"One what?" I reply.

"A virgin."

"A virgin?" I scrunch up my face at the word. "Honestly, that's such an archaic concept. It's just another way society labels women according to their sexual behavior."

"Oh, give me a break with your causes, Lettie. Just answer the question. Have you or haven't you?"

Since she's being truthful, or so it seems, I decide not to lie. "No, I haven't," I tell her.

Riley doesn't appear to pass any judgment. "That's cool," she says. "It's good to wait for the right guy."

"Or girl," I remind her.

Riley eyes me crookedly. "Are you—you know, into . . . ?"

"No," I say. "I'm not. At least I don't think I am."

Riley laughs. "Well, it's cool if you are," she says, and pauses before tossing out, "So are you into me?"

I roll my eyes. "Does everyone have to be into you, Riley?" I crack a smile, letting her know I'm joking, and we both laugh a little.

"But I'm serious," I say. "I'm worried about you. This older guy—can you give me a name?"

"Call him Guy," Riley says, and there's light dancing in her eyes that I think is the look of love.

"Okay, well, Guy makes me nervous," I say.

"I can handle myself."

There she goes with that lie again.

"Can you?" I ask, pushing because I'm genuinely concerned.

"I can."

I let it go because we need to focus on getting to Revere.

About an hour later we're driving down a narrow road with small houses crowded together. It's nothing like Meadowbrook, with its wide leafy streets and lawns cared for like golf courses.

Eventually we pull up in front of a single-story white house that looks like it could use a new coat of paint . . . and a new driveway, new fencing, shutters, and some window treatments, but I'm not here to judge. I'm here to find a father.

We ring the doorbell. My heart is pounding in my chest. I can only imagine how Riley is holding up. I put my arm around her shoulders to give her a brief reassuring half hug. She looks at me gratefully.

"It's going to be okay," I tell her. "We'll just introduce ourselves, explain who we're looking for, and that's it. Worst thing that happens is we have the wrong Monique."

Riley steadies herself. She wipes her hands on her jeans. Sweaty palms. Nervous. We both are.

"Guess I'm more worried that we have the *right* Monique," Riley says.

Moments later, the door comes open and we're standing face-to-face with a woman in her sixties (maybe).

"Monique LaSalle?" I ask.

"Yes. May I help you?" She sounds ready to be annoyed if this is a solicitation that she's not interested in hearing.

I'm looking at her closely—studying her, is more like it. There's almost no resemblance between the two potential relatives. Monique has dark hair, thick cheeks, and some extra weight on her short frame. I look more related to Riley than she does.

"I'm Lettie Fox, and this is Riley Thompson. We're from Meadowbrook, Mass."

"Meadowbrook? Okay, that's a long way to come to sell cookies."

Riley and I look at each other, perplexed. Then we break into uneasy laughter once we finally catch on.

"Oh, we're not Girl Scouts," I say. "We did a DNA test."

Monique's face goes slack. It appears she's put the pieces together rather quickly. "You got my name from the ancestry match. Is that right?"

We both nod.

"So which of you am I related to?"

"Me," Riley says in a tiny voice. "I think we're related."

Monique invites us inside. It's nicer than I expected—homey, even. I take note of too many figurines on display and too much floral-pattern furniture for my liking, but we're not here to assess the home decor, either.

We settle ourselves in the living room and pull out some of the on-line reports we printed to make the sharing of information that much easier. Monique studies the paperwork for some time while we sit on cushy armchairs, drinking soda water flavored with cranberry juice.

"So I think I got it," Monique says, but she doesn't sound particularly pleased.

"Do you know him? My father? It says here that you're a close relative."

"I think, looking at this report . . . well, I'm really sorry to tell you this, Riley. But I think your father was my nephew Steve."

I immediately key in on the word *was* and my stomach tightens.

"Steve was my sister's only son," Monique continues. "He passed away suddenly in a motorcycle accident five years ago. Heartbreaking for us all." Her eyes glisten with emotion.

Riley sits very still, her expression impassive. Maybe it's shock, I think.

"Steve was a truly wonderful man, troubled in some ways, with a touch of a wild streak. But he lived life to the fullest. I hate to be the one to tell you that he's gone. I'm sure he would have loved to meet you. I know it's not much consolation, but I'll answer any questions you have."

The next twenty minutes or so is a blur of the life of Steven Wachowski—aka Stevie the Wookiee, or Wookiee if you knew him well. We look at pictures in photo albums of Stevie in his younger days, looking all eighties hair band and dressed in tights that reveal way too much of the Wookiee for my innocent eyes.

"He loved his guitars—had about twenty of them that we eventually had to sell, couldn't find a place to store them all. My sister didn't have much room in her home to keep them, and what would she do with them all anyway?"

The weight in Monique's eyes seems to drag her gaze to the floor. "Stevie would have wanted them to be played. I'm really sorry, because I would have given you one to take home with you."

"That's okay," Riley says, "I don't play any instruments."

I have a passing thought about nature versus nurture. Might Riley have played something if Stevie had been around to guide her?

As we peruse more photos of Bio-Dad prancing about onstage, swilling beers at picnics, riding his motorcycle, and cavorting with all kinds of interesting tattooed types (many female and many young), it becomes increasingly obvious to me that Riley is struggling mightily.

It's hard enough to discover that you have two fathers, but to find out one of them is dead and was named the Wookiee would be hard for anyone to process, let alone someone not quite eighteen. It may well be that the Wookiee provided Riley with half her DNA, but based on these photos, it was a half well-hidden. Maybe Riley got the shape of her eyes and lips from her father, but that's about it. Certainly she didn't inherit his love for rock, kegs, or tats.

We end up leaving Monique's place with a copy of the Wookiee's one and only professionally produced CD, an album titled *Slather It On Thick*. The cover shows a shirtless Steve standing in front of a white background, a close-up of his bare chest covered in finger paint being applied with gusto by a group of hand models. Neither of us can play CDs, but we don't tell Monique this. We simply say thank you, exchange contact information, and away we go.

Riley is quiet on the drive back to Meadowbrook. I'm doing the driving because Riley's too rattled to be safe on the road. I appraise her gingerly while she holds her gaze forward, avoiding any eye contact.

Finally I break the silence. "How ya doin'? Wanna talk about it?"

She gives me a cool sideways glance. "Definitely not," she says. "Talking isn't what I need." Riley begins rummaging around in her bag. Eventually her hand emerges holding a pill bottle. Off comes the top and in goes a pill, which she chases down with a swig from her now-cold Starbucks drink. She puts the pill bottle back in her purse, knowing better than to offer me one.

"What's that?" I ask.

"Something to help me," she says.

I won't tell her that I already knew about her habit, but I won't let it go, either.

"Are those prescribed?" I ask.

"To someone they are," she says.

I think of Riley's dad, Evan, and his red-rimmed eyes, and have an idea whose prescription it might be.

"I know the pills seem helpful, but you're just masking the problem. Drugs aren't a solution."

"No offense, Lettie, but you don't really know what I need right now."

"No offense taken," I say softly.

We barely speak for the rest of the drive home.

Riley gives me a hug in her driveway. "Thank you," she whispers. "You're the best friend I have."

I'm sure she's high. She's not in her right mind. But that doesn't stop me from hugging her harder.

Chapter 31

Suddenly it was Christmas Eve. The day arrived as if Alex had entered a time warp. Hadn't she just been making soup with the leftover turkey? Now she was a baking a pie to take over to Emily's.

After New Year's, Alex would have a long respite—Valentine's Day didn't count much—until Easter and then the annual Memorial Day block party would come again, as sure as the earth spun around the sun.

First, though, she had to survive Christmas. Yes, it was a lovely holiday filled with some of her favorite memories. Tomorrow her mom and Nick's parents would both come again for another visit and stay a few days. They'd have another round of big meals, more wine, more desserts, after which Alex would make her annual get-in-shape pledge.

To her credit, Lettie joined Alex in the kitchen, where she helped make several pies that came out looking Instagram-worthy. Alex was relishing the moment of togetherness—until Lettie made an offhand remark about her drinking.

"Is that glass number three, Mom?" she asked. "You better pace yourself."

Alex huffed dismissively. "It's the holidays," she said. "I'm not counting."

"You never count," said Lettie.

Alex felt the bite of uncertainty, an unpleasant suspicion that her daughter's dig could be truer than she cared to admit. No matter. As she said, it was the holidays. She deserved to unwind.

Some time later, Alex and her family, all dressed in their holiday finest, arrived at Emily's house, which looked like something out of a Hallmark movie. It smelled even more comforting, with rich aromas of pine, mulled wine, and a host of spices—cardamom and cinnamon, cloves and nutmeg. A warm wood fire crackled in the living room while from the speakers wafted one of Alex's favorites, "The Little Drummer Boy," sung by Bing Crosby and David Bowie. A feeling of holiday cheer sank deeply into Alex, igniting a glow that warmed her from within.

After a series of quick hellos and even faster hugs, Nick went off to get beers with Ken and Logan, who was home for the holiday, looking strapping as ever. Lettie decided her phone was better company than anyone in the family. Rather than start an argument, Alex let it go because she wanted to talk privately with her sister.

In the kitchen, Alex helped Emily prepare the meal, where she also helped herself to mulled wine. "Do you think I drink too much?" she asked.

Emily gave her a look of indifference. "No more than I do," she said, and sipped from her own drink.

That was good enough for Alex. She wasn't about to put down the wine for good. She noted a heaviness about Emily, a worry that seemed fused into her sister's expression and dimmed the holiday sparkle from her eyes.

"Everything all right?" Alex asked.

Emily glanced about the kitchen as if worried someone might intrude. "Ken withdrew twenty-five thousand dollars from the checking account the other day," she whispered.

"Twenty-five grand?" Alex exclaimed, tossing the salad with involuntary vigor.

"That's right," said Emily.

"Did he say why?"

"Taxes." Emily made it sound like a lie.

"Is that a reasonable amount? Is it a normal thing?" Alex didn't think so, but she didn't know how much Ken pulled in—or Emily, for that matter.

"Not that I've ever noticed," said Emily. "But he assured me it's nothing to get upset about."

"Do you have the money? I mean, you're fine, right?"

"Of course," said Emily. "We're fine. We have plenty of money. But it was like he needed cash in a hurry. And then I can't find the emerald necklace Ken bought me. I keep it in my jewelry box, and suddenly it's gone."

"Do you think Ken took it? Shit, do you think he pawned your gift?"

Emily frowned. "I mean, maybe the chain broke when I wore it out, and I just didn't notice. But it's odd that the necklace vanishes, and so does twenty-five grand for . . . *taxes*." She put "taxes" in air quotes.

"What are you thinking?" Alex asked.

"I'm thinking a man acts like this when he has a mistress . . . or an enemy."

Alex relaxed before dinner in the comfy leather recliner by the Christmas tree. The lights on the tree had become blurry—or was it her vision? The mulled wine had really crept up on her. She'd had only . . . well, she wasn't sure how much she had. She remembered Lettie asking if she was on glass number three, but that was back home, hours ago.

Damn.

A buzz of conversation filled the room, while Alex remained in her own world, drinking from her mug. She surveyed the impressive evergreen, noticing that the star at the top was a bit lopsided. Hopefully it was just that, not the whole room tilting.

A crooked star on such a lovely tree simply wouldn't do. No, it wouldn't do at all, Alex decided.

She stood, a bit unsteady on her feet, appraising the tree from different vantage points, confirming what she'd observed. The star was indeed crooked. Standing at the base, she craned her neck skyward, then went up on her tiptoes, but couldn't reach high enough. It figured that Ken would have chosen a tree as oversized as his ego. Nick probably could reach it, but she might get a snide remark if he noticed she was a bit tipsy. Okay, maybe more than a bit. But no big deal. She was on a mission, and she'd solve the problem one way or another.

From the dining room where they'd soon be eating, Alex retrieved a folding bridge chair. The mahogany table came with six chairs, too cumbersome to move, but lucky chair number seven was light and easy to relocate.

Nobody took notice when Alex unfolded the chair in front of the tree. All were engaged in conversation—all except for Dylan, who was off somewhere, avoiding as much cheer as possible. Emily insisted that he'd be eating with them, but Alex remained worried. In her opinion, this breakup drama was going on far too long. It wasn't healthy. That was why the crooked star mattered! It symbolized that life in this home was out of balance. A problem Alex would rectify as soon as she managed to get one foot up on the chair, and then the other.

Her maneuvering attracted some attention.

"Alex, what the hell are you doing?" Nick asked.

"The star is crooked." She reached to adjust it. "You can't have a crooked star on Christmas Eve! What would Jesus think?"

"He'd think you had too much to drink," Nick shared as he came forward.

Ken said, "Careful, the tree's not secured to the wall."

"I'm fine," said Alex, ignoring the fact that the room seemed to be spinning.

She did manage to get a hand on the star, but to do so required that she step forward, just a little, enough to shift her weight on the chair. The change in foot pressure caused a reaction that physics could have predicted, but Alex, especially in her compromised state, could not.

The chair folded up like a bear trap snapping shut. One moment she was holding the star in her hand, and the next she was pulling it down as she tumbled backward. Reaching for something to help arrest her fall, Alex grabbed the nearest branch, which happened to hold the glass Rudolph ornament with a cherry-red nose that Emily had since childhood.

As soon as it was clear to Alex what she had done, the terrible mistake she had made, she threw her body to the side, lest she be crushed by a falling tree. Alex went down hard, the tree crashing beside her, narrowly missing Nick, who had tried to come to her aid.

A tree falling in a lonely forest may not make a sound, but this tree certainly did. The crash of breaking glass and snapping branches reverberated like an explosion, causing everyone to freeze in place— including Alex, who gazed in wide-eyed disbelief at the disaster of her making. Pine needles scattered across the floor, covering parts of almost every surface in the room as if a green glitter bomb had gone off.

As Alex tried to press herself up to sitting, she noticed long red scratches running down her arms. They were already starting to throb. She shook pine needles from her hair, hoping she might also wake herself up from a terrible dream. No such luck.

Everyone gathered around the fallen tree, stupefied by the destruction before them. Nick came over to Alex and gently helped her to her feet. "Oh my god, honey, are you okay?"

He looked her over the way a paramedic might, carefully assessing her from head to toe for signs of injury.

Alex, who wobbled a little once standing, held on to his arm for support. "Ken, I am so, so sorry," she said. "I was trying to help, and maybe I just . . ."

Ken didn't offer any response. He was too angry and too busy surveying the damage she had caused.

Lettie's red-faced embarrassment cut Alex to the bone. "The star's still crooked, Mom," she said.

The silent reproach in her daughter's eyes was the worst of it. If looks could kill, the tree would have fallen on her neck. Lettie marched herself out of the room, unwilling to endure another second in her mother's presence.

Once he established that Alex didn't have any obvious injuries, Nick whispered in her ear, "How much wine have you had?" He didn't wait for an answer. "Go lie down somewhere," he snarled. "Ken and I will clean up your mess."

Alex wasn't about to argue. Her head was spinning. If she tried to stay upright much longer, she would risk falling again. Some of her disorientation was from the alcohol, for sure, but some was due to the shock of her fall.

She went to the couch, which was the closest place she could plop herself down and not create another spectacle. Self-ridicule echoed in her ears, loud as a marching band.

Fool.

Drunk.

Idiot.

What the hell is wrong with me? she asked herself.

From her perch on the couch, Alex watched as Ken, Logan, and Nick righted the magnificent tree with a few grunts of effort. Miraculously, it wasn't in terrible shape. The lights still worked, thank goodness, and the garland barely looked out of place. Some ornaments had come off upon impact, but only a handful had broken.

Sadly, poor Rudolph was among the casualties. Emily cleared what remained of her childhood treasure off the floor with a dustpan and broom. She took it all in stride—bless her. Perhaps she was remembering the day she'd tried to stuff banana peels into the curtain rods of the Kumars' future home.

"It's okay, hon," Emily said. "Come to the bathroom. You've got pine needles in your hair."

After cleaning herself up, drinking water and a strong cup of coffee, Alex helped her sister finish setting the table, restoring some of her little remaining dignity. She put out plates of green beans bathed in butter, caramelized carrots, tender roast beef, chicken, gravy, and other savory dishes for their feast.

Emily said nothing more about Ken's potential infidelity or the twenty-five thousand he allegedly spent on taxes. No one said much about anything. What everyone wanted to talk about was Alex, but nobody could bring themselves to do so.

Nick, who'd normally be openly irate, was instead using the silent treatment. Probably for the best. No doubt they'd have a tense conversation later. Whatever. She'd handle it.

She played it out in her head. She'd make some promises. Maybe she'd even keep them this time. She owed him, especially because her mother was coming back in the morning. Every Christmas Eve, Alex's mother served dinner to the needy through her church. It was somewhat of a blessing, because it precluded her from driving to Meadowbrook after dark. The lens on the Hubble telescope wasn't strong enough to help her mother's vision at night.

Honestly, Alex and Emily worried their mother shouldn't be driving at all anymore. But for now, at least she'd arrive during the daylight hours of Christmas morning. One step at a time. And maybe by morning, Alex and Nick would be talking to each other again.

In a year, all of it would be different. Ken's grand plan for the in-law apartment would come to fruition—that is to say, if he and Emily didn't fall apart in the meantime.

Dinner began in silence, everyone still avoiding the elephant in the room. It appeared that Alex wasn't the only one who imbibed too much that night. Alex noticed Dylan's glassy eyes, which paired well with his thousand-yard stare. He swayed slightly in his seat, as if his chair were riding atop ocean waves. Alex wondered whether he'd been secretly spiking his eggnog.

As Ken took his place at the table, Dylan's expression seemed to darken. Though he was dressed festively, probably at Emily's insistence, Alex saw no holiday cheer in her nephew's demeanor.

"A toast," Ken said, rising to his feet before anyone had a chance to help themselves to the steaming food. He raised a crystal wineglass that had once belonged to Alex's grandparents.

"Every year I make this toast to remind us how blessed we are, but this year it feels especially poignant. Maybe it's because I'm getting more sentimental in middle age, or maybe it's because we didn't have to call an ambulance after Alex took down my Christmas tree."

Alex felt the sting. She hung her head as Ken chuckled at her expense, grateful that nobody joined him in laughter.

"First, let's toast Logan," said Ken, beaming proudly at his oldest son. "He gives us less and less time each year as he gets busier with his life. I know we're all excited for the upcoming lax season, Logan's last as a college player, and I wouldn't be surprised if he's named player of the year for the Atlantic Coast Conference."

Everyone toasted Logan, whose exquisite grooming made him look almost like a computer-generated graphic. He was broad-shouldered with a jawline to envy, lustrous dark hair, and teeth white as moonglow. His unblemished face bore no scars from his battles on the field, nor did it suggest any strain from his life off it. He looked as if he'd won some genetic lottery that blessed him not only with good looks and athletic prowess, but also with a brain capable enough to ensure him a lucrative career in finance after graduation. Logan was that rare breed who had it made, as Ken would take any opportunity to boast.

He was the fortunate son.

"And of course, I don't mean to overshadow Dylan, who should have a good season as well—assuming he doesn't quit lacrosse like he did wrestling."

Alex inhaled sharply while Emily went rigid in her seat. Lettie cringed slightly.

To his credit, Logan appeared more than a little uncomfortable. "Let's not pick on D," said Logan, placing his muscled arm around his brother.

Dylan flinched, as if Logan's touch were electrified, before glowering at his father. He stood, visibly unsteady.

Ken didn't budge. His towering presence made the already weighty atmosphere oppressive.

"I don't feel well," Dylan mumbled. He marched out of the room, his shoulders hunched forward, head bowed.

Alex's heart ached for her nephew.

"Go talk to him," Emily hissed at Ken.

Ken didn't budge. "I didn't say anything wrong," he said.

Emily shook with anger. "You embarrassed him."

"He quit the team his senior year," said Ken. "Who does that?"

"He quit because he's brokenhearted, you jerk," Emily snapped.

Everyone at the table, Alex included, averted their eyes.

"I'll go talk to him," said Logan, who got up just as a thunderous crash sounded from the window closest to Emily.

Glass shards, some sharp as knives, shot inward like shrapnel. As the glass fell to the floor, a misshapen object streaked into the room, landing on the table, right on top of the roasted beets, shattering the plate upon impact. Beet juice sprayed everywhere, peppering the white tablecloth with droplets of red as if someone had been shot. The object bounded over the chicken, smashed into the mashed potatoes, and came to a slow, rolling stop in front of Alex.

Nick instinctively turned his body to form a makeshift barricade that did little to protect his wife. Ken ducked as though there'd been a gunshot, but Alex knew that wasn't the case. She could see what had caused all the destruction because it had landed right in front of her. The room erupted into nervous, indiscriminate chatter.

"What the hell was that?"

"Oh my god!"

"Is everyone all right?"

Alex carefully picked up the projectile—a rock, which was wrapped in paper and secured with rubber bands. She hefted the stone in her hands, dumbfounded at the sight of it, the cold feel of it against her palm.

The room continued to buzz. Logan and Ken helped Emily, who had fallen off her chair onto the floor.

Dylan rushed back into the dining room. "What happened?" he asked.

All eyes fell on Alex, who fumbled to remove the elastic bands that secured the paper to the stone.

A crudely written message in red pen read: **Merry Christmas Asshole!!!**

Everyone seemed to be getting their bearings as the initial fright and confusion began to wane. Nick checked with Lettie, who appeared unharmed. Emily could be heard assuring Logan and Ken that she was fine as well. Dylan kept asking what happened, but Alex didn't answer him. She was still fixated on the note.

Logan went to the broken window. "I don't see anybody out there," he announced. He shined his phone's flashlight into the dark.

"Give me that," Ken said angrily, reaching over the table to snatch the paper from Alex.

"What's this supposed to mean?" he asked, pointing to the note. "Who's the asshole?"

"Have you pissed anybody off, Ken?" asked Alex.

"No," Ken said defiantly. "Why would you even think that?"

"Wait, haven't you been obsessing about getting *someone* fired?" Emily said. "My guess is this was sent by our neighborhood pest control salesman and *you're* the asshole, Ken. Did you get him fired?"

"I called the company and complained, sure I did," Ken snapped. "But I don't know what happened to that punk."

"I'm thinking your efforts were successful," Alex said, "and for that, Bug Man has retaliated."

"We need to call the police," Emily said.

"We're not calling anybody," Ken fumed. "I'll take care of this myself."

"What are you going to do?" Emily's voice quavered.

"I'm going to fucking kill him, that's what," Ken said.

Alex shivered, knowing full well that was no idle threat.

Chapter 32

Lettie

My grand plan to get Dylan and Riley back together—in other words, fix my giant mistake—involves me getting hammered on New Year's Eve.

I've never been a drinker. I leave that activity to my mom. And yes, I'm utterly mortified about Christmas Eve, but I'm glad nobody got hurt from the falling tree or the rock Bug Man tossed through the window. What the hell is wrong with people? At least Christmas morning was peaceful, and Grandma brought her cherry applesauce, which I'd honestly live off if I could.

With Christmas in the rearview, I've reset my focus on what I *can* control, or sort of control, or at least try to manipulate. Riley and I need to remain close friends (okay, besties!) for my efforts to work. Since we have zero things in common these days, I need an angle. Now that the Wookiee mystery is solved, I need something else to bond us.

Taking an approach that no sane person would ever endorse, I've decided to adopt Riley's partying habits. If all goes according to plan, tonight I'll get drunk with her, talk her into giving it another shot with Dylan, and Umbrella Man will be a thing of the past.

Riley drives me to Teagan's house. Yeah, Teagan was one of the Middle School Meanies, too, but in for a penny, in for a pound, as my grandma would say. Mom and Dad went to a party with Uncle Ken and Aunt Emily—big night for them. I sent Dylan a text urging him to join me at Teagan's. Somehow I neglected to mention that invitation to Riley.

Not surprisingly, Dylan asked if Riley would be there, and I lied. I told him I thought she had other plans. Oops.

I have no idea where my old crew is tonight. It seems the closer I get to either Riley or Jay, the more distance I put between myself and my former life.

If anybody from the climate committee knew I was at Teagan's, they'd be texting, asking if I needed to be rescued.

The party is twenty kids crammed into a finished basement. I feel bad for the carpet. Everyone is drinking beer out of red Solo cups. Totally environmentally unfriendly, but great for beer pong, which half the kids are playing.

Teagan's parents supplied the alcohol. It's kind of weird and unquestionably illegal, but nobody is going to make a stink about it. It is free beer, after all.

My first drink goes down without much gagging. It tastes bitter, with an aftertaste that reminds me of dirt. But I keep going. The second one doesn't taste as bad. By the third, I'm feeling a buzz. And after the fourth, I'm regretting all the parties I never attended. Now I know why everyone does this.

The music is loud and we have to press lips to ears to be heard. Two hours into the festivities and almost every surface is sticky from spilled beer, some of it my own.

I'm not entirely irresponsible. I've collected car keys from all the partyers and given them to Teagan's parents, who acted appreciative—not enough, though, in my opinion. My guess is they were embarrassed not to have thought of it first.

Around nine o'clock, Dylan comes strolling in. Two seconds later, he's double-fisting his beers. He gives a yowl to announce his arrival, drawing the interest of a girl who isn't Riley and several boys who surround him to grunt out greetings while thumping their chests against him.

Riley grabs my arm and pulls me aside. "What the hell is he doing here?" she says with alarm. Her pupils are dilated, and I'm sure it's not just the alcohol. "Who invited him?"

I shrug. "No idea?" I take a long swig of beer, avoiding eye contact with Riley. Can't get much down because my stomach has shrunk to the size of a pea. "Why don't you talk to him? Maybe it's a sign from the universe that you two can work some things out."

Dylan shoots a look our way. He's forlorn. Desperate.

My fault . . . my fault . . . my fault thumps in my head, like that guilty heartbeat from the Edgar Allan Poe story I read in ninth grade. Even so, I'm torn. Jay's warning that Riley is no good should carry some weight, but here I am, leading Dylan right back into the clutches of the femme fatale. There's every chance I'm going to make things worse, not better.

Right or wrong, there's no backing out now. He and Riley are both at this party, within feet of each other.

Riley and I pass some time playing beer pong. Dylan lurks nearby. I'm fast moving from buzzed to drunk, and I think I like it.

The booze may be bolstering my confidence, but it's not giving me any great ideas. Riley's acting all aloof now that Dylan's around. Not that she's been particularly chatty or open since our trip to Revere. She hasn't once brought up the Wookiee, Umbrella Man, or the pill habit. My guess is she's working hard to suppress it all. She's like a live version of your favorite train-wreck girl on a terrible reality TV show.

"Really, Rye, go talk to him." I nod toward Dylan when I notice her looking his way. She doesn't say no, so I press on. "Dump that older guy and get back with D. He loves you. Give him a chance. You two were great together."

Riley doesn't look particularly convinced. "Just leave it alone, Lettie, okay?"

It's sound advice that I wish I had taken a lot earlier.

I break away from Riley to talk to Dylan. "What do you have to lose?" I say. "If you want her back, you've got to *tell* her."

It doesn't take much prodding. Dylan approaches Riley with a confidence that I suspect is all show. I'm standing far enough away to see their interaction without calling attention to myself.

Dylan taps Riley on the shoulder. She turns. Her expression grows somber, like we've gone from a party to a wake. They talk, but I can't hear anything over the loud music and party noise.

As the conversation continues my hope dims. Dylan becomes

agitated. He's shifting his weight from foot to foot, nervously running a hand through his hair. He takes a forward step, invading Riley's personal space. She backs away. He leans in close, too close. More words are exchanged. Judging by Riley's furrowed brow and folded arms, she's not eager to hear much more. Seconds later, she turns her back and storms away.

Shit.

Riley doesn't come back for a long while. She's gone off with Teagan somewhere, probably to vent about Dylan showing up uninvited—or technically, semi-uninvited. Meanwhile, I keep an eye on my cousin while the party gets rowdier. It's an hour and a half before midnight, and already Dylan's wasted. I suspect he did some pre-partying.

Everyone is drunk, it seems. A couple kids have puked. I've seen some quality drama—boy-girl crap mostly—but my focus remains on my cousin. I'm not here to enjoy myself. I'm trying to set things right, but it's looking grim. I might even have made matters worse.

For the last ten minutes, Dylan has been slumped down against a wall, staring vacantly into his Solo cup.

"This party's lame, and I'm tired," I say, even though it's not yet eleven o'clock.

"Yeah, I can't stay here anymore," he says.

"Let's get an Uber."

He rises clumsily to his feet. "I'll never stop loving her . . . never."

And I'll never stop feeling responsible, I think.

I notice Riley across the room. Dylan sees her as well, talking to one of the cuter boys on the Meadowbrook soccer team. His body tenses, and he leaves my side. I'm worried he might start a fight, but he says that he just has to grab his stuff. He'll meet me outside.

"Okay," I say. "Our Uber is ten minutes away."

We're shivering as we wait for our ride. The moon is a whisper behind a thin cover of clouds. We barely speak on the trip back to Alton Road.

It's eleven twenty-five when we finally get home. My buzz is slowly wearing off. Now I just feel exhausted and a little sick to my stomach. I highly doubt I'm going to see midnight. Lights are on at the Kumars' house, but I don't bother texting Jay. That's over and done with, I remind myself, still wishing it could be different—a better kiss or another one, at least.

"Do you want to hang out?" I make the offer to Dylan even though all I want to do is go to bed. "We shouldn't be alone on New Year's."

"I'm always alone," Dylan mumbles before sulking back to his house. His head hangs low. His pain rips through me as though it were my own.

As it turns out, I can't sleep. The guilt keeps gnawing at me in a beaver-meets-tree kind of way. At midnight, I enjoy a glass of orange juice, along with a lonely solo toast to the new year.

Not long after that, my phone starts vibrating. I assume it's my friends from the other party, feeling bad that they forgot to wish me Happy New Year at midnight, but I'm stunned to see Jay's name on the display.

"Happy New Year," I say, surprised.

"Lettie!" Jay says with urgency. "Thank God you answered. I saw a light on in your room. Are you home right now?"

"Okay, that's a little creepy. Are you spying on me?"

"This isn't a time for jokes!" he shouts. "I'm being serious. I think there's an emergency at Dylan's house. Do you have a key? We need to check on him—right now!"

My heart cannons up into my throat. Aunt Emily and Uncle Ken are at the party with my parents, so Dylan's home alone.

"What's going on?" I ask.

"I was walking by and saw him outside. He fell over, didn't look right to me. Hardly got himself in the door. I'm afraid something is really wrong with him. Can you meet me outside?"

I hadn't thought Dylan was in that bad a shape when I dropped him off. But he's home alone, so maybe he hit his parents' liquor cabinet hard. Why would he have staggered outside? Was he looking for Riley? I rush out of my bedroom. "I'll meet you over there right now," I say. "I know where they hide the key."

I race down the stairs, calling Dylan's cell on the way. The phone rings and rings, but no one answers, and it rolls to voice mail. A drumbeat of fear fills my chest.

When I meet up with Jay, he looks panicked. "We need to hurry, Lettie," he says.

We rush across the street. I try the front door, but it's locked. I search the ground for the fake rock with the key hidden inside. A moment later, the front door is open and I'm calling Dylan's name as we enter his house.

No answer. All the lights are on, but it's quiet as a museum. We move quickly from room to room, checking the living room, the kitchen, before heading upstairs. I go straight to Dylan's bedroom. The door is closed. I move to knock, but Jay pushes past me and barges inside.

My breath catches when I follow him into the room. I can't make sense of what I'm seeing.

Dylan is sprawled out on his back on the floor. He appears lifeless. His face is frighteningly pale. His arms and hands are gray, as if the blood has drained from his body. His lips are tinged a deathly blue.

I scream, "Dylan! Oh my god, Dylan!" I rush toward him, not knowing what to do.

Luckily, Jay appears to be thinking more quickly than I am. He grabs something from his coat pocket and tells me to call 911.

I fumble for my phone. My fingers don't seem to be working right, I'm shaking so badly. Instead, I tell Siri to make the call for me.

The dispatcher comes on the line almost immediately. "Nine-one-one, what's your emergency?"

The words tumble out of my mouth. "My cousin, he's unresponsive."

"Okay, let me get you mapped." A moment later, the dispatcher says, "You're on Alton Road?"

"Yes, number 22 at the end of the cul-de-sac."

"Okay, we have help on the way. Is he breathing?"

As I push Jay aside to check my cousin's breathing, I see that he's spraying something up Dylan's nose. "What the hell is that?" I ask.

"Narcan," Jay says. "Just in case he took something."

I shake my head to clear my thoughts. "Is he even breathing?" I ask. "I need to know. Do we need to do CPR?"

Jay puts his ear to Dylan's mouth. He doesn't look relieved. Then he begins to press on Dylan's chest. I don't know first aid, so I can't say if he's doing it right or not.

By now, panic has engulfed me. I can barely talk, but I manage to tell the dispatcher that I don't think Dylan is breathing.

The dispatcher begins to instruct me as to how to administer CPR, but before I can relay that information to Jay, Dylan begins to stir. Already, I can hear sirens in the distance.

Relief washes over me with tears of gratitude. Good Lord, Dylan is moaning—barely moving, but moaning nonetheless.

"Talk to me!" Jay says forcefully. "D, come on. Talk! Open your eyes. You can do it."

Dylan's eyes open. "What's going on?" he mutters. "What's happening?" He makes a feeble attempt to sit up but doesn't have the strength.

The sirens are right outside the house. Red and blue strobe lights illuminate the room, like in a TV movie. There's banging on the front door. I sprint downstairs to open it. From above, I hear Dylan assuring Jay that he's okay.

"Upstairs," I tell the paramedics, who race into the house.

The EMTs work efficiently as a team. Everything becomes a blur as they get Dylan onto a stretcher and into the waiting ambulance.

I call Aunt Emily and then my mom. Everyone is freaking out. They say they'll meet the ambulance at the hospital. I'm outside now, but adrenaline has numbed me to the cold. I see Jay talking to someone by a police car. In a daze, I join them.

"He should be okay," the officer says. "He'll get the help he needs. You saved his life, young man, by giving him the Narcan."

I grab Jay's hand. My heart swells as fresh tears rise. It could be my imagination or a trick of the light, but I'm pretty sure I see tears in Jay's eyes as well.

Chapter 33

Alex gripped her seat as Ken drove everyone straight to the hospital at a high rate of speed, seemingly oblivious to the stoplights. Emily stayed on the phone with Lettie, who was already there, but had little knowledge of Dylan's status. The party mood felt like a relic from a different era.

"He's awake and talking, that's all Lettie knows right now," Emily said to everyone in the car. "They won't allow Lettie into the ER because she's not immediate family."

"That's just ridiculous," Nick said. "She's family enough."

"What the hell did he take?" Ken wanted to know.

"It was an opioid of some sort, because Jay gave him Narcan," said Emily.

"Where did Dylan get opioids? And what is Jay Kumar doing with Narcan?" Ken asked, giving the road only fragments of his attention.

"I don't know," Emily said. "I'm just grateful Jay had it on him. He saved our son's life. We should be thanking him."

"Yeah, yeah, for sure." Ken kept a white-knuckled grip on the wheel, not looking or sounding particularly grateful.

He pulled to a hard stop in a parking space outside the ER. Alex and Nick went straight to Lettie in the waiting room, while Ken and Emily checked in at admissions. Jay hovered near a vending machine, looking shaken and anxious.

Alex hugged her daughter. "Thank you," she said. "Thank you so much."

She opened her arms, inviting Jay into an awkward group hug. When the three broke apart, Alex assessed Lettie anew. Somehow she seemed stronger, more capable, more mature, than when she'd left her at home just hours ago.

"Do you know what he took?" asked Nick.

Lettie shook her head. "I called Teagan. We were at her house. I asked if there were any drugs going around, but she didn't think so."

Something about Lettie's demeanor struck Alex as evasive. Had she been drinking? Had *she* taken drugs? Before Alex could probe further, the automatic doors to the waiting room swooshed open.

In came Willow, with Riley at her heels. Judging by her clothes—a winter coat thrown over sweats—Willow hadn't had any New Year's plans, while Riley had obviously been partying. Alex could smell the booze on Riley's breath as soon as she was within arm's reach. Her hair was a mess, not her usual coif. Her makeup was smeared, and the dark smudges of mascara under her eyes were a clear indication that she'd been crying.

"Is he okay?" Riley asked breathlessly. "Is he?"

"He's going to be fine," Alex told her.

Willow expressed her relief as well.

"I tried to call you," Lettie said to Riley, "but your phone kept going to voice mail. Do you have any idea what Dylan took?"

"I can't find my phone," Riley said. "It's not in my bag. If your mom didn't call mine, I wouldn't have even known. And I don't know about any drugs. You were there, Lettie. Dylan and I barely talked all night. And he's never taken drugs before. Not that I know of."

"Were other people taking drugs at the party?" Willow asked.

Riley didn't answer, but her body language was defensive.

"Anyone want something to drink?" Nick asked.

"Riley, do you need water or coffee?" Alex's pointed look implied that Riley could use something to counteract the alcohol.

Before Nick could take any orders, Emily and Ken entered the waiting room through the ER's automatic double doors. Emily's eyes were swollen and her shoulders were rounded, hunched in on herself. Ken, normally the picture of health and vitality, looked gray and worn.

"We are so damn lucky," Emily said, wrapping her arms around Alex. "He's going to be fine—at least physically. But he told the doctors he took an overdose *intentionally*."

Riley choked down a sob as she turned to Emily. "He tried to . . . *kill* himself?"

Emily's soft gaze hardened. "What are you doing here? I'm guessing you're the reason this happened."

Riley would not have looked more stricken if Emily had reached over and slapped her across the face. She stammered, but no words came out. Willow put an arm around her daughter.

Ken straightened up and sent Emily a scathing look. "You can't blame a teenager for breaking up with her boyfriend," he said. "Just because Dylan went off the deep end, that doesn't make it Riley's fault."

His eyes fell on Riley, who looked up with gratitude. It was as though Ken's words had rescued her from her own worst fears.

A tense silence descended.

Nick cleared his throat. "Ken, why don't you come with me? I'm going to get some drinks."

Alex and Emily took seats on uncomfortable hard-plastic chairs while Ken left with Nick, his footsteps heavy as he retreated down the hallway. Alex took her sister's hand. Without words adequate to convey her feelings, she hoped the gesture said enough.

Riley and Willow didn't stick around for long. They offered a few more words of comfort and support and departed minutes before Nick and Ken returned from the cafeteria carrying four bottles of water and a coffee on a cardboard tray. Nick handed out the waters, keeping the coffee for himself.

Emily got up to use the bathroom.

To Lettie and Jay, Ken said, "It's getting late, you two. I can take you both home—Alex, Nick, you as well. There's no need for all of us to be here now."

Jay still looked haunted. He shuffled uneasily on his feet, hands stuffed in his pockets, barely able to meet Ken's gaze. "Thanks," he said, "but my mom is on her way. She can take us home."

When Emily returned, she said to Ken, "The kids don't need to stay here. Why don't you drive them home and come back?"

Ken took a sip of his water. "Amanda is coming to get them."

"Who?" asked Emily. "Who's Amanda?"

Ken stammered as he corrected himself. "I mean Mandy. Isn't that short for Amanda?"

Emily glanced at Alex, looking confused. "Yeah, I guess. Maybe."

At that moment, Mandy arrived with Samir. She pulled free from Samir to embrace Jay.

"What happened?" asked Samir. "Jay told us Dylan took an overdose. Is he okay?"

"He'll be fine, thanks to your quick-thinking son," said Alex. "If he didn't see that Dylan was in distress and know to administer Narcan, it could have been so much worse." She silently agreed with Ken: it was strange for Jay to have the lifesaving treatment on hand.

Samir eyed his son, nonplussed. "You have Narcan? Why would you have that? Jay, are you—"

Jay interrupted his father. "I don't use drugs, Dad. Don't worry. I saw an overdose in college once, and decided I'd always have it available."

"Very resourceful," Mandy said with pride and tears in her eyes.

"Thank God for Jay," said Emily. "We could have lost our son. I can't imagine."

"No, you can't." Mandy wiped at her eyes.

Her statement had a weightiness that made Alex wonder again what Mandy was holding back.

Emily looked to Ken, then back at Mandy. Her expression shifted from gratitude to suspicion.

Samir stiffened. "Mandy, let's go," he said. It was an order, not a suggestion. He turned to leave.

A police officer dressed in blue approached the gathering. He was young but carried himself with confidence. "Excuse me," he said. "I'm Officer Grady O'Brien with the Meadowbrook Police Department. I'm looking for Dylan Adair's parents." He scanned the faces of the adults present.

"I'm Emily Adair, Dylan's mother."

"I've heard your son is going to be okay," said Officer O'Brien. "But I'm wondering if you know an Evan Thompson."

"He's our neighbor," Emily replied. "Why do you ask?"

"I'd like to speak with him," said O'Brien.

"About what?" asked Ken. "What's he got to do with Dylan?"

"The pills Dylan took tonight," O'Brien said. "According to the prescription bottle we found at the scene, they belong to Mr. Thompson."

Chapter 34

Lettie

Sadness burrows into my chest as I watch snow fall outside the kitchen window. The flakes are big and fluffy, easily blown around, blanketing the town in white, as if Meadowbrook were encased in a snow globe. It's a picture-perfect scene, unlike the holidays themselves.

In another life, my dad and I would have made a snowman. Now we're fighting about college. Mom's still drinking. Riley's still popping pills. Dylan tried to kill himself. And I still feel responsible.

The doorbell rings and Zoe goes crazy. I'm sure she thinks it's the UPS guy, who always brings dog treats, but this time I'm surprised to see Riley standing outside. She looks an absolute mess—her hair flaked white with snow, face pale and drawn, eyes red and swollen. No question she's been crying.

"Can we talk?" Riley asks. "Sorry, I would have texted, but I still can't find my phone."

"Sure," I say. "Come upstairs."

My mom wants to know who's at the door.

"Riley," I yell as we hurry to my bedroom.

I close the door and Riley sits on the bed. I grab my desk chair, swiveling it to face her. Riley's looking around—checking out my space, seeming perplexed by the lack of mirrors and makeup products, not to mention the anime decorations adorning my walls.

"How are you holding up?" I ask. The answer is obviously "not very well," but what else am I going to say?

Riley surprises me yet again. "We broke up," she says as tears spill out her eyes.

I get up to give her a hug, and she sobs in my arms.

"The older guy?" I ask.

She can't speak. I worry she's going to start hyperventilating. I ended the year with an ambulance ride and don't wish to start the new one with another.

"I'm so sorry," I say, not meaning it at all, but I'm trying to de-escalate the situation. I have to force myself not to say "I told you so." Instead, I ask, "What happened?"

Riley continues to heave and sob, her face buried in her hands, trying to collect herself. Eventually she gains enough composure to speak. "He told me that what we're doing is wrong and we can't be together anymore. He says that he loves me, he really, really loves me, but that it has to end, and I don't know what I'm going to do now. It wasn't supposed to be this way."

I get that she's hurting, but the melodrama is off the charts. Even so, I keep my real feelings hidden so I can be a compassionate friend.

"What did he mean wrong? What's wrong? Is it the age difference?"

"No," Riley says. "It's more . . . complicated than that."

"Complicated how?"

"Lettie, don't be dense," Riley snaps.

"Are you pregnant?" I whisper.

She rolls her eyes at me. "No," she says. "He's married."

"Oh shit, Rye," I say. "What were you thinking?"

"I wasn't *thinking*, Lettie. It's love. We're in love. It just happened."

I suppress a groan while somehow managing to keep my expression utterly blank. "Falling in love with a married guy doesn't just happen, Riley," I say. "I believe it takes some effort."

Riley bites her bottom lip. More tears pool in her eyes. "But he's not happy," she says. "He's told me a million times that he's going to leave his wife for me. We're going to have this amazing life together. We're supposed to travel the world. He wants to take me to *Paris*." Her voice cracks with anguish.

Now it's my bullshit detector that's going off. I don't have much experience in the world of adult lies, but I've seen enough crappy TV shows to know that Riley's been fed a buffet of them.

"Riley, you're better off," I tell her. "Let him go. You're young, beautiful, brilliant . . ."—okay, that one was a stretch, but I'm trying to make her feel better—"and you've got your whole life ahead of you. It'll feel crappy for a while, but eventually you'll be better."

This is a lot of worldly knowledge for a girl who's never had a boyfriend, but I think I'm doing pretty well.

Riley isn't convinced. She shoots me a look that could cut flesh. "This is harder than you can understand."

Okay, condescending much? But whatever. She's upset. I let it go. "Does he have kids?"

Riley returns a grim nod.

I'm sure my look is disapproving.

"Please, don't judge," she begs. "I don't expect *virginal* Lettie to understand—" This time at least she catches herself. Her expression is mildly ashamed. "Sorry, that wasn't fair," she says. "And you're the only one I can talk to about this. You're the only one who knows. I'm just really upset."

"It's okay." I remind myself that the married guy holds most of the responsibility here. "It's a lot for you to process right now, on top of Dylan's overdose. It's too much for anyone to handle."

"Thanks, Lettie." Riley looks at me like I just endorsed her behavior, which I have not. I'm feeling sorry for her, is all. She has a lot on her plate.

She needs to know that more might be added to it, and soon. "Riley," I begin, clearing my throat, "I hate to even bring this up, but you should know that the police found an empty prescription bottle on Dylan last night."

"Do you know what he took?" she asks.

Her pupils are enlarged. I'm wondering what *she* took.

"The bottle, it, um, well . . . it had your father's name on it."

Riley blinks rapidly. "My father's name? Shit. Shit."

She flies off the bed, heading out of my room, moving faster than Zoe chasing a squirrel. "I'll be right back," she calls.

From my bedroom window, I watch Riley streak across Alton Road, her feet slipping for traction on the ice. She heads straight for her car, which is covered in snow. She vanishes inside her vehicle and emerges a moment later, holding her bag. I can't see her face from this distance, but as she nears my house, it's clear that she's deeply troubled. "Distraught" might be a better description.

I'm at the door to greet her when she returns. She pulls me outside. The cold air squeezes my chest, a feeling compounded by the look of fear in Riley's eyes. Snow falls on my eyelashes, causing me to blink.

"What's going on?" I ask.

"The pill bottle isn't in my purse," she practically yells, holding up her designer bag for me to see. "And it's not in my car, either."

"You think Dylan went through your purse and took it?"

"Lettie, you have to help me," Riley says. "And yes, I think Dylan took the pills at Teagan's party."

"Okay," I say, "just relax. You don't have to tell your parents about your . . . habit. Just talk to Dylan. Maybe he'll say he got them from your house one day. But, Riley, you do have to stop taking drugs. What are you taking, anyway? What are these pills?"

"It's OxyContin mostly, but forget the drugs," Riley says. Her face is bright red, and I'm sure it's not from the cold. "If he took those pills from my purse—do you know what that means? Do you?"

"Um, that he got oxy from you. But like I said, you can still dodge this bullet."

"NO!" she shouts. "It means he must have taken my phone, too. He took my phone *and* the pills. Lettie, we have to get it back. This is an emergency. We HAVE to get my phone!"

Chapter 35

Lettie

Dylan is finally home from the hospital. I'm nervous to see him. I feel sick to my stomach all the time. If he had ended his life over the breakup with Riley, it would have been my fault, and nobody knows the truth but Jay and me.

Maybe someday I'll find a way to forgive myself, but I'm not there yet. And it appears that I'm not done inserting myself into other people's problems. I've got a new mission now: get Riley's phone back from Dylan, who we suspect took it when he also took the pills from her purse. That phone must have images and messages that Dylan shouldn't see, things that might send him over the edge, maybe trigger a second attempt. That's all the motivation I need to stay involved.

I march across the street to Aunt Emily and Uncle Ken's house. No need to knock, I'm family, so I let myself inside before calling out my arrival.

Aunt Emily approaches from the kitchen. Her smile has dimmed, but she still greets me with a big hug, just as she would on any other day. She asks if I'm hungry and I tell her no, that I came to see Dylan.

My cousin Logan has come and gone, here for a few days at the start of the crisis. Still, I feel his presence lingering. Every room is something of a shrine Uncle Ken has erected to honor the one I suspect is his favorite son. A trophy case in the hallway is filled with hardware, most of which belongs to Logan. Gracing the walls near Uncle Ken's first-floor office are plaques and photographs honoring Logan's numerous athletic feats.

I want to believe other issues caused Dylan to take an overdose. Like that awful toast my uncle made on Christmas Eve, which symbolized the way he's treated Dylan his whole life. *Less than. Not worthy. Falling short. Never good enough.* That's why he took the pills, or so I tell myself. But I know better. I see the real reason every time I look in a mirror. He did it because of me. *I* messed up his life.

"I hope you can get him to open up," Aunt Emily says. "He barely speaks to anyone and hasn't said a word to his father since the— incident."

I note how she can't bring herself to name what he did. "I'll do my best," I say, and head upstairs.

I knock on Dylan's bedroom door.

"Come in," he says.

I enter to find Dylan lying on his bed, eyes glued to a phone. I'm hoping it's Riley's, that would make things a lot easier, but then I recognize it as his.

"Up for a visitor?" I ask, standing awkwardly just inside the threshold. I close the door behind me so we'll have privacy.

"Sure," Dylan says with indifference.

His room is quite neat, neater than mine by miles. His collection of sports memorabilia from the Boston teams—signed balls, posters, and cards—is displayed in glass cases, hung on his walls, or perfectly arranged on his bookshelves. There are no clothes on the floor, which is a bit unsettling. In my room, clothes are both carpeting and something to wear.

"How are you feeling?" I ask. The bottomless pit in my stomach won't go away.

"I'm okay," he says. He's already thanked me for saving his life, told me to thank Jay as well, but he didn't sound particularly thankful.

I smile at him, but really what I want to do is cry. He looks so sad, utterly broken. He may be breathing, thank God for that, but there's no life in his eyes. It's as if someone has pulled up the drain stopper, letting out all the things that had made up Dylan. He's not the same as he was. There's no lightness to him anymore.

"Why, D?" My voice cracks. "Why'd you do it?"

Dylan lets go a shaky breath. "I shouldn't have told them it was intentional," he says, irritated. "I didn't leave a note. It could have been just an accident. Now everybody knows." He sounds more upset about that than about having nearly died.

"D, everyone loves you," I say. "We just want you to be okay."

"Well, that's not going to happen," he says bitterly.

I sit down on the edge of his bed so our faces are closer. "Is it about Riley?" I ask. "The breakup? Or your dad? What happened at Christmas, I mean."

Dylan laughs harshly. "Lettie, just let it go, all right?" he says. "This isn't your problem."

It is, but I don't go there. Instead, I slide a bit closer to him. I want to hold his hand, though I don't dare touch him. He's so fragile, I'm afraid he'll break.

"I care so much about you," I say. A lump lodges in my throat, tears squeezing at the corners of my eyes.

"I'm okay," he says. "I've just got a lot on my mind."

"Let me help," I say. "You've got to talk to someone. It'll be between us. I won't tell a soul. If you keep everything bottled up, I'm worried you're going to burst from all the pressure. You need to release it."

Dylan doesn't take my bait, but I'm undeterred. I feel like I've been helpful to Riley, at least with the Wookiee, so maybe I can help Dylan as well.

"Just so you know, I think it sucks, what Riley did to you," I continue. "Cheating on you like she did."

Dylan keeps his chin to his chest, won't make any eye contact.

"You deserved better than that."

"Yeah, well, what's done is done."

"I know you don't believe it, but Riley really cares about you. She really does."

"How would you know? You two barely talk."

Dylan pauses, looks as if he's putting two and two together but it's not adding up to four in his head. "That day I confronted Riley at school," he says. "What were you doing with her? You were in the staff bathroom together. Why?" Instead of avoiding my gaze, his eyes bore into me.

This is my shot—my opening. "I've been helping Rye with something," I say. "Something personal, not related to you."

"What?" he asks—*demands* is more like it.

A warning bell is going off in my head. I hesitate a good long while. I shouldn't betray Riley's confidence, but I love my cousin, and I hope it will ease his mind.

"She took a home DNA test and found out that Evan isn't her biological father."

"Whoa!" Dylan bolts upright in bed, his eyes wide.

"It's true," I say. "Her bio-dad is a musician named Steve Wachowski, but everyone called him the Wookiee. Anyway . . . he's dead. Motorcycle accident."

"Damn." Dylan's expression turns somber. He's thinking something through or maybe feeling something deeply. I can't say for sure, because he's gone quiet on me.

Eventually he speaks. "She knew all this before she started seeing that guy?"

"Not all of it," I say, "but she definitely knew that Evan wasn't her father." Maybe I'm stretching the truth, but it might help Dylan to think Riley was in crisis when she cheated on him.

"I'm only telling you this because I don't want you to think the breakup is all about you. Riley's going through a lot right now, and she's not handling it well at all."

Dylan's demeanor shifts, seemingly for the better—not a lot, but a degree, maybe two. I'm encouraged.

"She's struggling, but I can promise you—and I know this, because I've been part of her struggle—that she's much, much better now because she's not keeping it all to herself anymore. I really think you should do the same and tell me what's *really* going on."

Dylan rises from his bed and goes to his closet. He comes out holding a gorgeous necklace with a big green pendant dangling from a silver chain. I'm thinking it's something he bought for Riley—an emerald, of all things—but never gave to her. "I took this from my mom," he says, handing me the necklace.

I'm confused. "What? Why would you do that?"

"Because I need to pawn it," he says. "I need money, and fast."

"What for?"

Dylan lets out a heavy sigh. "I'm being blackmailed."

"Blackmailed?" My eyes go wide. "For what?"

"Something I did," Dylan says. "Something I wouldn't want any-body to see."

"What is it?"

"Doesn't matter," he snaps. "I'm not interested in talking about it. It's something bad, *really* bad, something I wouldn't want anyone to know about, and that's why I need money—fast."

"Is that why you took the pills? Because of this blackmailer?"

"It was stupid and impulsive," he admits. "I grabbed them from Riley's purse at Teagan's party. I was drunk and feeling sorry for my-self. I just—I don't know, it just seemed like the only solution."

I get the sense that's not all there is to the story, that Dylan's hold-ing back, something big. But I'm not going to press my luck.

"Suicide is never the answer," I say, bold enough to take his hand. "It's a permanent solution to a temporary problem. You have to believe me. We love you, and we'd all be so devastated to lose you." He shouldn't need to see my tears to believe me, but out they come regardless.

"I'm not going to try again, if that's your worry. I'm done with that—I promise."

"Dylan," I say, "when you took the pills, did you also take Riley's phone? She can't find it. She's got a new phone now, but she'd like her old one back."

He nods. I get that hint again of something more.

"Yeah, I took it, but I don't know where it is," Dylan grumbles. "I was pretty high, so who knows. Maybe I tossed it into the woods. Can't say. But I don't have it anymore. You can tell her that for sure."

"Okay, okay." I give him what I think is a tender smile. "What are you going to do about the necklace?"

"I need to sell it. I feel horrible about it, but what else am I going to do? I have to pay up—or else."

I go quiet. Soon an idea comes to me. Will I ever learn? But I blurt it out anyway.

"Hold on to that necklace," I tell him. "Don't sell it. We can make up a story about finding it later after we fix your problem."

"The blackmailer?" Dylan asks. "How can you fix that?"

I smile at him, give his hand a squeeze. "I know someone who can figure out who's behind it," I say, thinking of Jay and his scorpion tattoo. "He's great with computers, and badass enough to make whoever it is stop, and stop for good."

Chapter 36

Lettie volunteered to do the dinner dishes that evening, but Alex gave her a pass as a reward for yet another college acceptance, this time into the honors program at UMass Amherst. She seemed quiet all evening, as if something was on her mind. Alex asked what was wrong but got the brush-off.

The only topic Lettie broached at the table was college. "I get an air conditioner in my room if I go to UMass," she said without much enthusiasm. Her plate of enchiladas that Nick had made, normally a favorite, had gone mostly untouched.

"And a state school means more money in your 529 account for graduate school," Nick added.

"I guess that means you won't pay if I do get into USC?" said Lettie.

"I'm just trying to teach you the value of a dollar," Nick said. "We both know a BA in environmental sciences from either school holds essentially the same weight, but one is half the cost."

"Sorry I'm not worth it to you," Lettie said under her breath.

Alex topped off her wine.

Nick looked stricken. "Honey, that's not what I mean," he said. "The courses are basically the same, is all. And you got six thousand dollars a year in scholarship funds for being in the honors program. That's amazing and awesome."

"Awesome because it's less money for you to pay even if it's not where I want to go." Lettie carried her plate to the kitchen, with Zoe trotting behind her as if in solidarity. She went upstairs to do her homework, leaving Alex to load the dishwasher while Nick finished clearing the table.

"Why do you have to make such a big deal out of money for college?" Alex asked. She closed the door to the dishwasher with force. "I'd understand if we didn't have it, but we do. You're kind of being a Scrooge."

Nick looked hurt. "I cooked a nice dinner, and you're calling me a Scrooge?"

"I already thanked you for dinner, and what does that have to do with the college argument anyway? She's leaving, Nick. Let's not add emotional distance to the distance we're already going to have. Can't we just support her and allow her to choose where she wants to go?" Alex finished that thought, then finished her wine.

"It's not that I don't want to help her out," Nick said. "It just isn't worth it."

Alex looked away in annoyance. "I think potentially saving your relationship with your daughter is worth a lot. Maybe instead of issuing mandates, why don't you try connecting with her? You tell her to see your point of view. Why wouldn't you try to see hers? Talk to her about this environmental science program. Find out why she thinks USC is better. Start acting like you care about things that matter to her before she's gone. You don't get this time back, Nick."

There. That put him in his place. Alex was feeling quite pleased with herself. And she wasn't wrong. Time wasn't something to take lightly. The end was fast approaching. Valentine's Day had come and gone, here they were already in March. The school year would be wrapping up in no time, and life felt like it was moving in fast-forward.

"I won't change my mind about teaching her the value of a dollar, but you make a good point," Nick admitted. "You're right—I need to connect with her more. I'll come up with something."

Alex took this as a small victory. "Thank you," she said. "I really wasn't up for an argument."

They resumed their seats at the table. Alex topped off her wine and offered some to her husband, who shook his head.

"Early day tomorrow—none for me. You should think about that, too," he said, eyeing her glass with concern. "I thought after Christmas you were cutting back?"

"First of all, I have cut back," Alex said.

"What, from two bottles to one?" Nick asked.

Alex wasn't amused. "Very funny. I'm just unwinding a bit. Work's been a lot recently, and I've been worried about everybody . . . Lettie, Emily, even Mandy Kumar. I know you think it's nothing, but I've been concerned about her more and more as time goes on."

"Do you still think Mandy and Ken have something going on?" asked Nick.

"It's certainly possible," said Alex. "And I don't think you're taking the red flags with Samir seriously enough."

Nick looked slightly disapproving. "Please don't take this the wrong way, honey," he said, "but you've talked about this before—with me, and I assume with Emily and maybe Brooke as well. But have you talked to the most obvious person? Have you reached out to Mandy?" He gestured toward the direction of her house. "Tried to be a friend? Maybe everything is just fine, and it's not what you think. Or maybe instead of accusations and innuendo, you can give her some support. It's a lot more helpful than gossiping about your neighbors."

The word *gossip* struck Alex like a punch. She wasn't that person. She *solved problems,* that was her job. She didn't add to them.

Alex sat up straighter. "You know, I think you're right," she said. "I've let Samir intimidate me. I'll just be more up-front with him. In fact, I saw Mandy coming home not long ago. I'll head over now—pay a surprise neighborly visit."

It might have been the wine emboldening her, but Alex stood with confidence, prepared to offer a helping hand—or if need be, confront the new neighbors. However it played out, she was ready. "Thanks, hon." She gave Nick a quick kiss on the cheek.

"Um, this isn't exactly what I had in mind," Nick said. "You're being a little impulsive, don't you think?"

"Carpe diem!" Alex called as she left the house with a purposeful stride.

Whatever bravado she'd carried across the street left her the moment

Samir answered the door. He was dapper as always, nary a crease in his khakis. His mouth attempted a smile.

"Alex, what brings you here?" he asked. His affect was as flat as his expression. There was no warmth in his voice. No cheery welcome. He seemed to be channeling the evening's cold March wind.

"I was hoping to speak with Mandy," said Alex. She wished her voice wasn't shaky, but no luck there.

"Well," said Samir, "she's not at home."

Alex could feel herself sobering up quickly. "That's odd." She peeked over Samir's shoulder into the empty hallway beyond. "I saw her come home not that long ago."

Samir leaned forward.

Alex wrapped her arms around her body, as if that might shield her from his intense stare.

"Are you asking to come inside, search about, see if I'm lying?"

"No . . ."

"Because I assure you, you won't find her here," he continued. "And I'm not sure I appreciate the insinuation."

"What insinu—"

"Let's not go there, shall we?" Samir interrupted. "We both know what this is *really* about, Alex."

Her nerves jangled. "We do?"

"Why did you follow me to the supermarket that day?" he asked.

"Me? Follow you? No, I was just—driving—to the market . . ." Alex placed a hand against her chest, her heart pumping on overdrive. She hoped Samir couldn't tell that her whole body was trembling.

"Down streets that took you in the opposite direction of the market?"

"I—I—" *I have no good answer,* Alex realized.

"Let me be clear about something," Samir said. "We like our privacy. We *cherish* it, in fact. Friendsgiving was a favor to Mandy, but it wasn't meant to be an open invitation to pry into our lives." His finger stabbed the air, too close to Alex's face for her liking. "Now, I would very much appreciate it if you would respect my wishes. It's fine to be neighborly, but we don't need friends."

That last word came out with notable hostility. Though shaken, she pressed on. She thought of Brooke—her secret life with Jerry, the hidden suffering she had endured at her husband's hand. Her radar was pinging too loudly for her to slink away. She wouldn't be able to live with herself.

"It was you who sent me that note attached to Zoe's collar, wasn't it?" she said scornfully. "You did it to send me a warning." She watched his eyes, looking for the tell.

Wide open, unblinking, they remained veiled. "Have a good night, Alex," Samir said roughly before closing the door firmly in her face.

Chapter 37

Alex slunk home as if she'd just lost the big game. She felt Samir's presence like a weight she had to carry with her. In the safety of her kitchen at last, she found Nick pouring a cup of coffee. Alex poured herself some wine.

"How did that go?" he asked with a half-cocked grin.

"Not well," said Alex. She replayed the conversation for his benefit.

"Wow," said Nick with mock surprise, "I can't believe that after you accused him of nefarious behavior, he was rude to you. Shocking!"

"Well, you suggested it," Alex said. The wine went down like apple juice.

Nick scoffed. "I suggested that you try to be *friendly* with Mandy," he said. "Be supportive, not accuse her husband of harming his wife and threatening you. How did you expect him to react? Jesus, Alex. I'm worried the wine has pickled your brain."

"What's that supposed to mean?" Alex's body vibrated with anger.

"It's means exactly what I said," Nick snapped, looking not at her but at the half-empty wine bottle on the counter. "Glug, glug, glug, every night. You're not thinking clearly. Hell, you're not *thinking* at all. Honestly, I'm surprised you still have a business to run."

Alex made a scornful sound. "My business is actually growing— I'm even considering hiring an assistant. The house is running smooth as always, Lettie is doing well . . . I'm doing a fine job with pretty much everything, better than fine in fact, so I don't really appreciate your commentary here."

Before Nick could offer his retort—and it was clear from his contemptuous look that one was coming—Lettie burst into the kitchen, clearly alarmed by something. She thrust her cell phone at Alex, who instinctively took it as if it were a baton in a relay race.

"It's Riley," Lettie said. "Something is going on at her house. She wants to talk to you, but didn't have your number."

Alex put Lettie's cell phone to her ear. "Riley," said Alex in the tone of a concerned mother, "what's going on?"

"I need you to come over to our house right away," Riley said, her voice pressured. "I think my mother is going to kill my father."

Alex bolted for the door. Lettie started to follow, but Alex stopped her. "There's trouble at the Thompsons'. You stay here. Call 911. Dad and I will go."

Riley was standing in the open doorway to her house as Alex raced up the walkway, with Nick close behind.

"What's going on? Are you okay?" Alex asked at the door. From down the hall, she heard a loud crash, glass shattering, and then another crash, more glass, an explosion followed by a scream.

"Get out! Get out of this house right now, you psycho!" That was Willow.

Evan responded in an equally loud voice. "Whose name is on the deed? Why don't *you* leave?"

"Because I'm not leaving my daughter alone with you, you sick asshole!" Willow bellowed.

Another loud crash followed.

"Okay," Alex said, taking a deep breath. *You do mediation,* she told herself, *not violent ones—but just be professional and calm this situation down.* "Riley, you stay here. Let me try to defuse this."

She headed for the kitchen, where she found Willow standing with her arm cocked, a sturdy drinking glass clutched in her hand.

In the opposite corner, Evan cowered. His black shirt was opened wide, as if he were a cover model for a romance novel—except it looked like someone had ripped the buttons off, probably the same someone holding the drinking glass. Near Evan's feet lay the remnants of other glasses Willow had likely thrown in a rage.

"Oh shit," said Nick, who'd come up behind Alex.

"You disgust me!" Willow shouted before throwing the glass at Evan like a pitcher trying to deliver a strike. Fortunately, her effort lacked in execution. The glass shattered nowhere near her intended target.

Evan spun toward Alex. "Will you make her stop?" His wide eyes pleaded for mercy.

Willow was rearming herself from the dishwasher. By the looks of it, she had a lot of ammo. She had pinned Evan into a corner. And she had just reloaded with a fancy whisky tumbler.

"Willow, don't," Alex said. "This isn't the right way. Especially not with Riley in the house. Think of her. Please—just tell me what's going on!"

"*Tell* you? How about I *show* you?" Willow said. "I was doing laundry and saw a leak in the basement, so I called a plumber. I thought it was coming from the darkroom, and Evan of course was out of town in New York, taking drugs and being a shit. The plumber found the leak, all right—coming from an old copper pipe in a room hidden *behind* the darkroom that I never go into. Anyway, I left that door open. Go see for yourself."

Red and blue lights flashed outside. The police had arrived.

"Nick, go talk to the police," Alex said. "Make sure they know things are settling down."

Willow put the tumbler back in the dishwasher. "I like this glass too much to waste it on you," she said.

Alex felt Evan was safe enough now that the police were on the scene. She left the kitchen for the basement, passing Riley on her way downstairs.

"You stay here, Riley," Alex said. "Everything is all right, but I have to go check something out."

The odor of chemicals sharpened as she neared Evan's darkroom—which wasn't dark at all, as the overhead lights had been left on. Evan, a fan of traditional film, had developed and framed many of the photographs hanging in the Thompsons' home. But Alex's interest wasn't in his darkroom supplies or in Evan's photography chops, but rather in the hidden space Willow had told her about, the one accessible through an open door at the back of the darkroom. Alex could see the door would be somewhat camouflaged when closed, blending in perfectly with the smooth white walls. Evan's secret lair.

Someone—probably Willow—had left a light on in the hidden room as well. Alex gawked, blinked, and shook her head in disbelief.

Covering the walls were pictures of Brooke Bailey, and *only* Brooke Bailey, in various levels of undress. In some she wore lacy, revealing underwear. In others she had on a camisole as sheer as cellophane. Everywhere Alex looked, she saw more pictures of her sexy neighbor, who seemed to stare back at her with a provocative, almost challenging expression. Alex could understand Evan's attraction to this strong and striking woman, but this was a display of pathological obsession.

The pictures were disturbing in their own right, simply for the sheer number of them, but other images turned Alex's blood cold. In addition to the professional photos on display, a collection of snapshots cluttered a small wooden desk to Alex's right. It was a collage of images taken from outside Brooke's home, the photographer obviously peering into Brooke's inner sanctum—the bedroom, the living room, and even the kitchen where Alex had stood when that alarming text message arrived.

She turned away, closing the darkroom door behind her, and headed upstairs. She wished she could forget what she had seen. At the top of the stairs, she nearly ran into Officer O'Brien, whom she recognized from the hospital. "Are you okay, ma'am?" he asked.

From down the hall, Alex could hear Willow and Evan pleading their respective cases to the police in the kitchen.

"I'm fine," said Alex. "Sort of. But I guess you should know that we've just discovered the identity of the Alton Road stalker."

Meadowbrook Online Community Page

Regina Arthur

Evan Thompson. Anyone . . . anyone?

> **Reply from Laura Ballwell**
> I don't think we should speculate, spread rumors, or make disparaging remarks about anybody, especially on a public forum.
>
> **Reply from Tom Beck**
> What else are we supposed to do here? Be nice?

Susanne Horton

Weren't Evan and Willow Thompson always fighting?

> **Reply from Regina Arthur**
> Like cats and dogs! But I was thinking more about his obsession with Brooke Bailey.

Henry St. John

I just checked Brooke Bailey's OnlyFans page. It's still active.

> **Reply from Ed Callahan**
> Oh yeah, do you pay for access, **Henry St. John**? Is she in your favorites?

Susanne Horton

Does anyone remember what Brooke did to her husband Jerry?

> **Reply from Christine Doddy**
> Or "didn't" do. She wasn't charged.
>
> **Reply from Susanne Horton**
> OK, does anyone remember what Brooke got away with doing? Wondering if she took care of the Alton Road stalker herself.

Regina Arthur

My bet is Evan killed Brooke, not the other way around.

Reply from Tom Beck

So now we're betting on who killed who? Way to keep it classy, Meadowbrook!

Susanne Horton

Willow and Evan didn't exactly have a great marriage. Can you say restraining order? And don't forget—it's always the husband.

Reply from Katherine Leavitt

This isn't a Dateline episode, **Susanne Horton**. These are our neighbors and friends!

Reply from Susanne Horton

Friends? The Altonites? Speak for yourself.

Reply from Katherine Leavitt

Nice. Way to be a good Christian.

Reply from Susanne Horton

Who said I'm Christian?

Janet Pinkham

That reminds me, the Congregational Church of Meadowbrook is having our annual bake sale next Saturday.

Reply from Ed Callahan

I'm wondering what they put in your brownies, **Janet Pinkham.**

Susanne Horton

Riley Thompson broke up with Dylan Adair. Young love can be obsessive, and that can be dangerous.

Reply from Joseani Wilkins

Now we're involving high school students? What is wrong with you people?

Reply from Ross Weinbrenner

You people?? You sound like an Altonite!

Christine Doddy

I still say it's the Bug Man. He's crazy! And if he's got some vendetta against Ken Adair for getting him fired—look out!

Reply from Susanne Horton

I've heard Ken's got a thing for Mandy Kumar. Won't

reveal my source, but angry lovers and spouses have motive for murder.

Laura Ballwell

Speaking of the Kumars, the husband has been to a few town meetings, and let's just say, it's his way or the highway.

Reply from Christine Doddy

Agreed! I saw him grocery shopping with his wife. He was holding her arm like it was a horse's rein. I work with abused women, and that was a red flag.

Reply from Ross Weinbrenner

And I think their son Jay is a drug dealer. Could have been a deal gone bad?

Reply from Joseani Wilkins

Talk about opening yourselves up to slander! Wow! I think we're spreading enough rumors as it is, people.

Reply from Regina Arthur

Rumors always have some truth to them—Brooke and Evan, Mandy and Ken, Samir, Jay, Riley, Dylan, the Bug Man—it sounds to me like any one of them could be the victim or the killer.

SPRING

Chapter 38

Alex was home, enjoying a little white wine with her lunch salad. With Nick at work and Lettie at school, she took advantage of a lighter calendar to enjoy the quiet pleasures of home. Her only obligation that day was a two o'clock interview for an office assistant, a position she needed to fill now that her business was going gangbusters. She'd been preparing for an upcoming mediation session, but stopped to review the candidate's résumé.

The back door off the kitchen opened, interrupting her concentration. In stepped Emily, true to form—unplanned and unannounced. "Got a minute to talk?" she asked, plunking herself onto a kitchen chair. Zoe emerged from beneath the table for a bark/tail wag before returning to her hiding spot.

"For you, I've got all the time in the world," said Alex.

Emily eyed the stack of papers in front of Alex. "This looks like my kitchen," she said. "I had to get away from work before my head exploded."

"And to think we women fought so long and hard for the right to make our lives miserable."

The sisters shared a laugh.

"Mind if I join you for a drink?" asked Emily. "Ken's home. We're still not comfortable leaving Dylan alone."

"I'd feel the exact same way if it were Lettie, but happy you found some time to visit."

Alex took the opportunity to refill her glass after pouring one for Emily from a bottle she'd picked up at Costco. Wine was probably an item she shouldn't be buying in bulk, but after Nick called out her drinking, Alex decided she was done hiding it. Now that everything was out in the open, maybe he would see that all was fine and he was overreacting.

Emily cleared space at the table.

"How are the plans coming for the addition?" asked Alex. "I'm worried about Mom. Have you noticed how her balance is getting worse? She's leaning on things for support. I'm worried she's becoming a fall risk."

"The plans are fine," said Emily. "They're done, in fact. And we got the committee approvals we need. If schedules hold, the contractors should break ground this summer." She took a drink and glanced out the window, her face turning sad. "It's my marriage that's the question."

Alex sighed. "I'm sorry, Em," she said. "Tell me everything. What's going on now?"

Emily inhaled a good portion of her wine. "The money is back in our account."

Alex looked surprised. "When?" she asked.

"Two weeks ago," Emily said. "I didn't notice it until today when I checked our statements."

"What's that all about?" asked Alex.

"Beats me," said Emily.

"What did Ken say?"

"He told me the IRS made a mistake."

Alex nearly spit out her wine. "The IRS doesn't make mistakes," she said. "Or if they do, they don't admit it that quickly."

"I said the same thing, or basically that."

"And?"

"And nothing. Ken stuck to his story."

"Do you want to ask him for paperwork?"

"And have him freak out on me? Accuse me of not trusting him again? We have enough problems at home as it is. No thank you."

Alex didn't disagree. "What do you want to do?"

"I think I want to use some of the twenty-five grand to hire that

PI, that's what," Emily said. "There's something up with Ken, but I don't know if it's related to Mandy Kumar."

"I suppose anything is possible," said Alex. "Did you ever think Evan Thompson would be a creepy stalker?"

"No, never," said Emily. "He's always seemed obsessive about his work, but I didn't think that extended to women. Why do you think Brooke protected him?"

Alex thought of Evan's character—despite his flaws, he was always endearing. It troubled her that she could still care for him when he was so clearly deranged. And he was dangerous, too. Willow had confirmed it was his handwriting on the note threatening Alex.

Back off or you'll regret it.

"I guess when it comes down to it, we want to believe people are better than they are," Alex said. "We cling to our hope for redemption—for change, growth, that sort of thing. I imagine Brooke had some of those thoughts about Evan.

"She must have known all along who was watching her. Otherwise she'd have been more cautious. Probably she felt stuck. If she outed him, he would have been humiliated, maybe escalated things . . . Maybe it would have ended his career, damaged Willow and Riley in the process. Since she couldn't make him stop and didn't think he'd hurt her, I suppose she hoped he'd get bored and outgrow his obsession."

"From what you told me about that Brooke shrine, there's no outgrowing that," Emily said. "How's Willow handling it all?"

"She kicked him out of the house. He went willingly—I think the shame humbled him—and she's filed for divorce. Finally," Alex said. "Evan's living in an apartment about ten minutes from here. I'm helping her with the divorce."

"That creepy shrine to Brooke would seal the deal for me, too," said Emily. "Let's toast—to Willow and to having the courage to move on." She raised her glass. "Speaking of moving on, I saw Lettie drive off with Jay Kumar."

Alex looked moderately pained. "Yeah, they're spending time together again."

"Because of Dylan?" Emily asked.

"Perhaps," said Alex, less than pleased. "Trauma bonding isn't exactly the gateway to a healthy relationship, but it seems the experience brought them closer together."

"Are you talking to Lettie?" Emily raised an eyebrow.

"What about?" asked Alex.

"Oh, I dunno," Emily said. "Condoms, IUDs, the pill—your not becoming a grandmother, maybe your daughter not getting an STD. That."

"Jeez louise," Alex said. "How about a warm-up question next time?" Her laugh was slightly nervous.

Emily wasn't smiling. "I'm serious," she said. "Lettie is almost eighteen. Have you ever talked to her about these things? I mean, *really* talked?"

Back came the guilt, along with memories of that dinner conversation with Nick before all hell broke loose at Willow's place. No, she hadn't talked to Lettie. She hadn't brought up birth control, Jay Kumar, or Dylan. She hadn't made any meaningful inquiries into her daughter's hopes, dreams, or fears for the future.

Of course they *talked*, but about things, not feelings. Things that had to get done in preparation for next year, not major life decisions. In a way, it was like living in that busy period after a death, when grief could be pushed aside for a long list of distractions.

Alex realized she was holding on to an illusion. Lettie was leaving. She was growing up—no, she *was* grown up. Almost an adult, nearly eighteen. Alex had to get ready to let her go.

She promised—first herself, then Emily—that she'd have a *long* talk with Lettie when she got home.

But for now, more wine. She and Emily kept talking until Alex's phone rang.

"I'm here, but the office is locked?"

The words confused Alex. Who was this? What was she talking about? Wine swam in her brain, fogging all coherent thought. Then, like the clouds parting, the buzz vanished and her memory returned.

This was her two o'clock interview. She checked her watch. It was 2:05. How long had she been chatting with her sister?

The apologies poured out in a rush. "Oh my god, I am *so* sorry. I was working on another project and lost track of the time." The lie came out without effort. "I'll be there in twenty minutes. Can you wait? There's a coffee shop right across the street. It's on me, of course." She had never hired someone out of guilt before, but there was a good chance this woman would get the job.

Flustered, Alex rose to her feet, a sick feeling in her stomach as she fumbled through her purse for the key fob. "I gotta run," she told Emily. "I screwed up an interview. Shit."

Out the door Alex went with a huff of air, blaming work stress for her absent-mindedness. She got into her car. Turned on the engine. Craned her neck to look behind her as she reversed.

She drove a quarter mile before taking a right onto Chester Street, which was the same route Samir Kumar took to the supermarket the day she had followed him. Nearing an intersection, Alex noticed bright lights in her rearview mirror. Her jaw clenched before her stomach dropped.

An instant later, her heart leapt to her throat. It was the police! The patrol car was directly behind her.

She pulled over to the side of the road. A fruity taste tickled her lips and tongue. Her head buzzed and thrummed. It wasn't work that made her forget the interview—it was wine. And now here came a police officer, strutting up to her car. His youthful appearance didn't fool her. He might have been in high school when Lettie was a freshman, for all she knew, but young or not, this individual had the power to upend her life.

Alex's mind raced ahead, glimpsing a dark future: herself in handcuffs, her mug shot posted to the Meadowbrook community page, her business imploding, friends turning their backs on her, a reputation in ruins.

As the vision faded, she took ever-deepening breaths, though she still wasn't getting enough oxygen to her brain. Fear flooded her. Her heart pounded as if it might break out of her chest. A thought came and went: a heart attack might save her from a field sobriety test. How much had she drunk? Two glasses, right? No. No. And no. She knew better. She damn well knew better—about everything, about it all.

Down rolled her window. She turned her head ever so slightly, enough to not seem evasive while shielding the policeman from her eyes—and breath.

"License and registration, ma'am." His voice was only a few years removed from puberty. Still, the words rattled her.

She fumbled with trembling hands for her ID and car registration. He took them back to his patrol car.

Alex felt certain he was calling for backup. That sick feeling settled in her stomach. *I did this to myself,* she thought. She clutched the steering wheel tightly, the sweat of her palms making it slick.

How will Lettie take it? What about Nick?

Her marriage felt shaky as it was. Could this be a tipping point? Down she went, falling into the abyss of fear, until the officer returned.

He handed back her paperwork. "You're due for an inspection."

Alex's expression of surprise was authentic. "Oh, I'm sorry. I didn't realize."

"I could issue you a forty-dollar citation," he said.

Have me blow into a tube and you'd issue me a lot more than that, Alex thought.

"But I'm going to let this go. I put a note in the system. You've got ten days now to get your vehicle inspected, okay? Otherwise, next time, it's a citation and that could impact your insurance."

"Yes, Officer," Alex said. "Thank you."

Off he went, back to his car.

Alex drove away slowly, her eyes shifting constantly from the road to her speedometer. She made it to the next street before finding a safe spot to pull over.

Enough, enough, enough, rattled a voice in her head. She called Nick.

"Hey, hon," he said. "What's up?"

Alex's hitched breathing could barely get out the words. "I need—I need you to come pick me up—right now," she said, her voice cracking. "I think—" She couldn't get out the words; sorrow blocked her lungs. Finally, courage found her. "I think I have a drinking problem."

Chapter 39

Lettie

It's April 20, which means I'm now eighteen years old. I don't feel like an adult, even though the law has deemed me one. I can legally vote, join the military, work full time, get a tattoo, and adopt a child. I've settled on doing only one of those things, at least come November.

Jay buys a scone at the local Starbucks, where we've met up to go over his progress tracking down Dylan's blackmailer. He places it in front of me. He's a croissant guy (still surprised by that), and me, I'm all about the scone. When he reaches into his pocket, I'm sure he's going for his vape pen. To my surprise, he takes out a small candle. He spears the end of it into the scone.

"Happy birthday, Lettie," he says. He's got a lighter on him, and just like that, the candle flame is flickering, enticing me to blow it out. "Make a wish."

I pause, then say, "I wish my parents would pay for me to take a gap year to travel."

With a huff, out goes the flame.

"I think if you tell me your wish, it won't come true," Jay says.

"Shit. Good point. Do-over?"

"I only brought one candle," he says.

I shrug it off.

"Where would you go, anyway?"

"Maybe Taiwan," I say. "Feels like a safe place to experience geopolitical turmoil without putting myself in too much danger."

"Solid," Jay says.

"Then I'd go over to Australia, learn to scuba dive, see the Great Barrier Reef before climate change bleaches it out of existence."

"Cheers to multinational corporations and uncaring, myopic, self-serving politicians." Jay raises his drink in a toast. We tap paper cups.

"Hopefully, you'll become a leading environmental scientist and help lead the charge to a brighter future. Speaking of, any word from USC?"

"Nope. Still waiting," I say. "Doesn't matter anyway. My father won't let me go."

"You're eighteen, Lettie. Your father doesn't control your life anymore."

"Yeah, sure," I say. "But I don't want to be saddled with hundreds of thousands in loans to pay back. And he won't pay if he thinks it's a waste of money."

"He has the money and he won't give it to his daughter?" Jay sounds appalled.

"Something like that," I say, though it's *exactly* like that.

Jay shakes his head. "Your father may be more rigid and unyielding than mine."

"What would you suggest I do? It's not like I can write a check for that kind of money, and the loans will crush me."

Jay leans in close. All the familiar triggers are still there—his swarthy good looks, that distinctive cologne (or maybe it's his natural smell, can't say for sure). His to-die-for smile sends a shiver through my body.

"Lettie," he says in a low voice, "how are you going to save the world if you can't stand up for yourself?"

I pull back because I don't like how close he is to the truth. "You don't know my dad," I tell him. "He doesn't give in when his mind is made up."

Jay offers a crooked smile—a devious look if ever there was one. "Everyone has a weakness you can exploit," he says. "*Everyone.*"

My mouth slips into a frown. "Jay, you worry me sometimes." Then I think: *What is my father's weakness?* Next thought: *What's mine?*

It might be Jay.

"Don't be so quick to judge," he says. "You've been on a revenge kick for as long as I've known you. Isn't that all about exploiting weaknesses?"

"Touché," I say. "But I did have *some* encouragement."

"Hey, did you ever get a grade on your revenge paper?" Jay asks.

"Yeah, just got it back," I tell him. "I got an A."

Jay claps.

"I changed my original premise from the biological and sociological benefits of revenge to a psychological analysis of the harm it causes. Basically, I just wrote my own story—names changed to protect the innocent—and then backed it up with quotes from pretty much every psychological study I found, all of which supported that claim. My teacher particularly liked my conclusion."

"Which is?" Jay leans forward on his elbows, his eyes probing mine, keenly interested.

"Revenge might seem like a good idea," I say, "but everyone gets hurt in the end."

Jay's eyes spark up, like he gets off on human misery. Meanwhile, I still get a sick feeling in my stomach any time I look in the mirror.

"It's a two-edged sword. It cuts both ways," he says.

"Yeah, a lesson learned the hard way," I answer. "In the end, everyone did get hurt—everyone including me. Dylan tried to kill himself because of what *I* did. Riley's a walking disaster, still in denial about her pill-popping habit, which, by the way, may have become worse because of the stress *we've* put her under. And she's back with Umbrella Man, did I tell you that?"

"No, you didn't. But I'm not surprised," Jay says. "Older men have a certain charm that's . . . hard to resist." He winks at me and I want to die. "Speaking of Riley, did she ever find her phone? Have you searched the woods around Dylan's house?"

"Four times now," I tell him. "And no luck."

"Well, I'm sure it will turn up at some point." He sounds quite certain, and I wonder why. "And at least you got an A on your paper. That's a win."

"I've been enduring bouts of guilt and general self-loathing for months. Definitely not worth the grade—that's basically what I learned."

"Hmm," says Jay, as if to say I care too much. "Well, maybe we can still set one thing right." He gives me a smile that's almost tender. "If I can help Dylan find his blackmailer, perhaps that will make you feel a little better." He fires up his laptop, starts typing like a man possessed.

Dylan allowed Jay access to all his computer files. But he's been pushing off this investigation for a while—too busy building his mysterious billion-dollar app to give it much attention. I still don't know what the blackmailer has on my cousin, and Dylan isn't saying.

Jay runs a bunch of software programs that trace data packets. He does some other stuff that's way too techy for me to comprehend.

"Whoever it is, this guy is good," Jay says. I hear something like awe in his voice. He stares intently at his laptop screen while our lattes cool. He shows me a screen full of meaningless jargon, as if I need the visual to confirm his assessment.

"How do you know it's a he?" I ask.

Jay raises his head. "Fair point," he says. "They're good, whoever it is."

While Jay works, I look at my phone and see an alert. There's a new message in my inbox. I switch over to email, have a look, and frown.

"What's up?" Jay asks. "Everything okay?"

"Yes and no." My throat closes up, tears threatening as I stare at my phone.

"What's wrong?" He sounds genuinely concerned.

I ball up a napkin in a tight fist. "I just got into USC."

I return from Starbucks to find the kitchen festooned with colorful balloons and streamers. There's a big cake on the table, impaled by two candles representing the numbers 1 and 8. Zoe is barking up a storm, and I give her some much-appreciated attention. After an off-key rendition of "Happy Birthday," my parents and I dig into the cake (carrot, my favorite) and I notice something a bit odd.

Something's been up with my mom for weeks, but I've been brushing it off. Biggest red flag is that she's started talking to me—I mean *really* talking, *awkwardly* talking—about things like sex and birth control, making a point to tell me that I can come to her with anything, she's there for me no matter what. One day she even got a little weepy and we had to hug it out. I reassured her that I loved her and everything was good between us. I guess that didn't satisfy her, because she keeps engaging with me—asking if I want to get our nails done (um, I *never* want to get my nails done)—and she's taking a real interest in my various causes. She bought all LED light bulbs for the house and then announced a major reduction in red meat because of the environmental impact.

Tonight I notice something else. Can't believe I didn't catch on to it sooner. Mom is celebrating my big day without any wine. In fact, I can't remember the last time I saw her drinking.

I'm thinking about this while I'm pairing my birthday AirPods to my iPhone.

Mom interrupts just as I get the music to play in my ear. "Honey, can I talk to you?" she asks.

My dad is off on a walk with Zoe, and Mom and I sit down on the living room couch.

"Sure," I say. "As long as we're not going to have the birth control convo again. I'm good on that."

Mom gives me a strained smile. "No, I actually want to talk about me."

"Okay," I say, a bit uneasy. I'm thinking, no more wine means cancer. My mom has cancer. She's dying and she's about to shatter my world. Oh my god.

My mom takes a big breath, holds it a second. My heart stops. I'm not ready for this. Whatever it is, I'll never be ready.

"I want to tell you that I have a drinking problem, so I've decided to stop drinking and seek professional help."

Phew, not cancer, and not exactly breaking news, but I'm relieved to hear her admit it and to know she'll get some help. "Okay," I say.

"Now, you may have questions—and I know you've brought up my drinking before."

"I don't have questions," I say quickly.

"Well, you may," Mom says in a way that implies I should come up with a question.

"Umm," I say. "Okay . . . what now?" There. That's a good one.

"Now I'm seeing a therapist," Mom says.

"What about AA? Isn't that how people quit?"

"Not always. I haven't had a drink for a month now. It's been going pretty well, better than I thought. I'm not saying it's been easy or without temptation, but I'm doing okay. And I'm sorry for keeping this from you, but I didn't want to tell you what was going on until I felt that I had a handle on it . . . though it's not something you ever just get a handle on. And yes, I'll go to AA if I need more support. Regardless, it's a daily commitment, and I have to be mindful. I have to look at the reason *why* I was drinking so much."

"And what's the reason?"

I admit, now I'm curious. This is my mom, and we've never talked like this before—like friends, two people connecting outside the roles of mother and daughter.

Mom lets out a heavy sigh, tosses her head back in dramatic fashion. "I don't know exactly," she says. "Stress, I guess. Not to make excuses, but it just became too easy to relax with wine. Whether it was pressure at work or worrying about family, I started using wine as a crutch. When you start drinking to cope with life, that's definitely when it's a problem. I'm working on that now.

"Mandy Kumar referred me to a psychologist she knows, so I have a therapist who's helping. Like I said, I may try AA, but I'm not quite sure if it's for me. I'll take this one step at a time."

"I'm proud of you, Mom," I manage to say, choking a bit on the words.

She gives me a hug, and then gets teary and, well, maybe I do, too—just a little.

After our embrace, I feel a heaviness of my own. Mom dropping that big old truth bomb shook me to my core. Her openness and honesty make my deceptions feel a whole lot worse. Some secrets are so heavy, they can bring you to your knees. I guess I'm done carrying this weight alone.

"Since we're doing the heart-to-heart thing," I begin, "there's something I should probably tell you."

Mom looks alarmed.

"Oh, Jesus, no, not that," I say. "I'm not pregnant."

She relaxes immediately.

"It's about substance abuse—well, sort of." And that's when I blurt it out—a dam bursts, unleashing a waterfall of secrets.

I tell her about my revenge plot to get back at Riley for ratting me out as the school vandal; about following Riley to some rendezvous with an older guy, and the pictures Jay and I took as evidence.

"I changed my mind after the fact," I tell Mom. "I knew if those pictures got out there, Dylan would end up being collateral damage."

"I'm guessing Dylan found out," Mom says.

I nod. "Jay sent them using an alias because he thought it would be better than Dylan being deceived."

"Maybe he was right," Mom says.

"But those pictures sent Dylan over the edge—and I feel responsible for it all."

"What do you mean . . . all?"

Now I have to tell her about Riley's pill habit, and how Dylan stole drugs from her at Teagan's New Year's party.

"I went to that party and got pretty drunk, too, trying to bond with Riley, stupidly thinking I could fix things between them."

Mom needs the whole unvarnished truth. I tell her about how I've been helping Riley track down her bio-dad, and Monique and the Wookiee, thinking Mom would be shocked. She is, but not to the extent I was expecting.

"Lettie, oh my goodness," Mom says, shaking her head. "That's a lot—a lot you've been dealing with, and a lot you've been keeping from me."

"Tell me about it—and for the record I'm not drinking, not seeking revenge, and I'm not taking drugs. But Riley's still using, and she's still seeing that older guy, too, and not dealing with her family stuff at all. At least Dylan is doing better now, and Jay and I are trying to help him out with something. But I still feel really guilty for my part in all this mess."

Mom nods slowly. "I feel like I really let you down, Lettie," she says. "I've been checked out, and maybe my drinking was keeping us from communicating better. I'm sorry you've been struggling and dealing with so much on your own—but revenge? Honey, you know better. That's never the answer."

"Are you going to say it's like a double-edged sword? Because I've heard that already."

"Well, it is," Mom says. "And I'm glad you're over and done with that. You should have talked to me instead of acting out."

The truth stings.

"And just for the record," Mom continues, "Willow told me Evan wasn't Riley's biological father, but I don't think Evan knows."

"Yeah, I'd second that assumption," I say.

"What Riley is doing is very, very dangerous," Mom adds. "We need to get her help—right away. We need to talk to Willow."

"Agreed," I say. Now *I'm* the rat, but at least I'm doing it for Riley's own good. Of course that's what Jay thought when he leaked the pictures to Dylan, and look how that turned out. I'm still hoping that finding the blackmailer will make amends.

We've both gone quiet, absorbing the magnitude of it all.

My face must betray my thoughts, because Mom asks, "Lettie, is that the whole story? You said you're helping Jay with something involving Dylan. Is there something else going on that I should know about?"

I sigh. It comes out, like I'm vomiting the words. "Dylan's being blackmailed for something he did—maybe something embarrassing that he doesn't want anybody to see. I don't know what it is, but it's something really bad, and he stole Aunt Emily's necklace to pay off the blackmailer."

"What?" Mom's mouth falls open. "Do you know if he took any money from her? Did he get into their bank account somehow?"

"No," I say. "He couldn't get any money—that's why he stole the necklace. Dylan said the blackmailer made him so afraid, it's one of the reasons he took the pills. Jay Kumar is trying to track down whoever is threatening him. Anyway, Dylan put the necklace back and he doesn't plan to take anything else. He feels too guilty about it, and there's some hope now that Jay can get him out of this mess."

"Holy shit," says Mom, who hardly ever curses. "Lettie, is this true?"

"No, Mom, I'm making it up," I say. "Of course it's true."

"We need to go talk to Aunt Emily," Mom says.

"Why?" I ask. "We can't tell her about the necklace."

"We *have* to tell her."

"Why?"

"Because Dylan is fragile and if he's being blackmailed, his mother needs to know."

Chapter 40

Alex and Lettie left the house together, with only a vague word to Nick as they passed him in the hall. Side by side, they hurried down Alton Road, getting to Emily's before the couple left for a big night out—their first time leaving Dylan home alone since New Year's Eve. Alex knew the plans because Emily had asked her to pop in and check on her nephew.

Letting herself in without knocking, Alex stepped into the foyer. A loud and unexpected voice from down the hall made her freeze in place. It was Samir Kumar, and he sounded irate.

Alex didn't linger in the entryway. She bolted down the hall, entering the kitchen to find Samir standing with his back to her. Lettie came up behind her mother, peering over her shoulder at the scene in front of them. Alex formed a physical shield between her daughter and what appeared to be a heated conflict.

A wrathful Samir faced Ken and Emily. "This is not a request," he said. "I'm telling you to stay off my property, and *especially* to stay away from my wife."

Ken and Emily were dressed for an evening out. They made a striking couple, Ken in a well-tailored suit and Emily in a stunning black dress with a plunging neckline that revealed, of all things, the green pendant necklace Dylan had stolen. The two stood still as they endured Samir's tirade. The look in Ken's eyes was sharper than daggers. Emily appeared to be fuming as well, though her hostilities were directed toward her husband.

Samir twisted at the sound of the new arrivals. His angry dark eyes bored into Alex.

Lettie backed up a step, while staying fairly close to her mother.

"I'm sorry you had to see this," said Samir. "But I have a serious issue with your brother-in-law that needs to be addressed, and *now*. I was hoping to do so in private, but it seems nobody on Alton Road minds their own business."

"What's going on?" asked Alex.

"Tell them, Ken," said Emily, her tone accusatory. "Or better yet, why don't you show my sister the video, Samir. Unlike my husband, I don't keep secrets from my family."

Samir didn't hesitate. He held his phone to Alex's eye level, which allowed Lettie a view as well.

"I've installed cameras around my property, and they captured this," he said.

Security cameras were not uncommon in Meadowbrook. Even Ken had installed a doorbell camera after Bug Man "allegedly" shattered that window on Christmas Eve.

The grainy footage from Samir's camera, recorded after dark from a high vantage point, showed Mandy Kumar on her back deck, standing intimately close to Ken. They were clearly having an animated conversation, but Alex couldn't make out any facial expressions. When Mandy made a gesture, as if pointing to the camera, she and Ken moved out of view. Alex couldn't tell if they went into the house or simply relocated to a spot where they couldn't be recorded.

When Ken reappeared in the frame, he was without Mandy. Moments later, he descended the stairs to the lawn and hurried away from the house, heading for the same wooded path Alex had seen him take before.

"When was this taken?" Alex asked.

"Last night," said Samir, still seething. "The time stamp showed eight-thirty in the evening. Conveniently during the hour or so when I left the house to go to the grocery store."

Ken stepped forward, looking more annoyed than embarrassed. "I don't see what the big deal is," he said. "There's nothing wrong with paying a friendly visit to a neighbor."

"The sexy neighbor I've been suspicious about for a year now, and you don't tell me about your little visit?" said Emily. "There's plenty wrong with that."

Ken's expression, one of protest, discounted Emily's accusations entirely. "I told you both it was harmless. I went there to talk to her about Dylan. She's a mental health professional, and I wanted her opinion. Sorry I was so concerned about our son."

"I don't see why that conversation has to take place after dark in the back of my home," Samir said. "And I'm a mental health professional as well. Why not talk to us both? But now, regardless of your needs and intentions, I want you to stay away from my wife. Is that understood?"

"Whatever, dude." Ken sounded like he didn't care. "I don't want anything to do with your wife. She can't help my screwed-up kid, anyway."

"Who are you calling screwed up?"

The wounded voice came from the hallway behind Alex. Dylan pushed past her and Lettie into the kitchen. "Well, Dad?" he asked, getting right in Ken's face. "Who's screwed up? Are you talking about me—or Logan?"

Samir locked eyes ever so briefly with Alex. His anger was gone. In its place, she saw compassion, as if Dylan's hurt had shifted everyone's focus.

"Don't answer," Dylan snarled at his father. "I mean, Logan is the all-American lacrosse player. He's a top guy in the whole ACC, right? How could someone like that be screwed up? So I guess that leaves . . . me." He pointed to himself.

"Dylan, I didn't mean—"

"Yeah, you did," Dylan said. "You meant it. You probably wish I did it, too—don't you, Dad? You probably wish the overdose took me out of the picture. I guess I didn't even do that right."

"Hey, Dylan, don't say that. Don't ever say that." Ken looked stricken. "Let's calm down, son, okay?"

"Yeah, okay, let's. Let's calm right down." Dylan nodded vigorously in mock agreement. "Let's just forget everything, okay? Pretend we're one big happy family. Is that what you want, Dad? Make more memories to share? I mean, family shares *everything*, right, Pop?"

"Dylan," Ken said in a low voice like a warning.

Dylan gave a short, mirthless laugh. "You want to know why I'm so screwed up? Go take a look in the mirror, that's why." With that, he fled the kitchen, tears falling as he left.

Chapter 41

Lettie

'm downstairs cooking scrambled eggs from pasture-raised hens—not the cage-free kind, which I know is a marketing ploy. I'm thinking about the craziness of the night before with Samir and Ken, when Willow enters our kitchen without knocking.

I'm so tense, I jump, dropping the spatula, sending bits of egg catapulting to the floor.

"Oh my god, Willow, you totally freaked me out." And then I think: *Oh my god, Willow!* This is the moment I've been dreading since Mom invited her over to talk about Riley.

It's alarming how Willow seems to have aged years in months, but honestly, I'm not entirely surprised. Evan's antics would make anyone look older. Word from my mom is that Evan left the house willingly, and he's crashing at a friend's place in Meadowbrook. He refused to press charges against Willow for assault with numerous kitchen glasses, and Brooke refused to do the same against Evan for stalking, so Riley didn't have to watch her parents get arrested. At least some good came of it, but still, I have this horrible feeling that adulting might kind of suck.

"Do you want any eggs?" I ask Willow, using a paper towel to wipe up the mess I made.

"No thanks, hon," she says. "How's everything? School's almost done."

"I still have some tests," I say, "but they don't really matter much anymore."

"Have you made your college decision yet?"

My heart wants to announce USC, but I end up channeling my father instead. "Yeah, probably UMass," I say. "I got into the honors program. It's a way better value for the money." I nod a bunch of times, like I'm reassuring myself.

"Sounds great," Willow says, her expression brightening. "And prom? Any lucky guy? I guess Riley is going with someone on the soccer team, but I wish it were Dylan."

"Yeah, me too," I say. "And no. No, no big date plans yet." Again, my heart is in conflict. It wants to say Jay Kumar, but I never asked him and that's for the best. As far as I'm concerned, no Jay, no prom, and that's my final answer, but Willow doesn't need to know all that.

Willow's expression shifts quickly from light to serious. "Your mom told me we needed to talk, and I'm glad. I've been worried sick about Riley."

A knot forms at the base of my neck as I imagine how she's going to react to the news. Thankfully I don't have to fret long because Mom appears in the kitchen. She smiles warmly and gives Willow a hug before we get down to business.

"So what is it about Riley?" Willow asks anxiously. "What's going on? What have you heard? She's keeping to herself these days, barely talks to me. Spends most nights at Teagan's house, and I've smelled alcohol on her breath several times now.

"I know teenagers keep secrets—I sure did at her age—but I'm extra worried, because she has so much going on. I mean with Dylan, the police coming to our house, her father's . . . um, behavior and all that on top of the divorce. It's so awful." Willow buries her face in her hands. "How'd everything get this screwed up?" she asks in a muffled voice.

I want to say: *Because we were born and life seems to go awry no matter what we do.* But I don't. Instead, Mom touches Willow's arm, guiding her to a seat at the kitchen table. She leaves her side only to get her a cup of coffee and a slice of banana bread, which she plates and sets out so fast it's like a magic trick. My eggs are going cold because I'm too nervous to eat.

"I agree, Riley's got a lot to manage," Mom says. Her natural compassion is evident as she takes a seat beside Willow, clutching the coffee mug I bought her for Christmas. "Lettie," she says in her best no-nonsense voice, "you need to tell Willow what you told me."

I might have left the room if I didn't feel nailed to the spot. I thought I was the backup, not the main event.

"Um, well . . ." Clamminess washes over me, making me sick to my stomach.

Mom smiles tightly. "Do you need me to start?" she asks.

But I don't give her the chance. "Riley knows about her birth father—the Wookiee," I blurt out. "And she's been taking pills, stealing them from her dad. Dylan got the pills he overdosed with from Riley's purse when they were at Teagan's New Year's party, not from your house." I speak without taking a breath, so when I'm finished, I'm a bit winded.

Willow looks winded, too, but it's more like she's been blown away. Eventually she blinks, so at least there's proof of life. "I'm sorry—you, she, what?" It's evident she can't quite grasp it all.

"She took a home DNA test," I say.

"Oh, shit," says Willow. "I knew she was interested in her ancestry, but I thought it was a phase and she'd forget about it."

"She took the test and got the results without telling you." My heart is doing a high-octane tap dance. "When she saw her Polish heritage and saw a list of paternal relatives she'd never heard of, that's when she knew Evan wasn't her father . . . or her biological father, I mean, because Evan is her dad—I mean he raised her, but I know he's been dealing with a lot, too, I mean you've both been dealing with a lot, and—"

A voice inside my head is screaming at me to shut up, so it's no wonder my words come out totally confused. Thankfully, Mom touches my leg, which won't stop bouncing, and that's enough to close my mouth.

"There's a lot to unpack here, Willow," Mom says sadly. "But I'm most worried about the drug use. I think Riley needs an intervention, and this revelation about her biological father is likely making her extra vulnerable."

Willow's the one who looks extra vulnerable to me. I don't know what to say, or how to help, so I sit quietly, hoping I've become invisible.

"Lettie, what do you know about this?" Willow asks. "I need you to tell me everything."

So much for being invisible. I let out a big sigh and look to my mom, who gives me a nod of encouragement.

"I just said I'd help her find her bio-dad," I begin. "I told her that she needed to take more DNA tests to increase the likelihood of finding a close relative."

"And you found one?" Willow guesses.

"A woman named Monique LaSalle who lives in Revere," I say. If the name means anything to Willow, it doesn't register on her face. "She told us about Steven Wachowski, and even gave us a copy of his CD."

"Oh my god—he's the Wookiee, all right," Willow says in a long exhale. Her expression goes blank, as if she's vanished into a memory.

"I think Riley was already taking drugs before she did the DNA test, but I'm sure the results are compounding her problems," I say. "On top of it all, we learned that Steve passed away."

"He's dead?" Willow went pale.

"It was a motorcycle accident," I say. "Happened, like, five years ago."

"I always hated those damn things," Willow says. "But Steve was kind of fearless."

"Well, I think Riley is full of fears, or insecurity at least. She took a pill after we met Monique. I'm sorry. I—I should have told you she was using drugs. She made me promise, and . . ." *And nothing*, I think.

The weight of the guilt I've been carrying around, keeping a secret I knew was wrong to keep, makes me burst into tears—either from relief or self-hatred or both.

Willow gets up from her chair and rushes over to give me a big hug, while I keep wailing like a newborn. She's shushing me, stroking my hair, being far sweeter to me than I deserve.

"It's okay, sweetie," she says as I continue to cry. "I understand why you didn't tell me. I get it. But I'm glad you shared. I needed to know the truth. I've been worried about Riley, and now I can do something about it. We had to get all these secrets out in the open."

I manage to stop crying long enough to spit out one more tidbit. "Then I guess you should know that she's been seeing somebody."

"The soccer player who's taking her to prom?"

"No, he's some older guy," I say. "I thought they broke up, but they're back together now. She told me she doesn't want to go to college anymore because she thinks they're going to be together, like, forever. I think half the time she tells you she's at Teagan's, she's really with him."

Willow puts her hands to her mouth, maybe to stop a scream from coming out. "Okay, all right," she says, collecting herself.

Willow picks up her mug. Her hands shake so violently the coffee might spill out. But something shifts as she sets her mug down by the sink—a kind of determination hardening. "Riley and I are going to have a long talk," Willow says. "Right now."

The sureness in her voice comforts me.

"She needs help," Willow says. "I'll make some calls. Hopefully find her the support she needs."

"And Evan?" Mom asks.

"He and I will have a talk as well, about everything. Evan has his issues, no doubt, but he loves Riley and has a right to know what's going on. I think there's been enough secrets for one lifetime—maybe two."

Chapter 42

Since Alex stopped drinking, she'd had precisely zero fights with her husband, but that could change if they couldn't come to terms about Lettie.

It all started with a seemingly innocuous comment from Nick one afternoon. "I've asked her to go to a movie and out to lunch, but she's always busy. It feels like she's avoiding me."

"Just keep trying to connect," Alex said. "She needs us."

"Sure," said Nick. "On her terms."

"Exactly," said Alex. "And that means giving up some control."

"Okay, the next time you can't sleep because she's not home, I'll simply remind you that you gave up control." Nick cocked an eyebrow with a "gotcha" kind of grin.

"I'm her mother," Alex said. "The rules don't apply to me. But on a serious note, you've been pretty strict with her for some time—so maybe she has lingering resentments?"

"What? You mean last summer or with college? She's fine going to UMass. She didn't get into USC, so it's settled."

"She seemed weirdly unfazed about the rejection, don't you think?" Alex said. "Something's up with her. Maybe she was relieved she didn't have to confront you about the money, but her reaction was still odd to me. I'm going to call USC admissions next week, find out if there's more to this story than we know. But perhaps you two need to have a talk about it as well."

Alex left the conversation feeling somewhat victorious, but she'd neglected to mention that she and Lettie were close to having a big blowout of their own—this one over the stolen necklace. Alex wanted to tell Emily about the blackmailer, while Lettie, fearing Dylan would never forgive her for breaking a confidence, did not.

Alex had consulted her therapist for guidance.

The therapist wasn't at all conflicted. "Your sister needs to know about the blackmailer," she had said.

So, a few days later, Alex told her. But she did so with a plan, or more like an approach, that might prevent further emotional turmoil.

"I thought it was strange that Dylan found it behind my dresser. So he took my necklace to pay someone off?" Emily couldn't believe her ears. "What do they have on him? Who blackmailed him?"

"Lettie doesn't know, and she says he's not under threat anymore," said Alex. "Even so, Jay Kumar is still trying to figure out who was behind it. But Em, Dylan's in a delicate place. Revealing his big secret might be detrimental to his recovery. We need to proceed with caution. Lettie is going to encourage Dylan to open up to us. Since there's no threat, let's just give it some time."

"I guess," said Emily.

"And maybe we should keep all this from Ken for a little while. He and Dylan are on rocky ground as it is. If Dylan's behavior changes drastically or we see something out of the ordinary, it could mean the blackmailer has come back, and we'll have to be more direct."

Emily thanked her sister for the plan and her honesty, which led to some honesty of her own. "Ken doesn't understand why I'm not interested in sex anymore, especially since Samir's visit. He insists it's totally innocent between him and Mandy—that he went to her place trying to help Dylan. Who'd believe that crap? When I'm certain Dylan is stable, when I know he's going to be all right, and this blackmailing nonsense is behind us, I'm going to divorce him."

For Alex, this was a bombshell.

Emily, however, seemed to have no doubts. "This is between us sisters," she said.

"I'll support you in every way I can," Alex said. The two shared a hug, Alex feeling extra grateful that the secrets she carried about Ken didn't matter much anymore.

On the Friday before the block party, Alex was thinking of that conversation with her sister when she saw, of all things, Evan Thompson's car coming down Alton Road. She was out front with Nick, trying to make the lawn look nice, when she spied his familiar BMW.

Nick had just finished pushing a wheelbarrow full of mulch up the driveway. He huffed like Sisyphus, hauling his stone up the hill. His white shirt—goodness knew why he'd picked that color to do yard work—was smeared with dirt. Sweat dripped from his brow. Mud streaked down his cheeks, looking like hastily applied war paint.

Alex thought he looked adorable as she worked the rake to spread his piles of mulch evenly in the garden bed. Finally, spring had sprung. The trees had their leaves again, and April's showers had indeed brought May flowers. Flowers weren't the only thing in bloom. Since she put down the bottle, the closeness Alex had once felt with her husband was slowly returning.

Only moments ago, she was breathing in the fragrant air, letting it soak into her lungs as it warmed her from the inside out. Nearby, Zoe sunned herself on the grass. Lettie was off somewhere. Alex didn't ask too many questions.

All was good in her world. Finally. For once. *One day at a time.*

But now Evan was here. Warning bells rang in her head. Alex didn't think he'd set foot on Alton Road since he'd moved out of the house. Maybe he'd come to talk to Willow. She had told him about Riley's pill habit and the older boy she was seeing. They certainly had plenty to discuss.

According to Willow, Riley had admitted to dating someone in college, but claimed the relationship was over. She hadn't told her parents because she knew they wouldn't have approved of the age difference. As Riley explained it, they'd broken up a month ago, but Evan wasn't buying it. He thought his daughter was still involved, and that this man was her source for the narcotics she denied taking.

"What's he doing?" Nick asked, smearing dirt across his forehead as he wiped sweat from his brow. "I thought he wasn't allowed back here. Or did Willow have a change of heart?"

"He told Willow he was going to find out the name of that college boy Riley was with because he's convinced that's her supplier. I'm like, whatever—just look in the mirror for that. But maybe she's got another source, so could be he's got some information to share."

Or maybe he knows about the Wookiee, Alex thought. Willow had sworn she wasn't going to tell him, but it could be that he found out on his own.

Evan drove by with a fixed gaze, not bothering to acknowledge Alex or Nick, who gave him a halfhearted wave. He seemed completely oblivious to their presence.

He made one slow trip around the cul-de-sac, his car zigzagging in the kind of erratic driving that would get him pulled over. Instead of navigating into the driveway of his former home, Evan drove by it without slowing, only to apply the brakes as he passed in front of Brooke's house. He didn't come to a full stop, however, and after making one complete revolution around the cul-de-sac, he began a second circumnavigation.

"What the hell? Is he high?" Nick asked.

They watched, and as Evan came around the bend, Alex got a better look at his vacant, glassy stare. "I'm going to go with *yes* and *very,*" she said.

"Um, should we call the cops?" Nick asked.

Alex wasn't sure what to do. They kept watching Evan make his ponderous circles.

Movement in a window across the street drew her attention away from the BMW and toward the Kumar home, where Mandy was observing the scene from a first-floor window.

The light was just right to allow Alex a clear view of her neighbor. The two women's eyes met. Alex raised her hands, as if to say to Mandy that she had no idea what was going on. Mandy returned a shrug, but Samir appeared in the window beside her. Alex could see him scowl even from a distance and watched as he pulled Mandy away.

Samir's behavior concerned her less than Evan's, who was now on drive-by number five, or maybe it was six—Alex had lost count. With each trip around the cul-de-sac, Evan slowed down in front of Brooke's house before speeding up again to make another pass. His driving seemed to be getting worse as he continued his rotations.

Alex positioned herself at the edge of the sidewalk to try to get Evan's attention, when she caught sight of Brooke, who had emerged from her house. Standing at the end of her driveway, Brooke waved at Evan. This time he put on the brakes, coming to a full stop in front of her.

Alex kept close watch as Brooke leaned her nearly flawless form into the open passenger-side window. She spoke to Evan at some length, but Alex couldn't hear the exchange.

Without warning, Evan hit the accelerator hard. With a squeal of tires, the car lurched forward, Brooke's body still halfway inside the vehicle. If it hadn't been for her quick reflexes, Brooke might not have extracted herself in time. She jumped back to a safe distance as Evan sped away.

Brooke hurried over to Alex, breathless.

"Are you all right?" asked Alex.

"I'm fine," Brooke said. "Do you have a phone? We need to call the cops. Evan's not in his right mind, and he shouldn't be driving."

"Do we have his license plate?" Nick asked.

Alex shook her head. Even after all those trips around the circle, she couldn't recite a single number.

"No worries." Nick turned to go. "We know the make and model. I'll call from the house."

"What was that all about?" Alex asked when she and Brooke were alone. "What did he say to you?"

"He was talking all kinds of nonsense. He thinks we're meant to be together. He can't live without me. He was just going on and on. I told him he needs help. That he's not well. He doesn't look right to me. I think the drugs are affecting his brain."

"Are you worried, Brooke? Do you think he might—you know, try to hurt you?"

Brooke's confidence had disappeared. "I don't know," she said. "It all started when I asked him to take pictures of me for OnlyFans. He's a professional, and I wanted my shots to look good. I figured he'd do the job without getting attached. He's done this kind of work plenty of times. When he started making overtures, I told him that we were done—that he couldn't be my photographer anymore.

"I think that's when his obsession kicked in. I felt bad for him, but I was never afraid of him. I just didn't want to lead him on. Now it's different. It felt safer when he was the secret stalker. Since it all came out in the open, something's shifted. He feels a lot more menacing."

"Maybe go talk to the police," Alex said. "Ask what you can do to protect yourself."

"I have all the protection I need from my friends Smith & Wesson."

Alex's jaw fell open. "You have a gun?"

"Sure," said Brooke. "I sleep better at night with it in my bedside table—and with all the craziness in our neighborhood, can you blame me?"

"Speaking of crazy," Alex said, "just now I saw Samir literally *pull* Mandy away from the window where she was watching Evan."

"What is up with the men on Alton Road?" Brooke sounded more annoyed than distressed. "When did they all go nuts?"

Alex felt the need to tell Brooke about the confrontation between Samir and Ken over secret liaisons with Mandy.

"That reminds me," said Brooke. "I started digging into Samir's background, looking online, searching for anything concerning—like past charges of domestic violence, restraining orders, that kind of thing. I have to say, I didn't find too much—just the usual: LinkedIn posts, some past employment info, but nothing noteworthy or nefarious. I did, however, stumble across their wedding announcement. I guess he and Mandy have been married over twenty years. Her maiden name was Gibson—Amanda Gibson."

"Interesting," Alex said. "That's how Ken referred to her when she came to pick up Jay at the hospital. He called her Amanda. What do you make of that?"

Brooke answered in a low voice: "I'd say at the very least, Ken seems to know Mandy a lot better than we do."

This left Alex feeling deeply unsettled. As Brooke walked away, Alex's phone rang. The number that came up was unfamiliar to her.

"Hello, this is Alex," she said.

"Alex, it's Meg Ruley from USC admissions returning your call from earlier today. Sorry it's taken a bit to get back to you. Crazy time of year."

Alex brightened. "Yes, of course. And thanks for the call. I was just curious for more information on my daughter's rejection. Not sure what you can share, but like I said on my voice mail, her reaction was odd, so I'm just wondering if there's more to the story than I've been told."

"Yeah, I checked into that," Meg said hesitantly. "I guess there really is some confusion . . . your daughter was accepted to the university. And there's still a slot for her if she wants to take it."

Alex felt a pulse of anger come and go. Lettie had lied to her, obviously, but this wasn't about Lettie—it was about Nick. "Thank you for letting me know," Alex said in a measured tone. "Yes, some misunderstanding for sure. We'll have a family meeting, and I'll be back in touch."

She ended the call feeling a storm was coming, a dark, swirling eddy of threatening clouds. A thought tingled at the back of her mind. She was going to have a candid, difficult conversation with Nick, but she knew how stubborn he could be. A different worry followed, a gnawing little fear that depending on how that talk went, it might not be so easy to avoid a drink . . . maybe two . . . at the block party.

Chapter 43

Lettie

I'm in my bedroom when I hear what sounds like a gunshot. Downstairs, Zoe starts barking like crazy. Dogs hate loud noises, which they perceive as a threat. In this case, I'm in full agreement with my dog.

I'm home alone, so I'm the only one who can investigate. My brain is already coming up with justifications for the noise. It was a car backfiring. A tree branch had splintered. It was a rumble of thunder, even though the day is clear and bright.

A series of pops follows in close enough succession to give me a moment's pause before I venture outside. It could be fireworks, I'm thinking, but it's also coming from the direction of Dylan's house, which makes me supremely anxious.

As I'm opening my own door, I hear yet another pop. The sound seems to dissipate as it moves outward into the pleasant afternoon. When I reach the end of my driveway, I decide the pops are coming from behind Dylan's house, and I'm almost equally certain about what's making the noise.

Riley comes out of her house. She frosts me with a stare. We haven't spoken since I ratted her out (even though she technically did the same to me), but I don't regret my actions for a second. I keep seeing more news reports about kids dying from taking what they think are Percocets and ending up with a fatal overdose from fentanyl. I'll take Riley's hatred in exchange for her life any day.

But right now we have a mutual interest, so her anger doesn't last long. She meets up with me at the end of Dylan's driveway. Our eyes lock as another pop tears through the air.

"What's that?" says Riley.

"I think it's what we think it is," I say.

She starts toward Dylan's house in a rush, but I lunge at her, grabbing her arm, pulling her back toward me. "What do you think you're doing?" I ask.

"I'm checking it out," she says, as if that should be apparent.

"Yeah, I get *what* you're doing, but did you think this through?"

Riley gives me a blank look, one I take to mean no.

"We don't know who's back there," I say. "But I highly doubt my uncle Ken, who has a lifetime membership to a firing range, is shooting a gun in his backyard."

Pop. Another shot.

"Obviously it's Dylan," I tell her. "I don't know why Uncle Ken would give a kid who tried to kill himself access to a gun, but he definitely has one. And you're definitely his ex-girlfriend, so you should think twice before marching back there."

"You think Dylan would—" Riley can't bring herself to finish the thought, and I don't feel a need to say it for her.

"Yes," I say. "This is how you make the news. Go home, Rye. I'll take care of this."

Riley doesn't move, but when I hear yet another shot, I lose my temper a little. "Go!" I order, and she sets off running.

I wait until Riley is safely inside her house before I call Dylan. I'm not going back there, either. I'm not stupid. He has a gun and evidently some aggression to get out—or he's in desperate need of attention, which I will happily give to him, but only when he's not holding a weapon.

My call goes to voice mail. I try again and it rings, but maybe he's wearing ear protection and can't hear the phone. So I send him a text and try DMing his social media accounts before I call for a third time.

Finally, he answers. "Hey, Lettie, what's up?" He sounds casual, like he's downstairs watching reruns of *Dawson's Creek* on the CW.

"Um, D, what the hell are you doing?" I ask.

"Target shooting," he says, as if that's no problem at all.

"Are you holding a gun right now?" I ask. My tone is a lot sterner than the voice I used with Riley.

"Yeah, I have my dad's Sig Sauer P365. Awesome gun."

"D, I don't care what the gun is, I care that you have one. You can't fire a gun in your backyard. What the hell are you shooting at, anyway?"

"Targets I made," he says, far too casually for my liking. "Some plates, a few plastic milk jugs."

"Dylan, listen to me and listen very carefully, okay?"

"Yeah."

"You can't do that!" My tone is scolding. My voice is firm. I am not sure what to say, how to defuse this situation, or how unstable Dylan might be. But my guess is he's damn unstable. I take one calming breath, then another.

"Listen to my words," I say, speaking slowly for emphasis. "Put the gun away. Put it away *right now*."

"Why?" he says. "I'm not hurting anybody."

"Dylan!" I yell into the phone. "You might kill somebody walking in the woods, or you might kill yourself—accidentally or otherwise. I don't know. But I do know you have to stop and stop right now, or I *will* call the police, and then I'll call your parents." My voice shakes and a sob catches in my throat.

"Hey, hey, okay," he says.

I guess it took my emotional distress to punch a hole through his thick skull.

"Take it easy, Lettie. I'm not going to do anything stupid. I don't want to upset you."

"Too late," I snap. "How did you get a gun, anyway?"

"From the gun safe," he says, making it sound obvious.

"That's insane," I say. "Your parents aren't going to give you access to the safe, especially when, well, you know—you tried to kill yourself." I have trouble saying the words. This is no time to layer on the shame, but I need to make my point.

"They didn't give me access," he says. "I guessed the new code."

"You guessed it? How?"

"The last code was Logan's jersey number and his goals scored last year. I just tried his goals scored this year and voilà, open sesame. I know how to handle a gun, Lettie. My dad used to take me to the range all the time."

"Yeah, and that's where you *should* be firing guns," I say. "At the range."

"I'm not going there—not with *him*."

"What's going on with you two?" I ask. "Is the blackmailer back?"

"Give me a sec, will ya?" he says. "I'll come over."

"Unarmed," I say in the strongest voice possible.

"Unarmed," he repeats.

Ten minutes later, Dylan is at my door. I make him show me his hands, and then I do my version of a TSA pat-down.

"Really, Lettie?" he says.

"Sorry for not being all trusting and cool, but that was pretty unsettling. You could have been arrested or much, much worse."

"Relax," he says. "I was just blowing off steam. I put the gun back in the case and locked it. Everything's fine."

We go to the kitchen, sit at the table. I get us two ginger ales, which my mom now buys instead of wine. I'm not sure it's a super healthy alternative to alcohol, but it's way better for her liver.

"Why did you start shooting up your backyard?" I ask him.

"I told you, target practice. I like shooting. And I don't like my father."

"Because of Logan?"

"Because he's an asshole, Lettie. Anyway, don't worry about it. I'm not going to shoot myself, if that's your concern."

"It's *one* of them." I'm still upset with him and the situation. "What's going on with you?" I ask. "Is it about the blackmailer? Did they come back for more money? Are you practicing shooting so you can—do something about it?"

Dylan gives me a cryptic smile. "I still don't know who was blackmailing me," he says. "But if I do find out, you bet I'll do something about it. Good news is I haven't had any more threatening emails, so he seems to have meant what he said about backing off. But I need to be more careful with my laptop camera."

"So it was a video?"

Dylan breaks eye contact, unnerved, while my neurons start firing.

Video evidence. Something to do with his laptop camera. Enough embarrassment to steal from his parents to pay up. Something bad enough to make him take up target practice in his backyard.

I think I have a pretty good idea what the blackmailer has on my cousin. I suspect it involves something a lot of teen boys do frequently—especially with the help of the internet. Something they wouldn't want their family or peers to ever see. I don't say anything, though, because he's suffered enough.

"What about Riley?" I ask.

"What about her?"

"Is this about your dad, the blackmailer, or the breakup?"

"Is what about it?"

"The gun. Playing *The Matrix* in your backyard. Taking the pills. Stealing Riley's phone. Everything!" I'm thinking: *Is this my fault for causing the breakup with Riley or something else?*

At that moment, the kitchen door flies open and Riley bursts in like a sprinter at the finish line. "Is everything all right? Is Dylan okay?" She stops herself from saying anything more and goes pale when she realizes who's sitting at the table with me.

"Well, there she is—Riley Thompson," Dylan says. He looks haunted, as if he did have Riley on the brain during target practice.

"Are you all right, Dylan? I'm sorry, I just—um." Riley is shaking. I feel all kinds of pity for her.

"It's okay," Dylan says with icy detachment. "I was just leaving. And believe it or not, Riley, you're not my biggest problem anymore."

He stands up fast, toppling his chair as he rises. The crash makes Zoe go crazy all over again. He pushes past Riley with a little too much aggression for my liking.

"Dylan," I call before he's out the door, "no more guns."

"Whatever you say," he replies. "See you both at the block party. Something tells me it's going to be the most memorable one yet."

Meadowbrook Online Community Page

Ed Callahan

Hope nobody is selling a house anytime soon. Property values in Meadowbrook are going down, down, down!

> **Reply from Laura Ballwell**
>
> OMG! Why would you even write that, **Ed Callahan**?
>
> **Reply from Ed Callahan**
>
> Because murder tends to have a negative effect on home buying. Think much, dummy?!

Tom Beck

Hey, Mr. Moderator! Are you reading this post? Can you please block **Ed Callahan** from the group? Isn't there some rule about name-calling? He's also spreading false information.

> **Reply from Ed Callahan**
>
> My apologies! It'll lower the property values on Alton Road. Sorry for my mistake. But that doesn't make you any smarter than **Laura Ballwell**. Ha-ha.
>
> **Reply from Tom Beck**
>
> Thanks for sharing your "enlightening opinion," **Ed Callahan**, under the mistaken belief that anyone cares what you have to say. Get a life!

Janet Pinkham

May I say something here?

> **Reply from Susanne Horton**
>
> I think we've heard enough about your trash bag complaints, bake sales, and stories about ambulance rides with your dad.
>
> **Reply from Janet Pinkham**
>
> Well, I just want to let you know that I heard

from my cousin, the EMT who rode in that ambulance with my father. He just texted me. According to him, there is more than one fatality.

MEMORIAL DAY, PRESENT DAY

Chapter 44

The shrieking of a siren woke Alex from her deep sleep. She felt as if someone had stuffed cotton balls into her mouth. Her head throbbed with a beat capable of cracking her skull.

Boom! Boom! Boom!

Blue and red lights blinked through a break in the living room curtains, attacking her corneas. Another siren blared in the distance.

Alex peeled herself off the couch like a Fruit Roll-Up separating from its cellophane packaging. She felt sticky and gross. The cushions had practically molded into the shape of her body. She had no idea how long she'd been asleep (okay, passed out). It could have been an hour, maybe two. Either way, she could still feel the wine on her tongue, souring her throat, sloshing in her stomach.

Memories came at her in flashes like strobe lights in a nightclub.

The block party had kicked off at the usual hour. She should know, she'd organized it. She shouldn't have—it wasn't her turn this year, but the neighborhood was in such disarray. There was so much trouble—between Evan and Willow, Brooke and Evan, Ken and Emily, Mandy and Ken, Samir and Mandy, even Riley and Dylan—that nobody else was up to the task. Brooke had helped out a little, but Alex did most of the work: putting flyers in mailboxes; managing the SignUpGenius page, the music, tables, chairs, drinks, buckets of ice, snacks, all of that, while Brooke took care of the desserts. Nick had bought the meat from a local farmer, earning his daughter's praise. She wouldn't eat meat, but she lauded his efforts around sustainability.

Nick.

Their big fight over USC.

His refusing to budge. Alex screaming that he should go back to school to learn how to be a decent human being. The tiki bar he hadn't stocked out of spite. The booze she snuck after she did the job for him.

Oh, crap.

It *all* came back to her. The flood of recollections and a torrent of shame. There she had been, staggering around the party, talking loudly, having the best time in ages, all while avoiding her husband. She remembered the little girl who had asked about hot dogs. She'd frightened the child with a caustic remark before escorting her to the grill. A kiddie pool full of pony-sized wine bottles was nearby. She'd grabbed one after she'd had so much to drink already. And she was talking to someone . . . who was it? Oh yes, the Bug Man! He was there!

That's when Nick had come to check on her. She had spilled her drink on him and had followed that shining moment with a fall on her ass into the kiddie pool, soaking her clothes and bruising her ego. Her husband's words—"Don't come back"—echoed loudly.

Ouch.

And now she heard sirens. Peering out the window, Alex saw not one, but two police cars parked on her street, their lights flashing. The bright light of day made her wince. The room seemed to tilt, just a little, and it wasn't because she was kneeling on couch cushions.

Alex stood, intending to go outside to have a look. One unsteady step later told her she was in that awkward middle place between drunk and hungover. But she wasn't in such bad shape; she could go investigate.

Nick had issued his mandate before all this commotion, Alex reasoned. Police on the scene changed everything, right? And who was Nick to tell her what to do anyway? She had every right to know what was going on.

Alex checked her phone. Maybe someone had tried to get in touch with her about the emergency. No calls or texts, but she noted the time. Five-thirty. Soon the party would be switching from afternoon fun to an evening vibe, which was always when things *really* got going. What the hell had happened while she was sleeping? The cul-de-sac had plenty of combustible relationships, but if she were to guess which one had brought the police, she'd bet on the escalating war between Bug Man and Ken. Had Ken been pushed too far? Had Bug Man retaliated for losing his job?

Alex slipped on new clothes, did a quick check of her hair—not quite a full Medusa, but close—and brushed her teeth before making her way outside. She blinked rapidly to ease the transition from the dark interior. Her legs felt like two rubber bands. She doubted she'd pass a field sobriety test.

Evidently it had taken Alex too long to get herself together. By the time she got outside, the crisis appeared to be over. Kids were gathered around the police cars, peering into windows, putting tiny hands all over the gleaming exterior, leaving greasy prints behind. One of the officers on the scene was actually entertaining the children with an occasional siren blast that made her already throbbing head feel like it was splitting in two.

Ken stood by himself, off to the side. He appeared to be storming mad. Alex approached him cautiously.

"That damn guy," he groused. Ken pointed to Bug Man, who stood in his green work uniform not too far away, talking to a police officer.

"What's going on?" asked Alex.

Her stomach lurched. Had she had anything to eat or did she just drink?

"Bug Man came to my house soliciting his crap service again, that's what," fumed Ken. "And we got into it. I gave him a little shove, barely anything." He demonstrated on Alex's shoulder. It didn't feel like barely anything to her. "And then he called the damn cops on me."

Alex had heard enough of his complaining. "Do you ever think that you're the problem here, Ken?" she shouted. "Has that ever crossed your mind? Maybe once? Ever?"

She returned the shove he gave to her shoulder, only harder.

For a second, Ken looked like the bully being confronted by his victim—slack-jawed, eyes full of surprise. "Hey, whose side are you on here?" he shot back.

"The winning one, of course," said Alex. "We both like *winners,*

Ken . . . but sadly, that pretty much excludes every man on Alton Road—including you."

Before Ken had a chance to respond, Officer Grady O'Brien, who had to be getting tired of the Alton Road dysfunction—approached. His expression was stern, eyes all but saying: *Adults should know better.*

"You're in luck," O'Brien announced, directing his words at Ken. "Bug Man says he's not going to press charges."

"You call him Bug Man, too?" Alex mopped her brow. She was sweating out wine.

O'Brien didn't answer. "Keep the temperature in check, Ken, will ya?" It sounded like an order. "We've been coming to Alton Road enough lately."

"Sure thing," Ken grumbled. He was still red-faced and angry, probably more at Alex than at Bug Man. "I'll be cool," he said. "But that guy needs to stay off my property."

O'Brien crossed his arms in front of his chest. "Remember, you can tell him to leave, but keep your hands to yourself. I mean it."

Bug Man, lurking close by, might have picked up a snippet of the conversation. He smirked in Ken's direction.

Ken stared back. "If anybody needs me," he told Alex, "I'll be in my office with Johnnie, cooling off."

Alex understood the reference to his prized bottle of Johnnie Walker Blue Label whisky, which he drank from only this day each year. To her knowledge—and true to his character—Ken never shared the ridiculously priced spirit at the block party, except for that one time he'd offered some to Mandy and Samir. Hard to believe that had been only a year ago.

Alex watched Ken storm away. "I'm sorry about my brother-in-law, he can be a little quick-tempered," she said to O'Brien, who seemed more congenial now that Ken was gone.

"Happens. Nobody got hurt. Not to worry," he said.

A blast of music exploded from the PA system and drew O'Brien's attention, and Alex's, to Lettie, who was working the controls. The song, instantly recognizable to O'Brien, brightened his expression. "Pearl Jam," he said with a slip of a smile. "Now *that's* what I'm talking about!"

"Lettie, maybe wait until the police are gone before putting the music back on?" Alex called.

O'Brien shook his head. "It's still a block party," he said. "There's no law against having fun."

Alex watched O'Brien get into his cruiser and drive away, the other cop car following close behind. Everything returned to normal almost immediately, but Alex still felt raring to go. Confronting Ken had delivered a rush of adrenaline blended with the alcohol still in her system, adding fuel to her anger.

God help Nick if he came at her now with some quip about being out of exile—or Samir, if he tried to grab Mandy again—or Evan, if he did who knows what to Brooke or to Willow.

All seemed fine, but Alex was not. She was drunk and pissed and spoiling for a fight. The police were gone, but Bug Man remained. Maybe he'd come over and start in on her.

If so, good luck to him.

Her neighbors had resumed talking, eating, drinking, and playing games as if no disturbance had occurred. But she saw no sign of Brooke, and the dessert table looked a little sparse. Even in her heightened state of agitation, Alex couldn't let go of all the party details. Perhaps Brooke was grabbing more desserts from the fridge. Alex headed toward her friend's home, on the pretense of offering a helping hand, while really needing someone to vent to.

As she was walking up Brooke's driveway, her friend was heading out the door. Instead of a dessert tray, Brooke was holding what appeared to be a large hardcover book. She quickened her pace to reach Alex. "I was just coming to find you," Brooke said.

"I'm glad you did," Alex said. "I need someone to keep me from committing a homicide. Between Nick and Ken, I'm not sure who I want to punch harder. Oh, and the dessert table is running low."

"I'd say the punches should be directed at Ken," Brooke said, holding up the book in her hand. "And forget the damn desserts."

"What's the book all about?" Alex asked.

"You know how I've been obsessed about the connection between the Kumars and Ken for ages now, right? Remember when I said that Ken seems to know Mandy a lot better than we do?"

"Yeah . . ." said Alex, wondering where this was headed. She wished her thoughts weren't so muddy. The wine was starting to wear off, her half hangover, too, but neither was ending fast enough.

"So I used Mandy's maiden name, Amanda Gibson, and did multiple Google searches, trying to find a past connection between her and Ken. I thought I was crazy, but I just needed to follow the thread."

"And?" Alex was intrigued but apprehensive.

"And nothing at first," said Brooke. "I couldn't find any obvious reason for their paths to have crossed."

Alex's eyes went to the book in Brooke's hand.

"Then I put Amanda Gibson's name into the search field and appended that with the name of every job Ken has listed on his LinkedIn profile and every school he's ever attended."

Brooke paused, leaving Alex tense with anticipation.

"You got a hit?" she asked, knowing the answer simply through Brooke's body language.

"I did," said Brooke. "But before I could believe it, I had to see it for myself. So I went up to the attic and got this."

Brooke held out the book so Alex could take a closer look. The cover was brushed with the yellow tint of time, the letters slightly faded, but she could still make out the words: *Westfield High School.*

"Is that your yearbook?" Alex asked.

"No," said Brooke. "It's Jerry's."

Brooke flipped the yearbook open to a marked page, holding it up so Alex could see the array of black-and-white photos featuring awkward teens, girls with uncertain expressions and goofy-looking guys, many in baggy, unbuttoned plaid shirts, sporting the grunge look from the nineties.

Brooke placed her finger on one image in particular, that of a fresh-faced teen with blond hair.

It took only a moment of close inspection before Alex saw it. She had no doubt. The girl looking out from the yearbook photo was un-questionably a young Mandy Kumar—or Amanda Gibson, as she had been.

"Exactly," said Brooke, reading Alex's reaction. "Mandy went to high school with Jerry."

"Which means . . ." Alex's voice trailed off.

"She also went to high school with Ken," said Brooke.

Alex and Brooke exchanged blank looks.

It was Alex who eventually broke the silence. "I don't get it," she said. "Clearly they recognized each other right away. That explains the look that passed between them at last year's block party. But what's the big deal? Why not tell us? Why keep it secret?"

Brooke's baffled expression said she agreed that those questions deserved answers.

Chapter 45

Lettie

I see the adoring look my father sends me when I play that Pearl Jam song. I also catch the dirty one he sends Mom's way. It's hard to miss, but Mom is too busy with Officer O'Brien to notice. Lucky her. Clearly, Dad's pissed about something, but I don't know what. Mom's been gone from the party for a while, so maybe he's angry about that, or it could be she tumbled off the wagon. That would be a crisis maker for the ages, but I'm not ready to assume the worst.

Mom marches off, heading for Brooke's house, doesn't even bother to engage with me, which is odd. I'm sure she's rattled given all the excitement with the police showing up over some dumb drama between Bug Man and Uncle Ken.

The Bug Man is sticking around, just to be a pest (pun intended). But now that the police are gone—as is Uncle Ken, who's retreated to his house to lick his wounds—things are getting back to normal. I'm trying to keep the energy going with more nineties jams. Up comes a song from a band called Toad the Wet Sprocket. What does that even mean? What the hell is a wet sprocket?

I see Dad heading toward me. He doesn't look angry anymore.

"Well now, this is a surprise," he says. "Last time you DJ'd the block party I think you were still in braces. To what do we owe this sudden enthusiastic involvement?"

"I dunno," I say, shrugging. "Everyone was distracted with the cops, so nobody was doing the music."

"You seem to be having fun." Dad eyes me with suspicion. "I'm worried about you." He smiles, but I can tell he's being semi-serious.

"I'm fine," I assure him. But I don't share my whole truth, which is that I'm feeling all the feels. This is my last block party as a high school student, and I guess I'm a little sentimental. For a moment I wonder if Dylan will make good on his pledge (threat?) that it would be the most memorable one yet.

"That sure was some excitement," Dad says, nodding toward the Bug Man, who for some reason is still loitering about, as if panhandling for trouble.

"Why won't he just go away?" I ask. "Nobody wants him here."

"He's making a point," Dad speculates. "Free country, all that."

"Yeah, free to be an asshole," I say, and that gets a laugh. "Hey, what's up with you and Mom?" I ask. I don't love the knot in my chest, but whatever. "I saw the look you gave her."

"It's fine," he says. "Just a little disagreement is all."

I don't believe him, not for a second, but I'm not about to press for details.

"However, there is something I want to talk to you about," he says.

The hairs on the back of my neck and my eyebrows go up at the same time. "What?" I ask.

"Your mom called USC," Dad says. He drops the bombshell like a microphone onto a stage, all nonchalant and cool.

It takes a second before I'm breathing again. "Um, yeah . . . um—" No words.

"Why'd you lie, Lettie?"

My eyes are drawn to my feet as though pulled there by gravity. "Why'd she call?" I ask.

"Your mom pays more attention than I do, I guess. She noticed your reaction to being rejected wasn't exactly—true to form. You got in. You even got some merit money. So . . . why the lie?"

I gather my courage to look him in the eyes, and the words just come to me. "Because what's the point?" My anger sparks to life. "You're not going to help me. You'll just tell me it's a waste of money.

That I don't understand the value of a dollar . . . that a BA from UMass is the same thing as one from USC. Why should I be excited about getting in when you've taken the possibility off the table?" My throat closes up like I'm having an allergic reaction, but the only thing I'm averse to is the truth.

Dad appears crestfallen, but I don't feel bad about what I've said. He goes quiet for a moment, then says, "You're right. And your mother said all the same things to me. I was going to tell her this news before I told you, but she went for a swim—and she's on board with it anyway, so now you'll hear it first from me. Your mom and I talked this over extensively, and I've been giving it a lot of thought myself. I can see now that I was wrong. I shouldn't have taken the option away from you."

"Exactly," I snap. "I mean, what's the point of telling you about USC if you're just gonna—wait, what?" I blink rapidly even though I'm sure I'm having an auditory hallucination. "Say that again?"

"If you want to go to USC, Lettie, I won't stand in your way," he says. "Admissions said they could still let you in."

"What about learning the value of a dollar?" I ask. "What about all the things we've been arguing over?"

"I guess I've had a change of heart. When I found out you lied about getting in, I had to take a good look at why. And that's when I realized . . . I was the problem. You couldn't be honest with me because I kept shutting you down. Clearly my priorities were out of whack. Now they're in whack." He smiles proudly at his own bad dad joke.

"For real, Dad?" I ask. "You'll help me?"

"You won't have any debt when you graduate," he says. "We're lucky, Lettie. We have the money. I shouldn't be holding you back to prove a point—my point. Your mother's right. We've been saving for this day for a long time now. It was wrong of me to stand in your way."

I let out a delighted scream, and suddenly I'm jumping up and down as though practicing for the upcoming sack race. I can't seem to contain my joy. I wrap my arms around my father in the biggest hug I've given him since I was about nine years old.

"I'll apply to be an RA," I tell him breathlessly. "It'll save so much money . . . see, I do get it. I'm not into drinking, either—well, not anymore, I can promise you that. I don't need to go to any big parties, and I'll rat out all the rule violators, all of them! I'm like a pro at ratting now." I'm thinking of Riley and Dylan.

Dad's jaw tightens. He seems to have taken a turn for the emotional worst. "I'm proud of you, Lettie," he stammers. His lips do a quiver thing that makes me profoundly uncomfortable. "I'm so damn proud. I don't always say it, don't know how to show it, and sometimes I feel pulled in too many directions to give you my full attention, but I'm watching, and I love what I see. You're an amazing young woman, and I'm truly grateful to be your father."

He's choked up, and okay, now there's this lump in my throat, too.

"Thanks," I manage. "I'm so grateful I can't even tell you, but don't go getting any crazy ideas. I'm still not doing the egg toss with you."

"Crush my heart." Dad clutches his chest as if he's having a heart attack. He seems relieved I've given him an out from expressing his more honest and raw emotions.

I'm glad, too. I don't need us acting like blubbering fools.

"I'm keeping the faith, regardless," he says. "Once an egg tosser, always an egg tosser."

I'm about to respond when Aunt Emily appears. The three of us talk about the police, Bug Man, and all of that, but I resist the urge to tell her about my new college plans. I need to sit with it awhile before I share. And I need to tell my mom.

Emily's about to go, but then stops as if she's remembered something. "Lettie, hon," she says to me, "can you grab some folding chairs out of our basement? We need them for the outdoor movie and Ken's refusing to come out until the Bug Man is gone, and honestly, I don't blame him. The chairs are on the unfinished side. There should be four of them."

"I'll help," Dad says, but I tell him no. I've had enough of his egg toss sales pitch for one day.

So off I go into Aunt Emily's house. I enter through the front door, calling out to Ken just to let him know I'm here.

"Chairs are downstairs," he calls back. Emily must have told him why I was coming over. He still sounds gruff.

I scoot down the stairs to the basement. I could have used the bulkhead entrance to avoid Ken entirely—they never keep it locked—but it didn't occur to me until now. Eventually I find the chairs tucked in a corner behind a bunch of smelly sports gear. They're light, and it won't be hard to carry them outside in one trip.

As I'm heading back up the stairs, I notice the gun case on a tool bench. I had already dropped a not-so-subtle suggestion that Uncle Ken should change the code. "I'm sure nothing will happen," I told him some days ago, "but I saw a YouTube video about a suicidal kid who knew the code to his parents' gun safe, and, well . . . I'm just suggesting you change it, just to be sure."

I can't stop looking at it—the case, it's taunting me. It's a sturdy black box that's big enough to hold a single gun. I know I shouldn't, but I also remember what Dylan told me about the code. All I want to do is have a quick look inside, make sure Dylan put the gun back like he said he did. It takes two minutes surfing the web to find Logan's jersey number and total goals scored—26—from his last season playing lacrosse.

I push the buttons on the safe based on my calculations and hear a satisfying beep. A red light on the front turns green. I look around nervously as if I'm going to be caught, but no one is around. Still, I'm freaked out as I undo the latches. Slowly, carefully, I flip open the case.

My eyes go wide while my mouth dries up. Before me is a big empty indent in the foam insulation where a gun should be.

Chapter 46

Evan Thompson drove his BMW slowly down Alton Road, while Alex and Brooke watched from the edge of the driveway.

"Oh shit," Brooke muttered under her breath.

The day had been eventful enough. Now Evan was back on the scene? They'd already had to call the cops once. His timing couldn't have been worse, especially since everything had just returned to normal. A tub full of squirt guns had been depleted and there was a war raging between the younger Alton Road residents and a few playful parents willing to get in on the action. Grills were going full steam, sending plumes of charcoal smoke skyward. Balloons tied to the backs of lawn chairs provided pops of color to the green landscape. Clusters of neighbors chatted easily together, eating and drinking (mostly drinking) as the afternoon faded away.

What should have been an idyllic scene of neighborhood fun was now tinged with foreboding as Evan navigated his car carefully around the cul-de-sac and into the driveway of his former residence.

"What's he doing here?" Alex wondered aloud. The yearbook had all but vanquished any lingering effects from the booze.

"Is Willow around?" Brooke asked with evident concern, but Alex was worried for Brooke as well.

Scanning the party, Alex soon spotted Willow idling by the tiki bar. Evan had to drive in front of the bar to get to the driveway, so she couldn't have missed him. She didn't look particularly alarmed.

"Let's see what's going on," suggested Alex.

Gently taking Brooke by the arm, the two joined Willow at the bar.

"Evan's here," said Alex in a warning tone.

Willow gave a nod. "He needed to get some things out of his darkroom. I'm out of the house for a while, so it's good timing," she replied.

Alex recalled the hidden room containing his shrine to Brooke. Maybe he left some other secrets behind that needed to be removed.

"Where's Riley?" Brooke asked.

Willow pointed to a gaggle of children who surrounded Riley like playful puppies, jumping up and down around her with unbridled enthusiasm. "The Nelsons are paying her to keep an eye on their kids," Willow said.

Off in the distance, Alex could see Nick playing a game of cornhole with some of the other neighborhood dads. He glanced her way, but quickly averted his gaze. Maybe he wasn't up for another confrontation, either. *Good.*

"Odd that Evan would pick today, the day of the block party, to get his things," Brooke said.

Willow took a long drink of her wine spritzer. "I'm out here, he's in there," she said. "What can go wrong?"

Before Alex could get out the word *plenty*, Samir Kumar came rushing over to the tiki bar. Tense and disagreeable on a good day, he appeared even more so in that moment. "Have any of you seen Mandy?" he asked. "I can't find her anywhere, and she's not answering her phone."

Brooke rolled her eyes. "God forbid she's out of your sight for a hot minute. She is a grown and capable woman, you know?"

Samir didn't flinch. "You don't understand," he said. "In fact, you have this *all* wrong. Alex, may we speak privately for a moment—please?"

Alex and Brooke checked in with each other, neither sure what to do. While Alex was more than willing to hear Samir out, she didn't feel comfortable being alone with him. Judging by Brooke's expression, she agreed. "We can talk right here," suggested Alex.

Samir shifted his gaze to Willow, making it obvious he preferred that she not be part of the conversation.

Willow extricated herself politely. "I'll go see how Riley's doing with all those kids."

After she departed, Samir's eyes darted among the partygoers, assessing the crowd with concern. "I prefer we speak somewhere a little less public," he said. "My son is at home, and I wouldn't want him to overhear what I need to tell you."

Alex said, "Nick and Lettie might be going in and out of the house, so I can't promise privacy at my place."

"I can," said Brooke. "My house is so private it sometimes feels like a mausoleum."

Alex peered across the way to where Evan's car was parked. "I'm not so sure you can promise no one will be spying," she said, "but I guess it'll do."

Chapter 47

Lettie

There's no gun in the case.

I'm no weapons expert, but I'm smart enough to know that there should be a gun in the foam imprint, and it's gone. I'm trying not to freak out.

Deep breaths, deep breaths, Lettie. There has to be a logical explanation, and the person going to give it to me is Dylan.

I close the lid. When I do, the case locks automatically. The green light on the front turns red again.

I need to find my cousin, so I text him—all caps loaded with exclamation marks. He deserves it.

WHERE ARE YOU???!!!!

He texts back almost immediately: *Outside setting up for the outdoor movie.*

Stay there, I text back.

Fastest way out is through the bulkhead door in the basement, so that's the way I go, which has the added benefit of avoiding Uncle Ken, who is still upstairs. I cross the street and meet up with Dylan, who is in fact helping Aunt Emily set up the projector.

Aunt Emily looks me up and down curiously. "Where are the chairs?" she asks.

Shit. The chairs.

"Sorry, I couldn't find them," I lie.

"No problem," Emily says with a smile. "It's a bit of a disaster down there. I've been telling Ken we need a massive yard sale to clean it out—certainly, before your grandmother moves in. I know where they are. I'll grab them."

Emily hurries off, leaving me with a brief opportunity to talk to Dylan alone. I pull him aside, finding a quiet grassy spot underneath the shade of an ancient oak tree near the Kumars' property. I have no idea where Jay is, but I suspect he's inside his house and will hide out there for most of the day. I can't believe it's been a year since I met him, but now isn't the time to dwell on my mild Jay Kumar obsession. Okay, a bit more than mild. But I have more important matters to address.

"What the hell, D? Where's the gun?" I bring this up only when I'm certain our conversation can't be overheard.

"I told you," he said, "I put it back in the case." He doesn't blink. Doesn't stammer.

Is he telling the truth?

"Well, it's not there now," I say.

Dylan's eyes go wide. He looks like I just kneed him in the nuts. "Lettie, what are you doing?" he says. "You opened the gun case?"

I nod, not feeling even a little guilty about it. "I was looking for the chairs in your basement, and the case was right there. I remembered the code, or what you said it was, so I decided to make sure you'd put it back."

"Why? You don't trust me?"

"No, I'm totally worried about you. There's a difference," I say. "But that doesn't matter. Where is the gun, D? Do you have it?"

Dylan brushes me off with a wave of his hand. "I told you, I put it back. You're making way too much out of this. My dad sometimes takes it out to clean it. I'm sure it's up in his office or something, but I promise you, I don't have it. Why don't you go get the egg toss set up—do something productive and leave me alone, will you?"

I can't say Dylan stomps off, but it wasn't the friendliest departure.

My instincts say to trust him. I've known Dylan my whole life and I think I'd know if he was lying to me. Still, I can't forget his comment about this block party being the most memorable one ever—and now there's a missing gun?

Something else Dylan said is sticking with me—not his words per se, but his egg toss reference makes me think of the conversation I just had with my father. *Once an egg tosser, always an egg tosser,* he had said. Basically, it was his cute way of implying that people don't really change.

I see Emily setting up the chairs as I'm lost in thought, taking bits and pieces of information and trying to connect them in a meaningful way.

Dylan and Riley.

Blackmailer.

Embarrassment.

A video recording.

Something private.

A *private* recording.

Who does that sort of thing? Who makes private recordings of people?

Who hacks and hides?

People don't change. My dad is right about that. And I'm stupid because I should have known it from the start.

The scorpion *always* stings the frog.

I see it all now. A fierce chill sets against my skin. Dylan is nowhere to be found. I look around, taking in the sights and sounds of kids running about, parents chowing down and drinking, music blasting, grills grilling, bikes biking—all our block-party norms—but I'm not feeling the party vibe. Instead, I catch sight of Bug Man walking toward Ken's house of all places.

Does this guy have a death wish?

I don't think about Bug Man for long. I have a more pressing concern.

I run toward Jay's front door, texting Dylan as I go.

He's not answering.

I call him, but I get voice mail. Now I'm terrified.

And that's why I need to find Jay Kumar right away, both to confront him . . . and to warn him.

Chapter 48

Alex settled herself onto the chilled white-pearled leather of Brooke's living room furniture, which was obviously intended more for show than for comfort. She glanced toward Brooke, who was occupying an adjacent armchair, before turning her attention to Samir.

"I'll be honest, Samir," Alex said. "Brooke and I have been worried about Mandy for a long time now. We've seen you behaving in possessive, controlling ways that, frankly, we find concerning. But we'll try and listen to what you have to say with an open mind."

Samir nodded. "Thank you. I can understand how it must appear from the outside. And you're not wrong. I *am* controlling. But not for the reasons you may think, and it's very important I explain why Mandy's absence is so alarming."

Alex leaned forward on the couch, as if to lean into Samir's story.

"I am deeply worried about my wife, her state of mind," he said. "She's left the house and taken all her medicines with her. *All* of them."

"You think she might harm herself?" Alex asked, sitting up straighter, eyes alert.

Samir shook his head grimly. "I don't know, but I don't think so," he said. "She's not well . . . she—" Emotion overtook him. He appeared to squeeze every muscle in his face to gain composure, but a strangled sob escaped nonetheless.

"Tell me what's going on," Alex said. "What's *really* going on, Samir?"

Samir managed a few ragged breaths, nodding several times in quick succession to indicate his willingness to be forthcoming. "We need to locate your brother-in-law, Ken, and fast," he said.

"I just saw him," Alex answered without hesitation. "After the confrontation with Bug Man, he went home to decompress."

Samir took this in. "Well, that makes me feel a little better," he said. "But I'm still concerned. I would have approached Ken myself, but—I know what he thinks of me, how his temper is, and I didn't want to instigate a volatile confrontation, so I came to you instead. Allow me to explain . . ." Again, he paused, needing to inhale a deep breath, wincing slightly as if in pain.

"Mandy and I . . . we are—well, we're not in a good place. I know you've suspected something is off between us, and you're not wrong, but again, it's not what you think. I'm not an abusive husband. I would *never* hurt my wife. Never. I love Mandy with all my heart. And for a long time, we were quite happy. We had so much in common—our careers, family goals. Our future was bright and full of hope. But all that was before Asher died."

"Asher? Who's Asher?" Alex asked.

"He's my younger son." The ache was audible in Samir's voice. "He died. Drowned in a swimming pool at my brother-in-law's house when he was just two years old."

The news struck Alex with the precision of an arrow. She flashed back to the disaster that was Friendsgiving, recalling the white plaster walls of the Kumars' home—and the cold, impersonal feel of every room, empty of any family photographs. She remembered asking Samir if he had more than one child, and how he became evasive when she dug deeper. Now she knew why.

"I'm so sorry," said Alex.

"Yes. Thank you," Samir replied. "We were all in shock, and deeply depressed as you can imagine, but nobody more so than Mandy." He cleared his throat, as though to clear the way for the words to come.

"Clinically, she was diagnosed with depression. Eventually, with lots of patience, therapy, and antidepressants, she *seemed* to improve. But she was never quite the same. I had hoped we could resume our lives to the best of our ability, and over time, Mandy appeared to move past the worst of her grief into what I thought was a place of acceptance.

"Naturally, we will forever mourn Asher's death, but life is for the living, as I have always said to Mandy and Jay. And we did just that—we began to *live again,* only now as a different family, a family of three, with a hole forever where Asher would have been. We managed like this for many years, but the hope I had envisioned for our future . . . I could see was just a mirage. Mandy was back, but she wasn't whole. My heart broke for her daily. It crushed me that I couldn't fix it, couldn't ease her pain.

"Ten years after Asher's passing, I decided to try something new. I planned a couple's getaway. Our anniversary was coming up. Jay was a teenager and had a trusted family friend to stay with. This trip was for Mandy and me to reconnect and hopefully rebuild."

"Did it work?" Alex asked.

"I thought so," Samir said. "By the end of it, she *was* a different person. Lighter. Full of excitement. She seemed to have rediscovered her life's purpose. Work inspired her again. Even Jay's troubles didn't derail her newfound energy. But . . . I remained wary. Something didn't feel—I'm not sure of the word . . . *authentic,* I guess. It was like she'd gone from too low to too high far too quickly. I felt as though she was better in some ways, but distant from me in others. It was as if she was on a mission and I wasn't part of the assignment. Clinically, something wasn't right, but I couldn't quite grasp it."

"From what I recall, she was very enthusiastic about moving to Alton Road," Brooke said.

"Which is why I didn't fight it," said Samir. "I wanted her to be happy. And the move to this neighborhood was something she felt quite strongly about—so much so that over time I began to feel extremely uncomfortable with the decision. Why this neighborhood? I kept asking myself. We didn't have any friends here, it's farther from our work, and we didn't need this big house with a grown son who eventually would be back out on his own—or so we *hoped.* Nothing really made sense. That's when I started noting her interactions with our new neighbors, trying to decipher her motivations."

"With Ken in particular, I bet," said Brooke. "You know about him—that he and Mandy went to high school together?"

If Samir was surprised that Brooke had learned of their shared history, it did not register on his face. "Yes, eventually I figured that out for myself—but *after* the move. I began asking myself: Did she *want* to be near Ken or was it simply a coincidence? None of it was adding up for me, which is why I looked into all of you. Each one—neighbor by neighbor, doing my research, compiling notes, inviting you to a get-together—"

"Friendsgiving—it wasn't Mandy's idea?"

Samir returned a slight headshake. "No, it was mine, but Mandy was happy to host," he said. "I learned some things at the dinner, but not enough to form a conclusion. It took time, research, and observation for me to develop a theory that honestly, I wasn't willing to fully accept—I *couldn't* accept it. But I couldn't sit idle, either. Best I could do was try to keep Mandy under my watchful eye and make sure she was taking her psychiatric medications—not only for her well-being but for the safety of others as well."

"Safety of others?" Alex repeated. "What does that mean?"

Samir's face looked so troubled that Alex found herself shifting uneasily in her seat. Brooke, too, looked tense and rigid. From somewhere close by, the gentle ticktock of a clock kept a steady beat that matched the rhythm of Alex's heart.

"I became convinced that Mandy had brought us here on a mission of sorts—that she wanted to move to Alton Road *specifically* to be close to your brother-in-law, Alex. She came here for Ken."

"Why would she do that?" Alex asked.

"I would not normally share Mandy's history, but these circumstances are indeed extreme."

"What happened to her?" Brooke asked with compassion.

"Mandy moved to a new town her junior year in high school," Samir began. "She desperately wanted to fit in, and one boy in particular paid her a good deal of attention."

"Ken?" Alex asked.

Samir nodded. "She got drunk one night at a party. Didn't remember saying yes—but she certainly was in no mind to give her consent."

"The next day, Ken stopped speaking to her. Mandy hadn't made other friends yet and felt very isolated and alone. There was whispered talk at school—you can imagine what was said. At her lowest point, a kind boy who ran in the same circles as Ken came to her rescue. He was extremely nice. Popular as well. He bought her flowers. Took her to the movies. Soon enough, she thought they were in love. But after they slept together, he stopped talking to her just as Ken did— 'ghosting' is the term for it these days. Back then, I suppose you'd say he gave her the cold shoulder."

"How awful for her," said Alex.

"It gets worse," Samir said. "Again, there was whispered talk. You can imagine the names they called her. Several boys made inappropriate overtures, expecting things from her. She didn't understand how the whole school seemed to know intimate details about her relationships.

"She would have remained confused were it not for a shy girl who approached her one day with some disturbing information. As it turned out, her relationships with these two boys were part of an elaborate game—it was all cold and calculating deception from the very start. You see, the boys had started a betting pool, with half the school participating, that they could both have sex with the new girl within a couple of months.

"The other girl showed her the sheet of paper used to track the bets and the money exchanged. It seemed everyone knew about the betting pool . . . everyone, that is, except Mandy. She was so distraught she thought of killing herself, but decided instead to tell her parents the truth. They were quite conservative, and no surprise, blamed Mandy for the actions of those two boys. The boys got a slap on the wrist, while Mandy had to transfer schools. But she never really recovered, never made any close friends at this new school, never escaped the shadow of what those boys did to her. On some level, I think she blamed herself for letting it happen. Either way, the ordeal followed her long after graduation."

Alex flashed back on the security camera recording of Ken and Mandy on the Kumars' back deck. She saw the truth behind that exchange—it wasn't romantic, it was hostile.

"Why would she want to be close to him?" Alex asked. "For revenge? To torture him with her presence? Make him uncomfortable all the time? Ruin his marriage? Why?"

"I have my theory," said Samir.

Before he could share, Brooke interrupted, her voice shaking with emotion. "The other boy," she said, "what was his name?"

"You know his name," Samir answered in a low tone. "And that anniversary trip I took Mandy on some years ago, the one she left feeling lighter, better, elated . . . it was a cruise."

Chapter 49

Lettie

'm a teen, so doorbells come second to texting, which I do while standing on Jay's front step. My patience in short supply, I eventually ring the doorbell. When he doesn't answer fast enough, I follow that up with another text, imploring him to come to the door.

Finally, he shows up dressed in a lavender button-down shirt and faded jeans, looking sexy as ever. He's got loafers on his feet, no socks—and no surprise, a vape pen in his hand. "What's up, Lettie?" he asks.

If my series of alarming texts disturbed him, Jay doesn't let it show. Bottling up his brand of cool would make the world a whole lot more relaxed, that's for sure.

"I need to ask you something, and don't lie to me," I say.

He invites me inside, but I'm not willing to go. I want an easy way to escape if everything explodes in my face. "I think I'll stay right here, thanks."

For a moment, he looks wounded, but I feel no sympathy. He strikes a defiant pose and I watch all the expression drain from his face, making him harder to read. He's going on the defensive. He knows what's up, and I suspect he knows why I'm here.

"I'm going to ask you one question, and I want a truthful answer," I say. "Are you blackmailing my cousin?"

Jay doesn't flinch, not even to blink. He holds my gaze with a penetrating stare.

I take a step back until my heels hover over the edge of the stone landing. "Are you?" I ask again.

Jay breaks eye contact. I feel satisfaction and confusion all at once. He's answered me, but I still want him to say it. "Why?" I ask. "Why'd you do it?"

I don't bother going into my shoddy detective work. No need to remind Jay that he once showed me a video of his parents' private conversation, which he obtained by hacking their laptop camera. I've no doubt that Jay did the same to Dylan, capturing him in some compromising position, for reasons still unknown.

"He's my family," I remind him. "I thought you were my friend."

Pressure builds in my chest and eyes, but I refuse to let my emotions get the better of me. I now think Jay is some kind of sociopath, and I won't give him the satisfaction of seeing me suffer.

Jay puts his pen in his mouth, takes a hit. I've had enough of his vaping, so I snatch the contraption mid-puff and toss it behind me, where it lands in the grass.

Jay spits out a plume of vapor.

"Tell me why," I demand again, through clenched teeth.

"Call it karma," Jay says.

"Karma?"

"Yeah, Dylan wasn't my big fish. That was your uncle Ken. But the sins of the father are visited upon the children," he says. I think he's paraphrasing the Bible. "Hurting Dylan caused more suffering for your uncle, so that's how I justified it—all of it, showing him that picture of Riley with Umbrella Man, and that video, too."

"What are you talking about?" I shake my head as if my ears are blocked. "What does Uncle Ken have to do with any of this?"

"Plenty." Jay smirks. "I got enough on him to get a twenty-five-grand payday."

"My uncle paid you twenty-five thousand dollars?" My mouth falls open. "Jay, you're a criminal."

He rotates his arm as if to show me his tattoo. "Yeah, I guess I am." If the admission bothers him, it doesn't register on his face.

My instinct is to step back, but I'd risk falling down the stairs. I stay put.

"I suppose your uncle and I have something in common—that criminal element."

"What does that mean?"

"It means he's not a good guy, Lettie. Look, I feel shitty about Dylan, okay? I got carried away, and I shouldn't have gone after him the way I did."

Jay might have gone too far, but I'm the one who brought the scorpion into the house. I'm no angel.

"You saved him . . . you saved Dylan's life. You called me, and—" I stop mid-sentence. My breath catches. The words won't come out. Then: "You were *still* watching him, weren't you?"

Dylan wouldn't be careless with his computer, not after being blackmailed. So how would Jay have known Dylan was in crisis? That's when I remembered the rock tossed through the window on Christmas Eve, and Uncle Ken's tough talk about better security and catching the shithead who did it. The lucky break that Jay just happened to be out and about at the same moment Dylan was stumbling around his lawn wasn't luck at all.

"You hacked their doorbell security camera, didn't you?"

Jay nods—no hesitation, but no pride, either. Merely a statement of fact. "Yeah, I have a feed from it running to my computer, so I was downstairs working when Dylan staggered outside. It caught my eye. He didn't look right to me, and I know an opioid high when I see one. I grabbed the Narcan and called you."

"That's why you stopped blackmailing him," I say. "Because you felt guilty he tried to kill himself, and you thought it was because of you."

"Yeah," he says. "I shouldn't have gone after him, and I'm sorry I did."

"He's a good person. He didn't deserve that." The guilt takes another big bite out of me.

"And my mother didn't deserve to be raped and humiliated by your uncle," Jay says.

"What are you talking about? That makes no sense." My voice rises in anger.

"I'm talking about your uncle and my mom going to high school together, where he preyed on her, lied to her, violated her, and nothing happened to him."

"How do you know that?" I ask.

"Because I not only hacked into my father's personal computer, but I also found all his notes, notes he's been compiling about your uncle—and all of you, in fact."

"Notes on us? On my uncle? Jay, you sound crazy."

My accusation doesn't ruffle him. "It's bad enough my family was all screwed up over Asher's death," he says. "My mom didn't need to suffer for years—*years*—because of what your uncle did to her."

I'm stunned into silence.

"It wasn't easy for me growing up in such a disaster of a family," Jay continues. "I had plenty of therapy, all kinds of medications shoved down my throat. My mom did, too. But your uncle Ken gets to have his perfect life, and Dylan's life looked awfully idyllic from the outside as well. So I decided someone had to tip the scales of justice to balance things out."

I can't process everything he's telling me. My mind's gone blank.

"I don't think you want to know everything I know," he says, bringing me back to my senses. "He's still your uncle. It's still your family."

"I think I deserve to know," I say. "Tell me everything."

Jay lowers his head, thinking, not saying a word. "Come inside," he says. "I'll show you something downstairs."

I take a step toward the door but stop myself. "No," I say. "I'd better not." I don't feel the need to explain.

"Okay," Jay says. "Suit yourself. Stay here. I'll bring it to you." He vanishes inside his house, closing the door behind him.

For want of something to do, I start looking at my phone, scrolling through random social media posts, not able to give anything much attention. The music is blasting, and a couple of eager dads are exciting the kids with firecrackers, a prelude to tonight's fireworks display, which is always something of a letdown. Fireworks are illegal in Massachusetts, but we do it anyway at the block party, keeping it intentionally small—a couple of bottle rockets, roman candles, and firecrackers that never seem to catch the attention of the Meadow-brook PD. Each loud pop of the tiny explosives makes me jump, re-minding me of Dylan and the missing gun.

Kids go screaming and scampering in all directions when a fire-cracker doesn't go off as expected. Eventually it blows up. A small cloud of smoke rises from the remnant. I flash on a memory of Dylan saying something about Uncle Ken sometimes cleaning his gun in his office. Then I think: Bug Man. Rocks through a window are one thing. Bullets are something else.

I text my mom. *I'm not panicking. Not yet.*

Where are you?

I don't check for her reply because Jay's come back, and he's got something in his hand. It's a phone, but it's definitely not his. The case is light pink—very feminine.

"New Year's Eve, Dylan threw this onto his front lawn. I saw him do it in my camera feed while I was watching him stumble about."

"Is that Riley's phone?" I ask.

Jay nods.

"You've had it all this time?"

Nods again.

"Shit, Jay. You are *really* messed up."

No nod from him this time, but there's no need. I can see in his eyes that he agrees. I think briefly of Asher, his brother, drowning, Jay blaming himself for his death, and what that must have done to him. It's not an excuse, but it may be the start of an explanation.

"I didn't ever want to show this to you, Lettie. I kind of hoped I could just let it all go, not burden you with it. I really like you—in every way. I think you're awesome. But your uncle—he's a different story. So I guess if you want to know, then you'll have to ask me again. You have to say it, Lettie. This time you're going to have to ask to be stung."

I want to walk away. Go back to the party. Make a veggie dog. Drink a soda. I want to step back in time to when I loved playing DJ at the block party, when I thought my mom and dad ruled this world as omniscient beings, back to a time when my family and extended family felt like one big happy unit. I want to inhale the innocence of youth and let it take over my brain, let me forget about all this craziness. But I can't look away. I have to know.

"Show me," I say.

Jay nods. "The phone was easy to hack. But it won't be nearly as easy for you to recover. Once I show you, there'll be no turning back, Lettie."

I nod again. My heart is beating in my throat.

Jay holds up the phone. He shows me what he didn't want me to see. I hear a pop of firecrackers, and another pop soon after.

And I let out a scream.

Chapter 50

Everyone jumped when the doorbell rang, including Samir, who was typically reserved. When Brooke opened the door, it seemed she got a second jolt.

"What are you doing here?" Brooke asked.

"I'm not selling anything, so you can drop the angry act," said a familiar voice.

Alex emerged from the living room to see Bug Man standing on the front step, holding his green cap in his hand. His big eyes bulged even buggier than usual. Sweat made his thin, dark hair look greasy.

"It's no act," Brooke said. "The police were here and nearly broke up this party because of you, or did you forget?"

"Hey, I get I'm not popular around these parts, but I'm not a bad guy. And I'm here doing a civic service, okay?"

"Oh? What service?" Alex asked.

"I went to try to clear the air with the guy who assaulted me," Bug Man said.

"The guy? You mean my brother-in-law?"

"Yeah, I know. Ken Adair. Aka the roach who got me fired. Whatever. I know who you all are. Which is why I'm here. I saw you go into this house, thought you should know."

"Know what?" asked Alex.

"There's some commotion over at your brother-in-law's place," Bug Man said. "I heard something. Raised voices—definitely an argument. It sounded heated, heard threatening language, but I couldn't make out any voices except Ken's. He didn't sound right to me, so I rang the doorbell, but got no answer. I could have left it at that, but you know—that's not what a good salesman does. A good salesman looks past grievances to always deliver a quality service."

"You called the police on him," said Alex. "That's not exactly letting bygones be bygones."

Bug Man made a big show of indignation. "I didn't press charges, did I? And I'm here to tell you something is up over there. I've got a nose for this sort of thing. You go to enough houses, you get to know the crazy, if you know what I mean," he said with a wink Alex found unsettling.

"You'd know the signs of crazy," Brooke muttered.

"Now, now, no need for name-calling." Bug Man made an overly theatrical bow, as if Brooke were a fair maiden. "But a warning is a warning. I could have left it alone. I don't like the guy, but I'm not looking for him to get in any major trouble."

Alex saw no need to wait any longer.

Samir, who had joined the gathering in the foyer, shared her alarm. "Mandy," he breathed.

"Alex and I will check it out," Brooke said to Samir. "No offense, but you might escalate things . . . inadvertently, perhaps, but you should keep away from Ken regardless."

"I guess my work here is done," said Bug Man in his oddly nasal voice. "Maybe I'll just leave you a flyer."

He reached into his satchel, but Brooke was already outside, closing the door behind her as Alex and Samir joined her on the front step. "Save it for later," Brooke said. "If you've been helpful, I promise to become a customer for life."

Bug Man beamed. "In that case—you mentioned Mandy's name, right?" He was looking at Samir. "You looking for her? Because I've seen her."

Alex and Brooke left it at that. They made their way down the driveway at a hurried clip while Samir stayed behind to hear what Bug Man had to say.

Alex noticed Lettie talking with Jay Kumar on the front step of his house as she rushed past. What was going on between those two? She didn't have time to give it much thought.

A burst of firecrackers went off as they neared Ken's house, causing Alex to jump. By the time they reached the front door, Alex heard it again.

Pop. Pop.

She jolted, uncertain where the noise had originated. She decided the blaring music and party commotion had made the firecracker's ricocheting echo sound like it had been lit off *inside* the house.

She entered the home with a mix of emotions—appreciation for the Bug Man (big surprise), concern for Ken's well-being, and an utter disgust at his abhorrent and criminal behavior with Mandy. And . . . fear?

Whatever commotion Bug Man had overheard, all seemed quiet now. Alex made her way tentatively down the hall. An odd smell hit her nostrils. Something burnt. *Had* a firework gone off inside?

"Ken, we need to talk," she called.

No answer.

Ken's office wasn't far from the front entrance. Alex headed there, with Brooke still in the rear. The glass-fronted French doors were open as Alex approached. She saw Ken standing inside his office, with his back to her.

"I've been calling for you," Alex said as she stepped across the threshold.

It wasn't until the figure turned that Alex realized she'd been mistaken, her mind tricking her into seeing what she'd expected to see.

It was not Ken who faced her, but Evan Thompson.

Evan's wide and glassy eyes—clear indications he was under the influence of something—fixated on Alex. His expression radiated a degree of madness that shook her before she even realized that he held a gun.

The unmistakable smell of gunpowder hung in the air, strong and pungent. Dazed as if he'd just been in an accident, Evan sidestepped to his left, revealing Ken's inert form lying facedown, motionless on the wood floor, his body soaking in a pool of fresh blood.

Alex let out a scream, cut short when Evan grabbed her by the arm, yanking her away from the door. He gave her a hard shove from behind that sent her stumbling until she crashed into a wall of bookcases opposite the entrance. Pain rocketed down her arm.

Brooke cried out as Evan hauled her inside, pulling with enough force to throw her to the floor, not far from where Ken lay still.

Alex whirled around but would not advance because Evan had the gun leveled at her chest.

"Oh shit . . . oh shit," Evan moaned. He ran his hand repeatedly through his hair, pulling at the roots anxiously. The gun remained steady in his other hand, though his breath came erratically. "You two shouldn't be here," he said, sounding more shocked than angry.

"Clearly," said Alex breathlessly, her heart racing. "Evan, is Ken alive? He needs medical help. Let me call for help."

Evan chuckled mirthlessly. "Yeah, that's not going to happen," he said. "Alex, throw your phone on the ground. Do it now. Brooke, you too. Then check for a pulse, will you?" he barked.

Evan's behavior left little doubt in Alex's mind that what happened to Ken was no accident, that her neighbor had most likely committed murder. Given he had a gun, Alex wasn't about to go against Evan's wishes. She had a daughter to think about, her own life to consider.

She tossed her cell phone onto the floor, but not anywhere near Evan. He'd have to ask for it, perhaps reach down to get it, and then maybe he'd be in striking distance of a well-placed kick. Brooke, who was still on the floor, seemingly in shock, got her phone out as well. She, too, placed it out of Evan's reach, perhaps having the same thought as Alex.

"Slide them over to me," said Evan, using the gun to draw an imaginary line from the phones to where he wished them to go.

So much for that plan. Alex and Brooke followed his orders.

"Now a pulse," said Evan. "I need to know."

Shaking with fright, Brooke did as she was asked, taking hold of Ken's limp wrist, then applying pressure with her fingers. "I'm not trained," she said after a moment, panic in her voice. "But I don't feel anything."

"Evan, please, let us help," Alex said. "He might still be alive."

"Yeah, yeah," said Evan. "He might." Somehow he managed to

sound relieved and disappointed at the same time. "Brooke, go stand near Alex, will you?" Using the gun as a pointer, he directed Brooke to where he wanted her to go.

Alex couldn't reconcile the incongruence of Evan's politeness with the seriousness of this situation. She and Brooke stood with their backs up against a wall of bookcases.

Evan maneuvered over to Ken's desk, where the architectural plans for the addition were spread out. His movement created an opening for Alex to escape, but she dared not make a break for it. It would take one second—less than that, even—for Evan to put a bullet in her back.

From atop the desk, Evan retrieved a half-empty bottle of Johnnie Walker Blue Label, Ken's sacred drink. He uncapped it, put the bottle to his lips, and took a long swallow. He was shaking badly. After downing a few sizable gulps, he took one last drink, decreasing the bottle's contents significantly.

Brooke spoke up. "Evan, please. You've got to be reasonable. We need to help Ken!"

"Help him?" Evan shouted. "Help? Okay, let's *help* Ken. I just kept him out of prison for rape." He surveyed Ken's motionless form, raising the bottle as if making a toast. He drank more. Pulling the bottle from his lips, he said, "There you go, Ken. Happy to help."

"Look, we know about Mandy," said Alex, "about what Ken did to her in high school, but that's no reason to—"

"Mandy?" Evan shouted, cutting Alex off mid-sentence. "What the hell do I care about Mandy Kumar? I'm talking about my *daughter*— I'm talking about Riley."

Chapter 51

Lettie

I see my mom walking to Uncle Ken's house with Brooke, so I follow. Jay knows where I'm going, and makes no attempt to stop me. I wonder if my mom knows what I just learned from Jay—the photographic evidence I can never unsee.

The moment I set foot into Uncle Ken's house, I know something is wrong. A strange smell hangs heavy in the air. I hear Evan's voice down the hall, coming from Ken's office.

"She's a kid," Evan says, and right away I know what he's talking about.

The pictures on Riley's phone were explicit.

Ken and Riley. The older man she was seeing—Umbrella Man—was her boyfriend's father and my uncle. I never got a good look at him, didn't notice Uncle Ken's car at the hotel or see his face at the bar on that foggy, rainy night, but now I know, and everything makes perfect, awful, terrible sense.

No wonder Dylan had stopped speaking to his father. No wonder he took an overdose and chucked the phone. His suicide attempt had far more to do with his father's betrayal than with any involvement of mine.

I'd seen Dylan use Riley's phone before. He didn't ask for her code back then, and I guess she didn't think to change it after they broke up. Dylan already thought of himself as a disappointment, but add to that the threat of blackmail and the sickening discovery that his father was sleeping with his girlfriend? That would be too much for almost anybody, I'd say, but especially someone as sensitive as my cousin Dylan.

But I can't think about Dylan or the pictures that Riley had on her phone—selfies of her and Uncle Ken in bed together, their naked bodies hidden by the bedsheets, thank goodness for that. All I can think about is my mother's safety. I saw her come into the house, and I hear a tone in Evan's voice that I don't like. I'm not sure what's going on, though I have a deep, dark feeling that my mother is in grave danger.

Instinct tells me to stay quiet, but the need to see what's going on keeps me inching closer to Uncle Ken's first-floor office. My back presses up against the wall as I work my way down the hallway, worrying my pounding heart is going to give me away.

"He slept with her. He's *been* sleeping with her. He's been having sex with my daughter," Evan says loudly. "Willow told me she was seeing some older guy, and I decided to follow Riley, check this guy out for myself since she wouldn't tell me anything about him. Stalking is something I'm good at—right, Brooke?"

Evan sounds insane—his speech is hurried, garbled, and his words are slurred like he's been drinking. "I didn't mean to do it," he says. "I didn't come here to shoot him. I just wanted to confront him. I told him I was coming over, that I wanted to talk—that's all. But he must have known or at least suspected what it was about, because he had his gun in his office, on the desk, right in front of him."

Evan pauses. I hear a slosh of liquid that I assume comes from him taking a drink. He coughs like it was rough going down.

At this point I'm about a foot and a half from the entrance to Ken's office, but I don't dare make myself visible. I'm panicked about getting out my phone, too, because I'm worried it'll make a noise if I try to text my father.

"So I said to him," Evan continues, "'Ken—you utter piece of shit—how could you sleep with Riley?' Next thing I know, he's got his gun pointed at me. *Me!* I'm the father of his victim and he's treating me like a criminal? So I grabbed for the gun. I was a lot quicker than he thought, and Ken always overestimated his athletic prowess. We struggled a bit, but I won out.

"Once *I* have the gun pointed at *him*, he's not so tough. He starts begging for his life, telling me we can talk it over. But I'm like, 'Talk what over? You can't fix what you did. You took advantage of a minor—my daughter, no less. It's called statutory rape, you know. You think you deserve forgiveness? You don't deserve a second chance. You can't take back what you've done.'

"And then I shot him. That's what happened. That's exactly what happened. I just shot him—three times in the chest."

I cover my mouth with my hand to keep a scream from coming out. As I do, I see the door to the basement open slowly—and silently, thank goodness. It's Mandy Kumar, moving stealthily the way I imagine a burglar might.

What's Mandy Kumar doing here? Why is she coming up from the basement?

I let it go. No time for that.

Our eyes meet. Before she can say anything, I've got my finger to my lips. The urgent look on my face makes it clear that she needs to keep quiet. I motion for her to get against the wall on the opposite side of the office door from me. She moves there as silently as a ghost.

"Evan, you shot him in cold blood," my mother says. "You may have *murdered* him."

Evan laughs almost maniacally. "Yeah . . . yeah, I guess I did. I really did," he says as if just coming to grips with it.

"You've got to turn yourself in," my mother says. "We've got to try and help Ken."

Brooke's voice is next. "You're not this person," she tells him. "There's a reason I never called the police on you. I was *never* afraid of you. You were just troubled, is all—but you're not a killer."

"Evidently that's exactly what I am, Brooke," says Evan. "And there's a big problem. I just confessed it to two witnesses." He laughs to himself like he can't believe his own stupidity.

I can't believe mine, either, because I'm reaching for my phone. There's a risk I'll give myself away, but I can't let fear keep me from getting help.

Mandy's eyes grow round as the moon. I'm sure she has the same concern I do. Thankfully, there are no beeps, but my hands are so shaky I'm worried I'll drop the damn device. I go to text—can't call, can't speak—and the last message I sent was to Jay, so it's that conversation I pull up.

Fear and terror don't keep my fingers from working.

I manage to type: *Call the police.*

And I hit send.

Next message: *911.*

Send.

Next message: *Murder.*

Send.

"What am I going to do now?" Evan asks himself.

Drink, I suppose, because I hear a gulp and more sloshing.

"Let the police handle this, Evan," says my mom. "You don't have to make this worse."

"Worse?" he exclaims. "Worse than life in prison? I can't do that."

"We won't say anything," Brooke promises. "It was self-defense. We'll back you on it."

"And I'm supposed to trust you, Brooke? You might not have been afraid of me before, but you'll be pretty damn scared of me now. My bet is you'll want me locked away for good. I'm sure of it."

"Evan, what do you plan to do?" My mom sounds anxious. No, make that totally terrified.

I'm looking at Mandy, who is motioning for me to check my phone. Sure enough, there's a message from Jay.

On it. Stay safe. Called the cops.

Okay, so I just need a few minutes—I can wait this out.

Then I hear Evan: "I've got it—Bug Man . . . that asshole's been here all day. He and Ken got into it. And you two showed up at the wrong time. I'll drop a few hints to the police about Bug Man, and that'll be that. Nobody but me knows about Riley and Ken, so I've got no motive."

"Evan, you're not making sense," Mom tells him. "That's a crazy plan, and it won't work. It could never work."

"Shit, you're right," Evan says.

The tight ball of fear in my chest deflates ever so slightly. Maybe there's hope.

"But . . . it's the best plan I got. It's all I got. I'm sorry to do this, Alex. I really am."

Everything slows down in that moment. I can't see what's going on inside Ken's office, but I hear it.

Brooke says, "Evan, you don't have to do this! We can work this out. You're not this person. You're not a killer!"

"Sorry, Brooke, this isn't what I wanted. I'll always love you."

"Evan, NOOOO!" my mom screams.

I have this horrifying image of Evan raising his gun, pointing it at my mother and Brooke—ready, aim, fire.

That's when my body and mind separate. I reach up and unhook a framed picture of Logan from the wall, one I know well from many viewings over the years. Logan's decked out in his lacrosse finest after some big game, with his arm draped around Uncle Ken's shoulders, his long hair glistening from the sweat of exertion.

Hoping I can create a brief diversion, give my mother and Brooke one more second of time, I throw the framed photograph hard as I can onto the floor in front of the office door. A loud crash follows, as the glass fronting the image shatters into countless pieces.

A second later, I hear a grunt from Evan, like something had hit him. Then comes another sound, as terrifying, heart-stopping, soul-crushing a sound as I'll ever hear.

Gunshots—not one, but two.

Chapter 52

Alex braced herself to die. She understood it would happen in mere moments. She saw murder in Evan's eyes, and God only knew what was swimming through that man's veins. She'd watched him guzzle down most of the contents of Ken's prized whisky, and the alcohol would certainly interact poorly with whatever narcotics Evan likely had in his system.

She could dive at him, Alex supposed. Or maybe she'd try to use one of the paperweights on Ken's bookcase as a weapon. But she couldn't risk it, especially not while Evan was raising his hand, bringing the gun level with her head, and certainly not when the look in his eyes showed his intent to pull the trigger.

Brooke bought them more time, pleading with Evan to reconsider, swearing that they'd keep his secret. *We can work this out. You're not this person. You're not a killer.* She tried all the clichés, to no avail.

Alex briefly imagined Nick coming to her rescue, crashing through the window like a warrior prince, disarming Evan with a single knockout punch. But that was nothing more than a flash of hope, a shimmering mirage that her mind had conjured to help her cope with the inevitable. It was hard to believe that their last interaction had been the worst of their entire marriage.

Alex braced herself for the shot. A desperate scream escaped her: "Evan, NOOO!"

Her chest caved in on itself when she heard a terrible crash, but it wasn't the gunshot she had expected. Instead, it was the sound of glass shattering everywhere.

Startled, Evan spun in the direction of the disturbance, looking through the office door and away from Alex, bringing the gun with him as he rotated at the waist.

Alex did not hesitate. This was her only chance. As Evan moved, so did she, reaching for the heavy glass paperweight on the bookcase. One moment she was without a weapon, and then just like that, she was armed. No sooner did she have the object in her hand—a clear glass orb encasing a kaleidoscope of small colorful beads—than she was fully engaged. Her arm came forward like a whip with her eyes locked on her target—Evan's head, to be precise.

With a rush of adrenaline, Alex released the paperweight to deliver a direct hit, or so she hoped. Evan turned away from the sound of the shattered glass in the hall toward Alex, who had just completed her throw. If he saw the paperweight coming at him, he didn't have time to move out of the way.

Indeed, Alex *had* delivered a strike, one that connected powerfully with Evan's shoulder. It was, unfortunately, the left shoulder—attached to the arm holding the bottle of whisky, not the gun. Evan dropped the thick glass bottle, which landed on Ken's antique area rug with a dull thud, as the gun in his other hand went off.

The bullet sank harmlessly into a nearby wall, splintering plaster but nothing more.

Evan adjusted his aim, staring directly at Alex. She thought of charging, but worried that would make her an easier target. Her thoughts dulled as the world around her lost all color, her field of vision blurring. She prepared once more for the sting of death, but instead heard a series of gasps and choking sounds come from Evan.

Alex's vision cleared in time to see him rocking on his heels, suddenly unsteady on his feet, as if a slight breeze could topple him over. His face turned gray. Each wheezing breath he managed came with great effort. Unable to hold his arm out straight, Evan could no longer aim the gun at any target. An odd gurgling sound bubbled in his throat as his eyes rolled into the back of his head.

What the hell was going on with him? wondered Alex. Was he having a heart attack? A seizure?

Evan finally lost his balance completely, falling backward as he went. He began to raise his arms in a pointless attempt to arrest his fall. For a split second, the gun was pointed straight at his own head.

A shot rang out. A spurt of blood exploded from Evan's skull as his body landed hard on the floor, not far from Ken's body.

Alex couldn't see exactly where the bullet had landed, but the blood pouring out, fast and steady, told her with absolute certainty that no bandage or first-aid technique she could employ would save his life.

Chapter 53

Lettie

'm frozen in place against the wall, trying not to think the worst of the worst.

Two shots.

My mother is dead.

Brooke is dead.

Wait.

I hear Brooke and my mother both screaming, but I can't make out what they're saying. My ears still ring from the loud shots in the enclosed space, but I don't care. I can hear well enough to know Mom's voice. My heart lifts.

As if we've coordinated our efforts, Mandy and I simultaneously spring away from our respective walls to take a peek inside Ken's office.

I probably should have stayed put. I've no idea if there's still a threat. But an irresistible need to see my mom, to make sure she's unharmed, overrules my better judgment.

A scream, this time my own, bursts out at the sight of the carnage. Two bodies lie on the floor—Evan and Ken. Blood is everywhere, with a grotesque aroma that I won't soon forget.

Mom rushes at me like she's going to make a tackle. In a way, she does, slamming into me so hard I nearly lose my balance.

Willow and Emily rush into the room moments later. My ears are still blocked, so I wasn't aware of their approaching footsteps. But I can hear, for the second time that day, sirens blaring in the distance. Also audible are Aunt Emily's throaty sobs as she drops to her knees beside Uncle Ken, who doesn't move a muscle. I glance behind to see Willow hovering just outside the office. Her eyes are glazed over, frozen with fear.

Jay must have told Emily and Willow something was going on. He probably relayed my text, which would explain why they'd arrived before the police. Everyone is crying, including me. A trace of gun smoke hangs in the air like a hovering mist.

Mom's checking me over as if I might have been injured, and I'm doing the same with her. We're simultaneously asking if the other is okay, and then my mom seems to figure something out. Her expression changes. "Did you break the glass in the hall?"

I nod.

Mom hugs me tighter. "That was so damn stupid and dangerous, and I can't love you and thank you enough. I think you may have saved our lives."

She leaves me to go to Aunt Emily, who is kneeling beside Uncle Ken. Emily searches for a pulse, placing her fingers on his neck. She tries to flip him over, but he's immovable.

"Wait for the ambulance," Mom tells her. "He might still be alive, and moving him could be harmful."

He's not alive, though. I'm sure of it. Same as I'm sure Evan is dead. The only dead people I've ever seen have been at wakes. The sight is surreal. My brain is working overtime to process the scene and, like it or not, I'm sure the memories of these smells, sights, and sounds will stay with me forever.

I've no idea what's happened here—how both Ken and Evan ended up in a pool of blood—but that's unimportant. Aunt Emily is in shock. We all are. Unfortunately, my aunt is in for more traumatic news. She doesn't know yet about Ken and Riley.

We're all hugging, crying, stunned and dazed. Mandy Kumar, who seems to have emergency training, evaluates Evan and Ken and somberly shakes her head, confirming our worst fears. The sirens grow louder.

Before I know it, the police arrive. They hold my father and Samir Kumar back, as well as most of the neighborhood who came to check on the commotion.

My mom is scanning the room. She checks all around—looking for something, it seems—but we're being escorted outside as police, firefighters, and EMTs swarm in.

Before we're forced to leave, she takes one last look, then shakes her head as if in disbelief. Maybe she's processing the scene, surveying the horror. But I think not. It's something else.

She starts to speak. I hope she's going to tell me what's on her mind—above and beyond the obvious. Instead, she puts her arm around me, pulls me in close. "I love you," she whispers. "With all my heart, I love you so much."

I'm crying. Rivers of tears streak down my face. I'm shaking, too, and it feels like I'll never stop. The EMTs are checking me over, asking all kinds of questions, but I insist I'm fine.

My dad is there, horror-struck, examining me for injuries as well.

Then Mom and Dad embrace each other—full love. Whatever trouble they had before, I think it's over and done with.

I'm all right.

She's all right.

Those are the *only* things that matter now.

Chapter 54

On an oppressively hot afternoon, as summer neared, Alex prepared the lunch she would bring to the lake. It was the first time the women who resided on the cul-de-sac—Alex, Emily, Willow, Mandy, and Brooke—would all get together since the funerals. It had been a difficult time for all, but Alex reserved most of her sympathy and heartache for Dylan and Riley.

She cut a tuna sandwich in half, thinking of Evan and Ken. Each had made fateful choices that led to their tragic ends, but the children were victimized. When Riley came to mind, Alex sliced a carrot with extra force, letting some of her anger out. She had been too young and naive to have been a consenting partner for Ken. Poor Dylan might never recover from his father's betrayal or from the confusing grief he was enduring.

Alex couldn't believe Dylan hadn't come forward when he found incriminating evidence about his father on Riley's phone. Perhaps he felt too much shame, didn't know how to process it all. At least he was in therapy, opening up to his family more. Despite the long road ahead, Alex felt optimistic that he'd get through this trauma.

Thankfully, the police did not release any motive, so social media was in the dark about Ken and Riley, and the same was true with the news. Nobody on Alton Road who was in the know whispered a word of it, either. There were no charges of abuse to levy, no crimes to be adjudicated, so Riley and Dylan were free to live their lives outside of the glaring media spotlight.

As always, Alex was concerned for her sister. As she finished packing the lunch, she wondered what would have happened if those involved had been more honest. Enough secrets for two lifetimes, Willow had said.

What if Riley had come forward about Ken? What if Dylan had told his mother what he'd seen on Riley's phone? What if Brooke had been more forthcoming about her stalker or confided to someone—a therapist, a friend—that her marriage to Jerry had been a nightmare? What if Willow had opened up to Riley about her birth father years earlier? Would that have altered the trajectory of her daughter's life or even that of the Wookiee's?

Alex was no saint herself, she knew. She'd hid her drinking, while Lettie did the same with her petty revenge plot against Riley. How much heartache could have been lessened, lives saved, if people owned up to their hard truths?

Outside, the lawn mower puttered by the kitchen window, with Nick riding atop like a king surveying his lands. He waved as he drove past. Alex returned a smile. She could not be more grateful for his steadfast support these past few weeks. He'd listened to Alex patiently and without judgment, knowing when to give her the peace and quiet of companionable silence. He was also a rock for Lettie and Emily as they tried to wrap their heads around their suffering and grief.

To Alex's relief, Emily was doing far better than she could have imagined. It wasn't long ago, over afternoon tea (and it was *only* tea these days), that Alex finally came clean with the secret she'd been keeping about her brother-in-law—two secrets, in fact.

"I knew about Ken looking at Brooke's photos before you did, and I didn't tell you," Alex had said.

"What do you mean?" Emily set her teacup down with a clatter.

"You know how the guys shared the pictures at poker night? Well, long story, but I found one picture on Nick's phone and asked him about it. He told me he got it from Ken."

Emily sat very still. "Why didn't you tell me?" she asked.

"Your marriage was so strained already, I didn't want that to push it

over the edge. Then you found out yourself, and I thought it didn't matter anymore. But I should have told you. And that's not the only secret I've been keeping."

"What else?" Emily asked, her eyes betraying a deep worry.

Alex drained her tea, buying herself one last moment. "I just wanted to protect you, and I feel sick about it. It's been a year now, and it's weighed on my mind the whole time. But we've all seen the damage secrets can cause—so no more of them for me."

Emily braced herself, eyes locked on Alex, jaw set tight in anticipation. "Well? Are you going to tell me?"

With an apologetic frown, Alex began. "Not long after the Kumars moved in, I saw Ken leaving Mandy's house early one morning. He seemed to be sneaking away, and it was odd—suspicious, even, but I didn't know what to make of it."

"Last summer? And you're just telling me this now?"

A pang of guilt twinged in Alex's chest. "You were already worried," she continued, "and I didn't have anything concrete to go on. I'm sorry . . . all of this was done out of love, but you have every right to be angry at me. I'm angry at myself. I'm so sorry, Em."

Alex saw only a quick flash of fury, extinguished almost as soon as it surged. The sisters held each other's gaze a moment longer, but Emily's expression softened and Alex breathed easier.

"I'm stronger than you think," Emily said. "I can take a punch, or two, or twenty—whatever. I can take it because I have you, and Dylan and Logan, and my friends, and Mom, and faith in myself, too. I want you to have faith in me as well, Alex."

"I do. So much I can't even tell you."

When they embraced, arms wrapped tightly around each other, Emily's tears began to fall, and soon after, so did Alex's.

All was forgiven.

The memory faded and Alex returned to packing up. She went outside wearing her backpack, a hat, and sunglasses to keep out the glare along with long pants and a long-sleeved jersey to keep the ticks away.

She saw Emily standing in front of Mandy Kumar's house with the rest of the women already gathered.

Zoe barked in greeting before rearing up to place her front paws on Brooke's perfectly muscular legs. There was no hiding from the ticks in Brooke's revealing attire. The hike was Brooke's idea, and she'd done the organizing, evidently with a purpose, although she was a bit cagey about what that might be.

"We need a cleansing," Brooke had said. "A group cleanse—a different kind of detox."

Alex wondered if it had something to do with the planned swim, as everyone was instructed to bring bathing suits. But was Brooke going to lead some kind of a ceremony?

There were hugs all around, but no tears were shed. At least for today, the crying was over and done with. In its place fell an uncertain weightiness, one that hung over the women like storm clouds, thick as the humid air. It was a reminder for Alex that the days could change, the seasons, too, but this heaviness would always be clinging to them.

They set off on the march to the lake, with Zoe trotting happily alongside Alex. There was muted chatter, the women pairing into smaller groups as they traversed the narrow path. As they approached the clearing, Alex found herself walking with Mandy, which gave her a chance to ask something that had been on her mind. She wasn't about to broach the topic of the cruise ship, which felt too confrontational and honestly a bit too dangerous, but something else had been nagging at her for weeks.

"I'm just curious," Alex said. "That day at the block party. Lettie told me you'd come up from the basement stairs. I've been wondering—what were you doing in the basement of Ken and Emily's house?"

It had been an open-and-shut case, with two witnesses hearing Evan's confession before watching his self-inflicted fatal gunshot wound. Police took statements from Alex and Brooke, took Riley's phone for evidence, and asked questions of Lettie and Mandy about what they had overheard, but it was hardly an extensive inquiry, as the facts of the case appeared equally evident and undeniable.

Mandy looked away for a moment. "Let's just say that I had a change of heart about something important, so I went to the house to set things right."

Alex knew that was all she was going to get. In some ways, Mandy would always be an enigma.

Alex glanced up from the trail to see the lake, and it was a good thing, too. The hot day and the long walk made her extremely happy that they were going for a swim. Alex wore her suit underneath her clothing, but Brooke changed freely in front of everyone, as did Mandy Kumar.

"You've inspired me to be a lot less self-conscious about my body," Mandy said.

Brooke gave her an approving smile. "This is the first phase of our cleanse," she said. "Last one in the water has to carry the cooler on the walk back!"

It was a sprint into the lake, and unclear who was last, but nobody really cared. The water was so refreshing it felt like a reset of mind, body, and spirit—a chance to start anew.

After the swim, the women took seats around a rustic picnic table shaded by a grouping of pine trees. Alex unpacked the sandwiches she had carefully wrapped, while Willow poured wine for everyone. As was her routine now, Alex brought a bottle of chilled sparkling water. Alcohol abstinence was a daily choice she made each morning. It was as simple and as hard as that.

For a time, the women ate and sipped their beverages, enjoying the company and the peace of their surroundings. Though they were in the shade, the hot day quickly dried everyone off—including Zoe, who had enjoyed her swim as well.

It was Willow who eventually broke what had been a stretch of silence. "Not to bring up darker matters, but I got Evan's toxicology report from the police the other day."

Everyone turned to Willow.

"And?" asked Emily.

"And he had a high blood alcohol content and amphetamines in his system. They think the combination triggered a seizure."

"A seizure that saved our lives," said Brooke.

Nobody toasted that sentiment.

"I guess now is as good a time as any for phase two of my plan," Brooke said.

"You mean our *cleanse*," said Emily, who sounded like she was in on the plan.

"That's right," said Brooke. She produced from her backpack a yellowing book that Alex recognized immediately. It was Jerry and Ken's high school yearbook.

"Now we all know what Ken and Jerry did to Mandy back in high school. And some of you know that I also suffered a lot under Jerry's abuse, and Emily has suffered from Ken's lies and deceit. Willow has also been deeply hurt because of Evan and Ken. And Alex, you are our glue in so many ways—you've brought us together and held us together, and for that you'll always be in our hearts.

"So my idea was to have a ceremonial burning of this yearbook—symbolically turning the darkest pages of our history into ash."

At last, a sentiment that could be toasted all around.

Brooke moved to the nearby fire pit and placed the yearbook in the center. She took a lighter out of her pocket and lit several pages on fire. All the friends gathered around, expecting to see a fireball, but instead watched a few corners burning slightly, a bigger flame failing to catch.

"Shit," Brooke muttered. "Not exactly the dramatic effect I was going for. Anybody have some lighter fluid?"

Most everyone chuckled at the irony of a small, pitiful flame for a big cleanse—everyone, that is, but Mandy Kumar.

From her bag, Mandy pulled out a quarter-full bottle of Johnnie Walker Blue Label whisky. "I was actually going to make a symbolic gesture myself today and dump the contents of this bottle into the lake, but I think we can put it to better use."

She doused the nascent flames with the liquor, which erupted into an intense blaze that engulfed the yearbook. The women stood enraptured as the fireball consumed one page after another, until the book was mostly ash.

Emily gaped at Mandy. "Where did you get that?" she asked.

Mandy looked directly at Emily. "I grabbed it from Ken's office," she said matter-of-factly. "Trust me, you wouldn't want to drink this. It's a little too . . . *potent* for anyone."

Emily stood straighter as her suspicious look gave way to one of understanding. Alex remembered Samir's desperate quest for Mandy, and his concern that she had vanished with all her medication. Had she poisoned Ken's prized whisky? Was that why she was in the house? Had she decided against such extreme revenge? Was that her change of heart?

If so, Mandy's plan had inadvertently saved their lives. Alex doubted that it was a combination of alcohol and amphetamines that caused Evan's seizure. She believed he consumed Mandy's missing drugs, which had been mixed in that bottle of Johnnie Walker Blue, causing a reaction that led to his self-inflicted gunshot wound. But evidence of that theory had just gone up in flames.

Brooke's expression darkened. She had heard Samir's plea and knew about the missing medication, as well as the cruise ship connection. She must have been thinking along the same lines as Alex.

Mandy said, "A few years back I was in a very dark place. Honestly, I wasn't sure if I even wanted to live. I had unresolved trauma added to the most painful loss a mother could suffer. Samir tried everything to help me find a way out of my depression, but there was no solution. Medications, therapy, nothing was working. And then we took that cruise. I know Samir wanted to rekindle things, but I just didn't see a way to get us back to normal.

"I was on the upper deck, thinking about jumping overboard and ending my life, when I ran into, of all people, Jerry Bailey. We recognized each other right away, even though he was as drunk as could be. And he was the same as he ever was. He told me in no uncertain terms that I better not get any ideas of dredging up old memories, using the #MeToo movement to come after him. He threatened me with his money and power, telling me I'd best keep my mouth shut. Then he put his hands on me and told me he could still take whatever he wanted.

"I pushed him away, hard, forcefully, and because he was so drunk, he stumbled backward, completely off-balance.

"The railing was about four feet high. He was a tall man, so it didn't take much to send him right over. There was nobody around, no witnesses, so I snuck away. Five minutes later I reported hearing a splash, but of course I didn't own up to my involvement. The ship turned around, a search got under way, but . . . they never found his body.

"This is horrible to say, but his death opened something up inside of me. I suddenly felt free of guilt and shame, sorrow and sadness—it was, in a word, *empowering*. I felt alive again. I got it in my head that revenge would heal me, and I decided to make that my mission in life—to seek justice on my own terms and in my own way. So I found Ken and kept a close watch on him, and when a house on Alton Road came up for sale . . . I was ready.

"It was tantalizing to torture him for a year—watching him squirm. I kept myself cool, very controlled, very methodical, except for one night, Christmas Eve, when I just snapped. I was spying, because our holidays aren't very merry—watching Ken through the window of his house, laughing, drinking, like he owned the damn world. I wanted to wipe that smug look off his face. Instead, I scribbled a note on a piece of scrap paper in my purse, tied it around a rock with a rubber band, and tossed it through that window. I could see that nobody was going to get hurt—I had a clear shot at the table, and it felt damn good to finally channel my anger into something tangible. I got a little release, along with some satisfaction, but the good feelings didn't last.

"I knew I couldn't play with him forever. I had to decide how to finish what I started, what I'd come here to do. I remembered that Ken had made such a big deal about his *prized* whisky, so an idea began to form. When the time came, however—I just couldn't go through with it.

"You see, I had snuck into your house, Emily, while everyone was setting up for the block party. I found the liquor cabinet easily enough, and poisoned Ken's bottle with my ground-up medications. Given the concentration of meds I dissolved, I knew it would cause a fatal reaction even if he drank only a few ounces, and since Ken made it a point that he didn't share the good stuff, I felt safe from harming others. I was safe from a tox screen, too, since the medical examiner would have to specifically test for the drugs I used."

Mandy's voice shook, her eyes glassy with unshed ears.

"I came to my senses. What happened with Jerry was an accident. With Ken, it would have been murder. Fantasy is one thing, but reality, well ... let's just say I found my guilty conscience. I knew right then it would be far easier to live with my trauma than the guilt that follows murder. While I waited for Ken to drink, I had time to reflect on what I was doing. I came to the realization that my pain and the relief I felt after Jerry's death probably had more to do with Asher, channeling my grief into something I could control, rather than what happened to me in high school. I was conflating one heartache with another, and I couldn't go through with it. So I went back into the house, sneaking up the basement stairs, same as before. Only this time I arrived too late for Ken's sake—and I guess for Evan's as well."

A pall settled over the group as the fire started to dwindle. The charred remains of the yearbook smoldered.

"What do you want us to do with this information?" Willow asked.

"I guess that's for you to decide," said Mandy. "I'm ready to own up to what I did—what happened. I'd like to be there for my son, Jay, and be the wife and partner to Samir that he deserves. But maybe I don't deserve that chance because of what I've done."

"What have you done?" It was Brooke who spoke up. "Jerry grabbed you and you defended yourself, then reported him as going overboard. You didn't do anything to Ken other than a little vandalism and make him feel uncomfortable—and as for Evan, you heard the tox report. It was amphetamines that caused the seizure."

Brooke looked over to Willow, who returned a nod. "Amphetamines and alcohol were his usual cocktail," Willow said. She moved over to Mandy and put an arm around her. If anyone had doubted Willow's inclination, that gesture dispelled it. "I think the bottle belongs in the lake where you intended to put it."

A few moments later, the five women and one dog gathered at the shoreline and watched in silence as Mandy threw the whisky bottle as far out as she could. The bottle landed with a splash, floating a moment on the water's surface before filling up and vanishing into the depths below.

Meadowbrook Online Community Page

Special Announcement from the group moderator.

The post about the tragedy on Alton Road has been permanently deleted.

I started this page as an information resource for the town of Meadowbrook. Bullying and insensitive comments will not be tolerated. If you're unsure whether your comment is appropriate, please refer to our posted Community Standards, or you will risk getting blocked like **Ed Callahan**.

MEMORIAL DAY,
ONE YEAR LATER . . .

Epilogue

Lettie

The object spins end over end, high above me. I've got my eyes on it. I'm not going to miss. No way. I'm locked in like a hawk on a mouse. And then, at the worst possible moment, a cloud shifts, exposing the sun's blinding glare. A bright light hits me so hard my vision turns white. It's a fraction of a second at most, but long enough for me to lose the target. *Damn it!*

Panic rises, but I've no time for that. *Got to focus! Find it!* My eyes dart left, next right. Searching . . . searching. Then, BAM! There it is. It hurtles toward me like a comet—impact in no time. The angle isn't perfect. It should have been thrown higher. Velocity will be a problem, that's for sure. I get my hands out at the last possible second, pinkies touching to form a cup.

Somehow I've timed it all flawlessly. I move my hands in the same direction as the egg's trajectory. This, I know, will slow its relative speed at the point of contact. I focus on catching the sides. That's where I want to cradle it in my palms.

The egg hits my hands with a thump, but I don't hear a crack. I wait . . . but nothing, no sticky coating against my skin. I look down at my hands. There it is—intact, perfectly intact.

I hold the egg up for all to see. Cheers and applause fill the air. Dad is about twenty-five feet away, jumping up and down like the Red Sox just won the World Series. The ten-year-old kid next to me looks like he's going to burst into tears, poor thing. Yellow egg runs down his hands like a sneeze gone wrong.

I go over to him, touch his shoulder. "Good game. Maybe next year."

After, I run over to my dad in a sprint. We hug like it'll be our last one ever. He's beaming—maybe on the verge of tears? Okay, that's an exaggeration, but he's super happy, no doubt about it. Even though we've won, there won't be any trophies this year. There'll never be trophies again. That was Ken's thing, and there will never be Ken again, either.

"Well done, Lettie," Dad says. "I knew you could do it!"

"Once an egg tosser, always an egg tosser," I say with a wink. "And you can thank my freshman physics class for the win. I knew exactly how to adjust for velocity. Next time, toss it higher, please."

"They teach you well at UMass," Dad says.

I smile. That's right. UMass, not USC. Guess what I really needed was the choice, not a mandate. A degree from those schools is essentially the same thing, or so some wise old man once told me. Dad has promised to help pay for graduate school with what we're saving. And I don't have to be an RA, so my ratting days are done.

Dylan trots over, his skin slick with the sheen of runny yolk. "Nice work there, Lettie," he tells me.

"Not too bad yourself," I say. "But you and Logan have a long way to go if you want to topple greatness."

He offers me a slight bow. "Think maybe this is good material for a short story."

I nod. "I read your last one—it was amazing. I had no idea you had that in you."

"Me either," says Dylan. "And thanks for the compliment. I've actually decided to be an English major. Bucknell has a great department."

"Who knew what one creative writing class would unleash?" I say.

"I can be a high school teacher—coach lax and wrestling, get the message out that wins and losses aren't all that matter."

"Oh, this loss matters," I tell him, holding up my unbroken egg proudly.

"Yeah, yeah," Dylan mumbles. He grows somber. "Feels a bit weird, doesn't it?"

I look around. Grills. Balloons. Kids. Music. Drinks. Food. Lawn games. The Alton Road block party. Same as it ever was. But not the same. It'll never be the same. This year everyone seems a lot more reflective. There are plenty of moments of joy and frivolity, but darker, painful reminders lurk just below the surface. In young and old alike, I see them bubble up from time to time as a look, a distance in the eyes, as though a memory had taken hold with force.

In some ways, I suppose the neighborhood has never been closer—as if we needed tragedy to become our authentic selves.

"Yeah, feels weird all right," I say. "It's more subdued, that's for sure."

Dylan nods in the direction of Aunt Emily. She's chatting and laughing with my mom and our grandmother. "Maybe my mom is right, and having the party *is* healing," he says.

"Maybe," I say.

I've healed a lot, I have to admit, though I'm still working through some guilt and maybe a little PTSD. I haven't lost my conviction to care for the planet, but I've realized it's equally important to care for other people.

I watch Grandma and Aunt Emily make their way up the drive-way to Willow's house—or what was once Willow's house. Aunt Emily bought it in the fall, after Willow and Riley moved away. The move made sense. My aunt couldn't bear to live in a house with so many haunted memories, but she didn't want to move away from my mom, either. She and Grandma live here now, Dylan too, when he's home from school. Logan moved to New York for a big finance job. Good news, there was no need for an addition, as Willow's place had the perfect setup for a one-floor basement apartment with its own exit—and a special room that Grandma uses as an "oversized closet." Lordy!

The new family who moved into the cul-de-sac have three young kids and full knowledge of what happened in the first-floor office—well, at least the parents know. I highly doubt they told their kids about two fatalities. All seems normal there now, idyllic even, with bikes, sidewalk chalk, sprinklers, and lots of laughter.

Willow and Riley come over to congratulate me on the win. They might not live on Alton Road anymore—they got a condo on the other side of town—but they'll always be a part of the "block." Riley has on her U Miami T-shirt. She's going there in the fall after spending a gap year traveling Europe with her mom.

I guess Willow came into a lot of money after Evan died. Since the divorce never went through, the prenup didn't matter, or something like that. My mom knows the details.

A few minutes later, Jay comes driving down Alton Road. He goes slow, being very mindful because it's kind of mayhem here. I haven't seen him much since he's gone back to college. He parks in his driveway, gets out holding two Starbucks coffees.

"Thirsty?" he calls out to me. "I got an extra spiced almond milk latte—no dairy—thinking you might want one."

Jay hands me the drink, which I receive with a smile and thanks.

"Long time no see," I say. "Didn't think you'd be here. How have you been?"

Jay gets out his trusty vape pen, as if needing a hit to share anything about himself. "You think I'd miss the block party? Someone has to look after you, Lettie." He gives me a wink paired with that smile of his—that damn smile. "I'm doing great. Straight A's my first semester back."

My eyebrows go up. "Without hacking into the system?" I'd found out why Jay had got kicked out of his last school.

He took the jab with grace. "Yeah, all effort, no screwing around this time."

"What about your big plans to take over the world with your mystery app?"

"Not there yet, but getting closer," he says. "And you'll be happy to know I think my business will help a lot of people. It's not just a money grab."

"But it's still a secret?" I ask, hoping that he'll finally share what he's been working on.

His sly expression tells me it's not going to happen. "Still a secret, but when I announce it, you'll be the first to know. I owe you a lot. You helped me become a better person."

He has a point. I'm the one who encouraged him to confess to Dylan about being the blackmailer. He assured Dylan that all the recordings had been deleted. But Jay had found his own conscience in returning the money he coerced from Uncle Ken without my prompting—though Aunt Emily still doesn't know who was responsible for taking and returning the funds.

"What's been going on at UMass? Have any of the guys figured out what an amazing person you are?" Jay asks.

I think I finally see some real emotion. "I'm totally into this guy with a spider tattoo on his arm," I say. "Guess I'm still hung up on arachnids."

Jay laughs. "They can be tricky, Lettie," he says. "If you ever need a somewhat dubious friend to help you out of a jam, anytime, you know where to find me."

He gives me a hug. I watch him walk away. He gets halfway to his front door before turning around to wave goodbye. I wave back . . . and then he's gone.

I'm returning to the block party mayhem when I spy an unfamiliar car—a blue Mini Cooper, cute as any car can be—driving down Alton Road. We have cones set out at the end of the street to deter nonresidents, but this car came anyway.

The driver pulls to a stop in front of Aunt Emily's new house, Willow's old, which happens to be right next to where I'm standing. A girl exits the Mini. She has dark blond hair, striking blue eyes.

"Hey," she says tentatively to me, "I'm looking for Riley Thompson. Does she live here?" Her blue eyes remind me of Riley's.

As it happens, Riley is actually standing nearby. She overhears her name and comes bounding over. "Hey, I'm Riley," she says to the girl, who looks to be about our age, maybe a little older.

The girl assesses Riley with a look I can describe only as nervous apprehension. She shifts her weight from foot to foot, not quite able to hold Riley's curious stare. "Um, hey," she begins, her voice soft and uncertain. "This is going to sound really weird, and I'm sorry to drop in on you unannounced and all, but . . . I took a DNA test. And well, um . . . I think you're my sister."

Riley's mouth falls open. Mine does the same. For a moment she's speechless—but then says, "You mean . . ."

The girl nods. "Steve Wachowski—the, er, Wookiee . . . he's my dad, and I think—"

Riley doesn't give her a chance to finish. "He's mine, too!" She starts jumping up and down like she's ten again. Willow comes over—there's talk, followed by hugs and laughter and yes, tears.

That's life here on Alton Road for you—plenty of surprises and a rainbow of emotions.

Honestly, I've had more surprises in the last year than I could even count. Enough that I'm thinking of becoming a double major in environmental studies and psychology. If there's anything more interesting to study than the planet, it's the people who live on it.

Acknowledgments

I set out to write *The Block Party* with a clear intention: I wanted to bring a little levity to the genre of domestic suspense, and couple that with family dramas to which many could relate. I should share that Meadowbrook, Massachusetts, doesn't exist, nor does Alton Road where the block party takes place. That's intentional. I wanted to write about a place that could be Anywhere, USA. To do that, I felt it best to invent a town. I love crazy, wild thrill rides as much as any thriller fan, but I gave myself a personal challenge to keep the suspense going without relying on an overly complex plot.

As the writer, I wouldn't want a product out in the wild if I didn't think I'd hit my mark, but I don't take full credit for that success. Writing a book is unique in that it is mostly a solo endeavor. There's no writer's room for novelists to go and hash out ideas. No team meetings break up our day. We don't have showrunners or actors to riff off in the process of creating. We simply write. That's the job. And yet, I'm surrounded by people who make sure I stay on course, and never lose sight of the most important person in the creative process—and that is you, the reader.

So with that introduction, I would like to thank my editor, Jennifer Enderlin, for believing in me and especially in this book. Her insights and instincts shaped the narrative profoundly and pushed me to be better. A book is only as impactful as its readership, and for that I must thank Christina Lopez, Lisa Senz, Brant Janeway, Erica Martirano, and Katie Bassel for spearheading the publication processes and spreading the word about the disastrous events that take place on Alton Road.

I'm grateful as well to have literary representation from Meg Ruley and Rebecca Scherer of the Jane Rotrosen Agency, and Lucy Stille for my film and TV rights.

While I may be mostly a solo operator when writing, editing and revising is more of a team effort. My mother, Judy, is a trusted first reader, and I'm always amazed at her keen understanding of story. Special, heartfelt thanks go to Kathleen Miller, to whom this novel is dedicated, and whose contributions to this book really can't be overstated. Thanks also go to Sue Miller for her eagle eye as a proofreader, Clair Lamb for her editorial brilliance, and fellow suspense novelist Danielle Girard, who always provides helpful suggestions and a vital sounding board.

As for the amazing cadre of writers who agreed to spend their time reading *The Block Party* with an eye to providing a blurb—Elin Hilderbrand, Megan Abbott, William Landay, Lisa Unger, Chris Pavone, Lisa Scottoline, Sally Hepworth, Mary Kubica, Lisa Jackson, Heather Gudenkauf, and Lisa Gardner—I'm deeply appreciative for the support. I'm a devoted reader and fan of each of these great writers, and their talents have informed my craft and taught me so much about what makes suspense stories hard to put down.

Last, I'd like to thank you for giving this book a try. You have a lot of great reads to choose from. I'm glad that you picked mine.

With gratitude,
Jamie Day